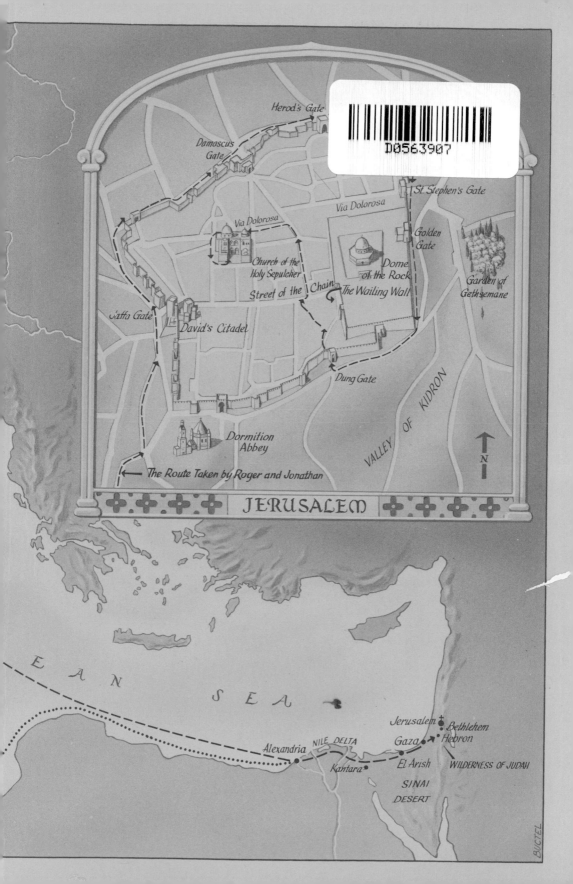

JERUSALEM

Herod's Gate

Damascus Gate

St. Stephen's Gate

Via Dolorosa

Via Dolorosa

Golden Gate

Via Dolorosa

Dome of the Rock

Church of the Holy Sepulcher

Garden of Gethsemane

Street of the Chain

The Wailing Wall

Jaffa Gate

David's Citadel

Dung Gate

VALLEY OF KIDRON

Dormition Abbey

N

← The Route Taken by Roger and Jonathan

BÜCTEL

EAN SEA

Jerusalem ● Bethlehem

Gaza ● Hebron

Alexandria NILE DELTA

El Arish WILDERNESS OF JUDAH

Kantara

SINAI

DESERT

AN ARMY
OF
CHILDREN

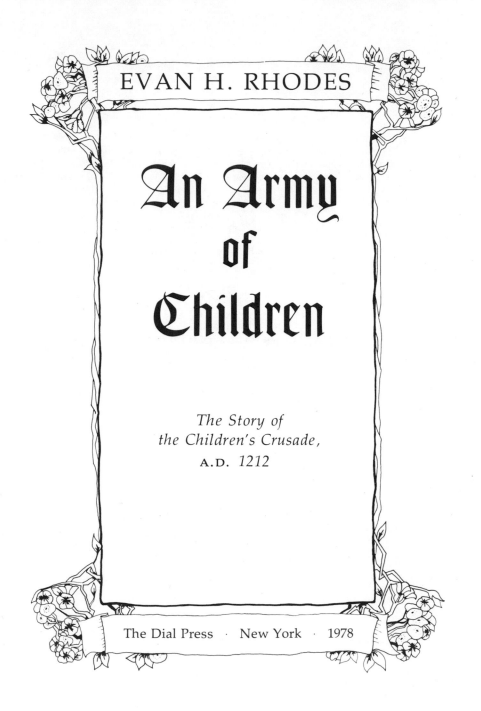

EVAN H. RHODES

An Army of Children

The Story of the Children's Crusade, A.D. 1212

The Dial Press · New York · 1978

Published by The Dial Press
1 Dag Hammarskjold Plaza
New York, New York 10017

Manufactured in the United States of America

First printing

Design by Francesca Belanger

Library of Congress Catalog Card Number: 77–25749

ISBN: 0–8037–0180–2

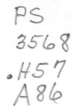
In memory of
Daphne Bunker Rhodes

NOTE

Extraordinary as it may seem, the phenomenon of the children's crusade is a documented historical fact. Wherever possible, primary sources were employed in writing this narrative. Actual names, dates, and places were used as recorded by the chroniclers of the times; indeed, several of the chroniclers appear as characters, as do the reigning monarchs, the princes of the church including the pope, and the two child leaders of the movement.

In many instances, records indicating the specific route of the children's army were vague or nonexistent; for example, by which mountain pass the Alps were crossed. The author traversed a number of these routes; from the known dates that the children arrived at certain monasteries and the estimated distance a child can walk in any given day, he determined which ones seemed most feasible.

In researching this book the author traveled the complete route indicated on the accompanying map; by ship, plane, boat, train, automobile, and some 571 miles on foot; only the small stretch of territory between Alexandria and Kantara was not covered. The Israeli war department was extremely helpful in supplying the author with an armed escort and transportation from Jerusalem deep into the far western reaches of the occupied Sinai desert.

PART

The Age
of
the Father

ONE

PROLOGUE

EUROPE PRAYED. PROPHECY HAD FORETOLD THAT BEfore the millennium could come, evil would first rule the world.

In this year of our Lord 1212, the signs were everywhere. On the continent, drought, famine, and war raged. France had wrested Normandy and much of the Angevin territories from her hated rivals, the Plantagenets, and now armed herself to invade their remaining stronghold, England. In Spain, Christian armies prepared to engage the advancing Saracen Almohads. The Holy Roman Empire writhed in the grip of civil war between the two contenders to the throne, Otto IV and Frederick II. And in Rome, Pope Innocent III cried out against all heretics, Beguines, Albigenses, and Jews, and daily preached for one last crusade to reconquer the Holy Land, once and forever. In the heavens, the streaks of comets, eclipses darkening the sun and moon, and unholy lights in the northern skies surely signaled the coming of the Last Judgment. But as had been prophesied, men would never see this day until the Holy Land was freed.

England was denied the comfort of prayer. For more than a thousand days and a thousand nights the bells of the churches had not rung. Neither to announce tidings of joy, nor to signal calamity, nor to call the faithful to prayer. The sick clung desperately to life, fearing to give up the ghost, for with the sacraments of the church denied, the good people of England feared for their immortal souls. Silence, and the leaden cape of interdict hung like a curse on the land.

In London, the citizens spoke in rebellious whispers and looked to the great square keep of the Tower of London, where King John had barricaded himself since Easter; they wondered what crime against man and God he would next commit. Long

ago, most of London's twenty thousand inhabitants had concluded that their choice of monarch had been a grievous error.

In 1191, when King Richard had led the Third Crusade to
the Holy Land, Prince John had won from the citizens recognition of himself as heir presumptive, providing he grant the
city the status of a free commune with the right to elect a
mayor, and grant every freeman the title of baron. For these
concessions, England had been taxed mercilessly to finance
John's wars with Philip Augustus of France, only to see "John
Softsword" lose all. Cursed with the mercurial Plantagenet
temper, John had become even more unpredictable with the
threat of invasion from France, rumors of plots against his life,
and Pope Innocent's most recent papal bull, which excommunicated him and absolved "all Englishmen high and low from
fealty and allegiance to this contumacious King." Against the
rising tide of rebellion John fought to hold his kingdom
together, but everywhere it was whispered that the king's enemies were as numerous as his barons.

LONDON

BARON THORNE SPURRED HIS WILD-EYED REARING horse through the warren of narrow lanes, racing from the fire behind him. Flames leapt from roof to roof, showering thatches of burning straw down upon the fleeing people. The baron beat at the sparks singeing his beard and hair. Across his saddle lay an unconscious lad no more than thirteen years old.

Shouts and alarms from the soldiers of King John added to the turmoil in the streets. They had just raided the dwellings of suspected enemies of the Crown, including the Hospital of St. Thomas of Acon, headquarters of the Mercer's Guild, in which Baron Thorne claimed membership. The baron did not know if he was one of their targets, nor did he wait to find out. He had galloped from the courtyard of the Guild moments before the guards' arrival. Others in the merchant complex were seized; those who attempted to escape were cut down on the spot, including women and children.

So engrossed in their raid were the king's lackeys that they paid scant attention to the fire which had been set earlier in the day in the tiny quarter of the Old Jewry. A Christian child had been found slain in a nearby alley. That it had happened on the eve of their Passover holiday had brought calamity down on the Jews. Screaming that the Christ killers were using the blood of Christian children in their unholy rituals, a rampaging mob had ravaged the quarter. But the quick April wind had spread the conflagration beyond the confines of Old Jewry; now it threatened much of the West Cheap Market District, and everybody fled before the common enemy.

Amid the screeching of hens and the screaming of people, Baron Thorne wheeled his horse onto Poulter's Lane, rode hard until he reached the Walbrook and then headed for the Thames. Once safely away from the direct path of the fire, he took a deep breath. He tried to collect his thoughts as he caught sight of the Tower of London hulking above the two-storied timber-and-daub dwellings. Built by William the Conqueror to keep the vexatious citizenry in check, the fortress was now used by another Norman for the same purpose.

"I fear the time to leave London must be this very day," Baron Thorne whispered to himself.

He had planned to journey to the continent the following week with his son, Roger. To throw off the king's spies, he had taken great pains to disguise this journey as a simple trip for the Mercer's Guild, informing the Crown that he intended to go first to Paris to enroll his son at the university, then on to the Champagne Fairs, and finally to Cologne, searching out new markets for English wool. The Crown had issued him the necessary permits, but events this day convinced the baron that if his true mission were to succeed he must leave at once.

"But what to do with this lad?" Baron Thorne shook the boy, but he had still not regained his senses.

Keeping to a moderate pace to avoid suspicion, Thorne continued on and soon reached the Steelyard at Dow Gate, home of the Guild of the Men of Cologne, the German hanse once headed by his late father-in-law. At the approach to London Bridge, impaled heads stared down at him from long pikes; he crossed himself, then slapped his mount and the horse's hooves beat out a rapid staccato on the stone roadwork of the bridge.

The Thorne house had been built between the Chapel of St. Thomas à Becket and the Drawbridge. The baron had chosen this location so that he could see the ships sailing up the Thames estuary and be first on board to bargain for their cargoes. He dismounted, lifted the still-unconscious boy from his horse, slung him over his shoulder, and strode into his house and was met at the door by his fourteen-year-old son, Roger.

"We saw the fire!" Roger said excitedly. "We were about to go look for you . . ." He broke off as he caught sight of the unconscious boy. "Who is this?" he asked.

Without answering, Baron Thorne carried the lad upstairs to the dormered main sleeping chamber and laid him gently on a pallet. Roger and his tutor, Brother Harolde, bounded up the stairs behind him.

"Shall I fetch a doctor?" Harolde asked, his fingers gripping his rosary. Then, staring at the child's ashen face, he added, "Or a priest?"

Baron Thorne shook his head as he slammed the window shutters. He herded Roger and Harolde toward the door. "Let the lad sleep for now. He is not badly injured. He will recover his senses shortly."

"What is his name?" Roger asked. "Who is he?"

"His name?" The baron looked surprised for a moment. "I do not know. Wait. Jonathan, yes, that is it."

"But where . . . ?" Roger began, only to feel his head pop with loud ringing as the baron boxed his ears.

"Heed me, the two of you," Thorne said to Harolde and Roger. "Gather your belongings. Take only what is absolutely necessary. We leave immediately for the continent."

"But we were not to go for another week!" Harolde cried. Being a Capricorn and ruled by the melancholy Saturn, the young monk was always thrown into a state of nerves by any change of plan.

"On my oath!" the baron exclaimed, "there are times when you act like an old woman instead of a grown man of twenty! Now do as I say."

Roger confronted his father, his mouth set in a determined line. "I told you before and I will tell you again, I will not attend that university!"

The baron's face flushed an apoplectic red as he slammed his fist repeatedly on the trestle table. Harolde grabbed the jouncing crockery. In the six months he had been in the baron's employ, as amanuensis and tutor for Roger, he had often witnessed these outbursts. Always he had prayed for a more proper balance of his benefactor's humors; clearly, the baron was a man ruled by the blood. But never had he seen him this disturbed.

Roger's clear blue eyes flashed as he shouted, "I will not waste four years of my life!"

Baron Thorne reached his son in two strides and gripped his shoulders until the boy winced. "We will discuss this later. At the moment, I am concerned for our safety. Now do as I say and without question! Or you will jeopardize our lives!"

"Do I not have a right to know the danger?" Roger said. "Or will you continue to treat me as a child?"

The baron took a deep breath and controlled his temper. "You are right," he said. "Well, King John has already placed some of my merchant confreres under house arrest, I may be next. Doubtless all ships departing London are being watched, so it is safest to go overland to Dover and embark from there. We leave at nightfall. Roger, you must accompany me. Our monarch is not adverse to punishing the sons for the supposed transgressions of the father—witness the murder of William de Briouze's family."

"But why?" Roger asked, excited now. "What have we done?"

"Nothing we need ever be ashamed of. Whatever happens, remember that." Then Baron Thorne turned to Harolde. "Now that I think of it, there is no earthly reason for you to risk your safety."

Harolde shook his head. "In these times, England is not a safe place for a man of the cloth. I will make this trip with you, for so have we contracted. After I leave you in Cologne, I will continue on my pilgrimage to Rome."

Much chastened now, yet also charged with the adventure, Roger left the bed chamber and Harolde followed. Downstairs, Roger said to the monk, "What can all of this really be about? And who is that strange boy? What does he have to do with my father?"

Harolde hurried around the room, collecting his belongings: his Bible; his guide to Rome, the *Mirabilia Roma;* an extra pair of sandals; a stylus; and a breviary. "You know your father has a weakness for sheltering strays," he said to Roger. "Did he not do the same with me?"

"But if we are leaving?"

"True," Harolde said. "He will probably drop him off at some monastery."

After Roger collected his things and packed them in his oversized leather wallet, he went into the small chapel in the rear of the house and knelt before the altar. A votive candle cast its flickering shadows over an enameled miniature of his mother, Gundred, hanging on the wall near a crucifix. She had died in childbirth just a year ago; Roger's eyes blurred as he stared at the painting. More than a mother, she had been a confidante and friend, forever calming the turbulence between him and his father. He missed her sorely.

"Mother, I must leave," Roger whispered, "but I have not forgotten my vow to pray for you in the temples of Jerusalem. Somehow I know that God will aid me in fulfilling my sacred oath."

A noise behind Roger made him whirl. Through the chapel archway he saw the boy Jonathan come stumbling down the stairs as if in a daze. "Where are you going?" Roger called, then raced after the lad and caught him just as he reached the front door.

The boy cringed away from Roger. "Father, come quickly!" Roger shouted. Rushing in from another room, the baron motioned Roger away and then approached Jonathan. The boy retreated like a cornered animal. Gently, the baron put his arm around his shoulder.

"Jonathan, no matter what you think, you cannot go back. Nothing you can do now can possibly help. You do understand that, don't you?"

The boy shivered; his dark eyes opened wide, not seeing, not comprehending. He struggled to break free of the baron's grasp, his face contorted with terror.

Baron Thorne slapped him hard. Recognition flooded back into Jonathan's eyes; he slumped and the baron led him away from the door. "Watch over him, Roger," the baron said. "We must decide what to do with him before we leave."

The baron continued his preparations. Going to a strongbox

hidden under a loose flooring plank, he removed all the gold and silver coin. Next, he burned a sheaf of personal papers in the fireplace, and finally, he buckled on his sword.

Jonathan sat huddled in a corner under Roger's watchful eye.

"By my oath, I do not know what to do with you," the baron said, approaching the boy. "Are you sure you have no kinsmen here? No one who can hide you?"

Jonathan shook his head.

"Another person makes it the more difficult to travel fast," Thorne said. "And a child at that. For my sins! Why did the Lord ever visit me with such a dilemma?"

Tears sprang to Jonathan's eyes. Terrified as he was of these strangers, he was more frightened of being left alone. He grabbed the baron's curtmantle and would not let go. "But you swore," he whispered, "I remember."

"Enough!" Thorne said sharply, with a swift glance at Roger and Harolde. Then he leaned close to the boy and whispered, "On pain of your life, you are not to speak of what happened to anybody. Not Harolde, or even my son. Do you understand?"

Jonathan's fingers twisted the cloth of the baron's cloak. He nodded his head. "But you did promise."

Baron Thorne loosened the boy's fingers and sighed. "So I did. And I will deliver you to your kinsmen on the continent."

"You mean he is going with us?" Roger demanded.

The baron nodded slowly. "I do not know why the Lord has placed this child in our care, but I cannot believe that it is mere coincidence. Surely there is a design somewhere in all this."

"The design of the Lord is in all things," Harolde murmured.

"It is settled then," the baron said. "Roger, I place him in your care, but be gentle with him, for he is not so sturdy as you."

They waited until dead of night. The baron opened a trap door in the storeroom, climbed down the rope ladder and dropped into the rowboat moored to the stone piling. Harolde came next, picking his way so that his skirts would not get caught. Roger scrambled down and waved impatiently to Jonathan who tripped and fell the final four rungs.

"Clumsy!" Roger muttered, swatting him.

They held their breaths, waiting for the alarm, but apparently the guards patrolling the bridge had not heard. Through the occasional breaks in the swirling river mists they could see the flame-lit horizon on the north bank of the Thames and hear the distant roar of the fire.

Harolde and the baron each grabbed an oar and rowed hard toward the south bank of the Thames, passing the dark forms of galley and drummond anchored in the estuary. The men were drenched with sweat when the rowboat finally scraped against the mud flats of Southwark, den of prostitute and cutthroat.

They had gotten no more than a hundred yards when shadowy figures surrounded them. The baron drew his sword, Roger his dagger, and Harolde brandished his Bible. The thieves slunk off to wait for easier prey.

At the Abbot of Hyde's Inn, called The Tabard, Baron Thorne commandeered three of the horses the Mercer's Guild had stabled there. The innkeeper thought them mad to travel at night.

"Highwaymen abound," he told them sleepily. "A party of pilgrims departs at dawn for Canterbury. You would be safe with them."

But the baron insisted they be on their way. He saddled an aging Great Horse named Tantor, Harolde a pack animal called Noname, and Roger and Jonathan shared a cantankerous donkey named Tortoise, who would not gallop no matter how hard Roger kicked or cajoled her. Jonathan sat behind Roger, clutching his waist.

"Not so tight!" Roger exclaimed, jabbing Jonathan in the ribs.

"I do not think I have ever been on such a beast before," Jonathan said, and clung to Roger even harder as they rode off.

DOVER

THEY RODE THROUGH THE NIGHT AND ALL THE next day, arriving in Canterbury in the late evening. Saddle-weary after the sixty-mile journey, they stopped overnight at the Conquest Inn, only to discover that not an available bed remained in the entire hostel.

They bedded down in the barn. Baron Thorne and Harolde spread their saddle blankets over some bales of hay.

"Let us sleep in the loft," Roger said to Jonathan, goosing him up the ladder. Roger had in mind to question the boy once they were out of earshot, but being bleary-eyed from the journey, he fell asleep almost at once.

Below, the baron gave voice to his fears. "Harolde, should anything happen to me . . . you are to proceed to the continent and enroll Roger at the university; this I charge you with. Despite his objections."

"They will be many and loud," Harolde said, rolling his eyes.

The baron gave a short laugh. "Yes, but he will be safe there. Ah, the boy is like some wild thing since his mother died. Only she knew how to calm him, though sometimes I believe she did more harm than good with her tales of saints and superstitions. These Germans! As practical as oxen yet as fanciful as the unicorn. He is his mother's son, without a doubt."

"A good lad nevertheless," Harolde said, "and he will outgrow these childish things."

"One hopes," the baron sighed.

Harolde coughed and cleared his throat. "And what about the other lad?" he asked, trying not to show his disapproval of Jonathan.

Baron Thorne weighed his words. "In that you must follow

your own conscience. But I pray you, let your judgment be tempered with mercy. The lad has suffered much. I would hope that you would deliver him to Cologne, where he should be able to locate his kinsmen. There will be a reward waiting."

Jonathan cried out in the middle of the night. "The knife!" he screamed, "the knife!" He bolted upright, scaring Roger half out of his wits. Roger crept to the edge of the loft and peered down at his father and Harolde; they were still sleeping. He crawled back to Jonathan.

"What knife?" he whispered.

When Jonathan did not answer Roger said softly, "We are friends, are we not?"

Jonathan nodded cautiously.

"Then you must tell me about yourself. Do not be frightened. How old are you? Under what sign are you born?"

"Thirteen," Jonathan answered. "Sagittarius."

"I am a Leo," Roger said with just a touch of pride. "But you are that old? I would not have guessed it, for you are mostly skin and bones. I am only a year older, but see how much bigger my arms are? Now then, who are you?"

Jonathan stared at his hands and said nothing.

"Are you a runaway slave?" Roger asked, feeling the boy's arms for any telltale branding marks. "Harolde thinks you are one of King John's hostages from Wales, newly escaped from prison. But I do not believe it." He regarded the boy's sallow face, his slight frame, his mass of dark curly hair. "Those hostages are sons of noblemen and you are not of noble birth, anybody can see that. Are you a Saracen then, that my father smuggled into London from one of his voyages to the Holy Land?"

When Jonathan failed to respond, Roger grabbed his wrist and twisted his arm behind his back. "Must I use force?" he demanded.

Jonathan drew in his breath sharply and then hung his head, resigning himself to the pain.

"Oh, stop crying," Roger said, releasing him. "I did not hurt you that much. Well, it is obvious that some demon has stolen your senses. I warn you, you might as well tell me, for I shall not give up until I have unearthed this mystery."

Shortly before dawn the travelers ate a hurried meal of cold venison and mead and, ever alert to the possibility of pursuit, were en route again.

It had been a vicious winter, with howling winds that burned the evergreens and froze the land; wolves and sheep alike had worn thick coats. But winter was done with now and spring more than a promise. Violets, sweet William, and baby's breath dotted the neat gardens of Canterbury.

As they approached the cathedral, Harolde said, "Is there land anywhere in England more hallowed than this? Here it was that Thomas à Becket suffered martyrdom at the hands of Henry II's knights, and here to this day the battle between Pope Innocent III and King John continues."

A quarter of a century before a great fire had melted the cathedral's lead roof, sending it crashing down into the nave. Rebuilding had begun almost immediately, only to be interrupted three years ago by Innocent's suspension of church services.

Harolde looked at the pilgrims kneeling in prayer before the barred and shuttered cathedral doors, his heart filling with sadness for these folk denied the Lord. But then he also felt a certain anger for his own denied aspirations. Believing that this less literate country of England offered a greater opportunity to rise higher and faster in the hierarchy of the church, Harolde had left the Benedictine monastery near his birthplace in Normandy and journeyed across the channel. But he had only been in London a short time when the investiture contest between king and pope erupted. For three long years Harolde had watched his fellow monks suffer as King John confiscated all church property.

"Only when the king submits to the wisdom of the Holy Father and allows Stephen Langton to become archbishop of Canterbury will Englishmen be able to live once more in the light of the Lord," Harolde said. "Remember, Roger, as I have taught you, such appointments are the sole domain of the Holy See."

But Baron Thorne also desired to instruct his son. "Harolde's view has merit, but lacks balance. Lord knows I have little love for our monarch, but there is much more involved here than the mere naming of an archbishop. What Englishmen must eventually decide is who will reign supreme in our land, church or state? And, can men reach God only through another man?"

"The pope is the earthly vicar of Christ!" Harolde exclaimed, scandalized.

"A man nonetheless," the baron replied equably.

Roger swiveled his head to and fro as the argument grew more heated.

Harolde said, "The church is like the sun, the state like the moon; and just as the lesser luminary takes its light from the greater, so must the state be guided in all things by . . ."

"Yes, yes," Thorne interrupted, "we all know Innocent's treatise *On the Sun and the Moon,* though you would do better, brother monk, if you did not quote the pope so much but thought for yourself."

Annoyed at this, Harolde cast about for a rejoinder and said, "Only the pope is armed with the mighty weapons that slay the soul!"

"Oh, what I would not give to go with you on your pilgrimage," Roger said to Harolde. "To Rome first, then I would press on to Jerusalem! Instead of just sitting in an old school for the end purpose of becoming a . . . merchant!" He made the word sound like an expletive. "Harolde, how can my father do this to me? You must intercede, convince him that I am meant for nobler things!"

"Just as Harolde listens to *his* father, so you must listen to yours," the baron said to his son, his eyes twinkling.

Roger made a face, then turned once more to Harolde. "Will you meet the Holy Father when you get to Rome?"

Harolde's face lit up with the prospect. "I do not know if I shall ever be lucky enough to meet the pontiff, but I do know

that within the year he will send out a summons for a new Lateran Council. For months the monasteries have been abuzz
with the news. If I get to Rome early enough and with just a
little luck. . . ."

In matters ecclesiastic, the Lord had graced Harolde with an
extraordinary gift. Long ago he had committed all the Psalms
to memory and now labored daily on the New Testament. He
could recite date and content of every major papal encyclical
and could argue the church's case against any extant heresy.
"With the proper connections," Harolde said, "I see no reason
why I could not advance to a position of importance in the
curia and perhaps eventually . . ." Harolde caught sight of
Baron Thorne's cynical smile; he blushed and added hastily,
"It may be that this Fourth Lateran Council will provide me
with the perfect opportunity to serve God."

Harolde's concentration on the letter of church law had, despite his youth, made him somewhat austere. Children especially were apt to find him forbidding; though Harolde adored
babies, they invariably cried when he assisted at baptisms. He
had somewhat the same effect on animals. At the Conquest
Inn, a wolfhound had lumbered from the room when Harolde
entered and a kitten would not suffer him to pet her, though
she played recklessly with Jonathan.

Cats being familiars for witches, heretics, and the like,
Harolde took this as further proof against the dark boy. From
the very beginning Harolde suspected Jonathan's secret. All
evidence pointed to his being a heretic. He never crossed himself, never said his prayers, averted his eyes from crucifixes. A
Beguine the child might be, or a pantheist, or, heaven forbid,
even an Albigensian, the wickedest of heretics, who believed
that the world had been created not by the Lord but by the
devil.

Harolde had wrestled mightily with his conscience about re-
porting Jonathan to the authorities once they reached the continent. Two things stopped him: first, his intense loyalty to the
baron, who had given him shelter when so many of his
brother monks starved because of the king's rape of the mon-

asteries. The second reason, and of paramount importance, concerned his sense of mission about the boy.

Harolde looked hard at Jonathan dozing on Roger's shoulder as Tortoise plodded along. They would be traveling together for at least six weeks on their journey to Cologne. "Forty days, more or less," Harolde breathed, "in which to lead him to Christ."

Harolde thumbed through his breviary searching for a prayer for the conversion of heretics. Goosebumps coursed along his body with the thrill of the challenge. Who among my superiors would not be impressed with such a feat? he thought. What greater glory can I attain than to bring the Savior's light into this lost and terrified soul? By God's wounds, by the time we reach Cologne I will have made a true Christian of him!

Leaving Canterbury, the band rode through the rolling countryside of Kent until they reached the seaport of Dover, some twelve miles distant. They found that the tides had not yet changed and they would have to wait several hours. The king's soldiers patrolled the wharf area, checking on all hostels and taverns.

"Where would we be least likely to arouse suspicion?" Baron Thorne asked, and then answered himself, "Why, right under their noses," and led his party up the steep winding road to Dover Castle, one of King John's strongholds.

High atop the chalk-white cliffs, the band watched the frenzied building in progress. New curtain walls were being erected, the dry moat dug deeper, the keep strengthened. All manner of knights rode across the narrow bridge into the fortress bristling with war machines.

The baron's party tethered their mounts in the shadow of the ruined pharos, a lighthouse built in Roman times, which stood just outside the castle walls. From here they had a commanding view of all the roads. Hundreds of feet below, the waves of the English Channel dashed against the cliffs, spuming up in a rainbowed mist.

Baron Thorne pointed across the channel. "Only twenty

miles separate us from the continent. If France does invade, her armies will doubtless cross here. He who controls Dover Castle controls the road to London, and whichever way London goes, so goes England."

"Will there really be war?" Roger asked hopefully, "for then I would surely be called upon to serve." That prospect was so much more exciting than his miserable struggles with the verb *sum;* after six months he was no closer to being able to conjugate it. And Aristotle's *Rhetoric* remained as elusive to him as the philosopher's stone.

"Many of us are doing what we can to prevent war," the baron said, making precise note of the new fortifications. "The coming weeks will tell."

Restless with energy, Roger pressed Jonathan into a game of follow the leader. He cartwheeled across the meadow; arms outstretched, he balanced himself on the narrow ledge of a retaining wall as he gazed at the pounding sea below. "Oh, that I could soar like the peregrine, or dive like the dolphin and be carried out to sea!"

Jonathan tried gamely to mimic Roger but balked when Roger began to climb the walls of the Church of St. Mary, which abutted the lighthouse.

"How will you ever learn to storm a fortress if you cannot do such a simple thing as scale a wall?" Roger asked, frowning. Then he made two swords from the construction debris and threw one to Jonathan. "Now I will instruct you in the art of fencing. *En garde.* No, no, blockhead, hold it like *this!* Never been on a horse? Never held a sword? You *are* a strange one."

Jonathan fell back before Roger's furious onslaught, trying unsuccessfully to defend himself.

"Stop now," Thorne called, "you have bloodied the boy's nose."

Jonathan stood absolutely still, staring at the bright stains.

Roger threw down his sword in disgust. "A fine knight you'd make if you had to stop for something as silly as a bloody nose. Come on then, let us tend to your wounds," and flinging his arm around Jonathan's shoulder, led him off.

"The lad is odd, is he not?" Harolde said tentatively to the baron. "At every moment he looks as if he is about to burst into tears. Yet he never complains, never cries. Never prays for comfort or guidance."

Baron Thorne looked evenly at Harolde and said nothing.

"Yes, he is afflicted," Harolde said as he felt himself being stared down. "But mark my words, in a few short weeks, perhaps less, you will see him reborn."

Shortly before dusk Baron Thorne spied a distant cloud of dust on the road below. "You have the eyes of a falcon," he said to Roger. "How do you make it?"

"Soldiers," Roger said promptly. "From the dust their horses are kicking up, I would guess at least a dozen."

"Quickly, then," the baron said. "They may be the king's men or not, but we cannot take the chance. We must get down to the docks before them and pray that the tide now be with us."

They rode down the steep path, presented their papers to the harbormaster, and boarded a small sloop about ready to sail.

"Faster, man, faster," the baron muttered, watching the captain cast off. Just as the company of knights rode into the dock area, the wind caught the sail with a sharp crack and the sloop sped from the harbor, past the ghostly cliffs of Dover and out into the blackness of the open sea.

ST. DENIS:
EARLY MAY

IKE A SENTINEL STONE IN THE GENTLY ROLL-
ing plain, the Basilica of St. Denis, mother of
churches, rose up before the travelers. Not quite a
week had passed since the baron and his party
had made good their escape from Dover. Fair
winds had carried them across a calm channel and into the
harbor of Calais, where a great number of ships lay at anchor.
Rumor had it that the French monarch, Philip Augustus, had
massed more than a thousand vessels in all the channel ports.
Invasion did seem imminent.

The need for protection against brigands had prompted the
baron to join a band of pilgrims journeying to the shrine of St.
Denis, some five miles north of Paris, there to worship its
sacred relics—a fragment of the crown of thorns and a splinter
of the true cross.

Now Baron Thorne shifted uneasily in his saddle. Paris was
only three or four hours away. He wondered how best to com-
port himself with the Capetian king; serious doubts had
begun to plague him about his mission.

Roger too was in a turmoil, though for very different reasons. He said over his shoulder to Jonathan, "How am I to escape from this university?"

"But why escape?" Jonathan asked. "I have heard tell that it
is a wondrous place."

Roger twisted and glared at the boy. "So that is why you are
so sickly pale!" he said, realizing for the first time that Jonathan's pallor bespoke books and studying, things he loathed
with a passion. "Then you attend!" he snapped.

"Would that I might," Jonathan murmured, "but such
things are not possible for me."

"Why not?" Roger asked, suddenly alert to the opportunity
of learning something about Jonathan.

Jonathan hesitated, and then with a swift glance at the baron clamped his mouth shut.

All this week Roger had tried every way he knew to win Jonathan's confidence, promising friendship, threatening torture, all to no avail. Sometimes the boy seemed about to respond to Roger's persistent questions, but then a blank look would glaze his eyes. And so the mystery surrounding him grew more perplexing.

Roger jabbed Jonathan hard with his elbow. "Touched you are, or dumb, I know not which, but truly you are a vexation to the spirit."

Jonathan nodded morosely, happy to get off with just a jab. In these few short days he had been intimidated and overwhelmed by this golden youth who seemed to draw the sun, who was so comely everybody turned to look at him. Roger's enthusiasms changed with the hour. Now he wished to be a knight, now a cardinal, now a hermit, a lover; each role he acted out for his captive audience. And though he thought Roger almost akin to a barbarian and was sore afraid of him, Jonathan was also dazzled by his wild dance with life.

Plumes of smoke drifted lazily from the fields where farmers burned their tares. Planting had been late this spring; for three months there had been no rain and the ground was baked hard from a sun too relentless for May.

The riders reached the north gate of St. Denis and waited while their credentials and goods were checked by the guards. Vendors from the tiny faubourg surrounded the pilgrims, proffering cheeses, bread, and flacons of wine.

All at once shrieks and curses cut the air. People scattered as a company of prelates and abbots galloped by with their armed escort, shouldering everybody off the road. Tantor stumbled into a ditch, Roger and Jonathan barely missed sinking into a sump of night soil, and Harolde landed in the dust.

Harolde brushed off his habit; his eyes flinched from his brothers in Christ, their gems winking on pudgy fingers, their jowled faces bespeaking good food and fine wines. "Come!" Harolde shouted, his voice trembling with derision, "leave what thou hast and follow me!"

An abbot wheeled at the insult and gave orders to one of the escorts. Whip raised, the guard charged the young monk. Harolde stood his ground. Baron Thorne spurred Tantor up from the ditch and brunted himself between Harolde and the guard, one hand resting on the pommel of his sword.

"Come ahead, then," Baron Thorne said mildly, "if you are so anxious to meet your maker."

The mercenary took in the baron's imposing physique, thought better of it and cantered back to his party.

Roger said to Jonathan, "If that coward had not fled you would have seen a fight. In his day, my father earned his keep fighting in tournaments. That was before my mother's people turned his head to trade. And universities."

Baron Thorne leaned from his mount and cuffed Roger good-naturedly. Then he turned to Harolde. "Are there not an uncommonly large number of churchmen about?" he asked, pointing to another group of priests and monks waiting at the gate.

"It is not the feast day of a local saint," Harolde mused, "for I know all of those. Perhaps there is a religious procession in St. Denis? Or a funeral?"

Harolde approached one of the guards at the gate and asked him.

"It has been like this all week," the guard said. "Never have I seen such crowds. From all over the province people have come to hear the words of this child. The Lord gave him the gift of speech so he could preach His message."

Before Harolde could learn more the gates opened and the press of people carried him and the others into the commune of St. Denis. As they headed down the rue de la Boulangerie, the cathedral loomed ever larger. Though it was market day, the stalls along the street were nearly empty of shoppers and many establishments were barred and shuttered.

"This young evangelist must indeed be a wonder," Harolde said.

Eager for any diversion, Roger said to Jonathan, "Do you not feel an excitement in the air?" but before Jonathan could answer Roger elbowed him again, and pointed toward a sling loaded with building blocks rising alongside the church tower. High above, two tiny laborers worked on the scaffolding and higher still, a gray hawk and its mate dipped and swooped in the cerulean sky.

Jonathan rubbed his ribs; riding behind Roger these many days, he had developed a sore spot.

When he came in full view of the basilica, Roger stopped short, struck with the huge expanses of stained glass that seemed to float between the stone buttresses. "But what holds this church up?" he asked, amazed. "There are hardly any walls!"

"It is miraculous," Harolde agreed. "When I was a lad in Normandy, many times I made pilgrimages to St. Denis, to marvel as this house of God was being built in the new style. See how different it is from the ponderous old Romanesque structures? See how it appears to float on light? Such churches are rising everywhere, to testify that the light of the Lord shines eternal!" Harolde finished in a burst of passion.

"We shall see a cardinal of you yet, Harolde," Baron Thorne commented.

Harolde dropped his eyes but could not control the blush that radiated up from his neck. He could never tell when the baron was mocking him. Exhausted from his speech he began to cough and it took him some moments to regain his breath.

When the band reached the south courtyard they saw a crowd of perhaps six hundred people listening, transfixed, to a boy preaching from a creaking platform. The lad stopped for a moment to let the new arrivals crowd closer. No more than twelve years old, he looked like an ordinary peasant boy. The thick brown hair that fell to his shoulders badly needed washing; his brown eyes were smallish and set far apart. Yet such an intensity radiated from him that appearances counted for naught.

Harolde reached down and tapped a monk on the shoulder. "Good sir, what can you tell me of this child?"

"Ask Brother Rigord there," he said, pointing to another monk standing nearby.

Brother Rigord, chronicler and physician of St. Denis, had

interrupted his major work, writing the history of Philip Augustus, to come hear the lad all France gossiped about. "It is the shepherd boy, Stephen of Cloyes," Brother Rigord said to Harolde. "Walked all the way from Chartres, he has, to bring us a message from the Savior. Why even the bishop of Chartres was so moved by this lad that he has petitioned the king in his behalf."

With a sudden urgency, Baron Thorne tried to get his party to ride on, but Harolde and Roger had already been separated from him by the crowd.

Roger edged Tortoise closer, at once attracted and repelled by the shepherd. "Who does he think he is?" he demanded, poking Jonathan. "Have you ever seen such a rude bumpkin? Why, I would not trust him to groom this donkey!" Still, Roger felt irresistibly drawn to the boy whose impassioned words once more resounded against the massive stone buttresses and flew toward the sky.

"Verily, I say unto you, there is not one soul in this land— not one!—who will be saved while the tomb of our Lord remains in the hands of the infidel. O infamous day that saw the devil in the guise of Saladin triumph over Jerusalem. Yet did we not deserve this cruel blow? Did not our knights journey to the holy lands of Outremer for gain and riches? Did they not pleasure themselves with foreign ways and foreign harlots? Forgetting the suffering of the one who died for our sins?"

Tantor whinnied as the crowd stirred. The baron did not like what he was hearing and again signaled the others to move on. Roger and Harolde, some ten paces ahead, remained oblivious to all save the shepherd, who now recounted how and why he had been guided to this mission.

On the twenty-fifth day of April, Stephen and his parents had journeyed from their village of Cloyes to Chartres. There, on the feast day of St. Mark, which had come to be called "The Day of the Black Crosses," Stephen had watched the procession of monks carrying the black-shrouded crucifixes, commemorating those Crusaders who had died to free the Holy Land. Upon returning to his village, he discovered that his sheep had trampled all the new plantings, a calamity in this time of drought. He raised his staff to strike them but before he could land one blow, the sheep fell to their knees and genuflected, begging his forgiveness. Everyone in Cloyes declared it a miracle.

"I sensed that great things were stirring in the land and waited for a sign," Stephen told the crowd. "Within days . . ."

The crowd surged closer, hungry for any miracle. Roger envied this boy his power to hold the crowd in his thrall. He punched Jonathan's thigh and demanded, "Who saw the sheep genuflect? Are we to take this simpleton's word?" Yet, annoyed as he was, Roger could not bring himself to move on.

"A gentle man appeared in the midst of my flock," Stephen continued. "This pilgrim told me he had just arrived from Jerusalem. He spoke of the trials of the devout who could not worship at our most sacred shrines. He said the Lord could not rest in peace as long as peace lived not in His land. When this traveler asked for a bit of bread, I gave him all I had. Whereupon this wondrous man said that after searching the length and breadth of France, he had found the one person to lead his new crusade, a crusade of peace, a crusade made up of children! For only the innocent, with no thought of gain, could free the Holy Land. And he told me that I had been chosen; that whereas once I could not speak, now I would stutter no more; and that whereas once I watched over a tiny flock, now I would lead multitudes; and whereas the Holy Land had been lost because of our sins, now it would be redeemed through our love!"

A white-robed Cistercian monk sang out, "Hallelujah!" and the crowd responded in ringing chorus.

"Well, it *is* a miraculous tale," Roger said grudgingly. "Though why our Lord should have made Himself known to a peasant . . ." He threw up his hands in consternation.

A beatific smile lit Stephen's face. "Furthermore, the Seignior said that before we can bring about the Kingdom of Heaven on earth, the Holy Land *must* be freed. To let all know His intent, my Seignior gave me this letter, charging me to deliver it into the hands of our good king. So that he would proclaim this crusade throughout the land. For the first time in all the history of the Crusades, we march not with sword in hand, but with mercy in our hearts. Not for revenge, but with trust in the Gospel of the Savior, who taught us to love our brothers. For I say unto you, if we are armed with the love of the Lord, have we need of any other weapon?"

As one, the crowd screamed back its affirmation. Despite himself, Roger joined in the cheering and even Jonathan added his shouts though an edge of fear sounded in his voice.

"Our Lord intended it this way," Roger exclaimed to Jonathan, "for has He not told us so? All we need do is *believe*! Oh, out of the mouths of babes! If only the Seignior had appeared so to *me*! If only. . . ."

Jonathan did not know what to make of this mood of Roger's. He could feel Roger's body trembling, hear his voice throbbing. He had not thought this bluff, hearty lad able to be so moved.

Then the child evangelist held out his arms so that his body became a living crucifix, waiting for that incandescent moment when one slogan would unite the mob. Just as they quieted, a jeering laugh floated down from the skies. A thousand eyes searched through the sun's glare, focusing at last on the scaffolding that hung from the south tower where two workers were repairing some stone ornamentation destroyed by heat lightning.

Pierre, the stonemason, continued lashing poles to complete the top level of the scaffold. He shouted to his apprentice and stepson, Guillaume, a lad of fifteen. Guillaume, cranking the windlass to bring up another load of mortar, interrupted his work and handed his master a mat woven of wood and twigs.

Pierre and Guillaume were stripped to the waist, their sweaty muscles flexing with their exertions. Pierre positioned the wooden hurdle over the crossbars, testing its strength before putting his full weight on it. All during this he continued his insinuating laughter, hurling insults down on the crowd.

"Who is that blasphemous knave?" Harolde asked Brother Rigord. "He should be put in the stocks for his foul mouth."

Brother Rigord nodded sadly. "You are right, but he is the

best stonemason in the province. He has the feet of a goat; some say the soul too. Last night he had to be carried home from the tavern again. But where other masons refuse to climb, Pierre dares and so the master builder and the bishop can do nothing but suffer his indignities. Now the lad next to Pierre, he is a gifted youth," Brother Rigord said, "wasted really on such menial work. He loves nothing better than to spend hours unearthing the hideous gargoyles or discovering the demure saints who lie hidden in our great blocks of Caen marble. Already one of his efforts has caught the eye of the master sculptor. But Pierre is jealous of the lad and will not release him from his apprenticeship."

High above, Pierre motioned for Guillaume to climb to the top level. Guillaume waited for the creaking scaffolding to stop swaying in the wind while Pierre continued to curse at him.

Jonathan, watching it all, suddenly gripped Roger's shoulder. "Look! The boy keeps slipping! Why does the older man not help him?"

Guillaume got one knee onto the upper platform but could not negotiate the other leg. Still his stepfather did not make a move to assist him. Guillaume finally reached the top level where Pierre clouted him for his slowness.

Pierre burped up the sour taste of last night's debauch, then turned his spleen on the crowd once more. "Fools you are and worse than fools to believe this young charlatan. Not the Lord who came to this idiot, but the devil! For only the devil could set a child to do the work that the greatest knights in the realm could not accomplish. And it is the devil speaking through his lips who beguiles you now!"

Harolde stood up in his stirrups, the better to see the stone mason. "Could he be right?" he asked Brother Rigord. "The shepherd boy might be soul-possessed, for everybody knows that the devil has a way with words."

An instant of fright contorted Stephen of Cloyes' boyish face. Voice quavering, he said, "As God is my defender, I call upon Him to judge who is telling the truth!"

"Child of the devil, go home!" Pierre shouted, going red in the face. "Do an honest day's work instead of trying to fleece poor people!" Pierre wrapped his bandy legs around an upright scaffold brace and leaned out into space. "Shame, shame, only the devil knows your name, only the devil knows your game!"

The crowd roared with laughter at Pierre's antics.

Stephen cried out defensively, "We must offer up prayers to the Almighty to exorcise the demons afflicting this poor being's soul!"

With a great rush of wings, a gray hawk returned to its nest atop the tower. The bird had flown in from the north so it had not been visible to the crowd. Perhaps Pierre had come too close to its young. Perhaps Pierre could no longer drink as in his youth and still keep his wits about him. Perhaps the bird was truly an omen. The crowd saw only a sudden fierce flapping of wings that seemed to fly out of the stonemason's head. They screamed as his frantic clawing upset the hurdle, leaving Guillaume dangling from the ledge.

Pierre hung in space for an impossible instant, then fell, hitting the earth with a fearful crump. Brother Rigord rushed to administer the last rites, but Pierre had already gone unshriven to his fate. All eyes flashed back to the tower where Guillaume hung from the scaffold, his feet fighting for purchase in the empty air.

"Hold!" Stephen cried, his arm shooting up.

Guillaume stopped struggling. Panic left him long enough to remember the windlass rope swaying just within reach. Guillaume's toes strained for the line, then his legs wrapped around it.

The crowd held its breath while Stephen called up prayers for the boy's safety. Slowly, Guillaume lowered himself toward the ground until he dangled very close to where Roger and Jonathan sat on Tortoise. Roger kicked Tortoise forward and reached up to help the apprentice. Guillaume, hands scored with rope burns, could no longer hold on and fell the final three feet, landing across Tortoise's neck. She let out an outraged bray.

Roger clasped Guillaume to his bosom as though he had found a long-lost brother. Then hands wrenched the boys apart to pass Guillaume over the heads of the crowd and finally set him down next to Stephen.

Stephen raised his arm in a gesture of triumph. "Again I implore you! Who will follow me and win everlasting glory?"

Guillaume, his bare body crawling with gooseflesh, dropped to one knee before the evangelist. "I will follow," he whispered.

A great stampede ensued as scores of people, young and old, surged toward the shepherd to take the crusading oath which would bind them until they set foot in Jerusalem, an oath they dared not break on pain of instant excommunication and loss of their souls.

As if in a trance, Roger urged Tortoise toward the evangelist, saying, "This is the path for me! *This* is my destiny!"

Jonathan's head reeled with the crush of hysterical people screaming, "Jesus!" "Salvation!" "Vengeance!" He saw not this cathedral square, but a looting, pillaging mob with drawn bloody swords while all around them the streets of London mushroomed into flame. "Oh, no, please," he whimpered, his hands reaching out in a gesture of pleading and then his fingers clenched into fists and he was punching at Roger's back, screaming, "No! Do not kill them! Stop!"

Hearing Jonathan's cries, the baron spurred Tantor through the throng. He grabbed Tortoise's reins and led the boys away from the basilica. Roger rose in the saddle, fighting to get back to Stephen but Thorne's hand clamped down on his son's thigh, pinning him to the seat.

Once away from the crowd, Jonathan gradually recovered his senses. In his own frustration, Roger pummeled and elbowed Jonathan for his attack on him, calling him fool and madman.

Behind them, they heard Stephen's fading voice. "We march now to petition the king of France. . . ."

The baron's party passed through St. Denis' south gate into the countryside. In the fields between St. Denis and Paris, where the Fair of Lendit would soon take place, a shocked Baron Thorne saw hundreds of encamped children. Each day, as news of Stephen's crusade of children spread through the provinces, hundreds more kept arriving.

"Truly a phenomenon," Harolde said in wonderment to the baron. "The lad's voice! One could be a cardinal with such golden speech. Did it not seem to you that the fine hand of the Lord was working through this young shepherd?"

The baron grumbled, "I do not know if the boy has been called by the Lord or the devil. Or if he is just mad. Ah, the young, the young," he sighed. "Every year the fevers of spring prompt such wanderlust. But a crusade of children? To Jerusalem?" He shook his head at Roger. "What madness will possess you next? Well, in any case, none of this concerns us, for we must be about our own work."

"What greater work is there save God's?" Roger demanded. "Did the Lord not make His will known when the mason fell to his death and the child was rescued?"

Baron Thorne frowned and said nothing. Secretly, he thought the entire event extraordinary. The king of France would have to do something, and quickly, lest the folly get out of hand.

PARIS:
THE PALAIS ROYAL

WHAT YOU DO NOT UNDERSTAND," BARON THORNE said as they proceeded toward Paris, "is that a crusade is not a game."

"You went," Roger challenged him.

"I went as a man," the baron replied.

Roger twisted around to Jonathan, "My father was only seventeen, not three years older than I, when he rushed off with Richard Coeur de Lion to wrest Jerusalem from Saladin."

"We did not *rush*," Thorne said wryly. "We set sail from Dover in the winter of 1189, but because of the intrigue between Philip of France and Richard, and Richard's insistence on conquering Messina and then Cyprus, our army did not arrive at Acre until a year and a half later! Philip had begun the siege several months before but it took Richard's magical presence to force the city to capitulate." The baron paused, his eyes fixed on a place distant in time. "An accursed, evil land that is; I saw men do things there. . . . After the Saracen garrison had surrendered, we slaughtered them—2,700 severed heads, all in the name of the Prince of Peace. My sword, my armor, my hands, all covered with blood. I grew old that day.

"Under the blazing sun trust withered. Philip, ravaged by jealousy and quartan fever, barely managed to make his way back to France, leaving the field with Saladin still in possession of Jerusalem. Twice Richard fought his way to the plains of Beit Nuba, within twelve miles of the Holy City! Only to be denied the goal by the Saracens who fought just as fiercely for their god."

"Their devil, you mean," Harolde muttered.

The Baron shrugged off this remark. "The best Richard could manage was the Truce of the Threes—Joachim of Fiore and the church having attached mystical significance to the number—the truce to last three years, three months, three weeks, and three days, allowing our pilgrims access to all the holy places in Palestine."

"Who is Joachim of Fiore?" Roger asked his father. "Why have I not heard you speak of him before? Is he a knight?"

"No doubt Harolde can tell you better than I," the baron said.

"Do you know nothing of the great men of the church?" Harolde said. "Joachim of Fiore has recently died, but his name will live on, for the Lord revealed to this poor Cistercian abbot from Calabria the hidden meanings of the Bible."

"What?" Roger asked, his clear blue eyes sharp and eager.

"All the prophets foretell that before the millennium can come three conditions must be fulfilled. First, that a new Kingdom of Jerusalem arise. Second, that the Holy City be free. And third, that the Temple of Solomon be rebuilt on its original foundations, now occupied by the infidel mosque, the Dome of the Rock."

Jonathan leaned from behind Roger and started to correct Harolde but then thought better of it and held his peace.

Harolde continued, "Further, Joachim of Fiore discovered that history is divided into three ages: the Age of the Father, which is the age of the law and of the Old Testament; the Age of the Son, which occurs with the Messiah and the New Testament; and finally, the Age of the Holy Spirit, which is to commence sometime after the year 1200."

"But that is right now!" Roger exclaimed.

Harolde nodded eagerly. "In this glorious age both the church and the Holy Roman Empire will wither away; with God in the hearts of all men there will be no need for artificial rule over body or spirit. Then will come the days of our Last Judgment. But before any of this can be brought about, Jerusalem *must* be freed."

Thorne shook his head sadly. "And more thousands of lives lost to fulfill a prophecy which may not be true. Roger, do you understand now why I could never permit my own flesh and blood to partake in such a doomed venture?"

"Don't you see?" Roger blurted. "It is because you went for *gain* that your crusade failed. But Stephen . . ."

"Paris," the baron interrupted, pointing to the massive thirty-foot wall that swept in a semicircle around the city.

Once through the Porte St. Denis, Thorne and his party passed into an intense world. Merchant shops competed for space with dovecotes and stables; the smells of leather, hay, and manure commingled.

"Never have I seen so many people, heard so many voices," Roger exclaimed to Jonathan.

At nearly every street corner, adding to the din, priests re-cruited able-bodied men for Pope Innocent's crusades for the faith. "Free the Holy Land!" one cleric shouted. "Crush the Almohads in Spain," cried another, while yet a third pleaded, "Wipe out the Albigensian heretics in the south of France!"

"If only I were a few years older," Roger said to Jonathan.

Above the cacophany of voices sounded a distant rhythmic rumble, steady as a pulse beat, which seemed centered in the great cloud of dust hanging over the heart of the city.

"Is it a fire?" Roger asked hopefully. Had his prayers been answered, was the university burning?

"You shall see what it is soon enough," the baron said.

The bells from the Charnel House of the Innocents tolled nones, and soon other church bells joined in until the air rol-licked with the clarion call.

"Only four more hours till dusk," Harolde said. "How good it is to hear the church's voice again. Living under the inter-dict, one might just as well have been deaf—never knowing the time of day, or *anything*."

Baron Thorne increased their gait. Ordinarily, he would have rested and refreshed himself before seeking audience with Philip. But these were no ordinary times. King John's spies were everywhere. For an instant he recalled the impaled heads on London Bridge and felt uncomfortably like a conspir-ator. "Well," Thorne muttered aloud, "King John has brought this down on himself."

"Brought what?" Roger asked. When his father did not re-spond, he shrugged and changed the subject. "Do you think we shall see Stephen at court?"

Thorne guffawed. "In truth, you *are* your mother's son! It is a small trick to impress a rabble in a churchyard, but it is a very different matter to confront a monarch with such nonsense."

Roger set his jaw doggedly. "It is no trick! I wager you that Stephen will go to the king as he promised."

The baron snorted. "My lad, I fear for your wits. Even the boy behind you has more sense. What say you, Jonathan?"

Caught between father and son, Jonathan broke out into a cold sweat. Though he could have bitten off his tongue afterward, he blurted, "Does it really matter where Stephen goes? Has not the Holy Land already been promised? And to bring about the end of days, the Bible says . . ."

"Blasphemer!" Harolde choked. "*You* dare to quote the holy book to me?" and smacked him smartly across the face. Tortoise bucked with the commotion and galloped away from the fuming monk.

"A lucky thing too," Roger said to Jonathan, "or surely Harolde would have brained you. You are stupid to contradict him on matters he knows best," and to drive the point home Roger jabbed him in the stomach.

Jonathan gasped and then said under his breath, "And no amount of cursing or punching will change the prophecy, for so it is written."

As they neared the Ile de la Cité, the noise they'd heard since entering Paris increased until it deafened. High above the broken line of houses they saw a superstructure of scaffolding, filled in with a beehive of building. They moved off the road to allow a convoy of wagons to rumble by; some loaded with timber, others with native gypsum so pure it took the name plaster of Paris. Most carts were drawn by plodding oxen, but Roger gaped at the sight of wagons being pulled by women and children doing penance. Though he knew of no sin he had committed, he sprang from the saddle and put his shoulder to the ropes.

Harolde also leapt in to help, mortified that he had raised his hand in anger, albeit against a heretic. "This boy's conversion will be more difficult than I anticipated," he groaned.

As they struggled with the wagonload, Roger's eyes met Harolde's, and in that moment he felt a rush of love for the monk.

Particles of marble, lime, and stone choked the air. Winches creaked, forges roared, carpenters sawed wood for centerings to support the arched ribbed vaults, hammers and chisels clanged carving column and statuary, while an endless stream of supplies moved toward the far end of the Ile de la Cité. And all to one common cause; to build the Cathedral of Notre Dame. Year by year, day by day, stone by stone it rose, until now it looked like some gigantic ark which would one day carry men's souls to heaven.

"If you do not leave be," the baron shouted to Roger and Harolde, "I will go on without you!"

Roger and the monk rejoined the baron.

At the Seine, two-storied houses overhung the Grand Pont, the river being the best sewage system yet devised. They passed the fine shops of goldsmiths and painters of miniatures, and the tables of moneychangers, where bankers from Lombardy, Cahors, and even an occasional Jew sang out the latest exchange rates for coin from all over the world.

On the Ile de la Cité at last, Thorne's party reined in at the paved courtyard of the Palais Royal. Leaving Jonathan in charge of the animals, the baron, Roger, and Harolde entered to seek audience with the king of France.

Roger stared in awe at the enormous council chamber: whitewashed, strewn with rushes and sweet herbs, and hung with brilliant blue wall hangings embroidered with the fleur-de-lis. Glass-paned windows, Philip Augustus's new innovation, stood opened to the river breezes; cloths soaked in honey hung at the narrow apertures to snare the ubiquitous mosquitoes.

The seneschal noted the baron's request for an audience with the king. Then the three dusty travelers stood in the rear of the Great Hall and listened to the proceedings.

At forty-seven, Philip Augustus, "hammer of the English

kings," was nearly bald and blind in one eye. His burly, well-wrought body had thickened, touches of russet tinged his beard, yet he still showed traces of the vital, handsome youth who had so intrigued Richard Coeur de Lion. He had wed three times; first Elizabeth, then Ingeborg, princess of Denmark, whom he had repudiated after one night of marriage, although the papacy had refused to recognize the divorce. Paying scant attention to this, Philip next took Agnes of Meron to wife and sired two children by her, both considered bastards by the church. When Agnes died, the papacy renewed its efforts to reunite Philip and Ingeborg; the battle had raged on for sixteen years.

On Philip's right sat his son and heir, Prince Louis, and Louis's wife, Blanche of Castile niece of King John of England. In Blanche's calm visage and regal hearing shone traces of her illustrious grandmother, Eleanor of Aquitaine.

"Eleanor herself brought her granddaughter to Philip's court to be betrothed to Prince Louis," Harolde whispered to Roger. "All the more remarkable because Eleanor had previously been married to Philip's father, Louis VII, known as 'the Pious.' "

"And probably the reason for their divorce," Baron Thorne interjected with a touch of levity he was far from feeling.

The warp and woof of feudal life was a complex fabric of marriage and alliance and none wove with more skillful hand than Eleanor, once queen of France, then of England, and the fount from which would flow kings, queens, and saints. What men could not conquer through war Eleanor won through her own art.

"Now it is her granddaughter Blanche who holds the key," the baron said to himself.

To end once and forever the battle over the succession to the throne of England, King John had, in a moment of drunken rage, strangled his nephew, Arthur of Brittany. When news of that crime first rocked Europe, John had been tried *in absentia* by twelve peers of the realm. Found guilty of murder, he had been judged unfit to rule. Consequently, many on both sides of the channel considered Blanche the rightful heir to England's throne.

In the places reserved for the princes of the church sat Eudes de Sully, bishop of Paris. "The man responsible for the continued building of Notre Dame," Harolde said, nudging Roger. In his gold and scarlet robes, de Sully looked even more resplendent than the king. Occasionally, the bishop dozed off, to be gently shaken awake by his attending priest.

Philip was listening to the case of Reynault, a long-faced chevalier who had borrowed money from Noah, a prominent Jewish usurer of unpleasant bulk and wheezing breath. Unable to repay his loan, Reynault had, Noah testified, "Come to my house on the rue Rossier and there did beat me on the head."

"The Jew incited me," Reynault said. "The drought has ruined my crops. If drought be an act of God, why then should I be accountable? I demand the debt be set aside."

Roger suppressed a yawn as the argument droned on. "Why can they not settle this with a trial by combat?" he asked Harolde, who promptly shushed him.

Under ordinary circumstances Philip would have found in the chevalier's favor, if only out of habit. Philip's relationship with the Jews had always been erratic. When he ascended the throne in 1180, at the age of fifteen, his first decree reversed the tolerant attitude of his father, Louis the Pious; in 1182 Philip banished all Jews from the realm; in 1187 he officiated at the burning of eighty Jews at Brie-Comte-Robert, on suspicion of the ritual Passover murder of a Christian child.

But after Richard Coeur de Lion had been ransomed in 1197, and begun his wars against the French on the continent, Philip needed substantial sums to fortify his kingdom, including his new fortress, the Louvre. Therefore, he gave the Jews permission to return to the Ile de France. So they had remained for the past fifteen years, in uneasy stasis, helping to supply the money for the Crown. At this decisive moment Philip needed a great deal of money and dared not alienate *any* moneylenders.

Philip said abruptly, "We find the drought bears no relevance in this case. Though it may ruin next year's crop, it is *this* spring that the debt became due." Philip found in Noah's favor, with one-quarter of the sum due to go to the Crown for court costs.

Baron Throne started as the seneschal called his name. He came forward, made his obeisance, and presented first the Mercer's Guild's petition for an increase of their goods allowed to be shipped to Paris. Philip referred the matter to the Parisian guild, the Marchands de l'Eau, with the Crown's recommendation.

"My lord," the baron said, trying to control the quaver in his voice, "what I am instructed to say next is meant for your ears alone." As Baron Thorne had been instructed, this should have been the signal for Philip to grant him a private audience.

Philip, however, had other plans. "I have no secrets from my subjects," he said. "Speak or not, as you wish." Philip saw no reason to let Thorne know that his spies had followed his every move since leaving London, and that all afternoon Philip had waited impatiently for his arrival.

"What is going on here?" Roger whispered to Harolde, but the monk could only raise his eyebrows and shrug.

Thorne broke out into a cold sweat, distraught at this new turn of events. Clearly this could constitute grounds for treason. Yet so desperate had the situation in England become that he had no choice but to deliver the message entrusted to him by the barons and guilds of London.

"As my lord must be aware," Thorne began, "the barons of England have asked King John to guarantee them the freedoms which they have always held. They have even talked of a charter to assure this, but the king has been deaf to our pleas. Should the pope declare King John deposed, then the citizens of London would be favorably inclined toward recognizing Blanche's claim to the throne. Provided, of course, that Blanche and Louis see fit to honor our request for our inalienable freedoms."

Long before the baron had finished, Philip bounded to his

feet. At last! The news he had waited for and out in the open for all to hear! Pandemonium broke out among the courtiers.

Baron Thorne felt weak-kneed and clammy, convinced that his open declaration had set forces in motion which would change his entire life. Despite a stab of apprehension about his own safety, he felt a certain relief about Roger. Thank the Lord the boy would be at the university, far from the revengeful arm of King John.

Roger clutched Harolde. "How can my father go back to England now? What will happen to him?"

Harolde patted the boy's hand. "Have no fear, Pope Innocent will shortly chastise King John and England will live under God once more."

When order was restored, Philip Augustus commended the baron on his bravery and told him that Blanche and Louis would take his petition under advisement. On the specific matter of the freedoms, Philip remained silent. Grant a charter of rights in England and the disease might spread, and Philip had not spent thirty-two years consolidating his realm only to have it rent asunder by greedy noblemen.

Baron Thorne rejoined Roger and Harolde. The king stood, about to adjourn the council, when an altercation broke out at the door. The guards crossed their pikes but all manner of children climbed under and around them. A swarm of urchins, led by the evangelist, Stephen of Cloyes, streamed into the Great Hall. Courtiers rushed forward, laughing as they tried to contain the ragged bunch. "Let them approach," the king commanded.

"You see?" Roger said to his father.

More surprised than vexed, Baron Thorne said, "Now you will see the king make short work of this."

At Stephen's side strode Guillaume, the apprentice stonemason. As they passed close by, Roger half-rose in his seat. Guillaume recognized him and broke into a wide grin.

"Look at Stephen!" Roger breathed to Harolde. "Surely he must have the protection of the angels to confront so mighty a monarch without the slightest trace of fear."

Though Stephen had walked the five miles from St. Denis, a

freshness still radiated from him. As Stephen dropped to one knee before the sovereign, he moved into a shaft of sunlight and was instantly clothed in a glow more dazzling than cloth of gold. The king motioned for him to rise, but the shepherd, through ignorance or design, remained kneeling.

Once again Roger and Harolde thrilled to Stephen's miraculous tale; the baron's face remained impassive throughout.

When Stephen finished, the king blinked his eye at the boy bathed in sunlight. Philip said, not unkindly, "Why do you believe that children will succeed when the four Crusades that have gone before you have failed?"

Stephen gazed along the path of light, head cocked as though listening to voices. Then he said, "For the last time have we heard of failure. Hereafter shall children show armed knights and proud nobles how invincible are youths when *God* leads them."

A note of challenge rang in Stephen's sweet alto voice and the court stirred uncomfortably.

"So you will walk to Marseille, that you may be able to do," Philip said on a rising note of irritation. "But how do you propose to cross the sea?"

"That is the most wondrous of all," Stephen exclaimed. "The Seignior promised me that the seas will part, as they parted for the children of Israel, and we shall walk across with dry feet to the Holy Land. All this will happen because we the children seek only salvation."

One small child cheered weakly and then sighed and sat down on the cold floor.

Harolde whispered to the baron, "Could it be that God has truly chosen the weakest in His kingdom to accomplish His aims? If the little ones do succeed where the mighty have failed, would that not be a clear sign of the Lord's might?"

The baron snorted, "Idiocy!"

But the question tormented Harolde. He resented Stephen for being so chosen, while he, who had loved and labored for the Lord these many years, had never received such acknowledgment of that love.

Bishop de Sully bestirred himself. "Child, how do we know that what you claim is truly the *Lord's* desire?"

"By His signals," Stephen answered promptly. "Have there not been tremblings in the earth? Have not the bridges of the Seine been swept away in His warning by water? Since we have not heeded, now He shows us the burning face of the sun. And worse shall befall us until our world be charred like Sodom."

With the recollection of those terrible days and the promise of worse to come, all in the king's court shuddered. How could this child know of such things? He had not been born when they transpired.

Stephen, sensing his advantage, pressed, "Did not the Lord tell us to leave everything, father, mother, and all earthly possessions, and follow Him?"

Bishop de Sully interjected, "He spoke thus to grown men. As a child, He Himself remained docile to the will of His parents."

Stephen bowed his head. "My Lord, I can only tell you what the Seignior told me. That the time of the sword has passed, the time of the cross is at hand. The only thing which will honor Christ is peace. 'Suffer the little children to come unto me,' He said, and at the risk of my immortal soul I must follow wherever He will lead."

Stephen got to his feet and approached the throne. "Here is the letter which the Seignior bade me give you."

Philip scanned the parchment; it looked like a letter written by some monk and then given to this gullible child. Philip handed it to de Sully, all the while wondering how best to be rid of the lad. With his plans to conquer England moving to a climax, Philip could not tolerate any interruption, let alone a simple-minded shepherd telling him to abandon all else and embark on yet another crusade to free Jerusalem!

Bishop de Sully handed the letter back to Philip with a shrug. "It is addressed to you, so you must dispose of it."

"How these men of the church stick together!" Philip said in an aside to Blanche and Louis.

The question of the children's crusade might have ended on this day had Philip been able to speak his true mind. But the king knew that Pope Innocent III was driven by his dream to regain Jerusalem, and to that end had, during the fourteen years of his reign, daily agitated for one final crusade. The pope was so vital in Philip's overall plan—first in deposing King John, then appointing Philip as holy avenger to invade England—that he dared not do anything which would in the least offend him politically.

"My child," Philip addressed Stephen, "you have presented us with a problem so weighty. . . . You say this letter was given you by the Seignior, but who knows in what guise evil may appear?"

A chorus of assent swept the hall, but Guillaume shouted, "The Lord guides Stephen's hand, for he saved my life!"

"I saw it!" Roger chimed in.

"It is not one life which hangs in the balance," Philip said, "but the lives of thousands of children whom we hold dear. And of what good is any nation without its children? Therefore, I give this whole problem into the hands of the masters of the university. Nowhere are there men of more compassion or wisdom and they shall be the ultimate judges."

With this pronouncement Philip extricated himself from a grave dilemma. Had he not granted the charter of privileges to the masters when they founded their university on the left bank? Had he not sided with them and the students in the town-and-gown massacres? Being indebted to the Crown for past favors granted and future favors sought, the masters could well be expected to render their decision in accordance with Philip's wishes, yet in no way could Rome place the blame at his doorstep.

For a moment, Stephen of Cloyes looked crestfallen; he had truly expected Philip Augustus to give him his blessing. But then he squared his slight shoulders and called to his followers, "The king has not said no to our holy cause, only referred us to another court. So let us take heart, for tomorrow shall see us triumphant."

Stephen, Guillaume, and the children marched out of the

Great Hall, singing. Roger watched them go with a sinking heart.

Never in my life have I encountered anything so unfair! Roger thought bitterly. They are as free as the wind, but what of my tomorrows? Have I naught to look forward to save the misery of the university? It cannot be! Somehow I must escape, he thought. Somehow I must!

PARIS:
THE UNIVERSITY

F OR TWO DAYS, WHILE HE WAITED IMPATIENTLY for word from Philip Augustus, Baron Thorne hammered out his business with the guild of the Marchands de l'Eau. During this time, Roger, Harolde, and Jonathan tramped through Paris, bedazzled by the "city of light."

On the afternoon of the third day, Baron Thorne gave his son a present, an overblouse of fine wool with stag-and-hound crewelwork on the neck and cuffs.

Roger clasped his father's arm, then had the blouse on in an instant. "It is the handsomest garment I have ever owned!"

"Watch over Jonathan until I return," Baron Thorne said to Harolde. Then he turned to Roger. "It is time."

The joy in Roger's face vanished; his eyes darted to the windows and door like those of some cornered animal.

Thorne took his son's elbow and led him firmly from their room in the pension. They'd gotten halfway down the stairs when Jonathan came running after them.

"I have no present for you save this," he said, holding out a tiny talisman with strange characters on it.

The baron snatched it from him. "Harolde! I told you to see to this boy!"

Harolde flew down the steps, grabbed Jonathan and hauled him back upstairs as the baron and Roger left.

"What did you take from Jonathan?" Roger asked. "Why can I not have it?"

"It is nothing but a nonsense charm," the baron lied, and tossed it into the Seine. He quickly went on to other things as they approached the Petit Pont, explaining how two years before the masters had thrown off the tutelage of the bishops of the Ile de la Cité, quit their lodgings in the Hotel Dieu, and set up their colleges on the left bank, land being cheaper there.

"A sound move too," the baron remarked. "Homage to God is one thing, but what sense is there in studying ecclesiastical matters for sixteen years, only to become an out-of-work doctor of philosophy? The new curriculum of arts is of this world and in just *four* years you will emerge an educated man. Remember, Pope Innocent himself studied in Paris, as did Stephen Langton and Thomas à Becket. I wish my father had given me such an opportunity."

"But you could have been a nobleman!" Roger exclaimed. "And instead you chose to be a *merchant*?" He shook his head at the madness of it all.

"Yes, we are of the nobility," the baron shot back. "But minor. And for a fourth son like me there is never anything left of the pie. That is why I sought my fortunes in the Crusades. But when I returned, what work was I fit for save to sell my sword to this or that nobleman and fight in their interminable squabbles?"

"But you were a champion in the tournaments!" Roger said hotly.

Thorne rubbed an old scar in his side. "Aye, and one grows old very quickly in the lists."

As he had neared thirty with no prospect save that of being either crippled or killed, fortune's wheel had provided the baron with another chance—marriage to Gundred, daughter of one of the Merchants of Cologne. Their guild controlled all the trade between England and the Holy Roman Empire. So quickly had this new class risen that they could afford to buy their way into everything, including the nobility.

Baron Thorne said, "At first I turned up my nose at the idea of going into trade. But within a year, why, I loved it. You see, Roger, its art of winning profits is not unlike that of war. Both are cutthroat!" he said, laughing.

Roger looked unconvinced. "But one *understands* a nobleman!" he exclaimed. "Or even a serf. But a merchant? He is neither fish nor fowl."

Stung by this, the baron retorted, "Look at this city, the largest, richest in all Europe. And who has made it so? Why, the merchant class! The faster it grows, the faster the old order

dies. 'Town air makes free!' " the baron sang out, quoting the
new proverb. For once within the protection of a town's walls,
a serf was freed from his enslavement to his feudal lord.

"A new breed of man is emerging," he said, "not quite a
lord, not quite a serf, but somewhere in the middle. And mark
me well, lad, these masterless men will one day hold the key
to power. Even now, with the exception of the reigning monarch, does not our lord mayor take precedence over everybody
else in London? Since both our mayors, Robert FitzElwyn and
Robert FitzAllen, came from the Mercer's Guild. . . ."

Roger started. "You mean you might be elected lord
mayor?"

The baron shrugged. "If this journey turns out well, who
can tell? And if so, I will have risen higher and faster than if I
had remained rooted in my old life." Excitement charged the
baron's voice. "In this changing world, one must change or
perish. If you are versed in letters and the law you will be a
formidable asset to our trade. For I envision a day when our
own isle will outstrip Genoa, even Venice. And we shall be
part of it, you and I. You will be my helper, and then inheritor
of all my dreams."

His father's excitement proved contagious and Roger saw
himself commanding a fleet of galleys, invading exotic lands
. . . only to have the bubble burst as they passed the Tavern
of the Two Swords.

A dozen students swarmed out of the inn. They immediately spotted Roger as a fledgling student and in good-natured
fun formed a running ring around him, calling, *"Bec jaune,*
little yellow beak, school is a cage! Fly away before it is too
late!" Then, intent on mischief, they ran off down the rue St.
Jacques, singing:

> *I a wandering scholar lad*
> *Born to toil and sadness*
> *Oftentimes am driven by*
> *Poverty to madness!*

Turning left after the bridge, the baron and Roger found the
streets thronged with students in their long robes. Everybody

had a tonsured haircut. Roger ran his fingers anxiously through his long blond hair. I shall wind up looking and thinking like everybody else, he thought.

Some twenty thousand students were crammed into the left bank's Latin Quarter: French, English, German, Norman, Poitevin, Burgundian, Breton, Lombard, Sicilian, ·Brabant, and Flemish.

"The Italians have the papacy, Germany the empire, but France—France has learning," the baron said. "The greatest number of foreigners here are the English, so you will not lack for company or friends."

Five minutes later they arrived at the rue du Fouarre—the Street of Straw—where the students attended classes in the strawmatted lecture halls rented by the masters. The baron located the building of Master Tournique, the administrator of the School of Arts of the English Nation, and they climbed a rickety staircase two flights to his rooms. The scabrous hallways were scrawled with irreverent and obscene sayings.

Perhaps I will not be so lonely here, Roger thought with a surge of hope as he read them.

Master Tournique's red eyes and running nose were a testament to the cold he had nursed for forty years. Though the sun warmed his study, he clutched a blanket about his shoulders. Spare of flesh and slightly squint-eyed, he sat at an ink-stained desk, incessantly drumming his long fingers. Behind him stood a grillework bookcase under lock and key.

"These are the texts you will be required to buy or rent," Tournique said as the interview progressed. "St. Augustine's *The City of God,* Priscian's *Grammar*—you have your Bible? No? Scandalous! Virgil's *Aeneid,* Innocent III's *De Contemptu Mundi,* and Abelard's *Sic et Non.*

"There are seven liberal arts," he continued in his droning voice while Roger fought to keep awake. "Grammar. Logic. Rhetoric. Arithmetic. Astrology. Geometry. Music. Repeat, please, in order."

"What?" Roger asked, startled, and received a rap across the knuckles with Tournique's thick ruler.

"It is forbidden to let the mind wander, it can only lead to sinful thoughts and unclean acts. You will arrive at chapel at five in the morning; six on Sundays and feast days. Attendance is mandatory. We at this school are not heretical freethinkers. We believe that faith precedes science, fixes its boundaries, and prescribes its traditions. Understood?"

Roger nodded, rubbing his knuckles.

"It is forbidden to be late at meals or to speak during them. Curfew is at eight, when lights go out. I make a bed check at regular intervals to insure against students sneaking out to drink, or committing abominations against nature with each other. The bearing of arms is forbidden; singing, forbidden; the playing of games and writing impudent sayings on the walls, forbidden."

Forbidden. The word bayed in Roger's ears as he watched the hounds pursue the stag around the cuffs of his blouse. Four years . . . how many thousands of hours listening to lectures that meant nothing to him? Of learning figures and letters which could only lead him deeper into the dungeon of his father's trade? Was this the end to his dream of one day accomplishing something truly great? The sadness in him grew so huge he barely felt the next rap on his knuckles.

Tournique looked at Baron Thorne as if to say, What kind of churl have you raised? "I do not know what has gotten into the young these days," he clucked. "They pay no attention. If they do not like something? They resort not to reason, but to riot. Each day we live in the shadow of another town-and-gown massacre. They care nothing for their elders, tradition is something to be destroyed. They question everything, honor nothing, care little for learning and less for honest work. But above all, the young exhibit no *sense!* Just two days ago, Philip Augustus presented us with a most sensitive problem. Perhaps you have heard of this shepherd boy, Stephen of Cloyes?"

Roger came alert.

Tournique sneezed, drew the blanket around his shoulders, and adroitly crushed a flea. "Night and day have we met over this dilemma. I am proud to say that my colleagues and I have shown great wisdom; we are unanimous that the shepherd not be encouraged in his aberrations. We in Paris have seen these false prophets before—and all with letters from our Savior. No wonder there is so much pestilence and sin in the land, the Lord is too busy writing letters to do anything else!"

Tournique laughed hoarsely at his little joke. "But in truth, these so-called prophets have all been incarnations of the devil. Emerich of Liengen, the Caputati, why we even had to dig up old Amaury and burn his bones at the stake lest his blasphemy of pantheism infect us from the grave!" His eyes narrowed. "In my opinion, if this shepherd were not a child he too would be burned at the stake."

"No!" Roger blurted. His words were cut off as the baron cuffed him.

Tournique rose with a sigh that had the weight of the ages in it. "Ah, me, the university would be a comfortable place," he sneezed, "were it not for the students. Follow me, I will show you to your quarters."

They climbed another flight to an attic dormitory that housed eighteen students of the English nation and assorted vermin. A bunch of freshman, alike as newly shorn sheep in a pen, looked up from their studies to take Roger's measure. One of the younger boys had a terrible cold. Sneezing again, Tournique led Roger to a pallet. "I have placed you between two older lads exemplary in their studiousness and not given to any of the . . . Eastern vices."

Before Tournique could introduce Roger to the others a scream of "Fire!" sounded from the street below. Everybody thundered down the stairs to do battle with the dread enemy.

Around the corner on the rue Galande, a candlemaker's shop had erupted in flames. A vat of molten tallow had spilled and rivulets of fire followed its random pattern into the roadway. The growing crowd milled about. The candlemaker, beating at the flames with his apron, only managed to spread it.

"A brigade!" Baron Thorne cried, remembering the conflagration in London. He organized a line to pass buckets of water from the well.

Clerics and citizens worked as though pursued by the devil.

If the wind were to come up, or blow in the wrong direction, the entire city could be leveled.

Baron Thorne took command, and Roger, watching him, felt the lack in himself for all his father wanted him to be. If only I could please him, Roger thought, be a student, become a merchant. But I cannot. He recited to himself a motto his father swore by, "There are no accidents in life." Quite clearly, this fire was a signal from on high. For here he was, out in the street, the breezes singing in his ear, "Town air makes free!"

Roger put down his bucket. Resisting the urge to run, he walked to the end of the lane and turned it, expecting at any moment to feel his father's hand close around his neck. Zigzagging through the rutted lanes, Roger crossed the rue St. Jacques and lost himself in the teeming market crowds. Through the less populated neighborhoods he hurried, passing vineyard and garden and came finally to the southwest gate of St. Germaine. The Benedictine abbey lay just outside the walls, and he broke into a run.

He had heard that Stephen and his disciples were congregating there. Now Roger saw the ragged children camped in the shadow of the monastery. The good monks worked ceaselessly to feed the growing crowd, numbering over a thousand. Roger began to search through the camp for Guillaume, the stonemason.

For the most part, this army looked very young to Roger, eight to fifteen years old—though many were younger and still more older. Some children wore the colors of the monastery of St. Jean Ronde, where unwanted children were abandoned by their parents. Some looked strong, fired with the adventure of being soldiers for Christ. Others appeared infirm, searching for the miracle which would make them whole. There were seedy-looking scoundrels who had come to prey on the innocent, and gaudily painted women eager to corrupt whomever they could; misfits, the hopeless, those seized with the mania to dance, the possessed. But in far greater numbers there had gathered the young faithful. They had come to offer their lives for the Lord.

Roger spied Guillaume just as the stonemason recognized him and ran forward, shouting for joy. The two boys gripped each other, slapping each other on the back. "I am captain of a band from St. Denis," Guillaume said, "and must see to sanitary conditions." Roger grabbed a shovel and fell to alongside Guillaume. As they worked, Guillaume told Roger everything that had transpired in the past few days.

"Stephen has chosen his missionaries and sent them to all the provinces, to preach our crusade. The army will gather at Vendôme, a village near Stephen's birthplace. Stephen himself has already left for Vendôme to prepare the way. When all is ready we will march to the sea. And there the most wonderful thing will happen."

A platoon of children dropped their spades and mouthed the words along with Guillaume, knowing the prophecy by heart: "The sea will part as it did for the children of Israel and we shall walk across to Jerusalem."

That night, the army slept under the stars. Guillaume and Roger lay side by side, their heads resting on their folded arms. From the next campfire came the soft call of a flute.

"You were lucky to find us today," Guillaume said, "for tomorrow we would have been gone."

"Luck?" Roger answered. "I do not think so. Surely fate guided me here, as I have been guided since the first moment I saw Stephen."

Guillaume nodded soberly. "You are right." He touched the cross of red cloth sewn onto the right sleeve of his tunic. "When we get to Vendôme, Stephen will administer the crusading oath and then you too will wear this badge. And so we shall set out together on the greatest adventure we will ever know."

Roger sat up abruptly. "I have just learned this news, and you must get word of it to Stephen." He told him of the decision of the masters of the university and their plan to halt the crusade.

Guillaume did not seem surprised. "Stephen suspected that

would happen. That is why he left Paris before they announced their decision, so they would not be able to stop us. Nothing can stop us!" Guillaume whispered emphatically.

The certainty in Guillaume's voice washed over Roger. He hugged his knees, feeling an exultation such as he had never known.

"It is so strange," Guillaume mused. "I met you only a few days ago, yet I feel that I have known you all my life."

Roger reflected on this. "Could it be it is because we met at the exact moment our new lives began?"

Guillaume rolled over to face Roger. "By the good Lord, you are right!" After a few moments he said haltingly, "I know I am not very clever. But I am strong. And I believe. And if you are of the same mind, then I will be as a brother to you on our pilgrimage."

"Agreed!" Roger exclaimed, and the boys clasped hands.

"We must cement this oath," Guillaume said solemnly. He took his knife, cut his wrist and did the same to Roger's. The boys pressed their wrists together, mingling their blood.

Then Roger pulled off the overblouse his father had given him and handed it to Guillaume. Guillaume's mouth fell open. "I cannot take anything of such great value."

"Would you deny me giving my own brother a gift?" Roger asked. "Take it, I beg you."

After considerable urging, Guillaume did, trading blouses with Roger. Then Guillaume tore two strips from his neckerchief and tied them into a cross. He gave the badge to Roger. "Keep this until we get to Vendôme and Stephen can administer the oath."

Roger slipped the cross beneath his undershirt and felt it lie burning against his skin.

"I will never fail you," Guillaume said. "This I swear."

"We will never fail each other," Roger answered. "And may the good Lord see us both safely to Jerusalem."

The two boys lay down then, and watching the stars fell asleep, warmed by each other's bodies.

PARIS:
NOTRE DAME CATHEDRAL

HORTLY BEFORE DAWN, AS ROGER MARCHED IN HIS dreams toward Jerusalem, gathering grateful multitudes until all humanity seemed to be streaming toward the Holy City, he was dragged out of his sleep and onto his feet by his father.

Baron Thorne had been led to the Monastery of St. Germaine by Harolde, who suspected Roger's intent. "You are going back to the university," the baron said curtly.

Roger shook his head, at the same time trying to gather his wits.

The baron's blow sent Roger reeling across the grass.

Guillaume immediately sprang to his defense, but Roger put out a hand to stop him.

"Will you heed?" the baron demanded, his eyes taking in the blouse Guillaume wore.

Roger got to his feet. "In all else but this." Blood trickled from the corner of his mouth. He wiped it away and confronted his father.

"I will not go to that school. I will not waste my life just to please you. The moment you leave Paris I will run off."

The baron gave him another blow on the side of the head; the ground flew up to meet him, a ringing sounding in his ears. As the spinning, upside-down world passed before Roger's eyes, he caught one last glimpse of Guillaume. We will meet again! he tried to cry out just before he lost consciousness.

Roger groaned and twisted on his pallet as the walls of the room took shape. He was back in the pension on the Ile de la Cité. The late afternoon light slanted through the window. "They have left without me!" he cried. He tried to get up but the room sucked him back.

"Hush," Harolde said. He applied a compress to Roger's forehead. With another wet cloth he bathed the boy's bruised and fevered face. The monk dropped his eyes when Roger glared accusingly at him.

Baron Thorne approached the pallet, towering over his son. He was angry not only at the boy but at the world. After all these days of waiting he had heard nothing from Philip Augustus. I should have guessed that a monarch intent on broadening his own powers would do little to champion the cause of anybody else, he thought. But the disappointment rankled deep and Roger's rebellion had infuriated him all the more.

"Prepare yourself to leave tomorrow," he said to his son. "Since you cannot be trusted here, you will accompany me to Cologne, then back to London when we are informed that it is safe. We shall see what to do with you then." The baron reached for Harolde's Bible. He grasped Roger's hand and slapped it down on the book. "Swear to me that you will not run off."

Roger yanked his hand away.

"You heard what the masters of the university decided! That shepherd is possessed by the devil!"

Roger had difficulty getting the words out. "Father, I cannot leave my life to the masters," he said hoarsely. "They see only what they want to see and believe only what they have been taught by their own kind."

Thorne dug his fingers into his son's shoulders. Tears of hurt and frustration welled to Roger's eyes but he would not give his father the satisfaction of seeing him cry. Once more he tried to make him understand.

"Father, this is as clear to me as a dream made real."

"Dreams!" the baron snapped. "You are too old for this nonsense of dreams."

"Did you not tell me of your own yesterday?"

"My dreams are sound and of the making of this world!"

"And mine are of the next!" He knew his father dared not challenge him on this with Harolde listening.

Crouched in the corner, Jonathan made himself as small as

possible. What did it matter which world the dreams were of? When father and son fought, somehow *he* always wound up with the beating.

The baron said, "If you do not take this oath, I will truss you up like a carcass and transport you to Cologne that way. It is all the same to me. Now which shall it be?"

Harolde came forward and put his hand on Baron Thorne's shoulder. He was frightened by the way Roger looked, and anxious to prevent another beating. "And if a nation be divided against itself it cannot stand," he said softly, "and if a house be divided against itself . . ."

"And blessed are the peacemakers," the baron interrupted sourly. "Harolde, spare me your homilies at a time like this."

Harolde would not be put off. "No problem is so great that it cannot be solved by prayer. Baron Thorne, will you and Roger go with me to the cathedral so we may confess our sins and pray for guidance? Come, I beg you. A priest is always there ready to hear confession and bring us back to God's house."

Thorne shook his head. "Of what use can such a thing be if the boy has sworn to run off? You heard him yourself."

Harolde lifted Roger's chin. "At least put aside your anger until we have prayed."

Roger, fighting for time, slowly nodded.

The three of them stood up, Harolde steadying Roger on his feet. As they reached the door the baron turned and said, "Jonathan, it is not wise for you to stay here alone." The baron had seen the innkeeper look suspiciously at the boy a number of times. "Come with us," he ordered.

Petrified, Jonathan fell into step behind them. He had never been in a church of the Catholics and feared that the instant he crossed the threshold he would be reduced to a cinder.

Harolde hurried them through the shadowed streets. With last light, the city's drawbridges creaked shut. Paris sounded with the slam of shutters as uneasy citizens barred themselves within their houses. Now was night given over to the powers of darkness which stalked the streets and roosted upon unsuspecting roof.

"Quickly," Thorne urged Roger and Jonathan who could not keep stride with the men. The houses wavered in Roger's sight and he fought to keep his gorge from rising.

The closer they got to Notre Dame, the greater the confusion in the streets. Coils of rope lay about, stacked timber, mounds of lime and sand, and great blocks of stone. They came to the environs of the laborers, whose crude huts huddled against the cathedral walls. The forges did not roar, the lead bellows did not hiss, the cries of workers—all silenced with darkness. But the brooding presence of the cathedral attested to a half-century of labor.

They approached the west facade, and in twilight's deepening haze were dwarfed by the immense bulk which had been completed up to the first porch. On either side of the facade, the stone towers were beginning to be visible. The portals of St. Anne and the Virgin were completed, their painted and gilded statuary standing out in bold relief against the whitewashed stone of the pointed arches.

Roger stared up at the figures that writhed along the arches of the unfinished central portal of the Last Judgment. Monsters with jagged tooth and rending claw tore sinners limb from limb. Roger touched the cross of cloth still hidden next to his skin.

Because I cannot fulfill my vow, I am condemned to hell eternal, he thought.

As they passed through the small door in the portal of the Virgin, Jonathan stiffened and held back, but Harolde's advancing body pushed him through the door. Jonathan's eyes widened; he braced himself, expecting the lightning bolt at any moment. Thorne saw the desperate look on his face, understood and gave Jonathan leave to wait for them just inside the door.

After genuflecting, Harolde, Roger, and the baron started the long walk down the nave to the altar. Roger stumbled and Harolde grabbed him under the arms. They crossed the transept and approached the choir. Bank upon bank of altar candles grew brighter with the gathering darkness. Through the great empty spaces in the walls, where one day the stained-glass windows would be fitted, Roger saw the dark massed clouds scudding by, symbols of a heaven now denied him.

Fever raced through Roger's body. Dimly, he saw his father move toward the confessional booth, heard Harolde tell him he would be next. After a time, Roger saw a white-robed figure motion to Harolde to come assist with the services. Harolde rushed forward, thrilled with the honor.

Roger lost sense of time, knowing only that he had come to this house of God to be judged. He fell on his knees and prayed as he had never prayed before. Desperate, he recited the Our Father, but it turned to stone on his lips. To ease the pain in his skull he methodically began to beat his head against the rail.

"If Guillaume were here, he would know what to do," Roger whispered. Guillaume, who in his simple faith knew a peace. . . .

A rope dangling nearby caught his eye and he followed it up through the gloom. The rope ended at the great wheel which stood on a platform set across the roof timbers. Above the wheel Roger could barely make out the wooden centerings for the ribbed vaults; some had already been encased in stone to form the arches, while others still showed their timbered skeletons to the peaked lead roof.

Staring up at the soaring arches, the answer suddenly came to Roger. His head throbbed with the sureness of it and he got up from his knees and drifted down the aisle. "Guillaume received his calling when he stood at the very top of the Basilica of St. Denis," Roger murmured, "and that is where it will happen for me."

He scanned the spiderweb of scaffolding that climbed the walls to the vaulted ceiling, searching for access. "To the top, closer to heaven . . . God will not deny me then," Roger whispered as he passed the confessional booth.

In a corner near the front door, Roger found a staircase that wound its way up into one of the incompleted towers of the west facade. Jonathan sat on the bottom step, looking determinedly at the flagstone lest the idolatrous statues everywhere seize his eyes. He started as Roger came upon him.

"Where is your father? Harolde?" Jonathan asked, standing.

Roger pushed his way past the boy without answering.

"Where are you going?" Jonathan cried, frightened by the strange look on Roger's face.

"To heaven!" Roger answered with an odd laugh.

Jonathan grabbed Roger's jerkin. "You must wait for your father. You must!"

Roger pulled free. "I am *going* to my Father." He extended his hand to Jonathan. "Come with me."

Jonathan backed off and Roger laughed, "Don't you want to test the Lord?"

Jonathan shook his head vehemently. "It is enough that I believe in Him. Please don't go. You are not well. That blow on the head. . . ."

Roger took the steps two at a time. Round and round the stone staircase spiraling toward the sky. Through the slotted windows he saw the ground grow smaller with each revolution, until the city's huddled houses looked tiny and the first stars ever brighter. Where the containing walls had not yet been completed, Roger glimpsed the cruciform shape of the cathedral stretching away before him and the massed altar candles glowing in the heart of the cross.

He reached the level of the great wheel; there it seemed to him that ghostly workers walked within its drum, winding the ropes around the outer barrel to haul up the great loads of stone and timber.

Ever upward he climbed, into the clouds, only vaguely aware of the burning in his body. All at once he came to a step that ended in space. For a moment he stood there, wrapped in wind, his outstretched hand reaching . . . then he regained his balance. And if I had fallen, he thought, my father would have mourned me then.

Directly to his left stretched the porch of the west facade, whose row of niches would soon house the twenty-eight kings of Israel. Pressing himself against the stone, Roger inched his way along the porch.

"Come back," called the moaning wind, but Roger knew this to be the voice of the fallen angel, trying to keep him from his destiny. He counted the niches and at last stood in the center of the facade.

Below, Paris spread out before him. The river coursed around the Ile de la Cité, sparkling with phosphorescence in the light of the rising May moon. He picked out the moon-shadowed landmarks: the Grand Pont, the Palais Royal and the university on the left bank. The events of the past days marched before his eyes, leading him irrevocably to this moment.

A sudden gust caught him by surprise, almost knocking him off balance. He molded himself into the niche, his arms aching with the strain of holding on. Yet at the same time, he wanted to fling off his clothes and launch himself over the balustrade to soar and wheel on the buffeting currents, then be let down gently to earth as Guillaume had been.

With a rush of wings, some demon set loose from the underworld came to claim him and Roger beat at the small furry creature that wanted only to enmesh itself in his hair. He managed to fight it off and heard its shrill squeaks fade away.

In the preternatural light of the moon, Roger waited to hear heaven's will. He felt himself being drawn upward in a blinding radiance, felt himself fall to land in a broken heap before the portal of the Last Judgment. He poised at the brink, suspended between earth and sky. . . .

Then the small dark statue in the next niche reached out for him. Roger recoiled, fighting off the hand. His glazed eyes focused on the figure until the statue came alive.

Jonathan said in a rush, "Whatever you are thinking—tomorrow it will be better. Come down, please." He was so frightened he could barely utter the words. I should have gone for the baron, he thought, then answered himself, there was no time. Reading the look in Roger's eyes, he cried angrily, "Go ahead, then, but think! Whom do you serve by doing such a thing?"

The words flew around Roger's head, attacking from every angle. He caught sight of the gargoyles grinning at him from the top of the porch. They hopped toward him on their grotesque legs, stone beaks stretched to tear at his heart and eyes.

Jonathan said urgently, "There are many ways to serve the Lord. Is it not a sin of pride to believe you know the only way?"

Fight Jonathan's words as he would, Roger found solace in them. His ears prickled to the strange yet familiar prayer that Jonathan was reciting ". . . hallowed be the name of God . . . may His kingdom come . . . and His will be done. . . ."

"Thy will be done," Roger repeated in a whisper. His arms dropped to his sides, and like a sleepwalker, he allowed himself to be led from the porch, then down the sounding staircase to the nave of the cathedral.

At the confessional booth and at the altar, both the baron and Harolde were still occupied and had not missed the boys.

TROYES:
THE BATHHOUSE

OME EIGHTY MILES SEPARATED PARIS FROM Troyes, the main city of the Champagne Fair. Being an eminently practical man (though he could scarce be otherwise with his sun in Taurus and moon in Virgo), the baron held them to a steady pace of twenty miles a day. The road was well-traveled with merchants and pilgrims, the counts of Champagne having guaranteed the safety of all who journeyed to the fair. The weather waxed fair and warm.

But this whole venture has been conceived under malefic planets, the baron thought, looking at his son riding some twenty lengths ahead of him. "Honor thy father and mother indeed," he complained to Harolde. "Moses might have received only the nine commandments if my son's behavior be any gauge."

Harolde took a deep breath before commenting on this, but went into a paroxysm of coughing.

Though Roger had given his solemn word not to run off again, the baron would not risk leaving him at the university. Always the danger existed that the call of Stephen and his crusade of children might prove too strong.

Riding behind Roger, Jonathan had tried any number of times to cheer him, but he remained glum.

"I feel like you," Roger muttered to Tortoise, "old, mangy, and just plodding through life." One thing had surprised him: Jonathan had never mentioned anything to his father about the incident atop Notre Dame. He twisted around to the dark boy, poking him in the ribs. "Though you are a peculiar one, you are trustworthy, and I shall not forget it."

· · ·

Late in the second day, they camped in a grove of poplar and elm. The baron threw some fur skins over a layer of pine boughs and they bedded down.

In the middle of the night a flailing arm hit Harolde in the nose. He started awake to see Jonathan's face contorted with nightmare pain. "Poor accursed pagan," he whispered, feeling a rush of pity for the God-forsaken boy. Harolde estimated that some three weeks remained before they reached Cologne. "If I am to convert him," he murmured, "then I must act quickly, and with inspiration." He prayed to the Lord for guidance, for as yet he had been unable to discover to which heretical sect Jonathan belonged.

An hour before dawn the baron got up and made water. When he returned, he lay down next to Roger.

Asleep, his son looked as innocent as a choirboy. Well-made, a golden creature, skin and hair. The black eye would heal soon enough. In all, a son to be proud of—"If only he would listen!" the baron swore under his breath. There were so many mistakes he could save him from, yet Roger seemed intent on making them all, and inventing a few on his own. Thorne stretched out beside his son.

Roger moved in his sleep, put his arm across his father's chest and burrowed against him. The baron dozed off then, but not before he breathed a prayer that this closeness, which only the moon had witnessed of late, would one day be seen again by the sun.

Five miles southeast of Nogent the road took the baron's party past a monastery.

"This is Paraclete," Harolde told them excitedly. "Here Abelard, the greatest logician of his time, founded his abbey of consolation; and his mistress, Heloise, became its abbess after she had borne their illegitimate son."

Harolde recounted the tale to the rapt boys—the scandalous seduction, flight, and Abelard's ultimate castration by Heloise's outraged uncle. "Thus does God punish those who transgress against the church's holy laws of matrimony," Harolde said solemnly.

"Castration," Roger repeated, feeling a twinge up his spine. "Sooner would I be devoured by a dragon than suffer such a fate! And you have sworn *never* to sin with a woman?" he asked Harolde, his mind overwhelmed by the enormity of the vow.

Harolde nodded soberly. "One night, long ago, as I lay sleeping, the devil came to me in the guise of a beautiful flame-haired woman, and drew from me the essence of my manhood. But before she could totally capture my soul I woke in terror. I realized then that my battle in life was to prove my spirit stronger than my flesh. And so have I vowed."

Roger reflected on that for a number of miles. He poked Jonathan in the ribs. "If I took such a vow, do you think God would reveal His will that much sooner?"

"No," Jonathan said.

"Why not?" Roger asked, startled by this unexpected response.

"God does not care about such things. Only men care."

"So you say," Roger snapped. "Yes, that is what I must do," he said resolutely. "I will never sleep with a girl."

Into a dense forest they rode where shafts of sunlight lanced through the leaves to touch the humus carpet. Near a still pool a doe and her fawn regarded the travelers. The gentle mood seemed to affect them all and they came out of the forest smiling. Rolling hills lay ahead and in their cup stood the capital of Champagne: Troyes.

The drawbridge led over the dry moat to the Porte de Paris. The narrow, dusty road took them past the city's new district and then to the Abbey of Notre Dame aux Nonnes, surrounded by a maze of streets. The Hot Fair would take place here in a month's time. Trade caravans loaded with spices from the Orient, gauze from Gaza, damask from Damascus, would cross the Alps from Genoa and Venice. From Bruges and London would come wool and tin, all to meet at the midway point of Troyes, the clearinghouse for all Europe.

A sudden shift of wind brought an overwhelming stench from the tanner's district.

"Who could live here?" Harolde gagged, hand to his nose.

Baron Thorne shrugged. "Those who spend their lives in that quarter know no other smell."

"Do you think it is like that in purgatory?" Roger asked, fingering Guillaume's cloth cross. "That after a while, one does not notice the stench or the torture?"

"Never," Harolde exclaimed. "The fiend must make the torment of the damned new with each day."

"Well, we shall all know soon enough," the baron said evenly.

Harolde crossed himself with fervor and told himself he must say a novena for the baron lest his flippancy be his undoing.

The street name changed to rue Grand and soon they were at the Pont Les Bains, which crossed the Moline Canal and led then into the old section of Troyes. On the right bank, above the bridge, stood the bathhouses, and next to them, l'Auberge du Chat Noir, where they would be spending the next few days.

"Come," the baron said with a grin, "we have not bathed since London. I fear the stench we smelled was not from the tanners at all. You too, Harolde; remember, cleanliness is next to godliness."

They left their horses at the stables, checked their valuables with the concierge, and were led into a warm, damp room in the bathhouse. They stripped off their dusty capuchons, blouses, and hose, and naked, went into a second room. A walk-in fireplace occupied one wall of the chamber; three large cauldrons bubbled over the fire. Nests of wooden tubs sat on the floor, with four to five men soaking in each. Serving maids drew buckets from the cauldrons and poured them into the tubs to keep the water at a pleasing temperature.

Men of every race and color frequented the bathhouse; merchants mostly, for trade rarely knew the barrier of skin. Some men had their servants with them; others hired the serving wenches of the establishment, who for a few sous scrubbed them with large blocks of pumice. When the bathers were done, a stopcock in the tub was opened; the water drained into the center of the concave floor to run off into the canal below.

A full, juicy young woman named Flamonde ruled the maids with a firm hand, ordering them about and laughing merrily as she avoided the pinching fingers of the bathers. Baron Thorne eyed her appraisingly, and Harolde was shocked to see the brazen red-haired hoyden eye him right back. She seemed so familiar to Harolde and yet he could not place her. And then suddenly it came to him: how much she resembled the woman in his nightmare!

As they climbed into the vat, Roger glanced at his father's naked body, then Harolde's, and then, gauging Jonathan's, became so confused that he almost lost his footing.

Roger's hand moved reflexively to make the sign of the cross to ward off the inherent evil. The mystery that had surrounded the boy these many weeks was now revealed. For Jonathan's body was marked—marked with the covenant that God had made with the Children of Israel.

Roger grabbed the baron's arm. "Father," he sputtered.

"I know," Baron Thorne said tersely. "But do not call attention to it any further." The baron cursed himself for having forgotten.

Harolde had also spied Jonathan and turned very pale. A heretic, yes, Harolde had suspected that. But he had never dreamed the baron would do anything as foolhardy as harbor a Jew!

But he could think on it no more for suddenly bucket after bucket of hot water cascaded on them, poured by Flamonde and a girl no more than thirteen years old. The child's sleeves were rolled to the elbow and her skirts hiked so they would not drag through the waste. The heat in the room had clustered her auburn hair in a halo and her flushed cheeks made her gray eyes seem even paler.

"That child would not be out of place in the court of a king," the baron said with an appreciative, appraising glance. "Never have I seen such fair skin."

"No, not in court," Roger breathed huskily, unable to take his eyes off her, "that is too worldly, for hers is the face of a saint."

"My name is Laurelle," she whispered in answer to Roger's query. She kept her eyes fixed on the floor, never looking at their naked bodies.

Harolde did not know what to do with himself. He would never have agreed to the baths had he known that maids would be privy to his shame! He studiously avoided Flamonde's twinkling glance.

Roger, on the other hand, felt as though he had swallowed a love potion and had fallen desperately and forever in love with Laurelle. Her lithe arms, long legs, and the delicate curve of her instep were almost more than he could bear. He crossed his legs quickly lest his love be visible.

But the Baron had already noticed and let out a guffaw. "That is how you would treat a saint?" he laughed and splashed his son.

Roger splashed back. The tension of the past weeks suddenly erupted and in an instant they were all splashing and laughing and creating such a nuisance that a rotund merchant in the next vat climbed out in disgust, muttering, "The whole country is going to the dogs."

In one corner, occupying his own bath, having paid handsomely for that privilege, lounged a man, his back to the rest of the chamber. One could see he was broader of shoulder than most, and probably taller. His skin, not quite olive, not quite white, gleamed a deep burnished bronze.

Hulking above him stood a creature of enormous bulk wearing flowing white robes, and, by his mannerisms, someone who had been deprived of his manhood. Roger stared, fascinated, for he had never seen such a one before. The eunuch anticipated his master's every wish, clapping his hands for the girls to bring more hot water, adding a drop of rare oil that floated in rainbow hues.

Laurelle hurried over, arms straining with two steaming buckets. With every other patron in the bathhouse Laurelle had kept her eyes determinedly downcast. But as she left this man's tub she could not help but glance back over her shoulder. Their eyes met and held and then she blushed at his sardonic, off-center smile.

"Why," Baron Thorne asked Harolde, "would a man of such obvious means choose to frequent a public bathhouse?"

The golden man stood up. The eunuch offered him a sheet but he brushed it away. He vaulted nimbly out of the tub, aware that every eye on the room followed him.

"Only once before have I beheld such an imposing figure," the baron said. "When Richard Coeur de Lion waded ashore at the siege of Acre, dwarfing every other soldier in our army." But it was something more than physical stature, the baron thought. There was about this man an aura of commanding presence, of someone who knew his value in the company of men. If the man had a flaw, it was not in his physique. His flanks were full but firm, and not an ounce of fat showed on his flat, corded stomach. Coated with bath oils, his muscles bunched and glistened as he walked slowly toward the hot room, vigor shooting from his body.

"To behold him is to believe that man is indeed fashioned in the image of the angels," Harolde said, and for once the baron agreed.

The man disappeared into the hot room. The eunuch stood outside the door, arms folded across his fleshy chest.

"Who is that man?" Baron Thorne asked a wizened burgher soaking in the next tub.

"Frizio," the burgher answered. "His slave is called Baalbek, from the city of the same name in Outremer. Frizio has come all the way from Jerusalem to sell his horses at the fair. Wonderful Arabians, smaller than our Great Horses, but far swifter. The stallion Frizio himself rides—Alexander's Bucephalus reincarnate. Today at the rue de la Corterie aux Chevaux, he challenged all to race against him. Three, four times he ran against the field, beating them each time. I tell you, the steed is tireless. I myself lost two livres. Count Thibault's constable offered him a ransom for the horse but Frizio refused."

"Is this man a Christian?" Harolde asked dubiously, suspicious because of Frizio's exotic look.

The burgher hunched his shoulders. "So he claims, but who can tell with these strange men from Outremer?"

Frizio, the baron thought, have I not heard that name before? He remembered then that years ago there were rumors about such a man, but even the papal court could not prove anything and all charges had been dismissed.

Baron Thorne stood up dripping from the tub and the others followed suit. Roger wrapped a sheet around Jonathan and then grabbed his arm. "Let us try the hot room," he said, dragging the boy after him. Thorne and Harolde followed them.

Roger whispered to Jonathan, "Do not worry, I will keep your secret. Because you never told what happened that night at Notre Dame. But you *must* convert! Otherwise, we are all in mortal danger. Till then, better keep covered as much as possible."

On entering the small room a blast of steaming air hit them in the face, sending Harolde into retreat. "Hell will come soon enough," he coughed. "I will meet you outside when you have done cooking yourselves."

Jonathan also wanted to leave but Roger would not let him.

So heavily clouded with steam was the dark room, it took some time before Roger could see anything. The swirling steam glowed red, as did the walls and beaded ceiling. And then Roger saw the reason; a small, intense fire in one corner heated a grill loaded with hot rocks, casting red shadows over everything.

Roger gulped for air, each breath drawing fire deep into his lungs. The baron motioned for the boys to sit on the floor. Roger hunched down. His eyes swept up to the wooden tiers and there he saw Frizio sprawled out on the top level, breathing easily. Slanted eyes, wide and yellow stared at him through the glowing mists.

Roger, fascinated and drawn by the strange man, blurted, "I have heard tell that you come from Jerusalem."

Frizio's off-center smile showed white, even teeth. "Yes, just arrived, and hopefully soon to return."

"Is it as beautiful as they say?" Roger asked.

"Of a beauty indescribable," Frizio answered.

"Leave the man be," Baron Thorne reprimanded his son.

"Oh, the lad does not offend," Frizio said. "It is always flattering to be sought out by the young. And glad am I for any chance to talk about the Holy City." Frizio brushed back his dark blond, sun-streaked hair. "When the Lord God created the world, He gave nine parts of the beauty to Jerusalem and the tenth part to the rest of the world."

"But to compensate for this inequity," Jonathan murmured, "He gave nine parts of the world's suffering to Jerusalem, and one part to the rest of the world."

Frizio's arched brows lifted in surprise. He reached down and raised Jonathan's chin with a crooked finger. "Ah, I see you know the old proverb. You read Arabic, then?"

"A little," Jonathan said, breathing heavily. "My father taught it to . . ." he stopped in midsentence.

Roger, finding it easier to breathe, got up from the floor and sat on the first tier. Jonathan, seeing Roger occupied, took this chance to escape from the room, choking for air. The baron followed him out. "Come, Roger," he called, "you have had enough."

"In a moment, father," Roger said, licking the sweat from his lips. Then Roger looked at the man whose muscles seemed carved in his golden skin. "Is it true that the infidel is defiling the holy places of the Lord?"

"There are many gods in Jerusalem," Frizio answered, his voice teasing. "Jehovah, God of the Jews. Mohammed, prophet of Allah. And of course—"

"The only true God," Roger insisted.

"Ah, then you mean Jesus," Frizio chuckled. "Tell me, do you wish to go to Jerusalem?"

The heat in the room made Roger's head whirl. "With all my heart," he whispered. "I made a vow to pray for my mother there. And I have many friends, young people like me, who are on their way right now."

"How is such a thing possible?" Frizio asked.

Roger explained about the crusade of children and Frizio listened with growing attention. "Thousands, you say?" Frizio asked. "Where may one find these worthy young souls?"

"Alas, I know not," Roger said, shaking his head. "For my father . . ." he broke off, swallowing hard.

Frizio stroked his chin, pondering. Then he stared deep into the glowing coals. "I would tell this to every young man: If you would find yourself and your god, then go to the center of the world, go to Jerusalem."

"Oh, how I have tried to explain this to my father!" Roger exclaimed. "Even to Harolde. But they will not listen, they will not understand. No one will." Tears started to his eyes.

"I understand," Frizio said softly. "But can your burden be so heavy for one so young? Surely tomorrow's sun will bring new hope?"

Flamonde bustled into the chamber just then lustily singing:

> *Swift age it overtakes us*
> *While duty holds us down*
> *It's young blood that makes us*
> *Frolic through the town!*

She poured a ladle of cold water onto the heated stones and clouds of steam sizzled up. The dampness made her blouse stick to her bosom and the line of her thigh showed through the wet cloth of her skirt.

"Are you ready then?" she asked Frizio.

"Whenever," he said, stretching.

She did a quick turn that flared her skirts and winked at him. "I will return in a moment."

"You stay at l'Auberge du Chat Noir?" Frizio asked Roger, and when he nodded, Frizio said, "I too. Then we shall have speech about this again. I will be pleased to tell you all you want to know about Jerusalem, from its holy places to its dens of iniquity. But now the wench will be back in a moment to . . . tend to my needs." Frizio's lips parted in his beguiling off-center grin. "You are welcome to stay, but I should warn you . . ."

Flamonde returned, carrying a bucket of cold water, a flacon of wine, and a switch of rushes. Frizio moved down to the lowest tier and stretched out on his stomach. Flamonde poured him a glass of wine. Frizio handed it to her with a gallant gesture. She curtsied with a laugh and poured another.

"Roger! You have had enough!" the baron shouted, poking his head inside the door.

"One more moment, father," Roger called, stalling while his heart beat in anticipation of he knew not what. Baron Thorne closed the door again.

Flamonde dipped the rushes in the icy water, then proceeded to beat Frizio across the back and legs. With each blow his body twitched and quivered. Frizio turned and whispered something to Flamonde, and then her high-pitched laughter twined with Frizio's guttural chuckle.

"Now tell me of your sister," Frizio said to Flamonde.

"Laurelle? Why choose the child when you can have the woman?" Flamonde asked, punctuating her laughter with the lash of rushes across Frizio's flanks.

Frizio twisted his head and his swollen lips parted in a wine-stained smile. "Is it for me to question why God made me prefer the flute to the hurdy-gurdy?"

Flamonde shrieked good-naturedly, "Imagine? I am considered overripe at twenty?" and gave him three more tastes of the switch. Then she said, "Laurelle has never been touched. She has just this spring come into her womanhood."

"To be sure," Frizio murmured lazily. "All the women in Troyes are virgins. Tell me, what price do you set on it?"

"No!" Roger exclaimed, starting forward, shocked that these two could even discuss such a matter about the angelic child.

Flamonde and Frizio stared at him in surprise.

Before Roger could say any more, the door swung open. The baron grabbed his ear and hauled him out of the hot room as the muffled laughter sounded more and more frequently from within.

TROYES:
L'AUBERGE DU CHAT NOIR

N THE CATHEDRAL OF ST. PIERRE AND ST. PAUL, Harolde had prayed for guidance as to what to do about Jonathan, but had received no clear signal, save that the child *must* be converted. Now his attention focused on Bishop Hervé as he inveighed against womankind, thundering from the pulpit, "These stinking roses! These pits of the devil!"

During the months of the Hot and Cold Fairs, the women of Champagne were notorious for their easy virtue. At all other times their behavior was no more or less circumspect than their sisters. But the fair was license for many to revel with the thousands of visitors who thronged Troyes. Maids, serving wenches, even strict merchants' wives were known to indulge in the bacchanal of the flesh. And if it happened to supplement the income, so much more the spur. Now Bishop Hervé took them all to task.

"Pit of the devil, that is what she is," Harolde muttered, fighting to keep from looking at Flamonde, seated a few pews in front of him. She had come to Sunday Mass with her sister Laurelle; Flamonde's tranquil profile glowed in the light from the stained-glass window, but Harolde knew this seeming repose was but another snare of the fiend's. He pressed his fists into his lap, determined he would not commit sacrilege, even involuntarily, in God's house.

Hervé, famous for his impassioned sermons, beseeched the women of Troyes to embrace the preachments of St. Bernard of Clairvaux, whose bones rested in the crypt. St. Bernard had elevated Eve to new and lofty heights with his revelation that the conception of Mary had been immaculate. That idea, though novel for these times, had taken root and proliferated throughout Christendom. In a world hungry for miracles, who would not want to believe that the Lord's mother had also been conceived without sin?

In the side aisle, hidden in the shadow of a soaring stone column, stood Frizio, eyes fastened on Laurelle. He had not been in a church in more than a decade, and only her presence had lured him inside.

Once services were over Harolde quickly left the church. He had managed to control his fevered young blood, but only with endless repetitions of Hail Marys. In the promenading streets he caught sight of Flamonde and Laurelle as they danced around a jongleur and his monkey, grinding a vieille. Harolde went off in the opposite direction lest the call of carnival prove more potent than cathedral.

That night, in their lodgings at l'Auberge du Chat Noir, Baron Thorne could not sleep. Each time he closed his eyes he heard the revelry thumping up from the tavern two stories below. Scrubbed clean, his face shaven, the baron felt ready for an adventure. "And I know exactly with whom," he said as he crept from the bed. He slipped on his clothes and went downstairs, unaware that Roger had been watching his every move.

The tavern ran the length of the narrow inn, with a row of cubicles against one wall; stacked along the opposite wall, a half-dozen barrels of red and white wine. The proprietor, a sharp-nosed man named Crevette, dispensed drinks to Flamonde and Laurelle, who wended their way skillfully around the tables, running the gauntlet of grasping hands.

Several oil lamps hung from the rafters, not quite illuminating the rear cubicles, where some drunken couples, the price agreed upon, where hammering out their bargains. For those desiring more privacy, Crevette had a room upstairs and a small shack in the backyard which could be rented for one full turn of the hourglass. The shack contained nothing more than a straw pallet, but then the goddess of love never required a more substantial altar.

Baron Thorne caught sight of Laurelle trying to tear herself

from the clutches of four leather dealers from Doubai. Flamonde came to her rescue, ruffling the hair of one, tweaking
the nose of another, laughing all the while. "Not even if you
pooled all your money could you afford her! The child is innocent! Now leave be!"

Laurelle looked miserable, her head bent and shoulders
stooped, as though praying for this night to be over.

A table of merchants from Montpellier were discussing, in
the mellow accents of langue d'oc, the course of the pope's
crusade against the Albigenses. Simon de Montfort, general of
the Holy Ghost, had laid waste to the countryside, killing
more heretics (and Catholics) than could be counted, and still
the war dragged on.

In a shadowed nook sat Frizio, beating time with his fingers
as a goliard troubadour accompanied himself on the harp and
sang:

> *Gather all the sweetness of youth as it flies*
> *Leave it to the old men to ponder and advise*
> *When summer starts to fail us*
> *Is winter far behind?*

Frizio turned slowly, following Laurelle's every movement,
struck with her sad expression, her supple grace. As she
passed close by he smiled at her and thought he glimpsed a
fleeting smile in return. "That one is a flower, is she not?" he
said to Baalbek.

Baalbek grunted disinterestedly. "You have plucked such
flowers in Rome, Venice, Paris . . ."

Frizio threw his head back and stared at the smoke curling
up toward the timbered ceiling. "No, Baalbek, not like that
one. I could love such a one as that."

Baalbek's thin, perfect eyebrows shot up. "You? Who have
known the choicest in the seraglio? Who have pleasured yourself with princesses? Would settle for a barmaid? Dear Allah, I
have put too much hashish in the pipe!"

"Much there was," Frizio nodded languorously, "but I have
also known there to be truth in the drug. She has been a dagger in my brain since the first moment I saw her. Those eyes!

As pale and elusive as a wraith's, begging to be captured! In such a one might I discover my true self."

Through some sorcery of the mind, Frizio slipped into a place where time had no boundaries. He saw himself as a frightened, loveless child, wandering the quays of Acre and learning the hard lessons of the bastard. Frizio's father, a commanding knight from Lotharingia in the Holy Roman Empire, had mated with a Bedouin slave girl in one of the Crusader's brothels. Born during a malefic eclipse of the sun in Scorpio, the boy had inherited the beauty of both parents and the sickness in their souls. From his father, the fair hair, the physique of a pagan god, and a streak of irrational cruelty. From his mother, the high cheekbones, a suppleness of limb, and the cunning to survive. His slanted, unblinking eyes came from a source beyond parentage.

When expedient, Frizio bent his knee to Christ; when necessary, he answered the muezzin's call; for he worshipped nothing so much as he worshipped survival. He had learned to steal to eat, and to kill to live, and somewhere in all this had learned the pleasures inherent in killing for pleasure. Yet there remained a part of him still hungering, still hoping.

Baalbek regarded his master intently. Hashish or no, he had never heard Frizio speak as he had this night, and it gave him pause. He shook him, "Come, I will put you to bed," Baalbek began, but Frizio paid no attention and waved impatiently to Flamonde.

She sauntered to the table, mischief sparkling in her eyes. "What will my beauty have this night?" Flamonde asked, making no effort to hide her naked admiration.

Frizio fumbled in his sleeve, took out a pouch and threw it on the table; gold coins, Byzantine in design, spilled out. "I am hopelessly bewitched by your sister," he began, "and I would—"

"Never!" Flamonde cried, shaking her head vehemently. "No amount of money will buy her. She is still a child!" and bustled away.

"I would post the banns . . . take her to wife," Frizio said to the empty air.

Upstairs, Roger lay staring at the pitched ceiling. The plangent twang of a harp sounded from the tavern. Jonathan lay beside Roger, teeth grinding in his sleep. Jonathan cried out, "No!" but did not waken.

Roger nudged him. "Wake up. You are having a nightmare."

Jonathan bolted upright, startling Roger half out of the bed. Harolde woke too, automatically mumbled the prayer for matins, rolled over, and went back to sleep.

Roger whispered in Jonathan's ear, "Let us go downstairs and see what is happening." Roger climbed out of bed, pulling on Jonathan's arm until he landed on the floor. Roger dressed quickly, urging Jonathan to do the same; Jonathan stumbled about like a puppet. Roger tiptoed to the door and carefully turned the latch. "Locked! So this is how my father trusts me?"

He peered out the window. A long fall, but stacks of straw lay all about. Climbing out, he hung from the sill and let go, his fall cushioned by a haystack. Roger held up his arms to Jonathan. "Come ahead, jump," he called.

Jonathan, seeing Roger safely on the ground, where he could not get at him, yawned and went back to bed.

"You tricked me! I will get you for that!" Roger said, shaking his fist. Roger circled to the tavern's back door, listening to the hubbub as the troubadour picked up his tempo:

> *Live then like immortals, worthy is the aim*
> *To seek at love's portals, heart's ease*
> *Without blame.*

Just then the back door opened and Laurelle stood outlined in the oblong of light. She went to the woodpile and loaded her arms. As she turned, Roger slipped from the shadows. Laurelle cried out and dropped the logs. Roger grabbed her arm before she could flee.

Laurelle recognized him then and sighed with relief. "I thought you were a spirit and that my days were over."

"Only of mortal flesh," Roger said, releasing her. "But you, you are so lovely, I did not think you were made of the same stuff." Whence those sweet words had suddenly come Roger did not know. But spoken to Laurelle they sounded as natural as any he'd ever uttered.

Laurelle blushed, recognizing this lad as a cut above the men inside, who wanted one thing only. No doubt Roger wanted that too, but his gentle manner and youth made him less frightening.

"I must bring in the logs," Laurelle said, "else Crevette will thrash me."

"When can you get out again?"

Laurelle shook her head. "I do not know."

"I will wait," Roger said, squeezing her hand.

When Laurelle had gone, Roger lay down on the haystack and whispered "Laurelle" to the night breezes. He added his own name to the refrain and thought he had never heard a combination more pleasing. Roger rolled onto his stomach, his fingers kneading the hay, head dizzy with the new sensations stirring through his body.

"I love you," he whispered into the straw.

The door to the shack opened and a bandy-legged drunk emerged, supported by Madame Crevette. "It is the wine," she consoled the man, biting the silver piece he gave her. "Next time you will do better. Do not fret, I will not breathe a word."

The moon had half risen when Laurelle appeared again. She flung herself on the haystack beside Roger. "I am so weary! Crevette is drunk, my sister is . . . occupied. They will not miss me for a bit."

"I knew you would come," Roger said, reaching for her hand. He pressed it to his thudding heart.

Laurelle pulled away.

Roger sat up. "Hush, I do not mean to harm you," he said.

Laurelle burst into tears. Roger put his arm around her shoulder and stroked her hair.

"It is not you," Laurelle sobbed. "It is Flamonde. I fear that she is about to sell me to a man in there."

"That cannot be!" Roger exclaimed. "Are we heathens for people to be bought and sold? We shall go to the prévôt . . ."

Laurelle shook her head. "It is nothing like that. It is for the night only. I saw her talking to that man from Jerusalem? And then he put a bag of gold on the table. Oh, Flamonde will do it, if not tonight, then tomorrow. Flamonde says it must happen to all girls sooner or later."

Laurelle told Roger that she and her sister lived in a faubourg outside Lille. Nine months of the year they took in piecework, fulling and dying cloth, eking out their existence. Then in early May, Flamonde headed down to Champagne for the fairs. Working two months in the public bathhouse and at l'Auberge du Chat Noir, she earned enough money to make the rest of their year bearable. "Everybody in Lille believes Flamonde so devout that she goes on pilgrimage each spring to the various holy shrines; St. Denis one year, Cologne the next. In this way, Flamonde is able to satisfy her wanderings." Laurelle dropped her eyes and blushed. "Both of travel and well, Flamonde is . . . spirited. You see, when she was seventeen, my sister wed a burgher in Lille. But after three years of not being able to bear any children, he repudiated her. More than anything in life, Flamonde wants children, but this is the cross God has given her to bear.

"This spring, she took me along for the first time, for I am at the age where I must earn my own keep. Flamonde told me I could earn enough for a dowry to attract some worthy man. Otherwise, she said both of us would wind up as withered prunes in a few years, marrying peasants, or worse, fullers like ourselves."

Laurelle dried her eyes. "But I do not hold with that. I mean to remain a maiden until the Lord . . ." she hesitated. "What I mean is, I am fated for other things."

Roger leaned on his elbow. "What things do you speak of?"

Laurelle began haltingly, "When I was a little girl, Flamonde, who believes overmuch in such things, took me to an old woman in Lille who could divine the future. First she asked the month and day of my birth—I am born under the sign of Pisces—and then she chopped off the head of the

chicken we brought her, slit open its stomach and read the en-
trails. To this day I remember what she said."

Roger waited, almost afraid to listen.

Laurelle's voice became a whisper as she said, "Innocent
you are and innocent shall you remain, and in the sight of that
place where other holy innocents were martyred, shall you
meet your maker and know of your last judgment."

Roger scratched his head. "What does it mean?"

"I do not know," Laurelle said, .her gentle gray eyes wide.

"Did you not ask the witch?"

"To be sure! But for that she wanted another chicken. I
know that one day I will discover the meaning, else why
would I have remembered every word?"

Roger whistled a tune through a blade of grass. "I do not
think your old woman a very good teller of fortunes."

"Why not?" Laurelle asked.

"Because she said nothing of me!"

Laurelle gave a little laugh and pummeled Roger with her
fists. She quieted then. Her long fingers reached out in the
moonlight and touched Roger's arm, sending goose pimples
along his body. "Will you help me?" she asked tentatively.

"Of course!" Roger said. "Anything."

Laurelle took a knotted handkerchief from under her blouse.
"I have saved some money. I must get away. You have a donkey."

Roger had not expected events to take such a sudden turn.
He wanted her with him, not gone somewhere. And what
would his father do to him if he gave away Tortoise? The
money Laurelle offered would not buy the donkey's feed for
one day. "Where would you go?" Roger asked lamely.

Laurelle pressed her hands to her forehead. "These many
months I have prayed to the Virgin to give me the strength to
enter a convent. But she has not answered and so this must
not be the way for me. All this week, with merchants arriving
from Paris, I have heard tell of a young shepherd who
preaches a crusade, and even though I am a girl . . ."

Roger punched his palm, beside himself with excitement. "I
know this shepherd! His name is Stephen and many girls

march with him. Stephen has a lieutenant named Guillaume— wait!"

Roger reached into his wallet and took out the crumpled cross of cloth Guillaume had given him. "Show this to Guillaume. Tell him I sent you. He is my sworn blood brother and will do everything he can to protect you."

In the baths, Roger had felt an overwhelming passion for this girl. Now he recognized it for what it truly was. Yes, he would have laid with her if she had given him the slightest encouragement. But his feeling went far beyond the call of the flesh. Their spirits had coupled in a common dream, and in this instant Roger knew that he would never love anybody in this way for the rest of his days. Surely this was God's design, to send her in his place, so that a part of him—the best part— would go with her to the Holy Land.

Roger took Laurelle's handkerchief with its meager coins and pressed it back into her hands. "If it is your wish to march with Stephen, then I give you my donkey. From my heart. I will repay my father somehow. Oh, God! If only I could go with you. But I have sworn on the Bible. . . ."

Laurelle flung her arms around Roger and he held her close, feeling her heart beat against his. Then for some reason neither understood, they both began to laugh and sob. "Do not cry, my heart," Roger murmured, crying.

All at once an elongated shadow fell across the children. Roger and Laurelle stared up at Frizio.

"I came into the garden to declare my intentions to you," Frizio said stiffly to Laurelle. "I thought you were pure, I thought to offer you all I had, instead I find you in a haystack rutting with another. Mother, daughter, sister, lass, you are a whore like all the others and like a whore shall you be treated."

But neither of the children understood one word of what Frizio had said, for his speech had been blurred by the hashish.

Frizio tapped Roger on the shoulder and jerked his finger in the direction of the inn. "Be gone, boy," Frizio said, "we are after men's work this night."

Roger scrambled to his feet, but even standing on the straw he reached only to Frizio's collarbone. Frizio's golden eyes were dilated and he swayed on his feet. Yet he does not smell of wine, Roger thought, his mind racing. Perhaps if I distract him long enough for Laurelle to get to Tortoise . . . "Good sir," Roger began.

Frizio's shove sent the boy sprawling. Laurelle started to scream but Frizio clamped his hand over her mouth. Roger lunged at him, but Frizio brought his whip butt down on the back of Roger's neck and he pitched forward, unconscious.

When Roger came to his senses, he found warm sticky blood covering his face. He groaned and sat up, feeling as though a horse had kicked him. Laurelle was nowhere in sight. The door to the shack creaked in the wind. Too weak to stand, Roger crawled on his hands and knees to the outbuilding.

Laurelle lay on the pallet, her clothes ripped asunder, a small pouch of coins on her chest. Roger knelt at her side, quickly covering her nakedness. Her body felt cold and her face, twisted in pain, had the pallor of death. He could not rouse her. "Oh, my merciful God," he whimpered, feeling that his own world had suddenly come to an end. He struggled to his feet and lurched to the tavern, barely conscious of the blood streaming from his mouth and staining his clothes.

He fell through the door, screaming, "Murder!"

Shock silenced the crowd, followed hard upon by shouting and general hysteria.

"That one there," Roger croaked, pointing to Frizio, just preparing to leave by the front door. "Laurelle . . ."

Frizio turned and regarded Roger with surprise; instantly, he collected his wits. "The boy is addled. Did you all not see her go into the backyard and wait for me? We arranged a price, willingly. I paid her, willingly. And the deed was done, all willingly."

"Murderer!" Roger shouted and spat out a chip of his tooth.

Flamonde came flying down the stairs, adjusting her skirts. "Laurelle?" she cried, and rushed to the bleeding boy. "What happened? Where is she?"

"The shack," Roger choked.

Flamonde ran out into the yard followed by a crowd of patrons.

Other people blocked the front door, preventing Frizio and Baalbek from leaving. Crevette wrung his hands, beside himself as he tried to calm everybody. One more charge of disturbing the peace and the count's council would close his tavern.

Baron Thorne thundered down the stairs then, tucking his blouse into his hose. Roger's heart leapt up at the sight of his father.

Wailing, Flamonde ran in from the courtyard. Two men supported Laurelle, half-carrying, half-dragging her in. Flamonde hurled the coins at Frizio's head. "What have you done to her? She is deaf, she is dumb! She will not speak, she will not answer. I told you you could not have her!"

Frizio, sensing the crowd turning ugly, said, "You cheated me. You swore she was a maiden and she was not. In fact, she had just finished with this young lout when I discovered them."

Roger's mouth fell open and he choked with frustration.

"If he denies it, he is a liar," Frizio said.

Baron Thorne wheeled on Frizio. "Why you maligning bastard!" he shouted. "My son may be many things but he is no liar!"

Bastard! The cry echoed through the twisted corridors of Frizio's memory. He heard the taunts of his playmates, felt the disdain and loathing of both Frank and Bedouin. His entire demeanor changed, his mouth fell slack and his breath came in short gasps as an uncontrollable rage blinded him. The voices in the inn grew to a roar that filled his head, then gradually receded as he heard the baron say, "Roger, will you take an oath on the Bible that all you claim is true?"

Frizio said with calculated deliberation, "The son lies and now the father asks him to swear to those lies?"

With a cry, Thorne sprang at Frizio, but he sidestepped and slammed the baron into the wall. The baron recovered and wrestled Frizio to the floor. The patrons tried to separate them but Baalbek blocked the way.

A curved knife flashed in Frizio's hand and Roger cried, "Father! Watch out!" but in one deft motion Frizio sliced off the baron's left ear. Before more damage could be done, the night watch of the count's council pressed into the Chat Noir and hauled the two men off to the *donjon*.

Roger ran after them, alternately cursing Frizio, punching at guards' backs, and trying to stem the blood from his father's wound.

TROYES:
THE TRIAL BY COMBAT

A T FIRST LIGHT, FRIZIO AND BARON THORNE WERE taken from their cells and brought before the court of the counts of Champagne. Those judges, acting for the eleven-year-old Count Thibault IV, deliberated all day but could not decide justice.

To complicate matters, the testimony of Flamonde and Laurelle could not be heard; both sisters had disappeared without a trace.

"All along I knew those two were evil," Harolde said to Roger and Jonathan as they listened to the proceedings.

"I do not believe it," Roger answered stoutly. "Something must have happened to them." But he was sore distressed that the girls were not here to tell the truth and vindicate himself and his father.

Not that their evidence would have changed anything; bad blood ran too deep between Thorne and Frizio. The baron's disfigurement had stirred up a rage for revenge in him, while Frizio swore he would not be content until he had the other ear.

The issue hopelessly drawn, the council declared, "We must leave the final judgment to God. In two days time there will be a trial by combat."

Stunned, Roger grabbed Harolde's arm. "Oh, Lord! What have I done to my father?"

Lest the upcoming fair be stained with blood before it had even begun, the council decreed that a fight to the death would not be required; this calmed Roger somewhat. The seneschal read the procedure to the two men.

"The rules of chivalry will be in effect. The warriors will tilt three times in the lists. Should that not decide the outcome, they will then battle with hand weapons of their choice. No blow is to be struck at the horses, any injury to a mount constitutes immediate forfeiture. The combatant who cries 'quarter' first will have admitted his guilt and will forfeit armor, horse, and ransom to the victor, such sum to be determined by the tournament judges.''

When the baron was released, Roger, Harolde, and Jonathan crowded around him. Roger stared at his father's bandaged ear and started to apologize.

"It is not your fault," the baron reassured him. "Now I am convinced that all the rumors I heard about Frizio are true. A goodly number of pilgrims whose transport he arranged to the Holy Land have since disappeared. Worse, he is suspected of dealing in the slave trade.''

Roger's eyes opened wide and Harolde crossed himself.

Baron Thorne said grimly, "It is God's will that this wicked man be chastised.''

The baron's Great Horse, Tantor, would do well enough for the contest, but Thorne lacked all the other necessary equipment. It would cost a small fortune, more than he could vouchsafe among his merchant confreres. He went first to the Lombard bankers on the rue de la Trinité.

The Lombards refused to loan him the money. "If you lose, you forfeit *our* armor and we are liable for *your* ransom as well. We are not gamblers, but businessmen like yourself. And frankly, you are not exactly in your prime.''

The baron pounded his fist on the table. "William the Marshall of England is in his sixties! And he has *never* lost a tournament!''

"Granted," the Lombard said, "but such a champion comes once in a lifetime.''

"This is a matter of honor before God!" Baron Thorne insisted.

The bankers shrugged, "Then let God finance it.''

Thorne wanted to knock their heads together but Harolde persuaded him that one fight at a time was all he could manage.

"Apparently not even that," the baron said in disgust, after two more moneylenders had refused him. Though nobody in Troyes had ever seen Frizio fight, disquieting rumors abounded about his strange powers.

"What will happen now?" Roger asked.

"Without armor I cannot take the field," the baron said. "I have no recourse but to beg Frizio's pardon and make whatever restitution the court decides."

They had come to the Broce-aux-Juifs, the Jewish quarter of Troyes. The baron did not have much hope that anybody here would finance him, but it was his last resort.

Troyes had once been a great center of Jewish learning and commerce. Here the philosopher Rashi had founded a talmudic school known throughout the world; his sons and grandsons had carried on the tradition. Here the Jewish bankers had rivaled other houses and stimulated trade from the North Sea to the Adriatic. But as in most districts in Gaul, with the preaching of the Crusades came the expulsion, the confiscation of property. Then, when more money was needed, the royal decrees allowed the Jews to return to their homes, provided they paid an additional indemnification. In this way were the counts of Champagne able to increase their treasuries twice.

On every door in the Jewish quarter hung a mezuzah, an enclosed parchment inscribed with biblical writings. Roger recognized this as the talisman Jonathan had tried to give him in Paris. At the house of Simon, master of the Jews of Troyes, Jonathan did not wait outside, but touching his lips to the mezuzah, followed the baron and the others inside.

An imposing man with a long gray beard and wearing robes of worked silk made them welcome with sweet wine and fruit in the immaculate house.

When Baron Thorne explained his predicament, Simon nodded his head gravely. "I have heard of this matter. But you understand, my people live here at the sufferance of the counts. After our long exile, I dare not do anything to jeopardize our community."

Jonathan spoke up then, addressing the patriarch in Hebrew, which startled everyone. "My father always told me the

Jews of Troyes honored truth and justice," Jonathan said, though for a fact his father had told him no such thing.

Simon's mouth fell open as Jonathan spoke. He looked from Jonathan to the others. "How . . . ?" Simon approached the baron and said, "I am an old man and have but a few years left. I would go to the grave happy if you let me buy the boy back from you."

The baron bristled, "Old man, do you think we are all swine? The lad is not my slave."   .

Jonathan nodded at the patriarch. "He is taking me to my kinsmen in Cologne. But if you will lend him the money, then . . . I will be your bondservant for however long it will take to repay the debt."

"A lifetime," Simon snorted. Then with a furtive look at the others, he said to Jonathan in Hebrew, "They are not forcing you to go with them?"

Jonathan blinked and said, "No. He has been a friend to me. I can do nothing less for him."

"So then," Simon said to the others, "I will do what I can. But you must promise never to reveal what I am about to tell you."

For every moneylending transaction Simon usually had a tale and for this occasion he decided to use the old widow's tale. "As it happens, a widow came to me not long ago and borrowed a sum for her lord's funeral. She left as collateral his hauberk, ball-and-chain, and shield. Now since you say you fight for truth and *your* god, which is *her* god, can she object if I allow you to wear the armor for one day?" Simon asked. "Oh, if you lose, I am ruined!"

"Do not be frightened, old man," Roger said eagerly. "My father will not lose. In his day—"

"Be quiet, boy," the baron interrupted. "Would that I were as confident as you."

Simon wrote a brief contract on a parchment scroll. He pushed the quill and inkstand toward the baron.

"Your percentage?" Baron Thorne asked tersely.

"Thirty percent of all you win, including the ransom."

"Twenty percent," the baron said, "and not a livre more."

Simon pulled back the quill, the baron started toward the door, and Roger's heart dropped. With one hand on the latch the baron said, "Twenty-five," just as Simon said, "Twenty-five." The two men smiled wryly at each other.

Baron Thorne made his mark on the contract and Simon affixed his seal to the scroll. "Done," Simon said. "Do not eat heavily at the evening meal. Avoid all strong drink, and no concourse with women the night before the battle." He handed the baron a packet. "If you have trouble sleeping, brew this in hot water."

"What is it?" Jonathan asked, taking it from the baron's hand and sniffing it.

"It is a concoction of camomile and lemon peel," Simon said.

Jonathan nodded and gave the packet back to the baron.

"What do you know of such things?" Roger asked Jonathan.

"Enough to know that the brew will help your father," Jonathan answered.

Roger nodded soberly and then put his hand on Jonathan's shoulder. "Thank you for your help in the matter of this loan. I am indebted to you again."

As they left, Simon called after them, "God be with you. Your god *and* mine."

Outside, Roger was beside himself with worry about his father and pressed him for battle plans. Roger's barrage of questions barely penetrated the baron's worrisome thoughts. True, he had been successful in the lists, but that had been fully twenty years ago. Frizio was younger and doubtless full of the guile of the East.

As they came to the Cathedral of St. Pierre and St. Paul the Baron went inside and lit a candle to St. George, patron saint of warriors. Prayer alone did not ease the Baron and so he made his confession, asking forgiveness for his carnal sins with Flamonde and for his harshness toward Roger.

The tournament lists were outside the walls near the Madeleine Gate. The field had not been used much in the past years; the church frowned on these war games which maimed and killed men unnecessarily. "If men need to fight," Pope Innocent III had decreed in numerous papal bulls, "let them use their swords against the Albigenses, or the Moors, or to rescue the Holy Land." But news of this trial had spread throughout Troyes and nearly the entire city had turned out.

Both combatants and their seconds arrived early and repaired to their separate tents at either end of the field. In the peaked space of his tent, Baron Thorne donned his armor meticulously. The day waxed exceptionally warm for the end of May.

"Too warm," the baron complained as Roger helped him squeeze into the too-tight chain-mail hauberk. Roger's diligence heartened the baron; at least a dozen times his son had checked to see that his spurs were properly affixed.

Roger's eyes sparkled as he surveyed his father. "No finer knight exists anywhere," he exclaimed.

"And no better squire," the baron replied, placing his weighted hand on Roger's shoulder. "Now I must warn you of something. With God's help we shall win, for we are in the right. But in such a tournament, there is always the possibility of accident. So, remember what I told you about this man Frizio and, whatever happens, avoid him at all costs."

Roger nodded soberly.

Father and son looked at each other, their bitter fight over the university and the children's crusade forgotten as they embraced.

In his tent, Frizio lay on a pallet while Baalbek massaged him. The eunuch's deceptively soft-looking fingers worked the ligaments and tendons dexterously. Baalbek flipped Frizio onto his back.

"And you have searched everywhere for the girl?" Frizio asked.

"Yes, master. She is nowhere to be found."

"By the prophet!" Frizio exclaimed, then asked, "do you have it?"

Baalbek nodded and handed his master a small brown square of baked hashish. Frizio chewed it slowly while Baalbek continued the deep massage. Within a few minutes Frizio felt the roof of his mouth go numb, felt the muscles throughout his body grow warm as the effects radiated down to his stomach and legs, felt the hashish begin to color his brain, the color of invincible.

Frizio had learned this trick of bewitchment in Syria from Alla-ed-din, the Old Man of the Mountain, to whom Frizio sold as many children as fell into his hands. Over the years, Frizio had watched the old master, with the aid of the sacrament of hashish, fashion these striplings into the dreaded Cult of the Assassins, human daggers ready to fling themselves on any man, king, caliph, or priest that the Old Man marked for death.

Through the flap opening in the tent, Frizio could see his tethered Arabian stallion. "You will carry me to vengeance and victory," Frizio murmured, and gave himself up to Baalbek's powerful kneading fingers and the magic of the drug.

Frizio had first seen the stallion galloping across the Sinai desert near El Arish, weaving in and out of the royal palms. That is, he thought he saw him. The horse was a pale amber in color with darker patches of beige. Racing over the dunes, the creature seemed to flow with the sands. Only when the stallion stopped on the crest of a hill, to be outlined against the Mediterranean, could Frizio be certain it was not the ghost of Mohammed's steed, al-Burak, on whom he had risen straight away to heaven.

Too beautiful to be of this earth, too much like a wish fulfilled for Frizio to ever believe the horse could be his, he had set about owning him. He hired men. Hired horses, camels, Bedouin trackers. He bankrupted himself to capture the stallion.

Part Arabian, part Frankish Great Horse, this steed had obviously inherited the best of both breeds, for he outran and outsmarted his pursuers for months. But in the end, Frizio's perseverance won. At that tremulous moment when Frizio first touched him he knew the stallion to be a gift from the winds of the Sinai, a fabled creature whose life was destined to be entwined with his.

Frizio called the stallion Mirage. He loved Mirage with an unholy love. He would whisper in his ear, stroke and fondle him until the high-strung animal would shy away.

When Frizio grew black with his moods, he would cut a switch, and defying the Bedouin law of the desert, would beat the animal until his flanks ran red. Mirage would rear on his powerful legs, eyes rolling in anger. After Frizio had exhausted the strength of his madness, he would love the animal even more.

Frizio now fixed the battle scene in his mind, saw the tournament field, sensed every rock and pebble, smelled the green of every blade of grass. He envisioned the gaily decorated stands jammed with the nobility in their finest dress, imagined Laurelle there, gowned in sable-trimmed silk, wearing his colors. Then he and Baron Thorne were galloping toward each other and blood spumed as his lance pierced the baron through. Laurelle leapt to her feet applauding, and with his lance at the ready, Frizio raced toward her. In full view of Roger and all the crowd, she reclined and opened her arms to him.

Baalbek glanced at the hourglass; the sands had almost run out. The eunuch increased his pace and pressure until the blood rushed to every cell in Frizio's body, until his entire being pulsed hard with the prospect of the kill.

Lifting Frizio to his feet, Baalbek began dressing him. Frizio disdained a hauberk. He thought it madness for a man to imprison his body in iron; he had seen hundreds of Crusaders fall because they could not maneuver as adroitly as the Saracens. Freedom and flexibility, Frizio knew, these were the keys not only to survival, but victory.

Instead of chain mail, he donned a specially stiffened leather breastplate and thigh guards, capable of deflecting most blows. Over this leather armor Frizio put on wide, amber-colored pants and a loose tunic also of pale amber, all designed to make his body blend with Mirage's.

Though ambidexterous, Frizio slung his shield over his right arm; the lance held in his left hand had always confounded his opponents. His round shield was sharply convex, so that when a lance did hit it, it deflected the blow and did not subject the wearer to full shock. Frizio had chosen the battle-axe, that being the weapon of the surest kill.

"You are ready, master," Baalbek said, drawing the tent flap.

Frizio stepped out into the brilliant prism of high noon. The crowd gasped when they saw him, for he appeared to wear no armor.

The baron protested, calling out, "I will not fight an unarmed man."

Frizio threw back his head and laughed. "Old man, I am just making the odds more even."

After a hurried conference the judges concluded that Frizio might dress any way he chose. The only binding rules were those applying to the three runs with the lance, and against injuring the horses.

Banners flapped in the breeze. The nobles and richer merchants fidgeted in the stands, placing their bets. Peasants and poor sat on the grass while the more agile climbed the nearby trees and the walls of Troyes.

While Tantor stood patiently, Harolde, Roger, and Jonathan struggled to lift the baron into the saddle. After two abortive attempts they managed to seat him. Roger handed his father his lance and ball-and-chain. The baron had had to settle for this weapon and felt ill at ease with it.

At the opposite end of the field, Mirage moved impatiently, tossing his mane, as though sensing from the crowd's energy that he would soon be called upon to perform.

Frizio's eyes swept the field, once more imprinting every detail on his brain. Then Frizio whistled. Mirage stood absolutely still. Frizio ran toward the stallion and in one bound leapfrogged over the haunches, landing perfectly in the saddle. The crowd roared its approval. Frizio's move was not lost on the baron.

Three trumpet calls would sound: position, prepare, charge. Baron Thorne guided Tantor to the beginning of the run. Frizio whispered to his stallion and Mirage pranced to his position in a precise half-step that delighted the crowd.

The blare of the first trumpet quieted the spectators. The baron lowered the visor on his barrel helmet. Frizio's antics had angered him and he grew eager to test the man's mettle. He patted Tantor's neck and the sturdy beast snuffled. At the second trumpet call the baron braced his ash lance against his shoulder and held it at the ready.

Charge! A roar went up from the crowd as the two horses thundered toward each other, their hooves kicking up the turf. Through the slits in his helmet the baron watched his adversary close the field. Sweat trickled down the baron's forehead and into his eyes. He felt he was being roasted in this metal carapace. He squinted, struggling to see where the horse ended and Frizio began.

For Frizio, no such separation existed. He felt the power of the stallion surging up through his thighs, and it seemed that he and Mirage were one, a two-headed centaur and one with the sun.

The baron's fear and indecision fled with the gathering hoofbeats; he was a knight once more, responding to the call of battle. Everything he thought he had forgotten sprang to mind. His hands tightened on his lance, feeling its reassuring roundness; he heard the rushing wind whine through the vents in his helmet. He aimed his lance for the center of Frizio's shield and braced himself for the impact.

As the horses thundered close, Mirage flattened his neck and head. Frizio offered his shield to Baron Thorne's lance and at the same time threw his weight to Mirage's far side. The baron's weapon skidded across the shield's convex face then cut harmlessly through the air. Frizio's lance shattered on impact with the baron's long triangular shield, jarring both horse and rider.

Frizio straightened in the saddle and grinned at the baron.

The horsemen took their places again, this time to charge from opposite ends of the lists. Tantor's sweat soaked through his protective caparison; the horse trembled from the exertion of the charge and the baron's weight.

For a panicked moment Thorne remembered galloping across the desert at Gaza. On the straight field, nothing could withstand the iron charge of the Frankish knights on their Great Horses. But the Saracens had learned to let the Franks gallop through their lines, then—on their swifter Arabian mounts—they would close ranks and encircle the knights, attacking from all sides.

It came to him then, that despite what Frizio claimed, he was no Christian. The man rode only the way a Bedouin could. Infidel blood flowed in him somewhere and this enraged the baron. He thought of flinging off his armor and fighting Frizio in his own manner. But the trumpet sounded the second charge and Frizio again came bearing down.

Baron Thorne started an instant later, an instant that made the difference, for Frizio's lance caught his shield dead center with such force that Thorne felt himself lifted from his seat. In a desperate move he grabbed the pommel and hung on.

Roger broke from the sidelines to help his father but a guard caught him. Harolde grabbed hold of Roger's arm. "Do that again and you will forfeit the match! You must leave this to God!"

The baron doubled over in the saddle, fighting to get his breath. Dimly he became aware that he had managed to hold on to both lance and shield, though how he did not know, for in the little iron cage around his head he kept seeing multicolored flashes of light. He heard a loud ringing in his bandaged ear and flung up his visor to take gulps of air.

All too soon, the third trumpet called. The baron prayed he would be able to make this run. He might have a better chance in the hand-to-hand combat. Once more the charge, and the baron's heart sank when Tantor stumbled. With the rocking, uneven motion, he missed Frizio's shield completely. He felt Frizio's lance slam against his own shield, then graze off his left arm.

The combatants moved out of the lists onto the free combat field. Frizio bore down, battle-axe raised. The baron had just enough time to free his ball-and-chain and raise his shield above his head. He reeled under the axe's fearful clang.

"One blow," Baron Thorne muttered. "All I need to land is just one blow!" Frizio wore no chain mail and the ball would break flesh and bone. But landing it proved next to impossible, for Mirage wheeled and turned and ran circles around Tantor. With each pivot Frizio battered at the baron. He managed at last to land a blow·with his weapon, only to see the studded ball bounce harmlessly off Frizio's chest. The man must be enchanted! the baron thought, and grew afraid.

On the sidelines, Harolde struggled to hold Roger, who kept yelling, "It is all my fault!" as he fought to get to his father. Jonathan had turned deathly pale as he followed Frizio's swift harassments. His lips moved in endless prayer, for he knew not what else to do.

Mirage did not show the effects of the three charges but seemed to grow swifter and more graceful with each maneuver. According to the rules of chivalry, this was not supposed to be a fight to the death, but the crowd realized that they were witnessing just that. Even the judges were caught up in it, for in this ritual, mercy had no place—the call of blood stronger than the law.

Frizio stood up in his stirrups. He whirled the battle-axe over his head, faster, until the brilliant weapon sang. He galloped across the field, axe still whirling, and swung up from the ground. The blade caught the edge of the baron's shield and knocked it from his hand.

Blood ran from Thorne's ear and from a wound in his thigh where the axe had crushed the chain mail into his flesh. He could not tell from which direction Frizio was coming. The next blow caught him on the side of the helmet and knocked him from the saddle. With an instinct born of preservation, Baron Thorne staggered to his feet as Frizio began his last charge.

"I am free of sin," the baron whispered, thanking the Lord

that he had made his confession the night before. "May God protect my son."

Frizio spurred Mirage, determined to finish this off before anybody could stop him. Hashish and his own need had inflamed him. In anticipation of the kill Frizio grew expansive, reacting to the homage the crowd paid him. The defeated figure stood like an iron man in the empty field, waiting for the coup de grâce.

Frizio hung low in the saddle, aiming for that juncture at the neck where helmet and hauberk met. As Frizio swung, the baron ducked and with the same movement swung his ball-and-chain.

The chain wrapped around the handle of Frizio's axe and as Thorne fell backwards he dragged Frizio off Mirage and down to the ground with him.

The crowd leapt to its feet, screaming. Roger went wild, jumping up and down, pounding Harolde and Jonathan, who were both screaming back at him.

The two men struggled in the dust. Whereas the baron's armor had been a disadvantage, now its weight alone constituted a formidable weapon. The baron rolled over on Frizio, pinning him. Frizio struggled to reach the dagger strapped to his leg. His hand closed around the hilt and with a sidewise motion he stabbed at the baron. But the blade could not penetrate the chain mail.

Baron Thorne got his forearm across Frizio's throat and with the last of his strength sank down on top of him.

Frizio's eyes popped as he writhed, struggling for air. He managed to croak, "Quarter!" and with that, the baron collapsed.

CHALON-SUR-MARNE:
ABBEY OF THE THREE FOUNTAINS

ESPITE BRUISED BONES, FEVER, AND A DRAIN-ing wound in his thigh, the baron limped from bed on the third day, eager to be quit of the Frizio affair. "I doubt I will ever attempt another tournament," he groaned to Roger as they made their way to the courthouse.

"But you are quitting the field a victor," Roger said, squeezing his father's arm.

The baron nodded absently. One thing saddened him; Tantor, who had served him so faithfully, had died of exhaustion.

In the courtroom, the seneschal read the sentence. "Frizio, found guilty. To forfeit horse, weapons, and ransom. To be branded."

Frizio threw a bag of golden ducats on the table. "The ransom," he said. He placed a second pouch beside it. "For my horse."

The baron addressed the judges. "Since my son is the injured party, only he can decide this."

Every eye in the chamber swung to Roger. Somewhere in his being Roger understood Mirage's importance to Frizio; without the stallion, never again would Frizio be able to kill in the lists. Roger shook his head.

Frizio's face did not betray any emotion. He snapped his fingers. Baalbek produced another pouch of ducats.

Baron Thorne wavered. "It is more than any horse is worth," he whispered to Roger.

But Roger had in his mind a young girl and her shattered dream. He took a step toward Frizio. "What happened to Laurelle?"

A look compounded of hurt and confusion clouded Frizio's face. Then he shrugged impatiently, "Is it my province to keep track of every trollop in Troyes?"

Roger stiffened. "Then no amount of money will ransom the horse."

Frizio turned livid. Such naked malevolence twisted his face that Roger edged back to his father's side.

The seneschal proclaimed the final decree. "Under penalty of death, Frizio, you are not to seek revenge anywhere in Champagne or her adjoining territories. If your paths cross you are to give way, thereby acknowledging that you owe your life to Baron Thorne and to God. The judgment will remain in effect for one year from this day."

Roger turned his face away as the executioner branded the fleur-de-lis on Frizio's arm. Frizio bore the sentence without flinching.

When Frizio and Baalbek left, the baron sat down heavily. "I am not ashamed to say I am glad to see the last of those two."

Roger nodded, absently weighing the pouch of gold in his palm. "Gladly would I give this all, if only I knew Laurelle was safe."

"I will not go to the hospital!" the baron exclaimed when Harolde continued to fret over his prolonged fever. "If it will make you happy, then get a doctor. Preferably a Jew!" he yelled after Harolde as the monk dashed out the door.

Within the hour, Harolde returned with a great find; an Italian who had studied at Salerno, with all the necessary degrees, and willing to make house calls. That he was a good Christian pleased Harolde enormously.

There exuded from Dr. Santori a grave, gray manner, which matched his stiff gray hat and long gray robe. He held a vial of the baron's urine to the light. "No sediment," Santori said. Then he put a drop to his finger and tasted it. "No sugar."

"Is not his manner at bedside most pleasing?" Harolde whispered to Roger and Jonathan.

Dr. Santori probed the baron's thigh wound. "What is your date and place of birth?" he inquired. When Thorne told him, the doctor leafed through a small ephemeris translated from the Arabic, detailing the position of the planets. "The thighs are the province of Sagittarius, controlled by the planet Jupiter," Santori mused, his finger moving down the table of figures. "Ah ha! Jupiter is in excellent aspect to Taurus, your birth sign."

"What are you going to do?" Roger asked, watching the doctor take a scalpel and leather thong from his black bag.

Puffed with pride for having attended the most renowned medical school in all Europe, Santori explained, "The body has four humors, and three spirits, of course, but here we are only concerned with the humors. Phlegm, blood, bile and . . . and . . ."

"Black bile," Jonathan said softly.

"Do not interrupt!" Santori snapped. "Where were we? My patient has a tertian fever which occurs when the hot and moist blood overwhelms the cold and dry phlegm. He must be bled to keep the humors in balance."

"He should not be bled!" Jonathan blurted. "He has lost too much blood already."

Dr. Santori dropped his lancet. "Who is this?" he sputtered. "Remove him immediately! Nothing is more dangerous than upsetting a patient with tertian fever."

Roger shoved Jonathan out of the room, Jonathan strongly protesting, until Roger punched him silent.

Santori said, "Thank providence we are in a waxing moon. One must never bleed with a waning moon." With the leather thong he bound the baron's right thigh. Knowing that a running commentary usually soothed both the patient and family, Dr. Santori explained, "The wound being in the *left* thigh, we must bleed the *right,* to achieve balance. Balance being the secret of medicine."

Santori cut a pulsing vein in the baron's thigh and let the blood flow into a basin. "See for yourself how purple and unhealthy it is?" he said to Harolde, who nodded vigorously.

Finished with the bloodletting, Santori prescribed a light diet. "The broth of a well-boiled chicken is always salubrious in tertian fever." Then, obviously pleased with his handiwork (and relieved that his patient had not succumbed), Santori packed his bag, humming a ditty from his college days:

Use three doctors still
First doctor Quiet
Then doctor Merryman and doctor Diet . . .

"That will be three livres," Santori said. "And you, good monk, should take care of that cough. Mustard plasters morning, noon, and night. No charge."

Baron Thorne slept heavily for two days. On the third, he managed to keep down some chicken broth which Madame Crevette brought him.

Roger questioned the innkeeper's wife about Laurelle and Flamonde, but Madame Crevette said, "The earth has swallowed them up."

"And good riddance," Harolde said.

One afternoon, while Harolde was in church praying for the baron's recovery and the boys had taken the animals to be reshod, Baron Thorne heard a commotion in the street. Moving stiff-legged to the window, he pulled aside the oiled parchment.

Over the canal bridge marched a young lad dressed in a gray pilgrim's habit, a red cross sewn on his right shoulder. "Rejoice!" he called. "I come in the name of Stephen of Cloyes to gather the children of this province, as they are being gathered throughout France . . ." The evangelist's voice faded as he turned the corner.

When the others returned, the Baron insisted they leave at once, complaining that he was too flea-bitten to remain in bed any longer.

The baron's wounds forced them to travel too slowly to join any of the pilgrim caravans moving along the Champagne Fair routes. Inns being practically nonexistent in the countryside, they stayed overnight at the guest houses of the various monasteries along their route.

The baron now rode Noname; Harolde, Tortoise; and when

the stallion wasn't galloping, Jonathan rode behind Roger on Mirage. On the open road, Roger gave Mirage free rein. Mane and tail flying, the stallion hurdled fence and ditch, weaving in and out of the haystacks dotting the rolling fields. Then Roger would prance back to the others, riding rings around them in a display of Mirage's speed and agility. Roger had never ridden so fast a horse, and though he was thrown innumerable times, he always climbed back on.

Every traveler who passed looked upon Mirage with envy. "Yes, it is you they stare at," Roger whispered and reached over to hug the stallion's neck. Mirage seemed to flourish under the attention lavished on him by Roger and Jonathan, and without the demands put on him by Frizio, gentled considerably.

On the eve of the Feast of Sainte Germaine, the band limped into the Cistercian Abbey of the Three Fountains near Chalon-sur-Marne. The hospitalier took them to the infirmarian who immediately put the baron to bed. The monk treated the baron's wounds with herbal potions and unguents concocted in the abbey's own workshops: agrimony to heal all cuts made with iron, a salve of lemon balm to lave the black-and-blue bruises.

Unbeknownst to anybody, Jonathan availed himself of a supply of divers herbs from the garden, secreting them in his wallet.

Over Jonathan's strenuous objections, the infirmarian bled Baron Thorne again, showing Harolde how it must be done should he require future bleeding. The abbot insisted the baron rest at Three Fountains at least a week. After two days Thorne was fit to jump out of his skin.

"It is these incessant bells!" he ranted to Roger. "At two in the morning they ring for matins, at four, for lauds. I am just getting to sleep at dawn when they ring for prime. It is a wonder that anybody ever survives, let alone recovers in a hospital!"

Worse still, the baron resented the monks' silent condemnation of his way of life, and their not so subtle insinuation that, as St. Jerome had proclaimed, "A merchant can rarely, if ever, please God."

During his meditations in the cloister, Harolde fell into conversation with Brother Albericus, a monk working on a chronicle of the times. "This past week," Brother Albericus said, "I have been writing of this occurrence in the Ile de France. There is this young shepherd . . ."

With all the excitement of an eyewitness, Harolde told Brother Albericus everything he could of Stephen of Cloyes. The two monks agreed that Stephen had been chosen. "But by God or the devil?" Brother Albericus asked.

"Only time will tell," Harolde answered.

When Harolde reported this extraordinary coincidence to the baron, he swore Harolde to secrecy.

Later that afternoon Roger and Jonathan tarried in the garden to watch a group of sculptors working on statues which would ultimately find their home in the monastery. Harolde sat in a quieter section of the cloister, reading from his Bible to the dozing baron.

"Guillaume of St. Denis told me he could do that," Roger said, as he watched a stonecutter wielding his hammer and chisel. "But how do they know where to cut?"

"God guides their hand," Harolde called to the boys and then came over to join them. "See, here is Simeon carrying the child Jesus. Next is St. John the Baptist holding the haloed lamb." Then came Esau with Jesse asleep under the pedestal, and Moses with the serpent. "This last one," Harolde said, "is Abraham about to sacrifice Isaac. Though as we know, the Lord stayed his hand."

Jonathan whispered something to Roger. Suddenly the two boys were wrestling on the ground, shouting at each other: "They are!" "They are not!" "They are so!"

Harolde pulled them apart. Still the lads fought to get at each other, Jonathan for the first time refusing to let Roger have his way.

Baron Thorne woke and limped over. "But why are you fighting?" he asked, coming between them.

"He blasphemed," Roger said hotly. "He said all the statues were of Jews!"

Jonathan glared belligerently at Harolde, daring him to deny it. Harolde glanced around nervously and drew the boys away from the workmen. "They are all Jews," he said, and added quickly, "but they all accepted Jesus as the messiah."

Too late Harolde realized his error, for Jonathan cried, "How? From the grave? Most were dead before Jesus was born!" Jonathan darted behind the baron as Harolde aimed a kick at him.

Harolde fell into a fit of coughing, unable to catch his breath. Jonathan became frightened and tried to help the monk, slapping him on the back, then quickly crushing some leaves of the feverfew herb and holding them under his nose. But this only incensed Harolde all the more.

Roger was mightily confused. All of them Jews . . . and the Virgin and Joseph and Jesus too . . . should one hate only those Jews who came after Jesus? And venerate those who had come before? Perplexing. He would have to question Harolde on it, but when he was not so excitable.

Harolde continued to cough in tearing gasps. When he finally managed to stop, his face had turned ashen, and the hand he took from his mouth was stained with blood.

IN THE FOREST
OF ARDENNES

POPPIES AND MUSTARD SPLASHED THE FIELDS northeast of Rheims, the red and yellow of the flowers making the very ground appear on fire. The days grew longer as the sun burned toward summer.

The baron's leg became a constant source of pain as they plodded into the dense forests of the Ardennes. A perpetual thirst plagued him and they were forced to stop more often. One whole day they traveled without seeing anyone save a leper, clacking his wooden clapper to warn all of his affliction. The next day, Roger spotted a quartet of horsemen keeping pace a mile or so behind them. Baron Thorne watched carefully throughout the morning, breathing a sigh of relief when they disappeared at the crossroads of Longwy.

They had hoped to rest at some hospice that night, but an hour before twilight the baron fell from Noname, too exhausted to continue. They camped in a glen where elm, oak, and ash grew in gloomed abundance and hurried to build a fire before darkness fell.

Jonathan tethered the horses on a long lead so they could graze and drink from the nearby stream. In a moment of play, Mirage bit Noname, deviled Tortoise, and butted Jonathan repeatedly before cavorting off to graze.

Shadows of trees lengthened across the glen. The wind quickened, stirring the leaves; flowers enfolded their petals against the gathering darkness. A nightingale sent out its fluting lonely call and then a hush fell over the land.

Roger mimicked the bird, hoping to break the silence. To no avail. Harolde, staring into the flames, said, "I have heard tell of a monk, a hellion in his youth, who came to be touched by God's grace. As a special gift the Lord allowed him to talk to birds and animals. All living things calls he brother and they do respond to him."

"Who might this miracle worker be?" Roger asked.

"He is an Italian, from the town of Assisi. His father is a rich merchant, but the son has given all his inheritance to the poor and become a mendicant friar. The Holy Father, not three years ago, gave his blessing to this new order. They preach poverty and the love of all things great and small."

Baron Thorne shifted his aching body against the tree trunk. He did not like it when Harolde talked thus with his impressionable son in earshot. He said, "It is a noble thought, but in this world of practical realities, it is no more than a form of madness."

"You say his father is a merchant?" Roger said. "What is this monk's name?"

"Francis. The brothers who follow his rule call themselves the 'clowns of God,' for they hope to be jongleurs of joy for the Lord. I have often thought this would be the best way to serve God. To live in poverty and travel the land, teaching, helping the poor. Is this not what our Lord did?"

Baron Thorne interrupted, "But Harolde, I thought you were going to Rome? To attach yourself to some powerful prelate when the new Lateran Council begins. Oh, I see, that is what you thought yesterday. Today it is this monk, Francis? Well, we shall see what tomorrow brings."

Harolde threw a pebble into the darkness, furious with the baron but even more furious with himself. For he knew the baron was right. Oh, Lord! What a cross to be afflicted with this changeable nature, never to know the right path!

Through the circle of trees they saw the constellations and the great white way of stars called the Path of St. James. A shooting star blazed across the sky, falling down and down.

Thorne said softly, "In Outremer, the Jerusalemites say that shooting stars are God's tears . . . for the evil that man does." Then he cleared his throat. "Enough! Else we shall become melancholy to the death."

The baron set up a watch for the night. He and Roger would

take the first; when the moon had half-risen, they would waken Harolde and Jonathan. The monk and the boy bedded down.

Baron Thorne leaned back against the tree trunk, his ears alert to every sound. He took his sword from its scabbard and laid it beside him. Roger watched Mirage's pale form drifting in and out of the moonlight. In the distance, a wolf's howl bristled the air. With a powerful rush of wings an owl swooped from its branch; as it rose, Roger saw a limp hare in its talons. He moved closer to the fire.

Jonathan cried out in his sleep and both Roger and the baron started. "Every night it is the same," Roger said. "Is he troubled because he is not a Christian?"

"That and other things," the baron said. "He relives a time in his life that causes him much grief, and in so reliving, attempts to exorcise it."

"What happened?" Roger asked. "Will no one ever tell me?"

The baron sighed. "Well, knowing as much as you do, I suppose there is no reason for you not to hear the rest. Do you remember the time when I had that abscess in my eye?"

Roger nodded.

"The infirmarians I saw at the monasteries did little for my affliction save pray over it. So I went to see one of the physicians in the Old Jewry, right across from the Mercer's Guild."

"A Jew?" Roger breathed. "Were you not frightened of their devilish ways?"

"Nonsense!" the baron snorted. "Do not listen to such old wives' tales. I first came in contact with Jews in Palestine during the Third Crusade. Richard Coeur de Lion set great store by their doctors, even going so far as to try to woo Saladin's personal physician, Maimonides, from him. Maimonides, however, preferred the civilized court in Cairo to that of the barbarous Franks.

"The doctor I saw in Old Jewry, Aaron Ben-Oni, cured my eye. Thereafter, whenever I had an ailment, I sought him out. I took to supplying him with medicinal herbs from the Levant and with surgical knives from Mainz. In time, I learned his story. He was born in Cologne and studied at the medical university in Cordoba. About twenty years ago, an army of knights marching through the Rhinelands to join up with other Crusaders destroyed the Jewish quarter of Cologne. Aaron Ben-Oni and his wife, Rachel, fled, and after a year of wandering settled at last in London, where our King Richard's policies were a little more tolerant. In time, a son was born to them."

"Jonathan," Roger murmured.

Baron Thorne nodded. "A number of times the family tried to emigrate to Palestine with groups of other Jews, but something always prevented them. And so they lived in London until this last uprising, when Jonathan's parents were killed. I managed to spirit the boy away from the mob. And the rest you know."

Harolde and Jonathan stood watch now. Jonathan shuddered; never had he spent a night in so dark and gloomy a place. That growl, was it a bear, or some evil spirit? He hoped a bear, at least such a beast could be fought off. But what frightened Jonathan most was the way Harolde kept staring at him.

Harolde had decided that this was the moment to bring the Savior's light into the boy's life. He called softly, "Jonathan, I beg you, attend to what I am about to say."

As Jonathan turned to look directly at the monk, the fire cast twin flames in his eyes. An ingrained terror of all Jews caused Harolde to make the sign of the cross. When he regained his composure, Harolde said, "Jonathan, do you believe in Moses?"

Jonathan blinked in surprise. When Harolde repeated his question with greater insistence, the boy nodded.

"And do you believe in the Ten Commandments?" Harolde asked.

Again Jonathan nodded, growing increasingly nervous. A sudden sound in the bush made him start. He put his fingers to his lips and began to get up, but Harolde pulled him back down. Having forced himself to this precipitous moment, he would not let the boy distract him.

Harolde's words came tumbling out in a rush. "My Jonathan, you can be saved, I swear it. All you need do is make one small act of contrition. Open your heart to the Savior and He will open His heart to you. If you will but confess . . ."

"To what? I have done nothing," Jonathan said.

"Then confess for your people. Just one act and the Lord will reach out and heal your soul. Never again will you be a pariah. Never again will paradise be denied you."

"And how much will that indulgence cost?" Jonathan asked, setting his jaw. "I tell you, I have done nothing."

"Have you no sorrow then for the murdered children whose blood you use in your Passover rituals?"

Jonathan's mouth fell open. He had never expected anybody as learned as Harolde to believe such a lie.

Jonathan tried to keep his voice from trembling. "I have never killed anybody," he said. "Nor have I ever seen blood used in our Passover ceremony. Such a thing would be an outrage against our commandment, 'Thou shalt not kill'!"

"Yet your people killed Christ!" Harolde exclaimed.

"And for a thousand years you yourselves have used that excuse to keep on killing!" Jonathan cried, the blood rising to his face. "When will you stop?"

Harolde shook his head sadly. It was obvious that Satan had a hand in this, so wedded to his lies had the boy become. Harolde began on another tack, but Jonathan cut him short at the sound of a snapped twig.

Jonathan shook the baron and Roger. "Wake up," he whispered.

"He is imagining things," Harolde said. "I heard nothing."

"You were too busy preaching," Jonathan said, and for that piece of insolence received a smart slap across the face.

Baron Thorne squinted against the darkness. Nothing sounded, nothing moved. Then he caught sight of Mirage. The horse held his head high, nostrils flaring to the message on the wind.

The baron had just enough time to grab his sword and haul himself to his feet when four armed men came crashing through the thicket. Their capuchons were pulled over their noses, masking their faces. Three of them concentrated their attack on the baron, while the fourth ran for the pasture.

"Harolde! See to the horses!" the baron shouted.

The baron parried the thrust of the attackers' swords and the clang of steel roused the forest. Then Thorne's blade cleaved one robber's collarbone. The other two men forced the baron back against the tree trunk.

Roger threw himself on one tall brigand but the man flung him off as if he were a sack of meal and he landed in the stream, stunned. Jonathan dragged him onto the bank lest he drown.

Lifting the hem of his robe so that he would not trip, Harolde ran to the clearing where the fourth bandit was already cutting at the ropes that tied the animals.

"For the love of God, sir," Harolde began.

The bandit, thinking twice about killing a man of the cloth, did not go for Harolde with his knife, but gave him a fearful clout that knocked him off his feet.

Seizing Mirage's mane, the bandit attempted to mount him. Harolde recovered and grabbed the bandit's foot. Mirage reared and threw the bandit to the ground where he received a kick that knocked him senseless.

"Oh, merciful Lord, what have I done?" Harolde lamented. He did not know whether to administer the last rites or help the others. Shouts from the continuing battle convinced him that he must do for the living and he ran back toward camp.

The baron was bleeding from a wound in his side and from a gash running from forehead to jawbone. His legs were beginning to buckle. The two remaining brigands, seeing their advantage, were attacking with renewed vigor.

Jonathan looked around wildly. Harolde was still nowhere in sight, Roger lay unconscious, and the baron was about to be overcome. Run! Save yourself! Jonathan's terror screamed at him and he dashed into the bushes, fleeing for his life. But once in the safety of the forest, an anguished cry from the baron stopped him in his tracks. "I cannot abandon them, I cannot!" Jonathan cried, regaining his senses. He dashed back to the campsite and moved as if one possessed. Grabbing a branch from the fire, he ran up behind one of the attackers. The brigand, sensing a presence, whirled, and Jonathan thrust the burning torch in the man's face.

The brigand screamed and, clutching his face, crashed off into the bushes, just as Harolde returned.

The last attacker, seeing that he fought alone, turned and fled.

With a groan, the baron collapsed. "We bested them!" Harolde gasped, feeling an irrepressible urge to cheer. Then he remembered who he was and added hastily, "With God's help."

Still in a state of shock, they began to care for their wounds. Harolde had a huge bump on his forehead; his eyes were already beginning to swell. Roger's face and shoulder were scraped raw from where he had landed in the gravelly stream. Ugly burns blistered Jonathan's puffed fingers.

Baron Thorne suffered most. Under inspection, the wound in his side proved superficial. As for the slash on his face, fortunately, much of that would be hidden by his beard for he would carry the scar to the grave. But the thigh wound proved to be serious. A sword thrust had opened it again and the inflamed area advanced all the way down the leg.

"I think it is festering," Jonathan said.

"The more reason to get to Cologne as quickly as possible," the baron said.

When Harolde brought the horses back to the glen he discovered that his fallen assailant had disappeared. Never had he felt such relief. "Oh, I am not branded with the mark of Cain!" he exclaimed, and fell to his knees and gave thanks.

They gave the slain robber a Christian burial, first searching his clothes to discover who he might be. They found only a gold coin of Byzantine design.

THE HOLY ROMAN EMPIRE

THE DAYS SNAKED ONE INTO THE OTHER FOR Baron Thorne as they proceeded on to Luxembourg, climbing toward the fortress city built on the ridge of an impregnable hill. They were within the boundaries of the Holy Roman Empire now, and the people spoke both the softer French and the more guttural German. The baron knew he was very sick and had but one thought: to reach Cologne. Should he not recover, there at least, Roger would be safely in the hands of his mother's people.

The third day out of Luxembourg, on a lonely stretch of mountain road, the baron slipped off his horse and into unconsciousness.

The sun balanced on a ridge of craggy hills. It would be dark soon. Feeling his inadequacy huge in his chest, Harolde began preparations for bleeding the baron.

Before Harolde could act Jonathan grabbed his wrist. "Bleed him once more and he will die."

"But the infirmarian at the Abbey of the Three Fountains," Harolde sputtered.

"Knows nothing," Jonathan insisted. "My father was a physician. Many times I have seen him cure ailments similar to this one."

Harolde looked at Roger helplessly. Roger pressed his lips against his father's forehead. "Fever rages within him," he said. "We must do *something.*"

Jonathan said, "You listened to that charlatan, Dr. Santori, and your father did not get better. Then to the infirmarian, and see how he is now? Bled so much his body is too weak to heal itself. I warn you, if you do not heed me your father will be dead by morning."

A moan escaped from Roger. Then his dagger was at Jonathan's throat, drawing a dot of blood. "I will tell you why my father has to live. Because if he dies, then you die."

Jonathan knocked the dagger into the bushes. "I will try to save him," Jonathan said. "Not out of fear of you, but for him. And to honor my own father. Now do as I tell you and without question."

Despite the danger from bandits, Harolde built a fire, and according to Jonathan's instructions, ringed it with stones. After retrieving his dagger, Roger went to a nearby stream and filled goatskins with water. Jonathan set the water to boil. Then he searched his wallet for certain herbs, supplementing them with others he ripped from the earth. Mandrake, the gnarled, split root that looked like an ancient homunculous, Jonathan steeped in the boiling water. He placed the potion under the baron's nose, forcing him to inhale the fumes. Jonathan said, "Mandrake root dulls the senses and eases the pain. He will sleep for a bit now."

"He is breathing a little easier," Roger said to Harolde.

Harolde watched it all fearfully, as if the boy with the slanted eyes and pointed ears were invoking all the black and mysterious forces of the underworld.

Jonathan labored through the night, applying compresses of hot cloths alternating with poultices of herbs. The area around the wound grew redder and angrier, but still Jonathan persisted. The baron cried out in his delirium, "He is no Christian!" and Roger sprang to his side.

Jonathan pushed him away. "More water. When you are done, stay out of the way." He pointed to Harolde, whose hands were clasped in prayer. "You could do worse," Jonathan said.

Had he dared, Roger would have struck Jonathan, so imperious had the little Jew become.

At that time of night when darkness is at its pitch, the baron seemed to stop breathing. "He has given up the ghost," Harolde said mournfully, and turned with accusation to Jonathan. "We should have at least gotten him to a church, to save his soul."

"He is not dead," Jonathan said tersely. "Look." He pulled back the baron's eyelid and the pupil rolled in reflex.

He amazed himself by remembering so much of what his father had taught him. And his father had taught him well, grooming him to take over the practice when he would be too old to continue. Jonathan had never thought he had much calling for the profession; he had flinched from the blind and diseased who came to his father's door seeking help. But without realizing it, he had absorbed much from his gentle but demanding taskmaster.

Another round of compresses and yet another. Roger grew bleary-eyed carrying water from the stream. The waning moon stared down, mute witness to the struggle as Jonathan held death at bay.

As he worked, Jonathan felt a rush of warmth for the baron, remembering how his father had spoken of him, saying, "The herbs and medicines he imports are of the highest quality, and at a fair price. A most honest man, for a Gentile." True, the baron had taken Jonathan along because he knew he would be well rewarded when they reached Cologne. Yet not many would have risked it even for that.

Shortly before dawn, the baron's limbs stiffened and he began to shiver violently. Jonathan took off his blouse and ripped it into strips. He wrapped the heated rocks from the fire in the cloths and placed them around the baron's body. Then he demanded that Harold remove his robe. "I must use it for a blanket."

Harolde threw up his hands in consternation. A pleading look from Roger persuaded him and he slipped off his habit. Where the sun had never touched his body, Harolde's skin was of a pallor almost unearthly. His arms were thin but with well-defined muscles, and his chest, though narrow, had the strongly etched outline of pectorals. But at the sternum bone there was a deep indentation.

Jonathan had seen such a chest before: on a man his father had been treating for hectic fever, the coughing sickness. A slow, lingering affliction, his father had told him, very difficult to cure . . . then Jonathan remembered the blood that Harolde kept coughing up.

The baron moaned and Jonathan turned his attention back to him. "Give me your dagger," Jonathan said to Roger.

"What are you going to do?" Roger asked, handing it to him.

Jonathan did not answer.

"You know that if he dies because of you, I shall have to kill you."

"Always it is thus," Jonathan murmured to the spirit of his father who had guided his hand through the night. "Help me, they cry. But if he dies, then you must die. And should he live? Oh, then it is God's will. And where are we in all this? Always blamed, never thanked. Thank the Lord we do it not for them, but to honor life."

Jonathan shoved the knife blade into the glowing coals. "Listen to me carefully, both of you. Roger, when I tell you, hold your father's arms. You, Harolde, hold his ankles; sit on them if need be. The thigh must be absolutely still when I make the incision. No matter how he fights—"

"You are not going to cut the flesh?" Harolde cried out, petrified at the very thought. Man being created in the image of God, marring that image in any way was tantamount to inflicting new, crucifying wounds on the body of Christ. He reached out to stop Jonathan, convinced now that the boy was in the thrall of the devil. "Church doctrine explicitly states . . ." he began.

Jonathan shrugged Harolde off. "Which is more important, your church doctrine or his life? See the cyst here on his thigh? The herb compresses have brought it to the surface. It must be lanced, for that is what is poisoning his blood. Now take hold of his arms and legs."

Harolde resisted. Roger said, "Unless you know of another way, we must do as he says. Otherwise, my father will die." Roger grabbed his father's arms and Harolde sat on the baron's legs. Jonathan took the knife out of the coals; the steel glowed a dull red.

Jonathan looked to the light of dawn, just beginning to band the horizon. Holding the knife like a stylus, he made a quick incision across the inflamed pustule.

"Not deep enough," he chastised himself. He steadied his hand and tried again. Along with the acrid odor of burning flesh came the baron's scream as pain brought him to consciousness. He thrashed about violently and Roger and Harolde fought to hold him. Roger could not believe his father had that much strength left and it renewed his hope.

"Hold him, now hold," Jonathan said through gritted teeth. "Once more and it is done." So saying, he sliced another incision across the first cut, making a cross on the baron's wound.

This time the baron knocked Roger aside. The boy scrambled back, begging his father to be quiet, whispering that it would soon be over.

Yellow, watery lymph mixed with blood oozed from the incision. Jonathan applied his thumbs to the baron's thigh and carefully pulled the wound apart. More blood flowed out now, streaked with pus. Jonathan increased the pressure, harder, until his arms ached with the strain, and still the core of the infection would not come. He stared at his hands. "I am not strong enough," he said. Sweat broke out on his forehead as he tried to think.

"What now?" Roger demanded, his voice ominous.

"You must help. Do as I do," Jonathan said. He put his hands on one side of the wound and directed Roger to put his hands on the other. "When I say, pull the wound apart as hard as you can. No matter how he screams. Do you understand?"

Roger nodded.

"Now, then," Jonathan said, "begin. Harder. *Harder!* Or it will not come!" In one final desperate jerk, Jonathan yanked as hard as he could and a great spurt of poison and pus and all foul humors shot from the body. The baron screamed once and collapsed.

"Dead," Roger said dully. He turned and sprang for Jonathan. The force of Roger's leap knocked the two boys head over heels. Jonathan tore Roger's fingers away from his throat long enough to gasp, "Only fainted. But he will die, unless you let me finish."

"Roger! Jonathan is right," Harolde called, his ear pressed against the Baron's chest.

Roger knelt at his father's side and clutched his hand. Some of the warmth seemed to be gradually returning and the fingers were losing their heavy waxen feeling.

Jonathan cleansed the wound, extracting the last of the poisons. He bathed the entire area with hot water, then patted on a poultice of mud and herbs. Then he wrapped the thigh with brown bandages that he cut from the hem of Harolde's robe. Finished at last, Jonathan slumped down and rested his head in his hands.

With sunrise, birds lifted their voices. Doe and fawn came to the brook to drink. Creatures of the forest busied themselves as every living thing made life anew with the new day.

Jonathan's head reeled with exhaustion and lack of sleep, and it seemed to him that he was not in this lonely misbegotten wilderness, but back in London, in the ordered household of his mother and father, Rachel and Aaron Ben-Oni. Even though his parents had battled constantly, their devotion to God and to each other had been the rock upon which all their lives had been built. Jonathan remembered the Sabbath eve, his mother's weary face aglow with candlelight as her fragile hands made slow circles over the flames, her lips moving in silent prayer, beseeching the Lord for health and peace, and concluding, "A good Sabbath, a good year." And when Jonathan went to sleep on Sabbath eve, he always found a small bag of raisins and almonds by his pallet. Despite the daily trials in the Old Jewry, the taunts from rowdies, the beatings, the rocks and rotten vegetables that had been thrown at their house, the family had had each other—it was this that had made London bearable, had made being a Jew among Gentiles bearable.

Then had come that day of wrath when Jonathan had run home from the tiny synagogue school to warn his parents of a riot. As he raced through the narrow streets, it seemed that the entire quarter was on fire, with roaring flames shooting skyward. Coming into the courtyard he had seen men with drawn bloody swords running from the burning pyre of their house. In the doorway, his mother, dead, fingers clutching her Bible; his father dying of gouting wounds, his head cradled in the lap of a stranger.

"Go with him," Jonathan's father had whispered, and died.

Unable to move, unable to cry, Jonathan had allowed himself to be led away by the baron. These many weeks he could not admit that his parents were dead . . . unable to say *Kaddish,* the prayer which would ease the journey of their souls through the unknown.

Jonathan cast his mind back to his prayer book, and the words, halting at first, and then with growing sureness, slipped through the fingers that cradled his face.

"Hallowed be the name of God . . . may His kingdom come, and His will be done in all the earth . . . To my father and mother whom I now remember . . . may peace and bliss be granted in life eternal . . . may their souls rejoice in that wondrous good which God has laid up for all those who reverence Him . . . may the father of peace send peace to all who mourn . . ."

The tears fell, unbidden at first, then great gushing sobs wracked his body. He cried for his mother, and for his father, for the unknown joys and the unshared sadnesses and for all the things which would never be.

Then Jonathan felt a gentle, familiar poke in his ribs and Roger put his arm around his shoulder, tentative at first, then stronger and the two boys looked at each other through blurring eyes.

"You were right," Roger murmured. "My father lives and once again I am in your debt."

Jonathan nodded and then stood up. A strange looking lot they were, exhausted and half-naked in their torn clothing. Jonathan moved off slowly and made his way to the brook. He splashed some cold water on his face and then saw Mirage's reflection in the pool. Boy and horse drank from the stream.

"Mirage, did you see," Jonathan asked, "how Roger offered his hand in friendship?"

The stallion bobbed and shook his head, splashing Jonathan all over.

Jonathan sat back on his haunches. "Still, I know my lot will not be easy. But now I know something more."

He jumped to his feet, wanting to dance and shout with the knowledge of it, but he was too exhausted. Instead, he grasped Mirage's neck and hauled himself onto his back.

Responding to the boy's excitement, Mirage began to canter around the clearing, then faster, and Jonathan clung to his neck as the stallion stretched out into a gallop.

"I know who I am!" Jonathan shouted, and the wind tore the words from his lips. "And nobody—king or priest, thief or murderer—can ever take that away from me!"

As Mirage raced around the camp where Baron Thorne lay, Jonathan realized that in saving the baron's life, he had somehow managed to save his own.

PART

The Age
of
the Son

TWO

COLOGNE:
LAST WEEK IN JUNE

JAGGED BOLTS OF HEAT LIGHTNING SHATTERED THE heavens as the four weary travelers first glimpsed the city of Cologne, nestled on the banks of the mighty river Rhine.

"Thank the Lord we have arrived in one piece," Harolde said with a cautious look at the sky.

They approached the Ulrepforte Gate, Noname dragging the litter of beech poles and woven rushes on which Baron Thorne lay. Bumping along the rutted roads had caused his wounds to weep, crusting his bandages.

"We must get some fresh dressings the first place we can," Jonathan told Harolde.

Just within the walls of the city they stopped in the courtyard of the Monastery of St. Panteleon. A monk sat hunched over a slanted desk set beneath a tree white with apple blossoms, laboriously illuminating a page of the Bible; a second monk, whose white tonsured hair surrounded a scalp as pink as his cheeks, laid down his stylus and greeted them.

"My name is Brother Gottfried," the monk said, "chronicler of St. Panteleon. Will you rest here this day? You are most welcome." Then he leaned over and peered at the baron. "This man is very ill and obviously in need of bleeding. Wait here, I will send for the infirmarian."

"Perhaps another time," Jonathan said hastily. "For the moment we have need only of new dressings."

"And directions to the hanse," the baron called weakly.

"I can help you on both counts," Brother Gottfried said. He went into the monastery and returned a short time later with the necessary bandages. As Jonathan dressed the wound, the monk kept up an amiable patter.

"The hanse is quite close to the Dom, and since I am going there shortly to chronicle the wondrous happenings, I will be glad to direct you. Have you come to Cologne then so that our young evangelist can cure your friend?" he asked Harolde.

A startled look passed between the members of the baron's party. "An evangelist?" Harolde asked.

"Have you not heard?" Brother Gottfried said. "Why, the entire province rings with the news. Already the lad has effected many marvelous cures. I myself have noted two authenticated healings in my chronicles."

Baron Thorne felt a stab of apprehension but could not make himself heard from where he lay.

"What is this lad's name?" Roger asked excitedly. "Pray God it be Stephen of Cloyes!"

The monk shook his head. "He is called Nicholas, and comes from a hamlet not far from here."

Roger's face fell. The baron breathed a sigh of relief.

Brother Gottfried went on, "Young Nicholas has truly been called by the Lord. Such a voice must David have had to soothe the beast in Saul. Do you know that he carries the mark of the chosen?"

"Let us to the church and see for ourselves," Roger exclaimed, while the baron protested feebly, "We must get to the hanse!"

After Jonathan finished tending the baron's wounds, they set out with Brother Gottfried. He led them through narrow roadways and finally into the Höhestrasse, Cologne's main axis. At every cross street they caught glimpses of the Rhine, intermittently glinting silver from flashes of heat lightning. Cargo-laden boats plied the river. Because of the city's location midway on the great waterway, Cologne had become the largest city in the Holy Roman Empire, boasting a population in excess of forty thousand.

Roger poked Jonathan, pointing up at the marble-faced mansions of the Lombard bankers. "Why, some of them are five stories tall! And see how clean everything is!"

Here a portly burgher whitewashed his timber-and-daub house; there a maid in braids swept the walk before a gleaming copper and brass shop. Doorknobs sparkled in the sun, fresh flowers grew in the carved, freshly painted window-boxes and herbs and vegetables in the tidy gardens.

"It is far cleaner than London, I am ashamed to admit," Harolde said, "and even more than Paris. Why, I have not seen one chamber pot being emptied out of a window!"

Brother Gottfried's cheeks glowed with pride. "All our citizens are hard-working and fastidious. Better Christians are nowhere to be found, which may be the reason that Cologne has been chosen for these miraculous events."

"You know, Brother Gottfried," Roger said proudly in German, "my mother was born here in Cologne, but her people originally came from Saxony."

The monk nodded appreciatively, then turned to Jonathan. "And you, my boy?"

"My parents also came from Cologne," Jonathan said quietly. "I think I still have some relatives here."

"From which parish? Perhaps I know them?" Brother Gottfried asked helpfully.

Harolde understood enough of the conversation to know it was heading into dangerous areas. "How much further?" he interrupted hastily.

"Only a short distance," Brother Gottfried said. "And you, good sir," he said, pointing to Baron Thorne, "are wise to enlist the healing powers of our evangelist." He went on to describe the boy's various cures, including lowering an infant's fever and restoring life to his own father, given up for dead.

This further piqued Roger's curiosity, and disturbed the baron greatly. He tried to think of a way to leave the monk, but before he could devise a plan they arrived at the square of the Carolingian church. A goodly crowd of people, young and old, noble, peasant, and burgher, had gathered to hear the child evangelist who had been preaching at the Dom all this week.

The boy could not have been more than ten years old, with eyes of the palest blue and fine flaxen hair that stirred in the June breeze. So comely a youth was he that even had he not been preaching, the townspeople would have turned to stare at him.

Harolde and Roger strained to see, enthralled, and even Jonathan grew excited. The baron felt his head whirl; he had dreamed this before, this nightmare that had followed him these many weeks and miles. "Press on!" he cried, but nature itself conspired against him and his voice came out a croak.

Up from the Ile de France and along the Champagne Fair routes had traveled the news of Stephen of Cloyes' crusade of children. When the good tidings had reached the environs of Cologne, the child Nicholas had come forward, announcing that he too had had a visitation from the Lord. Now as he stood before the Dom he recounted his tale in his flutelike voice.

"One day as I worked in the fields, I saw a blinding light in the sky that turned the earth white. Sore afraid, I ran to tell my father, only to find him lying on the ground, his clothes smoking, his body rigid as if turned to a pillar of salt. Nothing I did could rouse him from this stony trance and I mourned him as lost. Just then, a gentle man appeared. He gave me this cross of St. Anthony, patron saint of lost things"—Nicholas held up the cross in the shape of the Greek letter tau—"and this shining, beautiful man said that if I made the sign of the cross with it over my father's body, that he would rise again.

"I did as he instructed and when my father came instantly to life, I knew that this man could be none other than our Seignior!"

The crowd drew in its breath sharply. At the bottom of the platform, Nicholas's father, a lean handsome man with darting blue eyes, nodded vigorously. "That is *exactly* how it happened. Praise be, the Lord working through my son has raised me from the dead!"

Nicholas continued, "The Seignior told me that to wash the world of its sins, God had visited Noah with the flood. But since man had not heeded, now He showed us the burning face of the sun, and if we persisted in our sinful ways, then would the world be charred like Sodom!"

"Amen!" a priest in the crowd shouted, and the cry was picked up by many in the throng. But Baron Thorne recognized that this lad was mouthing almost the same words as Stephen of Cloyes.

Harolde shook his head in a daze. Brother Gottfried had not lied about the child. He thought this boy's voice even more compelling than Stephen of Cloyes' for though the Germanic words sounded guttural, Nicholas's sing-song had in it the call of angels.

"Only the innocent . . ." Nicholas hesitated in his tale and ran his hand across his forehead. "Only the innocent . . ."

His father whispered up to him, "Can save . . ."

"Can save the world from itself!" Nicholas said hurriedly. "And so the Lord instructed me to raise a mighty army of *German* children for Christ!"

During the past fortnight Nicholas had been spreading this message at the Dom, and, as Stephen had done in France, had sent emissaries to the various German provinces. "To raise such an army as will put the French effort to shame!" he sang out. "Who has been the great protector of the faith if not the Holy Roman Empire? Will we let others usurp the honor reserved for us?"

On other days, this challenge had brought forth cheers, but today the restive crowd grew unruly. Hungry peasants bunched together with unemployed day laborers; their heckling became boisterous and some rowdies made obscene noises.

They shouted at Nicholas's father, "A month ago you had the child singing in taverns for coins! And this week you set him to preach a crusade of children?"

"My son speaks the word of God!" Nicholas's father shouted. "Did not the Lord restore me from stone to flesh and blood?" He pinched his arm in confirmation.

"Enough of these lies of the clergy who batten on the poor!" shouted a carpenter.

"It is the worker who grinds the wheat but never tastes the bread!" cried a miller's apprentice.

"Now you wear fine clothes and glut yourself on food and wine from your child's ill-gotten gains?" cried a stable hand.

Harolde yanked Brother Gottfried's sleeve. "Is there truth in what these people claim?"

The monk hunched his shoulders. "Many contend that Nicholas's father is grossly venal. But even Archbishop Theodorich says what matters this if it has truly led the child to proclaim the word of the Lord?"

Nicholas shifted from leg to leg. He raised his hand to still his tormentors, but they shouted on, "Give us food, not words!"

Roger shook his fist at the hecklers around them and said to Jonathan, "Shall grown men always treat the young this way? Not heeding, when in their very hearts they know we speak the truth?"

As the shouting increased, Nicholas appeared on the verge of tears. His father called up to him; the child listened, nodded, and began to take off his clothing. First his jerkin, then capuchon, and finally his undershirt, until he stood naked from the waist up. Those who had seen this performance before thrilled with anticipation, the uninitiated were caught off-guard by the lad's strange behavior.

Nicholas's voice sang out, echoing off the Dom's stone walls. "Many among you doubt," he cried, "and wise you are to question. For among us in this year of peril walk the messengers of the Anti-Christ, some of whose voices you have heard here today." Then Nicholas slowly turned, showing his back. Etched deep into the skin between his thin shoulder blades was a golden cross.

When the crowd recognized the mark, many fell to their knees; still more shouted their thanks that the Lord had allowed them to witness this day.

"Charlemagne himself bore this sign of the cross that Christ carried to Calvary," Brother Gottfried said excitedly. "And the prophets have foretold that those who will lead the world to the final days will be so marked."

"Any charlatan can paint a cross of gold on his back!" Baron

Thorne called with a spurt of energy that left him exhausted and Roger fuming with anger at him.

Nicholas's father turned bright red. "Who calls us liar? Beware, lest the lightning sword of the Archangel Michael smite thee! Have you all not witnessed my son lay hands on the sick and the afflicted and restore them to health?"

"Show us, then!" Baron Thorne gasped, and an ironmonger standing near him picked up the demand until the crowd was chanting, "Show us!"

Nicholas grew pale. But his father motioned to two monks standing a little ways from the platform. They struggled with a young novice of the Ursuline order, alternately rigid with paralysis and convulsed with St. Vitus's dance. Betrothed to a young nobleman who had deserted her, she had entered the convent in a state of shock. After months of these seizures the Mother Superior had given her up for lost, for the girl could neither eat nor rest and was fast wasting away.

The monks laid the girl at Nicholas's feet where she groveled, cursing her faithless lover in guttural shrieks or crying out, "Oh, my body, how it burns!" all the while raking at her loins.

Nicholas knelt and cradled her lolling head in his lap. He pressed his Greek tau cross against her forehead. Lightning continued to zigzag across the heavens, limning the edges of the clouds. Nicholas crooned to the thrashing girl, "Lift up thine eyes to the heavens and witness the wonder of the Lord's light. He will enter you if you will but open yourself to Him."

Then Nicholas began to pray, "Oh merciful Lord, Thou who hast the power of life and death over us all, calm this your young servant. Cast out the demons tormenting her, fill her yearning body with the sweetness of your love so that she may be made whole again." The soft sing-song words continued to lull the girl, and gradually her fingers stopped clawing at her body.

Throughout, Nicholas kept laying hands on her body, massaging her arms and legs. After a few more spasms the girl seemed to grow less violent and soon her breathing became regular. She sighed and then Nicholas gently helped her to sit up. She looked in awe at her quieted limbs and then with a cry grasped the boy, crushing him to her bosom and covering him with kisses. "I am reborn!" she cried. "Saved!"

As the monks helped the trembling girl off the platform, the crowd cheered itself hoarse. A beaming Nicholas sang out, "Who will now deny that the Lord uses me as His instrument?" Truly believing that he had cured the afflicted girl, he made ready to bring his sermon to a climax. Voice rising and falling in his choir-boy plaint, he began reciting from Revelations passages known to all the multitude. For more than a thousand years they had waited for this prophecy to be fulfilled. Amid the continuing flashes of lightning Nicholas made the words his own, as if the heavenly host had spoken directly to him.

"And He carried me away in spirit to a great and high mountain, and He showed me that great city, the Holy Jerusalem, descending out of heaven from God, and her light was unto a stone most precious, even like a Jasper stone, clear and crystal."

Amid the wailing and the hallelujahs, Baron Thorne listened in stupefied amazement. Could this gullible crowd not see that the child had been drilled in all he said? Yet the dolts listened, so hungry were they to hear the Gospel preached. The baron looked to Roger and Harolde, his heart sinking, for they too were caught up in the contagion of the mob.

Nicholas continued, "And if our Holy Mother were to gaze upon Her Son's tomb, would Her tears ever cease, knowing that His last resting place is in the hands of the unbeliever?"

Then a voice cried out from the far end of the square, "And what would the Virgin say if She knew His sacred tomb was being used as a stable for the horses of the Saracens? I have just come from the Holy Land and have seen these desecrations with my own eyes."

Women shrieked and strong men fainted and a cry roared out for the blood of the Saracens. But Nicholas stilled them,

once again sounding the same plea as Stephen. "War and killing have not freed the Holy Sepulcher! Before we shall see
Christ risen, we must embrace His new commandment, that
we love one another. Only then will we bring about the Second Coming, and the Kingdom of Heaven on earth!"

No one could stop Nicholas now, for the spirit had entered
him. His eyes rolled back into his head. "Do the children of
France love Christ more than we do?"

"No!" the crowd screamed back, clenched fists raised, and
Roger's fist shot skyward also, his crusading fervor once more
inflamed. "Do you not see?" he said to Jonathan. "Now there
will be two crusades! One from France, the other from Germany, until soon children the world over will be marching to
Jerusalem!"

"Will Mohammed triumph over Christ?" Nicholas shouted.

"Never!" The word tore from their throats and Roger felt
his own throat grow hoarse from shouting.

The litany went on, rising to fever pitch. They were under
his spell. He was of their nation, elected by the Lord to lead.
For these Germans of the Holy Roman Empire were a people
driven by a tribal mysticism, ready to follow the commanding
voice blindly and without question. And somewhere deep
within Roger, part of him thrilled to this new call, for such
was half his heritage, now come to the fore. He had sworn to
pray for his mother in the holy shrines in Jerusalem, and fate
had led him to this place so he could fulfill his vow. And
nothing, not even his father, could stop him!

When Nicholas demanded, "Who will march with me to
Jerusalem and win everlasting glory?" the young in the multitude surged forward as one to take the oath.

The crush of people, the noon heat and the inevitability of it
all pressed in on Baron Thorne and he fainted.

On the far side of the Dom stood a man tall enough to stand
out from the crowd. It was he who had inflamed the mob with
his talk of the defilement of the Holy Sepulcher.

The arrival in the square of the dappled stallion and the
baron and his party had not been lost on this man. He ran his
fingers over the fleur-de-lis branded into his arm.

"I will have it all," Frizio swore to Baalbek. "My horse, my revenge. And more. Much more."

In the fiber of his being, Frizio knew that in this pilgrimage of children, he had found the opportunty he had waited for all his life. For him there would be a far richer kingdom to be gained, and of this earth.

COLOGNE

WHEN BARON THORNE REGAINED CONSCIOUSNESS he found himself in the quarters of the hanse. Roger, Harolde, and Jonathan hovered over him anxiously. "I am all right," he said weakly. "The excitement . . ."

Roger pressed his father's hand. "Are you sure?"

The baron nodded.

After a bit, Roger rested his head on his father's chest. "Father, you must release me from my vow," he whispered.

The baron stroked his son's fair hair. "Knowing that you journey to your destruction? You ask the impossible."

"Then do the impossible," Roger said, lifting his head. "My way is not the way of death. Even should I fall in this pilgrimage, is there any greater glory than to do the work of the Lord? What good are all your riches to me if they can not ease my burden? Father, I beg you . . . I confess, that when I first heard of the crusade, I had in my mind naught save glory. I would conquer lands, I would conquer men. I would return home and be first in your eyes for all I had accomplished.

"But that night at Notre Dame—I cannot explain it—there came a revelation, that if this were meant to be, then the Lord would show the way. Father, whatever you believe about this crusade, we cannot escape it. See how it has followed us halfway across Europe? Surely, this is the hand of providence guiding me to my destiny."

"Or the devil pointing to your destruction," the baron said.

Roger shook his head. "This is my own pilgrimage. For on the road to Jerusalem, I shall discover who I am, what I am meant to be. Can you deny me that? Father, by all that is holy, I beg you, release me."

Barone Thorne turned his head away. "You do not know the place. Holy it is, yes, but also accursed to have soaked up the blood of so many valiant men and women. And yes, children too. Now you ask me to consign my own flesh and blood to that purgatory? Have you no heart?"

"A heart I have," Roger whispered, "and a soul, too. And it is for its salvation that I must go. If I remain here, all the days left to me on this earth shall be as dross, for this day shall my spirit have died."

Tears streamed down Roger's face. The baron's heart was sorely moved; so much had he come to love this child who had proven himself more than a son. He reached for him, holding the budding boy-man body that had his own life flowing through its veins. Part of the baron exulted and part of him died when he whispered, "I release you."

Roger's face blossomed into radiance. He smiled and embraced his father. "You will never regret it, I swear. I will do you proud in the eyes of men and of God."

With a final embrace, Roger ran from the room.

"Take Mirage!" the baron called after him. Thorne listened to Roger's footsteps thumping down the wooden flights. The front door slammed, sounding like a final sentence.

Baron Thorne turned to Harolde, "If you love the Lord . . ."

Harolde said, "Do not exhaust yourself. I had already planned to join him. You know the way children are. They will walk only a few miles, ten, twenty at most. Then I will bring him back to you."

"What if they persevere?" the baron whispered.

"Believe me, they will not. But I shall watch over him until this is done. This I swear to you."

Harolde hurriedly packed his Bible and his other books and started out. The baron's faint call brought him back. "Take this," he said, handing him the last of Frizio's ransom money. "And Tortoise, too. The people at the hanse will care for me until I am well."

Harolde nodded, and with a last wave, departed.

Silence hung in the room. Baron Thorne wiped his eyes and let out a long, low groan. He turned to Jonathan. "So we are left alone, you and I. You have lost a father, and I a son." The baron paused, clearing his throat. "Will you be able to locate your kinsmen in Cologne?"

Jonathan nodded. "I thank you for all your kindness to me," he said gravely.

The baron smiled. "It is I who should be thankful to you. When do you go to your people?" he asked, the slightest trace of loneliness in his voice.

"If it is the reward you are thinking of . . ."

"No, no," the baron said hastily. "Could I take money from one who saved my life? Consider that debt paid."

"In that case, I will not seek my relatives," Jonathan said.

A spark of hope lit the baron's eyes.

"I go to Jerusalem also," Jonathan said.

Baron Thorne recoiled. "But this is madness!" He pulled himself up. "You? If you are discovered by the army, you will be torn limb from limb!"

"By those who preach love?" Jonathan asked quietly. "I must believe them when they say they will not kill. I must give them that chance. Besides, none need know. Roger will not betray me. Nor, I think, will Harolde, though we have had our fights."

"But why? Why?" the baron insisted, shaking his head. "You and your kind are safer here in Germany than anywhere else in Europe. True, there were riots during the early Crusades, but that madness is past. I have not heard of any serious incidents in Cologne for the past ten years."

"That may be," Jonathan said, "but that is today. Who knows how quickly men can change? As quickly as tomorrow."

"I cannot get this into my mind," the baron said, very distressed. "I fear for your safety."

Jonathan clasped his hands, and the faraway look came into his eyes. "Four years ago, many hundreds of my people left Carcassonne in southern France to journey back to Jerusalem. My mother and father had thought to go with them, but fearing I was too young to undertake such a long journey, decided to wait. Then just last year, Rabbi Meier and his brother organized another exodus, this time from Normandy and England. We were all packed and ready to go, but I came down with smallpox and so once again we did not embark. Had I not gotten sick, my parents would still be alive."

Jonathan blinked and focused again on the baron. His dark eyes glowed with a resoluteness Thorne had never seen before.

"It is my land no less than the other children's," he said. "Perhaps more. For more than a thousand years we have wandered the face of the earth. That is a long time to be homeless, to live at the sufferance of other people."

He stared at the candle burning near the baron's head, seeing instead the Sabbath candles in his parents' house. "Each year, at Passover, our prayer is, 'This year, oh Lord, we are wanderers, strangers in a strange land. But next year, Jerusalem.'

"If I remain in Cologne, I will always be waiting for the next uprising against my people. Oh, it is quiet now, but it will come. Always when there is calamity in the land we are blamed. I cannot live under that burden of blame any more. Not my fingers that wove the thorns! Not my hand that drove the nail! *I* am not guilty!

"Nor will I deliver myself into the hands of such people who kill in the name of one who preached peace. God has promised that one day there will be a new nation of Israel. So it is written. So it must be. It is inscribed in our book. It is inscribed in our hearts. If not this year, then next. If not this millennium, then the next. But it will come about as surely as there is a God. And, for me, that 'next year' must be now!"

Stunned by the boy's outburst, Baron Thorne leaned back heavily against the wall. Whether Jonathan was right or wrong, the baron knew he could not stop him. He said, more to himself than to Jonathan, "On this day have all my children become men, while I have been reduced to the strength of a babe."

The baron slipped his blue champlevé enameled cross over his head and handed it to Jonathan. "Wear this for me. If it offends, then take it as a token of my affection and the hope that it will protect you. It is a long and dangerous road to Jerusalem, and as I said, I fear for you."

"It does not offend," Jonathan said, slipping the cross into the leather wallet that hung from his shoulder. "But my Lord will have no other gods before Him. Thank you, though, for your thought. I will give it to Roger. As for my safety . . ." Jonathan shrugged. "It should not be hard to hide myself among thousands of children."

Impulsively, Jonathan kissed the baron's hand and then left to begin his journey.

COLOGNE:
EXODUS OF THE CHILDREN

NEVER HAD A DAY DAWNED MORE DAZZLING THAN this one at June's end. The very elements conspired to bestow beneficence on the thousands of children preparing to depart Cologne. A swarm of people filled the square of the Dom. From every corner of the Holy Roman Empire the faithful had foregathered: Saxony and Westphalia, Thuringia and Franconia, Holstein and Mecklenburg, all had heeded Nicholas's call for the glory of the empire and had surrendered their young to the crusade. Here also flew a banner from Brabant and Lorraine, there a cross with the colors of Flanders, yet another from Hainaut and many of the northern provinces of France.

Those children who had been able to manage it wore the pilgrim's costume: a long robe of gray wool and a wide-brimmed hat. Some carried a palmer's staff. Sewn on the right shoulder of the tunic was the red cross, symbol of their vow to free the Holy Land. Only Pope Innocent in Rome had the power to release them from this most sacred oath.

Roger had received the cross the day before. Harolde had not, believing the entire charade would be over in a week. The boy and the monk stood in the center of the throng, waiting for the archbishop to appear and bless their departure.

As Harolde's eyes swept over the army, he felt a distinct apprehension. The majority of the youthful corps ranged in age from eight to fourteen years; most were about twelve. Older boys carried their younger brothers and sisters, some rowdy lads played tag through the throng, a small child clutched a rag doll to her bosom, another carried a kitten. For the most part the children's faces glowed with purity. But there were girls and women, too, whose sly looks and lustful figures belied their pretense at holiness, reminding Harolde of the proverb concerning women on pilgrimage: "Depart a pilgrim, return a whore." Men there were, too, who would be judged criminals at any court of ministerials. The lame, the halt, and the blind had also gathered, never doubting that the Lord would cure their afflictions.

"Is it not a wondrous host?" Roger asked. Roger had been surprised and alarmed when Harolde had come running after him, announcing that he too was going. But the monk had made no demands on him thus far, treating him more like an equal than a student.

Roger looked at a company of children, obviously of noble birth, who had brought along their servants, tents, and richly caparisoned horses. "But none is more beautiful than you," Roger said to Mirage, stroking his beige velvet nose. The stallion's nostrils flared; he pawed the ground, irritated with the press of people. Roger calmed him, his chest filling with pride at the envious stares directed at them. "No wonder Frizio offered so mighty a ransom," Roger said to Harolde. "With such a horse, a man is truly marked above other men."

Roger had every reason to be happy this morning. His father? Alive. His dream? About to be realized. Why then did he feel this sadness? As though he had lost something. . . .

The ponderous wooden doors of the west portal opened. A procession of priests emerged swinging their censers and chanting the liturgy. In the center, magnificently garbed in his magenta robes and gold-figured chausable, strode Archbishop Theodorich I. Behind him, six monks strained under the weight of the golden reliquary which held the skulls of the three magi. The Emperor Barbarossa had brought these precious relics to Cologne from his sack of Milan in 1167, and they had made Cologne one of the most important pilgrimage centers in all Europe, second only to Rome in religious and political influence. Recognizing the holy relics, the crowd fell to its knees.

Theodorich held high his staff, the staff that had belonged to St. Peter, the oldest crosier in all Christendom. Invoking Cologne's patron saint, Ursula, who with her eleven thousand virgins had been martyred here, he cautioned the girls in the crusade to follow Ursula's chaste ways, then called on the magi to hear the prayers of the entire gathering.

Head bowed, Roger complained, "Will Theodorich ever be done? What good is all this talk when we could be on our way?"

But Theodorich was far too shrewd a politician to allow such a telling moment to pass. Civil war raged in the Holy Roman Empire with two anointed kings battling for the throne: Otto IV of Saxony, the Welf, and Frederick II of Sicily, the Waiblingen.

Otto IV, yet another grandchild of Eleanor of Aquitaine (and thus nephew of King John of England), had originally been supported and crowned by Innocent III. But when Otto began his incursions against the Papal States in the hope of forcing Innocent to lift the interdict imposed on England, Innocent had excommunicated, then deposed Otto. Innocent switched his allegiance to his papal ward, Frederick II of Sicily, the sixteen-year-old son of the late Emperor Henry VI.

Last year at Nuremberg, Frederick had been acclaimed emperor by the laity and at this moment rode north through Italy to claim his throne. Swift couriers had brought the news that he had been in Genoa in May, had avoided capture by Otto's forces, and would be on Rhenish soil in a matter of weeks. The issue was drawing to a conclusion: On one side, Otto IV, backed by the power and coffers of King John of England; on the other, Frederick II, supported by Innocent III and Philip Augustus of France. Otto's grand plan called for the Welf forces to launch an attack on France through Flanders, while King John advanced on Paris from the remaining Angevin holdings on the continent, thereby squeezing Philip in the pincers. At stake, nothing less than the political future of all Europe.

Cologne had always been a stronghold of Otto's and he had tried to stop the children's crusade, hoping to embarrass the church. Archbishop Theodorich, who had consistently waffled in his support between the two royal contenders, now took the safest course. "On this day we must bury the bitterness of our civil war, heal the breach between north and south, Saxony and Swabia, Welf and Waiblingen. Our Lord said, 'And a child shall lead them,' and so you children have laid aside these temporal matters to march for the greatest king of all!''

At last, the archbishop wound down. Nicholas, dressed also in a simple gray habit, raised his Greek tau cross, symbol of his divine calling. Pointing it south toward the city gates, he signaled the crusade to begin. From the Dom and the churches of St. Mary in Himmelfahrt, St. Geron, and St. Martin, the bells began to peal, announcing the army on the move. Nicholas raised his voice in song and the two guards protecting him joined in. More children picked up the melody until Cologne rang with bell and song:

> *Fairest Lord Jesus*
> *Ruler of all nature*
> *Thee of Mary and God the Son*
> *Thee will I cherish*
> *Thee will I honor*
> *Thee my soul's glory, joy and crown.*

From a dormered window in the headquarters of the hanse, Baron Thorne looked down at the river of children. For a moment he thought he glimpsed Mirage and Roger, and hung over the sill straining for a last look.

"I must save him from this madness, I must . . ." He stumbled toward the door but weakness betrayed him and he sank to his hands and knees. His tears, hot and blinding, fell to the floorboards as he whispered, "Oh merciful Lord, I have given my only son to you, for your glory. I beg you, watch over him and all these other little ones."

Down the Höhestrasse they came, past City Hall, where the town fathers, hard-headed and practical men, shook their heads in disbelief. Many had sons and daughters on this crusade, who could not be held back by bolt or bar. Herr Schneidermann tied his ten-year-old Inga to a chair, but she stood up, chair and all, and hopped out of the house. Neither force nor reason could hold these children, seized with the conviction that they—and only they—could bring about the third age of man: the age of the spirit.

Yet amid all the moaning and wailing and gnashing of teeth a certain relief flooded Cologne. In the past weeks, the population had swelled from forty thousand to eighty thousand. The city's original ponderings of whether Nicholas's call came from the devil or the Lord had given way to a more immediate concern: the growing scarcity of food.

Past the Church of St. George rode Harolde and Roger, in the crush of marchers. The sun sparkled off the gilded mosaic tile above the oval Romanesque doorway, depicting the saint slaying the dragon. The tableau seemed to move in the glitter of the sun and the impaled dragon writhed before their eyes.

"Is it an omen?" Roger breathed to Harolde. "Shall we thus slay all evil with this crusade?"

Harolde paled, believing the Lord had seen the serpent of his innermost thoughts; for just then, for some unaccountable reason, his mind had wandered to Flamonde.

After leaving Baron Thorne, Jonathan had spent the afternoon and night searching for Harolde and Roger. But with the city so crowded, he had no luck. This morning, Jonathan thought he spied Mirage across the mobbed Dom square, but could not get within shouting distance.

Jonathan then learned that the army planned to separate once outside the walls. One segment would cross the river and head deep into Swabia, planning to reach the sea via Splugen and the other eastern passes of the Alps. The other legion would follow the Rhine to Basle, thence over the Alps and down to Genoa. In this way, as they journeyed through the far-flung provinces, the children hoped to gain more adherents to their cause.

He began to despair. "If I do not find Roger and Harolde before the armies separate," he told himself, "how will I know which route to follow?" When Jonathan saw Nicholas point toward the Severinstore Gate, he started for it immediately. He avoided the crush in the main thoroughfare by taking the street closest to the river, the Altemarket Place.

Jonathan ran until the pain in his side slowed him to a walk. "If I reach the gate before the army, maybe I will see everybody passing through," he told himself, to keep his courage up. Will Roger let me join him? he thought. What of Harolde? What if they were happy to be rid of me? What then? Go back to my relatives in Cologne? These thoughts tormented Jonathan as he started running again.

"This column moves too slowly!" Roger said to Harolde. Always there lurked the fear that the baron might suddenly appear, as he had at St. Germaine in Paris, and snatch him away from his destiny. In his mind, Roger made up, "If I get through the gate and out into the open plain, I will be safe."

The words of "Schoenster Herr Jesus" mingled with the pealing bells as the fortress of the Severinstore Gate came into view. "Soon, soon," Roger said to Mirage. "Freedom is almost within grasp."

Nearing the vicinity of the Monastery of St. Panteleon, they caught sight of Brother Gottfried, the chronicler, waving frantically at them. "Can this be possible?" he cried as they came abreast. "You are going on the crusade also?"

When Roger nodded the monk clasped his hands. "Can there be any doubt that God causes miracles to happen?" Then an idea came to him. "Wait here for me, I will bring you something that will be invaluable on your journey," and he rushed back toward the monastery a short distance away.

"What could it be?" Roger asked, but Harolde did not know. But they could not wait, for the press of people behind them carried them along the narrow street.

Brother Gottfried returned as fast as his short legs could carry him, fought his way forward through the ranks and caught up with Roger and Harolde. "I have gathered these maps for you," he puffed, thrusting them at Harolde. "God go with you."

"Come with us!" Roger shouted. "There are many clerics along."

"If only I were ten years younger," Gottfried lamented, as the surge of oncoming children forced them to separate.

Roger yelled, "Then write in your chronicle that we go to get the cross beyond the sea!"

"And to baptize the Moslem and all other infidels in the name of the Lord!" Harolde cried, carried away by the moment.

Atop the three-mile wall that enclosed Cologne in its semicircle stood the stunned citizenry, watching the army stream through the narrow gate and out into the countryside. Fathers wept, mothers wailed and tore their hair, but the children's ears remained deaf to all save their inner voices.

As Roger and Harolde were about to exit, Mirage veered off to the left. Pull as he might on the reins, Roger could not turn the stallion. Mirage followed his own lead. Suddenly, Roger caught sight of Jonathan, pressed against the wall.

The boys' eyes met and held. Without a word, Roger extended his arm. Jonathan grasped it at the elbow, and in one fluid motion vaulted into the saddle. Mirage tossed his mane, content with the familiar weight.

Though Roger could not have said why, his feeling of sadness suddenly evaporated. "Where have you been?" he asked gruffly and poked Jonathan in the ribs.

All these weeks, Jonathan had hated that jabbing elbow. Why it should now fill his heart to overflowing he could not understand. He slipped the blue enameled cross over Roger's head. "From your father," he said. Jonathan shifted to get comfortable, one hand caressing Mirage's flank, the other hand resting lightly on Roger's shoulder.

When Harolde caught sight of Jonathan, he near fainted. In that instant, such a premonition of disaster swept over him that he could scarce control himself. Jonathan? On this crusade? What if the others discovered the truth about him? They would crucify him! Harolde's apprehension reached such a peak that he broke into a tearing cough that speckled his lips with blood.

The spires of Cologne slowly receded. In their backward glances the children could no longer distinguish the people atop the wall. Nicholas, aware of the growing sadness of separation, broke into song again, and the column followed in step and word:

Fair are the meadows
Fairer still the woodlands
Robed in blooming garb of spring.
Jesus is fairer, Jesus is purer
Who makes our saddened hearts to sing.

First a dog, then a cat followed the exodus of children. Joined soon by small woods creatures, then birds and butterflies. The butterflies grew so numerous they formed a bejeweled, undulating banner in the gentle breezes. Some folk claimed they followed the trail of detritus left by the army. But those who really knew, agreed that butterflies were known to be the souls of the departed, and that all the Crusaders who had been lost in the Holy Land, all those brave Christians, had come back in the form of these flying flowers to be guardians of this host of young innocents.

ALONG THE RHINE:
FIRST WEEK IN JULY

HE SLOW ARC OF THE SUN SAW THE ARMY FOL-
low the meander of the Rhine. The halt and the
sick soon fell by the wayside, unable to keep
pace. From the terraced hills, farmers looked
down with amazement at the procession. They
watched the endless line of banners and crosses and listened
to the hymns floating on the wind. Here a child serf dropped
his hoe and scrambled down the hill to join his kind; farther
on, a farmer left his vines and joined the marchers. Thus were
the ranks of the army swelled.

By nightfall, the twenty thousand children in Nicholas's
army camped outside Bonn. As it is natural for birds to flock,
fish to school and all animals to congregate with their own
kind, so those children from the same provinces gravitated
together. Where an acknowledged leader did not exist, a bloodied nose or well-aimed kick usually sufficed to determine
who would take command.

There were not many pilgrims along from England, though a
dozen or so monks who had fled Britain because of the inter-
dict had joined the crusade. Roger did not feel comfortable
with their unending prayers, and surprisingly, neither did
Harolde, though his reasons were different.

"We must avoid older and wiser eyes," he told Roger and
Jonathan. He also instructed Jonathan, "Avoid all religious
services, enter no church. If questioned by anybody, pretend
dumbness or madness." In this way Harolde hoped to hide
Jonathan's identity. Each night at his devotions, Harolde
begged forgiveness for shielding a Jew.

Roger, Harolde, and Jonathan finally joined a contingent of
children from Liege, Bruges, and the Nether Lands. A motley
group of fullers and weavers, the stained arms of many attested to their being dyers. Roger chose this particular com-

pany because of their laughter and the hearty smell of soup coming from their camp. A young woman juiced with life stirred the cauldron and fed the footsore children, wiping a nose here, patting a head there. All the while she kept an apprehensive eye on a lad with close-cropped auburn hair who sat staring at the river. The boy's shadowed profile looked so beautiful in the drifting twilight that Roger thought it almost unnatural.

Roger reached the head of the food line and as the woman ladled out the soup, he saw her close up. He dropped his bowl and sprang at her, knocking her to the grass. They rolled around, legs kicking, arms punching, screaming at each other. Then many hands pulled them apart.

Roger shouted, "It is Flamonde!"

Harolde's head reeled with the recognition of the woman from the bathhouse in Troyes! His stomach knotted as he took in her creamy skin and flaming hair. A wave of loathing so violent came over him; it was all he could do to keep from striking her himself.

The beautiful boy ran up from the river bank and Roger's heart thudded. "Laurelle!" he gasped. Hair shorn, she wore disguising shepherd's clothes. Roger's hand moved with a will of its own and swung out to slap her.

Laurelle reeled away, recovered and slapped Roger back.

Flamonde laughed and shrieked in a kind of fit. "Surely it is a wonder! And part of the devil's design that he has brought us together again."

Laurelle touched Roger's sleeve. He jerked his arm away. She said, "As I love the Lord, it could not be helped. But what happened of old must be put aside. Now we must answer to a higher cause, is that not true?"

A ripple of assent came from Laurelle's compatriots, with the underlying message that Roger had better be reconciled, or face their fists. They closed in a menacing circle, but Laurelle stopped them.

"You could have at least stayed and told the truth," Roger spat. "It is a miracle that my father did not die because of you."

"Before you condemn, will you hear me?" Laurelle asked.

Roger kicked the turf and gave a grudging nod. Laurelle led him from camp down to the river bank. Across the Rhine reared the dark presence of the Seven Mountains; high atop one crag, the Castle Drachenfels lifted its towers to the moon.

"After Frizio . . ." Laurelle stopped, choking on his name. Her voice held the sound of tears, but her eyes shone bright and hard, eyes that would never cry again. "Flamonde and I thought to go immediately to the prévôt and tell what happened. But the eunuch Baalbek burst into our room and smothered our senses with a magic potion he had on a cloth. When I woke, I found myself bound and gagged underneath a wagonload of hay. The eunuch threw us out of the cart in a remote forest, warning us that if we tried to testify, he would slit our throats. He left us there to die of starvation, for we stayed bound and gagged for three days before being discovered by a woodsman. It took us two full days to walk back to Troyes, but by then the trial had been fought. Madame Crevette told us you had left. Flamonde said we must forget the whole thing since God had taken it out of our hands. So we returned to Liege."

Laurelle's voice dropped and Roger had to lean forward to hear her. "But I could not forget," she said. "Nor could I go back to our old life. I knew God had caused this to happen, to show me the error of our past ways. Now rumors abounded in the faubourg about us, the two wicked sisters. Taunts and jeers that grew louder with each day, for I wore my shame on my face and the people did not mistake it. When I heard that the children of northern France, the Lowlands, and the Holy Roman Empire were assembling in Cologne, I knew what I must do. You see, Roger, once I walk in the footsteps of the Lord, I know I will be cleansed."

Roger started to say something but could not put his thoughts into words.

When Laurelle had informed Flamonde of her plan, her sister cried, threatened, finally beat her, all to no avail. "I told her the only way she could keep me from joining the crusade was to kill me." In the end, giving in to Laurelle's single-mindedness and the growing pressures in the faubourg, Flamonde decided to join her sister. "To protect me," Laurelle said, looking back at the campfire where Flamonde tended to three ragged orphans who had adopted her: Rudolph, a thin nine-year-old; Little Luke, not yet six, with a perpetual grin and unending questions; and six-year-old Constanze, an indentured servant who had escaped her lecherous master.

"But I do not need protection any longer," Laurelle said. Her knuckles whitened as she strained to break a twig. "So Flamonde takes care of anybody in need. I did not want her to come with me. Even her presence reminds me . . ." She broke off, then hung her head. "But who am I to prevent anybody from seeking God? Perhaps this pilgrimage will help her. Since we left Troyes, she has not been with a man. Sometimes I think her mind is wandering, and have told her so. Flamonde agrees, saying yes, we are going mad together, all of us, and that is the cause and reason for this crusade."

"Do you believe that?" Roger asked.

Laurelle thought for a long while. "No, I am not going mad. For the first time in my life I begin to sense who I am, what I need, what brings me peace. It is the rest of the world who will not listen, they are the mad ones!"

Roger nodded eagerly. With Laurelle's first sentence, he had been ready to embrace her. To find that she still felt the way he did inflamed his feelings for her even more. In a gesture of forgiveness, he put his arm around her shoulder.

Laurelle stiffened and ducked out from under. "Never," she whispered fiercely. "Never!"

Roger drew back in surprise. Then he understood. "But you resisted! You did not willingly sin. You . . ." He looked at her face in the moonlight. Her gray eyes grew dark with pain and anger and something more.

Seeing that recognition in his face, Laurelle pummeled him with her fragile fists. "It is not true! I hated it! I will never let anybody touch me again!" He let her beat at him until she exhausted herself and fell limply to the grass.

Never had Roger felt such pity. She has turned hard, he thought. He liked her less this way than before, but still he liked her more than anybody he had ever known. He made a vow to himself, one as important as his crusading oath.

I will reach you, he swore silently. You will come to trust me again. We will forget what happened and make our lives anew. For if we are marching to renew our world, can we do less for each other? I will bring you back from your hell. This I swear to you on the first night of our great adventure. You shall be my beloved, and I, yours. By my eyes, I swear it.

That night, everybody fell into an exhausted sleep. In the various camps, the smaller children began to cry for their mothers and the comfort of their beds. For the faint of heart, the game was over; they did not want to play anymore. Some two hundred sneaked off into the night to make their way back to Cologne.

The camp began to stir with first light; within the hour, the army stood ready to strike out. In spite of their late start the first day, they had walked over thirteen miles, buoyed by the novelty and their irrepressible passion. They could manage between twelve and fifteen miles a day, depending on the terrain.

"But it is almost seven hundred miles to Genoa!" Harolde tried to explain, tracing the route on Brother Gottfried's map. "Up the Rhine river, through hostile territory, then over the mountains of the Alps, which have defeated armies of grown men. And will the sea *really* part for us at Genoa?" Harolde asked, fully expecting that the army would disband with the news of these overwhelming obstacles.

None of this deterred the children. Many sensed they would fall by the way. But if this was the sacrifice necessary to free the Holy Land and thereby gain the world's salvation, this they would gladly do.

The second night saw the army encamped at Rolandsek, within sight of the ruins of Roland's fortress. As they swapped tales around the campfire, Harolde recounted the legend of the knight. "Finally, Roland escaped from Roncesvalles, but ar-

rived too late at the island of Nonnenwerth to prevent his betrothed from taking the veil. She, believing him dead, had
married Jesus. In despair, Roland withdrew to his castle overlooking the island, and daily stared out at the nunnery, pining
for the love which might have been."

"What a fool!" Flamonde exclaimed. "Why did he not row
out to the nunnery and . . ."

"Pit of the devil!" Harolde muttered, got up and stalked off.

Roger had grown pensive during the tale of Roland. Now he
stared at Laurelle as she searched Little Luke's scalp for lice.
"She has retreated into the nunnery of her own wounded
self," Roger said to Jonathan with a love-sick sigh. "But there
is still hope for she has not yet taken the vows. During today's
march did you not think she warmed a bit toward me? Though
she would not ride with me on Mirage, she did let me walk
beside her."

Jonathan nodded to please Roger, but at the same time felt a
growing confusion about his own feelings for Laurelle.

"I shall die if she refuses me," Roger said somberly. Then he
called in Laurelle's direction, "Alas poor Roland! Alas poor
me!"

But Laurelle would not be drawn into his game.

When he persisted, Laurelle scooped up clods of turf and
threw them at him. Roger feigned great pain as each clod
sailed harmlessly past him, hopping and falling about until
Laurelle had no recourse but to laugh.

Roger paused in mid-leap and let out a whoop. He picked
up Laurelle and whirled her around until they both fell dizzily
to the grass. "That is the first time I ever heard you truly
laugh!" he exclaimed, and his whole being sang with the gift.

The following afternoon, Mirage came up lame. While
Roger, Harolde, and Jonathan stood arguing about what to do,
a broad-shouldered boy fell out of the line of marchers.
"Gunther is my name," he said, "and I was apprenticed to a
blacksmith." So calm a manner did Gunther have that Mirage
stood still when the boy lifted his right foreleg. "The trouble is
this shoe," Gunther said.

Gunther had rich brown hair that fell to his shoulders, a wide gap in his front teeth, and eyes so gentle that animals and children clustered to him. His big hands, callused from working forge and bellows, were surprisingly sensitive. A simple soul, without guile and with trust in all, only in one thing was Gunther set in his ways. He had a small wooden cross strapped to his back and would not take it off except to sleep.

"The children in my village gave it to me," he said. "They begged me to plant it in Jerusalem, and I have sworn to do just that."

While he reshod Mirage, Gunther told them his story. "My home is near Aachen. With this drought, my master did not have enough to feed his own family and so released me from my apprenticeship. I did not know where to go—my family all died of plague two years ago—and so I trudged to the cathedral at Aachen and lit a candle to Charlemagne whose bones rest in the crypt. While praying for guidance, I heard two clerics talking about a crusade of French and German children for peace. What can this be but a sign from on high? I thought. And so I have joined this march to honor our Lord."

"Does he not remind you of Guillaume, my blood brother from St. Denis?" Roger asked Jonathan.

Jonathan did not answer, envious as he was of Roger's ability to make close friends quickly.

When Roger suggested that Gunther join their band, Gunther embraced them all, saying it would please him for he liked their merry ways.

Gunther took to them as if he had always been part of the group. He carried tired children, fetched water for Flamonde, dug for tubers to add to her soup stock. Flamonde carried a big leather wallet slung over her shoulder and always had something in it to feed the young who came to her campfire.

One evening, while Flamonde threw cabbage leaves into the the iron pot hanging on its tripod over the fire, she tried to engage Laurelle in small talk. "Laurelle, play your flute for us?"

Laurelle did not respond.

"What is the matter with you?" Flamonde chided her. "Once you laughed, you sang. Now you look as if you dined only on vinegar and gall."

Laurelle held her sister's gaze with her clear gray eyes. "I sang?" she repeated. "That must have been in another life."

Flamonde turned from the pot. "I suppose you blame me?"

Laurelle did not answer and Flamonde said angrily, "What happened to you has happened.to many," she said. "You yourself know you could not have gone another year without catching the eye of all the lecherous nobles. And they would have had you as their right, God curse them!"

"That may be," Laurelle answered, "but I did not need you to throw me at them."

Flamonde cracked her sister with the wooden ladle. Laurelle did not flinch. Then, with a cry of repentance, Flamonde threw herself on the child and covered her with kisses. "You are right, it is my fault. I led you to this. You never wanted to go to the fair. I thought only to protect you, for if I had left you alone in Lille . . ."

Laurelle gently put her sister away from her.

Flamonde dried her eyes, picked up the ladle and continued stirring. "Ah, from the moment you were born, heaven fated you for trial. Did I not tend our mother when she came to her time in the fields? Other babes know the sanctuary of a roof over their heads; you had only the shade of a bay laurel. When Maman died in childbirth . . . you were all mine."

Laurelle nodded absently, having heard the tale a thousand times before.

Flamonde ladled out the cabbage stew into trenchers of stale bread and gave it to the starveling children clustered around her skirts. "You were not like any other babe I had ever seen," she said to Laurelle. "So clean and sweet you smelled, with skin so fair I hid you from the neighbors lest they give you the evil eye. To be as beautiful as you—that is surely a curse. But to be beautiful and poor? Ah, that is the Dark One's triumph."

When the stew was gone, Flamonde scraped the pot and

handed the last of it to Laurelle. Laurelle broke the trencher of bread and gave half to her sister. They sat close together, eating.

"Chew each morsel for a long time," Flamonde advised. "That way you fool your stomach." When she had finished, Flamonde wiped her lips and hands with a handful of grass. The fresh green smell lingered, sweetening her scent. Then Flamonde took a wooden comb from her wallet and began to groom Laurelle's hair.

"You must get over this," Flamonde said gently. "Will you torment yourself all your days for the misfortune of one night? Could the world go on if we all did that? Especially since it was not your fault?"

Laurelle winced under the tugging comb. "Oh, my sister, I know you are right, yet I cannot forget." She glanced up at Roger, who had climbed an apple tree and was picking the unripe fruit. And I almost loved him, she thought. Then Laurelle murmured, "It has come to be a sickness with me. I can only pray to the Lord that one day He will see fit to cure it."

To keep out of the way, Jonathan took to tending the animals, rubbing down Mirage and Tortoise at day's end, feeding them choice morsels of grass and flowers. While Mirage and Tortoise grazed, Jonathan scoured the fields for herbs, adding to the supply he carried in his small pouch. He would talk to the animals about the days when he was apprentice to his father, reciting the lessons he'd learned. "Aloe for burns, betony for bleeding—I must find some for Harolde—strawberry wild to destroy the web in a man's eyes, wormwood to assuage the wicked winds of the stomach. Oh, that cabbage stew."

Sometimes Jonathan would sing to the beasts, songs his mother had taught him; of the wheel of years, of wanderings in strange lands. One evening, while leading the horses to water, Jonathan sang them a tune from his childhood, of raisins and almonds, and began softly to cry.

Mirage stood very still while Jonathan clung to his neck and cried himself out.

ALONG THE RHINE:
SECOND WEEK IN JULY

HORTLY AFTER LEAVING REMAGEN, THE WALLS OF the Rhine massif became bolder, thrusting their rock into the cloudless sky. The heat grew intense, felling scores of children with sunstroke and heat prostration.

By nightfall the following day, they straggled into Koblenz, where the Mosel River empties into the Rhine. The army massed around the Church of St. Castor.

Much to the children's astonishment, Koblenz's clergy proved hostile to the pilgrimage. "An army of simpletons," they called them, and insisted they had no food to spare. As if hunger were not enough, a disquieting rumor swept camp. A tinker wagon, clattering with pots and pans, had just arrived from the Rhine territory. "Castles of robber barons lay two or three days march up river," the tinker said, "and travelers disappear there, never to be seen again." Rumor turned to panic and Nicholas had to make an appearance to calm the army.

Somewhere along the route, Nicholas had cast off his simple gray habit and now wore as a cloak a resplendent, if threadbare, scarlet velvet altar cloth. He appeared not weary at all, for his disciples had built him a litter (called a char) which hung between two horses, donated by noblemen. Like every good leader, Nicholas knew his army needed a hero to worship, and selflessly rose to that need.

Nicholas called, "Who would dare harm us on our holy mission? Who would dare risk burning in hell? As for food," he continued, "we only need faith, and God will provide." So saying, he faced the church's facade and lifted his voice in a Te Deum. His golden notes blended with the Angelus bells. The townspeople, who had locked themselves in their dwellings at the invasion, opened their shutters and doors, then gradually stole into the square.

The hot yellow sky cooled to a calm blue as Nicholas finished his prayer. A burgher murmured, "The child's voice is heaven-sent." A merchant came forward with a sack of flour. Bakers fired their brick ovens; poulters offered squawking chickens; butchers, fresh-killed meat; and like the miracle of the loaves, from nothing soon enough appeared to feed one and all.

With muscles sore from the trek, but with bellies content for the first time since leaving Cologne a week before, the army slept peacefully, their faith in Nicholas once more reaffirmed.

Beyond the hamlet of Spai, the rushing Rhine began its torturous turns, carving its way through the massif. Approaching St. Goar, Roger saw the eerie promontory of Rhinefels Castle. The mountains were shrouded with mists, which rolled down to obscure the river. The children kept their voices low, terrified of arousing the spirits. Somewhere in the graveyard of the river, Harolde told them, lay buried the treasure of the Niebelungen, and it seemed to Roger that he heard the clash of steel of Siegfried and Hagen, as well as of the descendants of Attila the Hun, who lived in the fortresses spiking the peaks.

Once around the bend of St. Goar, the children came upon the enchanted Lorelei jutting into the Rhine. The river squeezed narrow at this point, and the low waters revealed the rocks of the seven virgins, so hard-hearted they had been turned to stone. They exacted revenge by luring boats onto the reefs with their siren call. An uneasy tension gripped the army as it hurried through the gap.

Astride Mirage, Jonathan kept trying to calm the skittish stallion. "You are right," he murmured to the horse, "it is strange here. One can almost see demons lurking behind every boulder."

Laurelle and Roger were walking together and arguing. Laurelle clutched her arms and rubbed them, though her chill came not from any known wind.

Flamonde was carrying pigtailed Constanze piggyback. She peered up at the ominous towers of Soonek and Reichen-

stein castles and muttered, "The Lord protect us from this benighted place. Why did I not marry Odo the miller and become
a woman of property instead of all this marching nonsense?"

Suddenly the ground thundered with hoofbeats. Down from
Soonek and Reichenstein swooped bands of robber barons,
charging among the screaming children. One baron with a
black eagle atop his helmet spurred his charger toward Flamonde and tore Constanze off her back. Another crimson-
cloaked horseman made for Laurelle, snatching her up onto
his mount.

"Laurelle!" Roger shouted, turning frantically for Mirage.

Jonathan had already seen what happened and spurred
Mirage to Roger. In a running jump, Roger leaped into the
saddle. They raced after the marauder, who fought to hold on
to the kicking, screaming Laurelle as he headed for the cliff
path to Reichenstein Castle.

As Mirage overtook the other horse, Roger leapt from the
stallion, knocking both the robber and Laurelle to the ground.
The warrior drew his sword. Roger thrust Laurelle behind
him. Then Mirage charged between, his flashing hooves cutting the air as he reared over the attacker. The robber baron
fled for his life.

With the suddenness of a summer storm, the attack was
over. Forty children had been killed or wounded and at least
another sixty-five carried off. Twice the children's army tried
to storm the castles, only to be met with a hail of arrows and
cometlike catapults of fire that killed a dozen more.

"We have no recourse but to abandon these captured children," Nicholas said. "Their fate is in God's hands."

But Flamonde would not leave, and tearing at her hair
charged the slope again. Roger and Harolde intercepted her
and forcibly carried her away.

With night falling, the grieving army hurried on. The narrow slits of the castle towers blazed with light. The sound of
drunken laughter echoed through the valley, punctuated by
the scream of a used child being hurled from the battlements.
The fairest would be kept alive for further amusement, to provide sport first for the barons, then for their mercenaries, and

finally given to the serfs. Somehow it made a serf's life easier to be able to inflict on others the torment he had borne all his life. With wailing and gnashing of teeth, the army prayed for its martyred comrades.

Every few steps, Flamonde's hand would jerk to her back and she would cry out, "Constanze! Oh my Constanze!" Her eyes fastened on Harolde and she spat, "And why does God sleep through all this?"

Terrified that they might be set upon again, the exhausted children pressed on. Finally, they heard distant church bells ringing complin and came at last to the town of Bingen. They huddled against its walls for the rest of the night.

At dawn, Roger strode to Nicholas's tent to propose a plan. He could not get within fifty feet of him; a dozen guards protected him. The captain of the guard was a robust, handsome youth from Holstein named Leopoldus, called Poldus. A bull of a boy, Poldus had a high forehead and small regular features, save for a pouting, sensual mouth. He sported a fresh scar on one cheek, won in a fight over a girl named Germaine; the scar only made Poldus more handsome.

Because of his position as head guard, Poldus had developed a lucrative sideline. He managed to filch threads from Nicholas's robe and also collected the evangelist's long flaxen hairs. These he sold to the faithful, eager to possess any relics of their leader. The other day Poldus had been appalled to see Nicholas's bath water dumped. Such a waste, he thought, when a goodly sum could be made selling it as an elixir.

"A hundred people a day want to see Nicholas," Poldus said to Roger. "Can a leader lead if his time be taken up with petty demands?" Poldus suggested, "If you want to donate some coins, or your blue enameled cross, I will see if I can arrange an appointment."

Roger answered by punching Poldus in the head, and was immediately wrestled to the ground by four bodyguards. Hearing the commotion, Nicholas emerged from his tent and called in his sing-song voice, "Stop this wickedness! We march in peace, for peace!"

"He started it," Poldus grumbled. Never having lost a fight, Poldus was more shocked than hurt that Roger had landed the first blow. "That will never happen again," Poldus swore to himself.

Roger knelt before Nicholas. "If we are truly an army, then we must act like one. We must have lines of communication, so that the tail will know what the head is about. The devil has his own plans in this matter and we need to be prepared for him. Every day sees us hungrier," Roger said. "An advance guard could not only warn the army of danger, but also enlist the aid of the clergy in each town, forewarn them that we approach. Instead, we have descended on them like a plague of locusts."

As he spoke, Roger surprised himself with the sense of his arguments. As his father had taught him, an army was much like a business.

Nicholas chewed his lip. "I talked of such a thing only yesterday, did I not?" he said to his disciples. They looked blank for a moment and then hurriedly agreed. "Before I give my final decision, I shall seek divine guidance. But now I am tired and require a bath."

"Yes, my leader!" Poldus exclaimed.

The following day Nicholas announced that an angel had visited him and told him to send out an advance guard, and a rear guard as well to protect the flank. Mainly because Roger had a horse, Nicholas allowed him to pick which detail he would lead. Though he knew it was by far the most dangerous, Roger chose the advance guard; for his company, he selected, Laurelle, Harolde, Gunther, and Jonathan.

Flamonde insisted she be included, with Harolde paling at that prospect. But Roger refused. He knew Flamonde would do nothing except worry about Laurelle and that would distract everybody. He said, meaning it, "Flamonde, you are too much needed here. Surely, the very little ones would perish without you." When Rudolph and Little Luke began to cry at the prospect of her leaving, Flamonde gave in.

Then Nicholas did something which infuriated Roger. He

appointed Poldus to accompany the advance guard, "to act as my representative and report back to me regularly. Poldus, you will be given a mule and you and Roger will share the responsibility of leadership."

Roger swore and argued. Poldus himself did not want to leave the main army and his lucrative sideline—nor his girl Germaine—and tried in every way to get out of it. But Nicholas insisted. Roger and Poldus had no recourse save to swallow their frustrations and go along.

Between all the languages and dialects the children of the advance guard spoke, plus Harolde's command of Latin, Roger had every hope that they would be able to make themselves understood as they passed through all the territories on their route.

Later that morning, the advance guard rode out. The prayers of the army went with them, for it could easily be that the fate of the entire crusade lay in the hands of these six scouts.

Golden Mainz, merry Mainz, seat of the archbishopric, was presided over by Archbishop Seigfried von Eppstein III. On hearing Roger's petition, the clergy promised to throw open the granaries when the army arrived. Secretly, the archbishop hoped such an act of charity might bring God's relief, for Mainz sweltered in the grip of the most devastating heat wave in its history.

Jonathan had had a wearisome day. First, he had searched in all the apothecary shops for the balm of aloe for Laurelle's sunburn, but found nothing. Then, a nasty confrontation with Poldus. Poldus had tried in turn to intimidate Roger, Gunther, and Harolde. Failing with each, he then concentrated on Jonathan. When Jonathan did not respond quickly enough to Poldus's orders, the bigger boy knocked him down. Jonathan sprang to his feet but Harolde jumped between them. "Peace at any cost," he whispered to Jonathan.

Lest his friends be put in jeopardy, Jonathan retreated, which only increased Poldus's taunts and demands.

Now, as Jonathan and Roger passed the cathedral, Jonathan

caught sight of the merchants and moneylenders in the midst of their transactions, bargaining shrilly over grain and grape crops, flinging ducats on the balancing scales. A devil got hold of Jonathan's tongue. "When your messiah appears for His second coming . . . Suppose He would come back right this very minute. What would He do with these moneychangers in His temple?"

Roger could not believe his ears.

"And what of those people there?" Jonathan plunged on, pointing to a clutch of beggars. "What would He say about the poor going hungry in the shadow of this splendid church?"

Roger smashed him in the face. "Jew!" he barked. "You dare take the name of our Lord in vain?"

Jonathan wiped the blood from his swelling lip. "You have eyes," he said, feeling an oblique sense of victory. "Think on what I said."

Roger stormed away. Poldus, who had witnessed the fight from a distance, ran and caught up with Roger. "What happened?" Poldus asked eagerly.

"Nothing," Roger muttered, barely able to control his rage to tell all.

"You acted in the right," Poldus said. "Never have I met a more insolent churl, acting like he is better than us. Well, we shall soon straighten him out, you and I, eh?" Poldus said, and throwing his arm around Roger's shoulder, fell into step.

That night Roger could not sleep. When Harolde woke to say prayers for sept, Roger questioned him on what Jonathan had said.

Harolde shook his head wearily. "Ah, the Jews, the Jews. Will they never cease? They are the ferment of the universe. You must shut your ears to their ceaseless questions. Leave all such issues to our shepherd. Pope Innocent is wiser than we, for he is the vicar of Christ on earth and we must be guided in all matters, spiritual and temporal, by him."

Comforted somewhat, Roger drifted off to sleep. The next morning, when he and Jonathan went to the cathedral to make final preparations for the arriving army, Roger shoved Jonathan hard. "That's for nothing," he said, feeling very virtuous.

As though in retribution, strong hands grabbed Roger. Guards of the ministerials surrounded the two boys.

"What are you doing?" Roger shouted, pointing to the cross sewn on his shoulder. "Can you not see that we are part of the pilgrimage?"

"Does that give you leave to steal?" a guard demanded.

"Steal?" Roger exclaimed. "What did I steal? Who accuses me?"

"I do," said a man coming out of the shadows. "I accuse you of stealing my horse."

Roger and Jonathan turned to stare into the golden eyes of Frizio.

MAINZ:
MID-JULY

ERR RITTERMEIER, THE MINISTERIAL, RUBBED HIS watery red eyes, perplexed. On the one hand, it seemed perfectly absurd for so young a lad to own such a magnificent steed. On the other hand, the man called Frizio did have the fleur-de-lis burned into his arm as the boy claimed. But the bag of golden ducats Frizio slipped Rittermeier convinced him that, as Frizio explained, "The brand is really a very old one and has nothing to do with the boy's fabrications."

Yet thousands of children roamed the streets of Mainz, sure to take offense should one of their army be deprived of his rights. They could riot, or worse, never leave, and eat the city out of house and home. Herr Rittermeier poured another goblet of brilliant ruby Mainzer wine. What would Solomon have done, he wondered. Suggest they cut the horse in two, each taking part? When after the third goblet the solution came to him, he jumped to his feet and called the guard. He gave orders that a judgment would take place in two days time. "It is so simple," Herr Rittermeier exclaimed. "Let the *horse* decide who is master!"

That evening, Gunther's life took a troubled turn. As was the army's practice, the children had broken up in small groups to go begging for food. Usually, they avoided the houses of the rich, for those haughties would not even open their doors, as if fearing some sort of contamination. The poor, who knew the value of a crust of bread, were more likely to share what little they had. This twilight, Gunther found himself alone on the Augustinerstrasse, a district of solid two-story stone houses.

A door opened and a woman dressed in cloth of emerald

beckoned him in. "I am called Ermengarde," she said, "and my husband has gone to the cathedral for the latest news."

Gunther's eyes opened wide at the grandness of the house. "Why, there is no livestock anywhere! Not even a chicken or a pig," he said in awe. Gunther had heard tell of such palaces, but he had never seen one. An even greater wonder was the woman, with skin powdered white and smelling of attar of roses.

On her index finger, Ermengarde wore an intricately fila-greed ring. She noticed Gunther staring at it with vague recognition and gave him her hand to examine it.

"Yes," Ermengarde said softly, "it is fashioned in the shape of the edicule of Our Lord's Holy Sepulcher; my husband paid a pretty penny for it."

Gunther pressed her hand to his forehead, imprinting the tomb's design on his skin. He closed his eyes, overcome with devotion and hunger.

"Even our saints took time to eat," Ermengarde insisted briskly, seating Gunther at the trestle table and making him take the cross off his back. Ermengarde reached for a pitcher on a high shelf, contriving to show Gunther a trim ankle. Her bosom heaved as she watched Gunther's callused hands tear apart the breast of cold chicken; when his spaced white teeth bit into a thigh, she could stand no more and feigned a swoon. As Gunther rose to catch her, she melted against his rocklike body, so different than the soft old flesh of the burgher who had brought her to wife.

Still chewing, Gunther held her in his arms, not knowing quite what to do. The startled matron found herself being laid down on the table. Coming alive, she pulled the boy down on top of her. Gunther's hands moved with a knowledge born of instinct, while Ermengarde peeked at him from under her half-closed lids. With a warning creak the trestle table col-lapsed under their combined weight just as the master of the house returned. He rushed at them, brandishing his staff. Gunther had barely enough time to flee. He heard Ermengarde yelling: "He forced his way in! If I wanted to deceive you, would I do it on the kitchen table?"

Gunther felt stricken with shame. He had left his cross in the burgher's house. Back at camp, he confessed his sin to Harolde and Flamonde. Almost at once, Gunther felt better for having shared his guilt, though he could not understand why Harolde smiled, then sobered, and smiled again; nor why Flamonde kissed him so soundly.

"You are a wise man," Gunther said to Harolde. "What shall I do about my lost cross? Go back for it? How can I face the merchant?"

Harolde shook his head. "Too dangerous. There is a simpler solution. You shall make another cross and promise not to sin again."

A beatific smile lit Gunther's face. All through the night Gunther labored, and the next morning showed everyone his handiwork. This cross was bigger than the one he'd carried for the children of Aachen. "For my sins are bigger," Gunther explained matter-of-factly. "I have seen the beast in me. Only a heavy cross will keep it subdued. When I reach Jerusalem, I shall plant it in the garden of Gethsemane, and all my sins shall be taken from me. Is that not so, Harolde?"

Harolde nodded, feeling oddly close to tears. Later, Harolde prayed at his devotions, "Oh, Lord, if you would but grant me the faith of this simple youth. . . ."

The night before the trial, Roger did not close his eyes, beside himself with worry. "That Frizio should have risen from the past claiming I stole the animal from him in Cologne, and that he followed me all the way to Mainz to recover it? How is it that God does not strike him dead for these lies?" Roger asked Harolde, who could only shrug helplessly. Worse than the injustice was Roger's overriding fear that he would lose Mirage, for he had grown to love the stallion. "And how can I lead the advance guard without a horse?" he demanded of Jonathan.

At dawn, Harolde took Roger to the cathedral to offer their prayers. "At which end do we pray?" Roger asked, confused by the double choir at either end of the nave.

"This is the way churches are built in these parts," Harolde said. "The eastern choir represents the papacy, the western choir, the authority of the Holy Roman emperors. Ever since the investiture contest between Henry IV and Pope Gregory, the emperors have insisted that their sphere of influence remain inviolate, demanding its recognition even in the architecture of the cathedral."

The judgment of Mirage was to take place before the cathedral, in full view of the entire army; so whatever Mirage's decision, all would bear witness that justice had been done.

The jumble of market stalls around the square were crowded with the children. Poldus could not wait for the event to begin. "I always suspected Roger of stealing that stallion," Poldus told Nicholas and his lieutenants. "Without that horse," Poldus muttered to himself, "I will be the undisputed leader."

"The rules are simple," Herr Rittermeier explained. "The stallion will be placed equidistant between the two contenders. Man or boy can do anything to bring the horse to him, except cross his own position line. Whoever touches the animal first will be considered owner."

Baalbek quickly suggested a number of foolproof plans to Frizio. "There was a mare in heat in the stables," he said. "I soaked a cloth in her urine, so Mirage will surely come to you first."

"Did they cut off part of your brain also?" Frizio interrupted the eunuch. "Mirage is *mine,* my other self. We have no need of trickery. Of course he will choose me!"

Herr Rittermeier signaled for Mirage to be brought. "Begin!" he shouted with a hiccough.

Mirage pawed the ground, uneasy with the thousands of staring eyes. Frizio called to him in mellifluous Arabic and the stallion swiveled in Frizio's direction just as Roger shouted, "Mirage! Come."

The horse turned one way then the other. "Mirage, my beauty," Frizio called, extending his arm.

Mirage's nose twitched. His tail stood straight out as he ambled toward his former master. Roger shouted frantically, but Mirage came within an arm's length of Frizio. Had Frizio allowed the stallion to cross the line on his own, victory would have been his. But in his eagerness, Frizio reached out with a sudden motion. Mirage, perhaps reacting to the long-ago nights when Frizio had exhausted his rage upon him, reared back just as Jonathan whistled the call that meant food.

Mirage wheeled and trotted to the boys, stopping just short of the line. Jonathan whistled again and patted his wallet. Mirage stepped across the line and Roger flung his arms around the stallion's neck. Mirage paid no attention, but burrowed his nose into Jonathan's wallet in search of what the whistle had promised. He found only a withered carrot; one gulp finished that, and when he did not get anything else, he bit Jonathan.

Jonathan was too delirious with joy to care. During the afternoon, he scavenged through the alleys and dumps, preparing a feast for Mirage. That night there was much rejoicing in camp, with a constant retelling of how it had happened, and how indeed God did protect the innocent. Poldus was loudest in his congratulations.

In Frizio's quarters, there was no rejoicing. Baalbek cowered in a corner, fearful for his life. Frizio kicked the slop jar across the floor. He uncoiled his whip with a sudden flick, slicing a candle in two, then repeatedly slashed the wall above Baalbek's head. Flecks of spittle flew from Frizio's mouth; he shuddered, then slumped to the pallet.

At last Frizio said, "I cannot believe it. We are two grown men and yet we have been outwitted at every turn by mere boys." The recollection of Mirage turning away from him brought tears to Frizio's eyes. "They have bewitched him," he said, swallowing hard. "Baalbek, we must do something."

Baalbek slipped a long curved knife from the folds of his jalaba and stabbed it into the top of an iron-bound chest. "Say the word, master . . ."

Frizio shook his head impatiently. "Yesterday, perhaps, but that is no good now. The entire city would know we were responsible." He rubbed the branded fleur-de-lis on his arm, all too conscious that the next conviction could mean his death. "I must think on this."

Preparing for a deep meditation, he drew a circle on the floor, then a five-pointed star, and sat down within the pentagram. Baalbek lit candles at the points of the star. Frizio murmured an incantation and then, breathing deeply of the patchouli incense Baalbek burned, slipped into a reverie.

"What would I have not given if the boy had been captured when the robber barons raided the army?" Frizio whispered. Remembering the foray he'd planned and led for the barons at Soonek and Reichenstein castles soothed Frizio somewhat. He had realized a sizable sum of money that day, more than enough to pay for his trip from Jerusalem, and the ransom he'd lost to Baron Thorne. But not enough to compensate for the loss of Mirage, or the injury to his pride. No, Frizio thought, his mind drifting off to omnipotent dream, that scale would never be balanced until he had the boy in his power; to that end, Frizio called upon the ancient dark spirits to guide him. In the becalmed, breathless city, a sudden gust of wind extinguished the candles.

Baalbek wakened Frizio early the next morning with a dish of apples and plums. Frizio gobbled the fruit, his body craving the sweets after his exhausting night. He cocked his head at the persistent noise in the lanes below and went to the window.

The army of children streamed along the thoroughfare on their way out of Mainz. His heart shriveled at the sight of Mirage. Beside the stallion, Roger walked hand in hand with—another boy was it? Something about the pair seemed so familiar to Frizio. And then suddenly Frizio realized who the child was. "Laurelle!" he exclaimed. "Baalbek! Come here this instant and see if I am not right!"

A very surprised Baalbek confirmed that it was indeed the serving maid from the bathhouse in Troyes.

Frizio's whole being sang with exultation. "That the wheel of fortune should have brought us together again! Ah, this time I will not lose her!" Frizio's eyes followed the children until they were lost in the throng.

Many of the younger and weaker children remained behind,

unable to cope with the terrible heat. Many others had died. But the strong and dedicated marched on and, as Frizio watched them, it seemed to him that the army was in some strange process of purifying itself.

The vague plan he had dreamed slowly took more definite shape. "It is contingent on so many things," he said to Baalbek. "Whether the army manages to stay together. Whether or not they reach Genoa and the sea.

"In Cologne, I thought only to capture as many children as possible and sell them to the local barons. But now . . . If all goes as I plan, there is the distinct possibility I could become a rich man. A very rich man," he said to Baalbek. "Help me with this, and if it is concluded to my satisfaction I will give you your freedom."

Baalbek's tiny eyes glinted in the folds of fat. "Tell me what you plan so I may help. Shall I steal Mirage from them?"

"No time for that now," Frizio said. "Besides, it is much too dangerous."

Baalbek pulled his knife from the chest. "What then? Kidnap the girl?"

Frizio shook his head.

"It is good that you forget her. She is as gaunt as a scarecrow now, and with no hair, very ugly. I can buy you a finer wench anywhere."

Frizio sprang for Baalbek's throat, forcing his head against the wall. "Attend me! Should I ever discover that you have laid hands on her again as you did in Troyes when you spirited her away, I will have your heart! Do you understand?"

Baalbek nodded, his eyes rolling in fear.

Frizio released him, and breathing heavily said, "Now pack. We leave immediately."

WORMS:
THIRD WEEK IN JULY

WHEN THE ADVANCE GUARD CAME WITHIN A half-mile of the city of Worms, they sensed something drastically wrong. "Why are there no people on the roads?" Roger asked.

Nearing the walls, Jonathan exclaimed, "See there!" and pointed to the turgid moat, alive with rats. Shuddering, the band proceeded through the open gates.

"Why is it so quiet?" Roger called to the bowman on the walls.

The guard turned away as though he had not heard him.

Along the Mainzerstrasse, all the shops were shut tight. "It is not the feast day of any saint I know of," Harolde said, consulting his church calendar. In a dark deserted street near the center of town, they came upon the ruins of a still-smoldering building. "Too large to have been a private house," Harolde said. "See this raised section?" He squinted at the sun. "Yes, it is the east. It must have been a church."

Jonathan reached into the embers and pulled out a charred scroll. "Not a church," he said slowly, "but a synagogue."

"Lord be praised!" Poldus sang out.

"Let us go from here," Harolde said, with an uneasy glance at Poldus. That one was as sly as Reynard, and though he could not read to tell the difference between Hebrew and Latin letters, Poldus might take to wondering how Jonathan knew the difference.

At an urgent sign from Harolde, Roger dragged Jonathan away. The street, empty save for an occasional feeding rat, led them to the massive red-brown Church of St. Peter. Dwarf galleries and blind arcades circled the building. Quartered by its four round towers, the structure looked more like a fortress than a church. A crowd jammed the south porch. The bells tolled, a slow rolling dirge that signaled death. A series of pallbearers filed out of the arched doorway, coffins high on their shoulders.

"Seven in all," Roger counted. He addressed a lame beggar, "Tell me, old father, what happened here?"

The cripple squinted at him. "Who are you? Don't touch me!" and, manipulating his crutch, he dragged himself off.

A group of mourners followed the coffins. An elderly man lifted his arms to the sky, "They murdered my son, just as they murdered our Lord! I will not see my boy in the grave until he is avenged!" He looked around franticly and fastened on the thing closest at hand, the cemetery of the Jews, just two blocks away. Crazed with grief, he started running toward it. More people joined in until hundreds streamed after, shouting for revenge. Into the cemetery they charged, knocking over tombstone, desecrating the grounds and committing whatever other mischief came to mind.

"Let us go help them," Poldus said eagerly.

"Did you not swear to march in peace?" Roger said to him.

"Not for the Christ killers," Poldus snapped. "Never for them. Need I remind you of the cry of every Crusader who has gone before us? 'Convert a Jew, or kill a Jew!' Am I not right, Harolde?"

Harolde stuttered something unintelligible and then began to cough violently.

Roger grasped Poldus's arm. "Hear me. The old ways have failed. And that is why *we* march."

Harolde nodded and gasped, "We have more important work to do."

A priest came out of the church just then; the hem of his heavy linen robes stirred the dust.

Roger approached, kneeled and kissed his hand. "Father, we are in sore need of your comfort and wisdom. An army of Crusaders, children, mostly, is less than two days away. They count on getting food here in Worms, but all we have met is confusion. Pray tell us, what is happening here?"

The priest shook his head woefully. "Calamity, that is what. For our sins in harboring the Anti-Christ, God visits us with the plague. It struck our city two weeks ago. Thirty-three dead so far and who knows how many more must perish before the Lord is appeased?"

Fear flashed across the faces of the advanced guard.

The priest continued, "We hope we have put an end to this, for three days ago we burned the temple of the Jews, the source of the pestilence. And after all we have done for them in Worms! Do you know that last Friday they preached in their synagogue that all our Crusades were doomed to failure, because God had promised Jerusalem to *them*? And now the Jews have been poisoning our wells. There can be no doubt about it, for none in their quarter were afflicted."

A nervous twitch contorted Jonathan's mouth; he had turned so pale that his lips appeared blue. "How will burning the synagogue purify your wells?" he wanted to ask, but he caught the desperate look on Harolde's face and bit his hand lest he scream out his rage. Long ago, his father had told him that he believed plague came not from poisoned water, as commonly held, but from filth; his observation being that places kept clean were stricken less often. Jonathan wanted to pound this knowledge into the priest's head, but fresh shouting interrupted.

The mob had circled back from the cemetery and now stampeded toward the Jewish quarter.

"We must flee from here," Roger said. "Poldus, ride back and warn the army not to come through Worms. Better to go hungry than risk plague. Harolde, what is the next city?"

Harolde consulted his map. "Speyer."

"We will wait for the army there," Roger said.

"This mule," Poldus complained. "I would get to Nicholas much faster if you gave me your horse." Roger hesitated and Poldus said softly, "The lives of all our brothers . . ."

Roger flushed. "You are right, Poldus," he said, and dismounted.

Poldus got one foot in the stirrup and Mirage bucked.

"I guess you will have to ride your own mule," Roger said happily to Poldus, who lay sprawled on the ground.

With a curse, Poldus trotted off to intercept the main army.

Roger led his band south along the Speyerstrasse. Behind

them, a plume of smoke rose from the quarter of the Jews. At the gate, Jonathan hung back. Roger motioned for the others to go on.

"I know what you are thinking," Roger said, "but you dare not." Jonathan started to interrupt and Roger spat, "Idiot! Plague rages here! And rioting against your people. If one doesn't kill you, the other surely will. Did you come all this far only to die in Worms?"

Jonathan reached out and touched Roger's arm. "I know you are right. Yet, I must go back. Would you do anything less?" Then he reached up and stroked Mirage's nose. "Good-by, my beauty," he said, then turned and started back.

Roger watched him go, not knowing what to do. Then, silently begging Jonathan's forgiveness, he picked up a rock, ran up behind him and hit him a blow on the head that knocked the boy out. Roger slung Jonathan over Mirage's back and hurried through the gate.

By the time Jonathan regained consciousness they were many miles from the plagued city. At first, Jonathan snapped at everybody and would not talk to Roger at all.

"This will pass," Roger assured Laurelle. "In some small way, getting Jonathan out of Worms helps repay the debt I owe him for saving my father's life."

"But why would he want to remain in Worms?" Laurelle asked.

Roger bit his lip and quickly talked of something else.

Night into day, day into night into day, the miles disappeared beneath the plodding feet of the main army. Their voices were seldom lifted in song as before; they marched silently, husbanding their strength. Perpetual hunger knotted their stomachs, for in this new territory, so far from the source of the crusade, the inhabitants looked upon their venture as a kind of madness and did little to help them. Only the children of the nobility, who still had some gold left, could afford to buy food. This they did in secret, lest a thousand outstretched hands snatch all away.

Clothes became gritty with dirt and sweat. In the oppressive heat the children discarded their pilgrim's habits. Blisters gave way to calluses which did not feel the cutting edge of stone or the sting of nettles. Those children with fat on their bones now grew as supple as stalks of wheat. But daily the army dwindled; exhaustion, death, and despair decimated the ranks.

Poldus delivered the news of plague to Nicholas, led the army wide around Worms, and then, at Nicholas's orders, rejoined the advance guard, though he would have much preferred to stay with the main army. Poldus caught up with Roger and the others just before they reached Speyer.

On July 25, the feast day of St. James the Greater, the advanced guard entered Speyer, made arrangements with the city fathers for the care and feeding of the oncoming army, and then pressed on toward the next major city: Strasbourg.

All day Roger led his scouts through the heavily wooded countryside. Stands of oak and elm marched down the hilly slopes to the Rhine's edge. At twilight, he chose a campsite on a small plateau halfway up the hillside.

Everybody fell to his appointed task. Roger and Poldus went hunting.

Much as he disliked Poldus, Roger could not help but admire his ability as a hunter. He could spear a rabbit on the run, or knock a pigeon from the air with his slingshot. This time they returned with a pheasant which Laurelle plucked, cleaned, and roasted with a seasoning of fresh rosemary and thyme. Afterwards, they ate a salad of dandelion greens which Mirage kept trying to snatch from Jonathan. Jonathan pulled his trencher of stale bread away. Mirage whacked the boy on the head with his chin and trotted off.

"Better tie him down or he will run away," Poldus said.

"He will not go far," Jonathan said, and whistled. Mirage ambled back and went after the greens again. This time Jonathan shared.

After dinner they sat around the campfire and listened to Poldus's news about the army.

"The weak have deserted, or disappeared," Poldus said, his voice edged with contempt.

"About how many remain?" Roger asked.

"Some monks who claim to know about these things say a little more than fifteen thousand," Poldus said, "but these are the true warriors of Christ."

"And what of the thousands fallen by the wayside?" Harolde murmured sadly. "Is this always to be the fate of the innocent?"

Gunther clasped Harolde's hands. "Do not be sad, my brother, for the Lord has gathered them to His bosom."

After a bit Laurelle said to Poldus, "Have you by chance seen my sister? Have you any news of her?"

Poldus grinned wetly. "That one makes news every day."

Laurelle thrust her head angrily at him. "What do you mean?"

"Nothing, nothing at all," Poldus said placatingly.

Soon they settled down, listening to the chirp of cicadas. Laurelle studied Roger and Jonathan as they repaired the cinch on Mirage's saddle. The fire reflected off Roger's blond hair, grown long and bleached lighter by the sun. Jonathan's dark curls twined with highlights of copper, and his eyes seemed brighter in his tanned face. Jonathan looked up, saw Laurelle watching and smiled.

Roger noticed this and stiffened. During these past days, Jonathan and Laurelle had fallen into an easy friendship which rankled him.

Laurelle touched Jonathan's arm. "You look like a piece of brown velvet," she said. Roger's face clouded with jealousy and Laurelle nudged him. "But you, you are like a bolt of gold brocade."

When Jonathan left to check the horses, Roger took Laurelle away from the campfire. "He is getting too familiar with you and I do not like it," Roger said.

Laurelle chose her words carefully, "He means no harm."

"You like him then?" Roger asked, and when Laurelle nodded, he demanded, "But why?"

Laurelle hunched her shoulders. "He is gentle, and maybe because . . . he wants nothing from me. While you, you want everything."

Jealousy buried deep within Roger flared up. "Take care, he is a Jew!" Then, realizing what he had done, he looked around anxiously. Fortunately, nobody had heard.

Laurelle looked at Roger for a long moment. "I know he is a Jew. He told me shortly after what happened in Worms."

"He *told* you?" Roger exclaimed. "Whatever possessed him to tell you?"

"Why did you?" she challenged him.

Flustered, he stammered, "That is different. I am only trying to protect you."

Laurelle stared into the darkness where Jonathan gamboled with Mirage and Tortoise. "That is what he said. He warned me, so he might not appear in false guise. He said that if he was discovered, I must not risk my own life defending him."

"Would you?" Roger asked.

Laurelle thought for a long moment. "I do not know," she said, and rested her hand lightly on Roger's knee. "Who else knows?" she asked.

"Only Harolde," Roger said.

She sighed with relief. "Of all people, it must be kept from Poldus. He would turn it to his own end, even if it meant Jonathan's death."

Roger and Laurelle went back to the campfire and stretched out. Roger, feeling very unhappy about this new development, finally managed to doze off.

But Laurelle felt so unclean she could not sleep. The dust of the day's march clung to her hair and tickled her throat. She turned and twisted, trying to drift off, but the night, heavy with memory and humid air, pressed down on her fevered flesh.

She waited until the others were asleep, then slipped from camp and climbed down the steep path to the river. The wet sand felt cool on her bare feet and cooler still on her ankles as she ventured a little way into the current.

"Oh, demons of the river," Laurelle whispered, "I come not

to seek your treasures or your hiding places. I come only to cleanse myself." She waited for an answer, but heard only the benign croak of a bullfrog.

But Laurelle knew the spirits of the wood and rock were watching, for pinpricks of light flitted through the trees and along the river bank. One lit up close by her nose. Laurelle shied away and then smiled, "Only fireflies." They twinkled behind her as she waded deeper into the Rhine. The water crept up to her thighs, around her.waist, then billowed under her loose overblouse. She slipped off the blouse and swirled it against the current, fanning an arc of white water toward the quarter moon. A school of silver minnows flashed phosphorescent as they darted by in a long line. Laurelle moved slowly toward them and let them play through her fingers.

The water lapped around her taut breasts, sign of her budding womanhood. She touched them tentatively, then sank down into the water, as though the river would wash away all that had happened to her and make her as new as the new moon. She turned onto her back, arms outstretched, and the cross of her body floated slowly downstream, while the fireflies followed, marking passage.

Laurelle looked to the midnight sky with its infinity of stars. She dared not hope that the Virgin would attend her prayers, but she prayed anyway, her mind flashing always to that moment of anguish in Troyes. Laurelle prayed for absolution, she prayed for her violator, but most of all she prayed for strength to conquer this terrible, aroused passion.

The twinkling fireflies seemed to blend with the constellations as tears rolled from her eyes to mingle with the waters of the river.

Somewhere in this net of events, Laurelle sensed the Lord's design, sensed it drawing her ever nearer to the Holy Land. She saw it all clearly as she lay staring at the stars as numerous as grains of sand. Endless sands and men in flowing white garments, and chains and strange humped beasts. . . .

All at once the spirit of the river reached up from the deep and fastened its talons around her leg. Laurelle screamed and swung repeatedly, feeling her fist connect with solid flesh. She swam desperately for the river bank and as she ran along the shore, struggled into her overblouse.

Then Roger and Gunther and Jonathan came crashing down the hillside, surrounding her, as a wet Poldus limped up, holding his split lip. "Does she own the river?" Poldus bellowed when the three boys pinned him to the ground. "Is no one else allowed to swim on a hot night?"

"He grabbed my leg," Laurelle said, shivering from fright.

"The next time you touch her, I'll . . ." Roger broke off, mortified by what he had almost said after their crusading vow of peace. How could one use only the weapon of love, when others did not honor it? Roger released Poldus.

All the way back to camp, he kept yelling at Laurelle. "How could you do such a stupid thing? A wonder it is that one of the river monsters didn't swallow you up. And you would have deserved it!"

"They sound like they are married," Gunther said happily, and settled back on his bed of rushes, one hand resting lightly on the cross beside him.

Poldus curled up on his side, so mad he choked on his gall. They would never have gotten him down if there hadn't been three of them. Poldus could understand Roger trying to defend Laurelle; after all, she was his property. As for Gunther, the simple-minded fool did what anybody told him. But Jonathan? "I will settle with him," Poldus swore to himself.

After the others had fallen asleep, Laurelle and Roger sat by the fire, Laurelle turning every now and then to dry her clothes and brush the wetness from her hair.

At last Roger said gruffly, "I am sorry I shouted at you in front of the others."

Laurelle gave one last shudder. "Each day, you become more like Flamonde," she sighed. "Beware, for I fled from her."

"It is just that . . . I love you so," Roger blurted.

"And I love you, too," Laurelle said quietly.

Roger's head snapped up, not quite daring to believe what he had heard.

Laurelle rested her head on her knees and stared into the

fire. "You have been father, brother, and protector to me, and all without the rewards."

"Will you marry me?" Roger asked in a rush, desperate to bind her before she could change her mind. "We can go to the first priest, announce our betrothal, then when we are of age—my cousin Cnuteson married at sixteen. That is only a year or so off."

Laurelle put her finger on his lips. "I do love you. But I am not yet free. I will marry you, I swear it. But only when we get to Jerusalem. Until then, we must not touch, or kiss, or do anything to make me forget my vow. Will you swear to this?"

Roger smacked his head and groaned. "Are you made of stone? Even the Lorelei had more heart!"

Laurelle turned away.

Roger grabbed her hand and pressed it to his lips. "Anything you want," he said. "Anything."

Laurelle withdrew her hand gently. "Will you swear?"

With a glimpse of the torment he was consigning himself to, Roger took a deep breath and said, "I swear."

Laurelle looked at him; his face was beaming. She did love him, this golden creature who would dare anything, even love her, worthless sinner that she was.

"Jerusalem, then," Laurelle said, and Roger answered, "Jerusalem."

STRASBOURG:
EARLY AUGUST

IN THE OPPRESSIVE HEAT, THE DAYS DISSOLVED ONE into the other.

"Christians they call themselves," Laurelle said sadly about the people who had denied them food.

At every hamlet along the way, the advance guard had begged food, barely scrounging enough to keep them alive. Some villagers threw stones to keep the children at a distance. The rumor of plague and the reality of famine had turned the countryside hostile.

Gunther patted Laurelle's arm. "Be of good cheer. Though we may not see the reason now, it is all part of God's design."

Laurelle ran her fingers along Gunther's welted shoulders. "That cross—could you not put it down? You have carried it for so many miles. Surely your wish to plant it in the Holy Land will more than make up for the deed?"

"Oh, it is really not very heavy," Gunther said. "I hardly feel it anymore."

The fields parched under the seering sun, and Mirage's ribs began to show through the dapplings in his hide. Jonathan plucked wilted daisies and fed them to the stallion as they plodded along. He wove a wreath out of some other stunted flowers and placed it on Laurelle's head.

"Your betrothal crown," Jonathan said, bowing low. Roger had told him the wonderful news. With the overflowing of Jonathan's joy for them had also come a pang of sadness. During the day, he warned himself that he must never aspire to her. Not only did she belong to Roger, she belonged to another God. But, at night, when dreams heeded no warning, she belonged to him.

Laurelle's shriek interrupted Jonathan's daydreaming. Mirage had sneaked up behind her and eaten the wreath right off her head.

In the tedium of the blazing days, the Rhine proved a blessing. Without its water and fish, they surely would have starved. Whenever they could not stand the heat, they plunged in. Even finicky Tortoise waded until the water stood belly high, swishing her tail and braying. Then they would continue their trek, letting the clothes dry on their bodies. At these times, Roger could not bear to look at Laurelle, her lithe arms and legs showing through the thin stuff of her clothes.

They beguiled the hours telling tales of their youth, and all agreed that despite these daily trials, never had they been happier. When their spirits flagged, they sang crusading hymns, Roger in his cracking baritone, Gunther in a voice gravelly from inhaling too much smithy smoke, Harolde in his reedy tenor, Poldus booming off-key, and Laurelle in her sweet tones, which wove silvery phrases around the others':

> *I must go to a place*
> *Where I shall bear pain*
> *Where God was made to suffer . . .*

Jonathan hummed along, but mostly he did not know the stirring martial music. So he would sing to himself: psalms, and verses from the Song of Solomon, so as not to forget who he was.

On a twilit evening at the beginning of August, one month after setting out from Cologne, the advance guard approached the heavily fortified Rhine-fed canal-moat surrounding the city of Strasbourg. Flags with the insignia of the bishop of Strasbourg flew from the battlements. All the bridges were drawn and the gates shut.

"But it is not even dark yet," Poldus shouted to the guard in the tower of Quai St. Etienne. "Let us in!"

"There is an early curfew in Strasbourg," the guard called back. "You cannot enter until dawn tomorrow."

"What is that smell?" Laurelle asked, crinkling her nose at the heavy acrid odor that hung in the air.

"It is like burned horseflesh," Gunther said, recognizing it from his days at the blacksmith's shop.

Poldus called up to the guard, "Good sir, have you fresh meat up there? We pray you, throw some down to us, for we have walked far this day and are sore hungry."

The guard roared with laughter. "That is the flesh of heretics you smell. The priests have been at their fires all month, getting rid of the troublemakers. Tomorrow at noon you shall see more burned at the stake."

Laurelle clutched Roger's arm. "Let us be gone from here at once."

"Would that we could," Roger said, "but unless we get fresh supplies here for our army, God knows how many more will die."

"But there is trouble here, I feel it," Laurelle said.

"We will conduct our business early and then depart as soon as possible."

When the gates were opened the following day, the children hurried down the rue des Frères. They turned a corner and the cathedral rose up before them, bursting out of its old Romanesque shell into the new style. Wooden scaffolding enclosed the entire eastern end, where the choir and transept had already been completed. Stained-glass windows of many shapes and sizes interrupted the ponderous walls supported by flying buttresses.

Roger wasted the morning trying to speak to the authorities about provisions for the army. Everybody told him that all such business must wait until the trial by fire be done.

In front of the south porch, Roger counted five stakes. Almost noon now, and the charred, fire-blackened stakes cast no shadow. The band joined the waiting grim-faced crowd, which grew ever larger.

"Who is being burned?" Gunther asked a gritty day laborer.

"Heretics," the worker said.

"What are heretics?" Gunther asked.

The laborer gave Gunther a hard stare, but when he realized

the lad was serious, the man said, "If there be a battle between religions? The man who loses is a heretic."

Gunther nodded, but did not understand one word.

The crowd began to shout its displeasure, apparently hostile
to the upcoming executions. Moments later, they quieted
when Bishop Heinrich von Vehringen appeared, leading a procession of gorgeously attired priests. Behind them walked five
black-robed monks.

"Look," Gunther gulped. "They cast no shadow either."

When the chain-laden condemned were led to the square,
Laurelle clutched Harolde's sleeve, "But one is only a child.
She cannot be more than seven or eight years old!"

Harolde said lamely, "Well, evil knows no age."

A momentous time this was for Bishop von Vehringen. Not
too many years before, the citizens of Strasbourg had risen up
against him and he had had to deprive them of all ecclesiastical offices. Beguines, Beghards, Cathars, Jews, witches, Waldensians, freethinkers—all manner of misfits had flocked to
the city until it had become a hotbed of sedition. Witness that
inflammatory piece of trash written by Strasbourg's poet,
Gottfried; minstrels sang his epic *Tristan* in every tavern. The
mad rebel had the audacity to claim that the annointing of
king and cardinal, the holy sacraments of marriage and communion, all of these were dross beside the supreme sacrament
of love between man and woman. Von Vehringen knew that
such talk of free love, if left unchallenged, could destroy all the
church had achieved. So he sent for the church's new inquisitors, the disciples of Brother Dominic. *Domini canes* they had
come to be called—the hounds of God, trained to root out
heresy in all its guises.

After months of investigation, the inquisitors declared
Strasbourg riddled with heresy. To establish guilt in question-
able cases, they employed the time-honored ordeal of the hot
iron. The accused had to pick up a red-hot iron bar in his bare
hands and carry it three paces. If at the end of three days the
burns did not show signs of healing, he was judged guilty. Of

the eighty people accused, all had been put to the test. All had failed. Sixty-five, so far, had been burned at the stake.

Noon had been chosen by the bishop for the purification of the damned, for this was the daylight hour when evil was known to be at its height. "And if the devil be strong at mid-day," von Vehringen intoned, "then we will prove God more powerful still."

Of the five heretics scheduled for today's auto-da-fé, one was a woman old beyond years. She had changed herself into a raven during mass at St. Pierre le Vieux and flown from the church to a barn, where she soured the milk of a nursing cow. It had not been necessary to put her to the ordeal. To all questions she had nodded vigorously and with a toothless grin.

"As the good book commands us in Exodus, 17:18," von Vehringen cried, "thou shalt not suffer a witch to live."

Von Vehringen's greatest coup had been the unearthing of four Cathars. All had confessed, without torture, to being Albigenses, as they were called, after the city of Albi in southern France. Of Eastern origins, the cult had spread from Asia Minor to Hungary, and thence to Western Europe, finding particularly fertile soil in Languedoc and the Lombard plain and also spreading as far north as the Rhinelands.

Harolde whispered to the others, "No less a saint than Bernard of Clairvaux tried to teach these heretics the error of their ways. But for more than fifty years they have rejected the true church. Pope Innocent III tried to reconcile them, even sent Dominic and his brethren to preach the true gospel, but these sinners responded by murdering the papal legate, Arnulf. What could Innocent do except destroy the sect? See, it has even infected Strasbourg."

Of the Cathars awaiting burning, three were members of one family: a scrivener, his wife, and their eight-year-old daughter. The fourth Cathar, the leader, was an emaciated man of imposing mien. A count of the Palatinate nobility, he had answered Pope Innocent's call for the Fourth Crusade in 1204. But instead of recapturing Jerusalem as planned, the army had been diverted by the wily Venetians to Constantinople, there to conquer and pillage that Christian city. Horrified by the wanton killing of fellow Christians, the count had been a ready candidate for the preachings of the Cathars. He became so obsessed with the new religion that after seven years of prayer and fasting, he had attained its highest office, that of a perfect.

As the guards led the count to his stake, von Vehringen shouted, "Take care, lest he touch any of his fellow heretics!"

"So strange are the tenets of their religion," Harolde explained to the others, "that they believe a man can be absolved of his sins simply by laying on of hands and the perfect's recital of the Consolamentuum: 'As a disciple of Christ, do you give yourself to God and the Gospel?' With an affirmative answer, the fools believe the sinner receives back the Holy Spirit, which he lost when he first fell from paradise."

The scrivener winced as his wife and child were bound to their stakes. The perfect's voice throbbed with righteousness. "Blessed is he who is persecuted for the sake of truth."

"Amen!" the mother and father called out. But the child, terrified by the ropes which cut into her flesh, began to cry.

The crowd stirred angrily. A cooper with barrel hoops hanging around his neck shouted, "Let the girl go. She is too young to know sin!"

"Oh yes, *please* let her go," Laurelle cried. "They must *not* burn her! Roger, can we not take her with us?" Laurelle's fingers began to rake at her body as though trying to tear away imaginary ropes.

Bishop von Vehringen called, "Let the purification begin!"

The chief inquisitor approached the perfect. "Once more we plead with you to renounce your pagan ways and return to the bosom of mother church, who loves you."

The perfect answered, "Does she love us so much that she must burn us? We renounce *you*! Neither the church nor secular princes have the right to judge anybody, still less condemn him to death. 'Judge not lest ye be judged,' sayeth the Lord."

The inquisitor unrolled a scroll and read the charges in a flat monotone. "Do you deny that you use an effigy of Satan in your blasphemous rites? That you kiss the Prince of Darkness under his tail and on his privates?"

The perfect's eyes burned at the inquisitor. "The only kiss we exchange is the kiss of peace."

"Do you deny that once every month you meet in secret caves, there to perform orgies and other abominations?"

"Our creed is prayer and celibacy," the perfect answered, "more than can be said for your hedon priests. Once a month we do meet, but for confession of our sins. And if we gather in caves, it is because of your persecutions. We remind you that the very first worshippers of Christ were forced to do the same."

The crowd shouted its approval. The inquisitor said quickly, "Do you deny that you permit women to preach? That they can even grant your last rites?"

"We are all children of the one God, woman no less than man."

This had a great effect on the women in the crowd. The inquisitor grew flustered and played his strongest card. He thrust a crucifix before the perfect's face. "Do you deny that you commit sacrilegious acts against the holy cross?"

"Take that abomination away!" the perfect thundered. "Do you not have eyes to see that His broken body is but a symbol of the devil's victory?"

The crowd gasped at this and the inquisitor said triumphantly, "Do you further deny that the world was created by God the Father?"

"He who created this terrestrial world and this weak flesh—he is called Satan! His hand it was that helped God to create this earth, which is why there is both good and evil in it."

"Cease your blaspheming!" the inquisitor hissed.

The perfect plunged ahead, "It is the task of all of us to root out the evil in ourselves. Not in others, but in ourselves! And by leading a pure life, to return to God, purified."

"Enough of this," von Vehringen interrupted. The inquisitor was not faring well; the crowd's sympathies were leaning toward the perfect. "Begin!" von Vehringen called.

"No!" Laurelle cried out. "Not the child!"

Roger held her fast to prevent her from running to the stake. "You must be quiet," he warned her, "lest they accuse us."

"Let them!" Laurelle cried. "Can you not see that the child could be you? She could be me?"

"And what of our responsibility to the children of our army?" Roger demanded. "What of Jerusalem?"

But Laurelle, deaf to everything save the child's cries, fought to twist from Roger's grasp.

The soldiers piled green wood around the condemned. Priests and monks began to chant, but the perfect's voice carried over theirs. "The devil created this material world for the purpose of entrapping the soul and imprisoning it in a cage of flesh. With the death of Christ, Satan brought into being the church of Rome; this whore of Babylon now persecutes 'the pure,' the true believers in Jesus."

"Amen," the other Cathars called, and the old woman nodded her gummy grin.

"Light the fires!" von Vehringen shouted.

Roger fought to hold onto Laurelle as the monks moved forward to put the torch to the brambles. With a crackle, the flames licked slowly around the sap-wet wood, chosen to intensify the heat.

"I welcome the flames," the perfect called. "With them, I am released from my body, and purified, I go to God." The fire advanced to the hem of his robe and his words came faster. "I say unto you that there are two gods, the evil and the good. The evil hides behind the name of Jehovah, Baal, Jupiter and the god of the Roman church. True knowledge is the only way to redemption. The children of darkness . . ."

The perfect began to cough. In the crowd, Harolde started to cough also. The perfect, half-hidden by a wall of fire, continued, "The children of darkness . . . will forever do battle with . . . the children of light. Christ was such a messenger of the light, a spirit of the higher order sent by God to instruct man in the ways of purity. Christ is the soul of mankind. Christ is . . ."

Laurelle's scream twined with the child's last agonized cry.

The perfect slumped forward, and the priests and the inquisitors of Brother Dominic continued the monotone of prayer in rhythm to the roar of the consuming fire.

Laurelle buried her face in Roger's chest. "And we just stood here and watched!"

Harolde cleared his throat. "Is it not better for them to be cleansed this way rather than spend all eternity in the fires of hell? After their time is served in purgatory, they at least have a chance to be redeemed."

Gunther shook his head slowly. "I do not understand. For if they believed in Jesus . . ."

"It is not the same," Harolde said quickly.

"Are there two then with the same name?" Gunther asked.

"Only the one, the true Son of God," Harolde explained. "But these Cathars have perverted His teachings to mean something He did not intend. And so the church judged them for their sins."

Jonathan toed the ground. "But for what reason do we march?" he asked softly. Roger locked eyes with Jonathan. The unspoken thought flowed between them, conjuring up their confrontation at Mainz Cathedral.

Roger turned to Harolde. "My dear brother, do not be angry with me, I beg you. But I must ask you this: if our Lord had witnessed this sight today, would He have lit—?"

"Beware! You have been listening to sinful voices!" Harolde snapped, with a scathing glance at Jonathan.

Roger touched the monk's sleeve. "Harolde, did we not take an oath of peace? Do we not march for a different world than the one we see in this square?"

"You speak like the child you are!" Harolde cried, yanking his arm away. "I took no such oath!" He stormed off.

The rest of the afternoon, Harolde seethed. A dozen times he verged on quitting the pilgrimage; only his promise to Baron Thorne stopped him.

The archdeacon of Strasbourg Cathedral allowed the band to spend the night in the church, "providing you make no noise. As for food for your army, only the bishop can decide that and right now he is taken up with the pressing matter of the heretics."

The advance guard bedded down on the stone floor of the transept and watched the day's last light pass through the stained-glass windows to bejewel the soaring interior. With darkness, the old and new parts of the cathedral blended into a single quiet gloom.

"How is it that Jonathan does not sleep in the church with us?" Poldus asked sleepily.

"Why do you ask?" Roger said, his mind racing for a reason that would sound convincing.

"I ask because I ask," Poldus grumbled. "In all these weeks, he has not slept indoors once. Do you not think that strange?"

Laurelle said hurriedly, "Oh, you see, Poldus, long ago we decided that it was Jonathan's job to tend to the animals. So, naturally, he sleeps with them."

Poldus's grunt did not sound as if he had been convinced.

While the others dropped off to sleep, Laurelle stared at the votive lights banked on the altar. They were tended by the monk who had been the inquisitor. Laurelle stood up slowly. Her eyes widened as she watched the wax of the candles melt together to run in fiery rivulets down the altar steps, along the transept and nave, building in intensity until a wall of fire raced toward her.

In the advancing flames Laurelle saw the charring faces of the scrivener and his wife, the death's head of the perfect, and heard the echoing scream of the child.

Laurelle waded through the flames until she reached the black-robed inquisitor. She began to beat at him with her small fists. The startled monk fought her off and shouted for his brethren to rescue him until the entire cathedral rang with his clamor.

Roger and Harolde started awake and ran to Laurelle. They grabbed her flailing arms but she kept cursing the inquisitor and straining to get at him.

"The devil has taken possession of her senses!" the inquisitor cried, nursing his bleeding lip.

"Laurelle, what is it?" Roger asked.

"The child," Laurelle choked.

Roger nodded. "Yes, you are troubled. We all are. But you will see, it will be better tomorrow."

Laurelle shook her head wildly. "No, it cannot be tomorrow. For you see, the fire has eaten tomorrow!"

After an hour of trying to talk sense into Laurelle, the inquisitor threw up his hands. "This is hopeless. She must be given the cure. For unless these devils are exorcised from her body. . . ."

Despite Roger's protestations, two *Domini canes* spread Laurelle's arms and lashed her up onto the rood screen of the altar.

"Pray God this cure for madness works," the inquisitor said. "Otherwise, we shall be forced to drill a hole in her head to let the demons out. Failing that . . ." He said no more, but Harolde and Roger clutched at each other, for his meaning was clear.

The inquisitor sprinkled holy water on Laurelle, intoning, "Here in the heart of God's house, we pray that the Holy Spirit will enter this poor sinner and calm the madness that afflicts her. We pray that—"

Laurelle's cries cut off the inquisitor. Her body cringed, her mouth worked as though gasping for air, and long after the monk had stuffed a gag into her mouth, Laurelle's eyes continued to scream at him.

Throughout the long night Roger crouched at Laurelle's feet, sobbing and praying for her, whispering that he loved her and that everything would be all right if only she would get well. In time, Laurelle's body gradually lost its tenseness; then she slumped and fell into a coma.

Harolde awoke at the tolling of the bells at midnight, and again two hours later, his chilled bones aching from the stone floor. Each time his eyes sought out Laurelle still tied to the rood screen. He suffered with her in her agony, but he was also consumed with anger; especially with Roger, for the boy had challenged him at the heart of his belief.

"And as for the little Jew!" Harolde muttered to himself, "is he not the cause of all this hard feeling?"

Falling on his knees before the altar, Harolde prayed for Laurelle's sanity, prayed for his own soul to be cleansed of doubt, prayed for the Holy Spirit to enter him. Already weakened by days of hunger, he felt his mind begin to wander. The flickering light of the altar candles played over the wooden crucifix high above him, and the body, weighted by its own mortality, hung from the cross in a triangle of death.

"It could *not* be the devil's triumph!" Harolde cried out.

But as to whether or not the Lord would have lit the fires, the answer came back with such a resounding "No!" that Harolde buried his face in his hands and began to sob.

"And the sweet helpless child. . ."

Exhausted from his tears, Harolde went back to the rood screen where Laurelle hung in twisted unconsciousness. Roger huddled at her feet, his mouth working in his sleep.

"You are right," Harolde whispered to the sleeping boy. "We do march for a better way." Then Harolde looked up at Laurelle, tears filling his eyes again. "Laurelle, forgive me . . . if I could but change places with you . . . the child should have been saved . . . I swear I will never let this happen again."

Armed with his new resolve, Harolde searched the cathedral until he found a priest, woke him, and insisted that he administer the crusading oath to him right then and there.

On his knees, Harolde clasped his hands and gazed up at the crucifix. "On pain of my immortal soul, I do solemnly swear that I shall not rest until I set foot in the Holy Land and walk in peace in the footsteps of the Lord . . . so help me God."

At dawn, the black-robed monks returned to the rood screen to find Laurelle awake but silent. The inquisitor undid the ropes binding her to the screen and Roger caught her as she fell.

The *Domini canes* looked on intently, waiting for the slightest sign of a relapse. Laurelle opened her mouth to speak but Roger said urgently, "Hush, my heart, hush, it has all been a bad dream."

With Roger gripping her hand to the hurting point, Laurelle managed to control herself.

Through the double file of black-robed monks Roger led Laurelle out of the cathedral and into the light of day.

BASLE:
EARLY AUGUST

I N THE NEXT TWO DAYS, TEN MORE OF THE CONDEMNED were burned at the stake. During the time of this purge, a total of eighty heretics were killed. The ecclesiastical courts were well pleased with their work; the inquisitors of Brother Dominic could now report Strasbourg free of heretics. So, when the army of children appeared, the city's gates were thrown open and they were greeted with cheers and food.

"Surely, the Lord has sent these young warriors as a sign," Bishop von Vehringen said. "With such an angelic host, can there be any doubt that God created the world for good?"

Flamonde and Laurelle had a tearful reunion. "Yes, I am still with our countrymen from Flanders," Flamonde told Laurelle and the others. "Though after our company lost more than half its members, we allied ourselves with a contingent from Normandy. It is best to be with the strong," Flamonde sighed. "They are the ones who usually get the food."

Flamonde looked wilder than ever, and yet more beautiful.

Her original reason for joining the Crusade, to protect Laurelle, had broadened to include any needy child, and legions flocked to her. Passing through Lauterberg, she had bargained with a farmer; a half-hour of her time for a pail of milk. For the first time in her life Flamonde felt guiltless about her transgressions, for with every sin she gave another day of life to her children.

In Strasbourg, a baker heaped her with loaves of bread and a costermonger with vegetables, much to Harolde's consternation. Now sitting at the campfire of the advance guard, Flamonde's demanding children clustered around her skirts. Somehow she managed to find the strength and time to tend to each one in turn, kissing Little Luke's scraped knee, picking burrs from Rudolph's long hair.

"Is it wise to give of yourself so unsparingly?" Laurelle asked her sister. "You look so much thinner, you seem so weary and sad, not at all like my laughing Flamonde."

"Weary I am, yes, but are we all not weary?" Flamonde murmured. "And who would not be sad after all we have seen?" Then slowly Flamonde straightened her shoulders. "But I am a strong tree with many branches, and there is room for all in need."

Harolde regarded Flamonde with a growing sense of unease, knowing that if he did not speak out against her sinning ways, he too would be guilty, if only by his silence. He took her aside and began stiffly, "I feel I must remind you that this is a holy crusade, for God's glory. But by your actions—Flamonde, I beg you, desist, for the salvation of your own soul."

Flamonde whirled on him. "Let each of us look to his own salvation! For me, I know of no greater homage to the Lord than to save the life of a child. And to that end I will do what I must!"

Harolde was taken aback by her vehemence but he would not be put off. "And should you conceive? What then? Do you dare burden an innocent soul with such shame?"

Flamonde lowered her gaze. "Have no fear on that account, monk. For His own reasons, the Lord has seen fit to deny me the joys of bearing a child. And so the children of the world must be my children."

"Oh, doubtless that is a pretty conceit for you," Harolde said angrily, "but surely you know that you are setting a wicked example for the little ones. You say you transgress for the children, but could it be that it is just an excuse to pleasure yourself?"

Flamonde's green eyes flashed in the fire-lit shadows. "In the beginning, perhaps. But no more. Now there are only lives to be saved. And if I have any guilt at all, it is that you and I and people like us . . . well, if we had lived by the spirit, would these children have had to march? We have caused them great harm . . . But what is your concern in all this? Why do you plague me with your shalts and shalt nots when there is so much to be done?"

Flamonde returned to the campfire and began to prepare the vegetables. Harolde followed her back and Flamonde glared at him every so often.

"Who would guess that this was our same army?" Roger said, shaking his head at the ragged groups camped in the square.

"How long since you last saw us?" Flamonde asked. "Two weeks? Much has happened since then. Soon after we left Mainz, discipline fell apart. Dicing and wenching and beatings. We pleaded with Nicholas to intervene, but he and his guard were having a hard enough time protecting what they had. Then the army cleansed itself by banishing the most wicked from the pilgrimage."

Flamonde swept the thick fall of hair from her face and went on. "Food became scarce and the army depended on the kindness of the villagers. The peasants gave willingly, for the poor have always been God's elect. But there was never enough to feed all, and so Nicholas divided the lion's share among his lieutenants and to those children known to him. In this way did the fawning over Nicholas grow even stronger.

"When we received no provisions at all at Worms, hundreds deserted. A like amount died of fever, though Nicholas insisted that his angel had told him it was not plague. Then, a terrible tragedy." Flamonde stared into the fire, remembering. "A child wandered off into the forest, hoping to find some berries, and a pack of wolves . . . oh, merciful God, the screams," she whispered, and pressed her hands to her ears. "We rushed out to rescue him but found only pieces." She rubbed her hand angrily across her eyes.

"But the most frightening thing—scores of children have simply disappeared. Right from camp. They bedded down with us at night, but in the morning?" Flamonde snapped her fingers. "Gone! Some say they sneaked off and went home, but I do not believe that. I myself have seen dark demons circling beyond our campfires, and heard children screaming as they were snatched off."

Harolde clasped his hands. "Why, oh why, are we being afflicted this way?" he asked, his eyes glancing over Jonathan.

Of the twenty thousand who began the crusade, only twelve thousand remained. And this hurt Harolde sorely. But what pained him to the quick was the dramatic change in Nicholas. At the meeting with their leader to plan the next leg of the journey, Harolde and Roger saw that Nicholas's attendants had grown into a court of more than thirty. Nicholas had long been accepting gifts from the devoted, the Greek cross around his neck now hung from a heavy gold chain. Children shoved and kicked to touch the hem of his robe so they might later brag about it. The choicest food went first to Nicholas, still round-cheeked, then filtered down to his lieutenants.

"The army must keep its guiding light safe, no matter how many others fall," Poldus explained, as he gnawed on a venison bone Nicholas had thrown him.

When Roger and Harolde finally emerged from the tent, Harolde shook his head, confused. "I love him still," he said. "But I loved the child more when he was one of us."

The advance guard left Strasbourg a day before the main army. The terrain became quite flat and the guard made good time.

Having been lavishly praised by Nicholas for his liaison work, Poldus was full of himself. "See this phial of holy water?" he said to Jonathan. "It is known to guard against fevers and to ward off demons. Our sainted Nicholas blessed it himself. Already I have been offered four sous for it, but because we are comrades, I will let you have it for two."

"I do not have two sous, nor even one," Jonathan said.

"Oh, there are other ways you can pay it off," Poldus said with a grin, and rubbed his thighs.

"Even if I had money I would not buy it," Jonathan said.

With a lightning move, Poldus grabbed Jonathan's arm and twisted it behind his back. "You dare question Nicholas's sanctity?"

Laurelle saw the commotion and came between the struggling boys. She drew Jonathan away on the pretext of helping her dress a pigeon for their meal.

Jonathan rubbed his numbed shoulder. "One day I shall have to face up to him."

"I beg you, do not," Laurelle said. "Flamonde told me that when Poldus got back to camp, he found that his Germaine had taken up with another boy. The next day they discovered the lad all beaten. Though nobody could prove Poldus responsible, the wise ones avoid him. Please, I beg you, do the same, if only for my sake."

The town of Kolmar had heard reports of the children's crusade, both French and German, from Lorraine and Burgundy. At the monastery of Marbach, the chronicler of the Augustinian house cried out against the dementia. "It is doomed to inevitable failure," he wrote, "for it is undertaken without the balance of reason or the force of counsel."

Throughout the area, the clergy preached this message; consequently, all towns within a twenty-mile radius barred their gates and locked up their children.

Then one morning, beyond Mulhouse, the advance guard woke to find the air lighter and not as cloying as it had been.

Harolde spread his map on the ground. "The city ahead is Basle," he said. "Beyond it lie the mountains of the Alps."

Gunther hefted his cross to a more comfortable position on his back. "These mountains, are they very high?"

"The highest in all the world," Harolde said. "And there is no way around. We must climb them to reach Genoa and the sea."

"We are coming then to the most dangerous part of our pilgrimage," Roger said soberly.

"Never fear, God will guide us through," Gunther said.

"When it is dark and they go to sleep, it would be a simple matter to . . ." Baalbek drew his finger across his throat.

"How many times must I tell you?" Frizio said irritably. "I have other plans for them. Do not worry, Baalbek, when this is over, you shall have your chance to toy with one of them, I promise you."

From his vantage point atop the Basle Cathedral bell tower, Frizio watched the army approach. The church stood on a cliff fronting the river, at the point where the rushing waters turned sharply north to flow into the Rhineland. Across the Rhine, some nine hundred feet wide here, lay the deep sha-dowed green of the Black Forest, and to the southwest, the pale beginnings of the Jura Mountains.

Frizio stared down intently at the golden speck that was Mirage. The stallion, with Roger astride, rode in the vanguard of the army. Thousands of children jammed the square, flow-ing around the cathedral to fill the eastern terrace, which ran right up to the cliff's edge.

In honor of the army's arrival, work this day had been sus-pended on the cathedral, now in its final stages of construc-tion. At every flying buttress stood a carved stone statue from the Old and New Testament, making it appear that a host of angels supported the diamond-patterned tile roof.

Frizio did some quick estimating. "Ten thousand, perhaps a thousand more or less. These milling children remind me of our annual roundup of wild horses in the Sinai. The weakest of the herd are always snared first. One has to persevere to capture the hardy stock. But it is that flesh that brings the highest prices, eh, Baalbek?"

Now the army massed below made Frizio tremble with the possibilities. It seemed as if his meditation that night in Mainz had sprung full blown from his head into this reality. "If we lay our plans well and have just a little luck," he said to Baalbek, "not only shall we have our revenge, but what a price they will bring in the slave markets!"

Each Crusade that Europe mounted had whetted the appe-tites of the Mideast for these pearly-skinned, fair-haired Franks with their sturdy bodies and unending energies. As Frizio watched them, he saw not the children, but the gold that would buy him a house in Jerusalem, staffed with slaves and concubines. He imagined a flaxen-haired lad as his body servant, and a gray-eyed wraith as the prize in his harem. A stone house with date palms in the atrium and a reflecting pool to cool the days and bring the moon to earth at night. He knew of such a place—on the hill of Golgotha, overlooking the Church of the Holy Sepulcher.

For all his thirty-three years, Frizio had wandered from one end of the earth to the other, seeking his fortune. "Now at last I will be able to strike roots in the fairest city in all the world, devote myself to a life of ease and pleasure. Time also to father some legitimate sons instead of the bastards I have seeded everywhere. Mirage, too, will be put out to pasture, to sire a race of unparalleled Arabians." Frizio smiled at the turn of the wheel which had brought it all within his grasp.

An argument had begun in the square below and the shouts of "Mt. Cenis!" and "St. Gotthard!" floated up to Frizio.

"They are deciding which route to take," he said. "Come, we must make sure they go the safest way. The greater the number who reach the sea, the greater our profit." Frizio started down the circular staircase, Baalbek lumbering behind.

Frizio reached the square at the peak of the argument. A Premonstran monk who had journeyed to Rome the year before argued passionately for using the St. Gotthard pass. "It is by far the shortest route to the Lombard plain, and from there Genoa is but a few days away."

The archpriest of Basle Cathedral pleaded with Nicholas to go via the Mt. Cenis pass. "It was over Mt. Cenis that Emperor Henry IV went to prostrate himself before Pope Gregory at Canossa. And Philip Augustus also chose this route when he led his army on Crusade."

"But it is longer by more than ten days!" the monk cried.

"True," the archpriest agreed, "but the Mt. Cenis pass is not as high nor as treacherous. Of what merit is it to gain a few days at the cost of your lives?"

Frizio nudged Baalbek. "They will go by way of Mt. Cenis, that is the sane thing to do. Remember our trek over the St. Gotthard? Never again! It is too dangerous, even for grown men."

Quiet fell over the crowd as Nicholas pondered. "I have heard your voices," he sang out. "But no voice has been as clear as the voice of my angel. And he said to me, 'Have you not been guided this far? Have you not survived the trials of nature and the inhumanity of man?' " Nicholas raised his arms. "Speak not to me of popes and emperors! Speak to me only of the Lord! And I say that every moment we delay puts off the day of judgment! Let those of faint heart go by way of Mt. Cenis. For myself, my angel will guide me over the St. Gotthard! Who will march with me?"

An affirmative roar answered Nicholas, and the palmer's staffs and the crosses beat against the sky.

"But this is sheer madness!" Frizio exclaimed to Baalbek. "Many more than necessary will die in the attempt to cross the St. Gotthard! It is as if they actively seek their own destruction!" Infuriated, he kicked Baalbek.

"Come," Frizio decided impulsively. "We will no longer follow the army. We have too many arrangements to make to bother with the capture of a child here or there. We go to Marseille."

In Marseille were the offices of two shipowners, Hugo Ferrus and William Porquierres; they also had branch offices in Venice and Genoa. Having done profitable business with Ferrus and Porquierres before, Frizio felt certain that the merchants would jump at his proposal.

"Fresh horses and supplies," Frizio said to Baalbek. "We leave at once."

Disappointment pulled at the corners of Baalbek's mouth. "Then we will not get Mirage back?"

"Yes, yes," Frizio said impatiently. "But not right now. Nothing must interfere with the master plan. Marseille first. Then time enough to settle all accounts when the children reach Genoa. For we shall be waiting for them there."

LAKE LUCERNE

ROGER TURNED AND WAVED TO THE RHINE, A silver slash in the pale gray dawn. "It is like leaving an old friend," he said, "that has guided and fed us for more than a month."

The advance guard headed south across the plateau country wedged between the Jura range and the Alps. The early morning fog dissipated with the rising sun, revealing tiny villages nestled at the foot of the heavily wooded hills. For a day, then two, the guard moved ever upward in this hilly region divided by ravines and steep-walled valleys.

Buff-colored cattle and woolly brown sheep grazed in rolling meadows of lupine and poppy. Poldus galloped off on his donkey "to get our night's food!" only to come crashing down the slope moments later pursued by a snarling dog. The shepherd, outlined against the brilliant blue sky, kept a wary eye on the travelers. All strangers were suspect here, the houses of Zahringen and Hapsburg being in constant conflict with the local forest cantons for control of this shortest route to the plains of Lombardy and its wealth.

The people of this region were appreciably shorter than the Rhinelanders, with thick legs, bony heads, and cheeks pinked bright by sun and wind. They shared their food unstintingly. When Roger tried to persuade the young shepherds and farmers to join their cause, he found no recruits. Though life was hard, the children in these parts were not so harshly treated and there was always enough to eat.

If Roger was unsuccessful with his recruiting, Poldus fared far better with his endeavors. With determined door-to-door peddling, he managed to sell three bottles of holy water.

Beyond Zofingen, a gentle bell tinkled through the forest, then a brown cow appeared, tagged after by her newborn calf. The cow would not suffer anybody to milk her except

Gunther. She followed the band until dusk, the bell sounding behind them, until Gunther gently, but quite firmly, told her, "No, you cannot come to Jerusalem with us; it is much too far for the calf."

Four days after leaving Basle, the advance guard reached the wild, mysterious shores of Lake Lucerne. A scrubbed fishing village straddled the lake's northwestern tip. A series of tall square towers connected by crenolated walls protected the northern approaches. Jagged mountains ringed the lake, their ice-capped peaks changing color with the changing light. On the horizon lay an endless series of seemingly impenetrable blue-on-blue mountains.

Merchants with their armed guards thronged the town. Despite the dangers of the St. Gotthard pass, the opening of the route some years before to pack-horse caravans had made Lucerne an important staging point between the cloth-weaving cities of northern Europe and the trade routes in Italy.

The old deacon at the Church of St. Leger near fainted when Roger informed him that ten thousand children were a day's march behind the advance guard. A venerable man, he threw up his hands and stammered, "Lord protect us! How will you pass? After the town of Brunnen there is no road; the cliff goes straight down into the lake!"

"How do others pass?" Laurelle asked.

"One must take the ferry down the Bay of Uri to Flüelen."

"Then we shall take the ferry also," Roger said.

The deacon kneaded his hands anxiously. "There are not enough boats for ten thousand! And what of the toll charges? It would cost a king's ransom for so many!"

"Have no fear," Harolde said, "the Lord will provide."

"And beyond?" the deacon cried. "Strong men have died in the gorges of the Schonellen, and the St. Gotthard pass itself! Two months ago a caravan of merchants set out to cross it, and have not been heard of since."

Then tears sprang to the deacon's eyes as he looked at the cross strapped to Gunther's back. "The climb is terrible enough without that additional burden. Surely the Lord will not mind if you lay it down?"

Gunther comforted the old man, and promised he would consider it; but the following morning, he set out with the others, the cross tied firmly to his back.

A haphazard road took the guard around the wild and craggy shores of the lake to the town of Weggis. Mt. Rigi, with its outcropping of red rock, stood directly behind them; across the waters, the sun flamed the ice cap of Mt. Pilatus, while the lake reflected the shimmering upside-down mountains.

From Weggis, the flower-strewn path formed a continuous quay along the steep lake shoreline. Though at an altitude of almost fifteen hundred feet, they were facing due south, and the dreaded and revered Foehn winds made the vegetation near tropical.

The terrain grew wilder still and they made camp in a copse of evergreen and larch some fifty yards from the shore. A red fox and her kits eyed them warily from their burrow. The traps Poldus set snared two brown hares. Laurelle skinned them, and while the meat was roasting, fashioned the hides into makeshift shoes. The sun dropped behind the peaks, and lake, sky, and mountains turned all shades of blue. The smell of sizzling meat and burning wood mingled with the sharp blue twilight.

The clear, thin air made Harolde's head spin. His cough had diminished since leaving Basle; why, he did not know. But now he was given to spells of mind wanderings. Today, as he rode on Tortoise, he had been obsessed with a continuing reverie. The college of cardinals first offered him the mitred hat, next the papal tiara, but he rejected them all. Instead, holding aloft a palm frond, he had ridden Tortoise through the Golden Gate into Jerusalem.

Somewhere in the forest, a wolf bayed its mournful call, answered by another, then another, until the children seemed ringed by the pack.

"It is hunting time," Poldus said, "and they are brazen with hunger. We must keep the fire high or they will sneak right into camp."

"Especially watch the horses," Roger said to Jonathan.

Laurelle felt so weary her fingers and jaws buzzed. A wave

of heaviness, of the body and spirit, overcame her and she reached out for reassurance. "Harolde? Tell us again how it will be when we reach Genoa."

Harolde looked at her dreamily. Why Genoa? he wondered, when he was already moving from the Golden Gate toward the Via Dolorosa?

Roger said in counterpoint to the baying wolves, "We will find our way through these mountains. We will reach the sea. Nicholas will raise his voice to heaven. God will attend and cause the sea to part as He did for the children of Israel. We will walk across and so enter the Kingdom of Jerusalem."

Gradually, as Roger spoke, his voice lost its weariness. The others listened intently, their need to believe shining in their eyes.

Roger leaned toward the fire, conjuring what would come to pass. "Armed only with God's mercy, we shall win the enemy over. Not a fist raised in anger, not a sword drawn for blood. But as the prophets have promised, we will be the messengers of that day when all men shall join hands."

Slowly, Roger extended his arms and they all joined hands around the fire. "We will live in peace," he went on, "and as it has been foretold in the Book of Daniel and Revelations, the world will have passed from the age of the father, which is the age of law, to the age of the son, which is the age of mercy, to the age of the Holy Spirit, which is the time of our final judgment."

The children's hands gripped tight with the bond of brotherhood. Then Jonathan whispered, "Amen," and the others answered, "Amen." Gunther leaned over to Poldus and kissed his cheek, Poldus turned to Laurelle, and so the kiss of peace traveled around the circle.

Harolde and Jonathan took the first watch. Harolde wrapped his arms around his chest, stifling a cough. "You know, don't you?" he said to Jonathan. "You will not tell? After all, I have kept your secret."

"I will not tell," Jonathan reassured him.

"Is there nothing I can do? No herbs you know of?"

"There is much you can do," Jonathan said. "Foremost is rest. Every step you take robs you of strength. If you could remain here at a monastery for a few months. . . ."

"Impossible," Harolde whispered vehemently. "I pledged my word to the baron."

"He would not want you to risk your own life," Jonathan said.

Harolde shook his head. "It is more than that. There is also my crusading vow. I *must* go on. Rather would I lose my life than deny my oath to the Lord."

Jonathan did not say anything to this. After a bit, Harolde nodded off and Jonathan covered him with Mirage's saddle blanket. The wolves howled again, closer this time, and Jonathan threw another log on the fire. Then he got up and checked the horses. He peered into the forest and thought he saw burning eyes under every bush. He threw a rock and the bushes rustled as some creature slunk off. Jonathan collected a pile of rocks and heaved one into the darkness each time he heard something. In this way did the hours of his watch pass.

Poldus had been wakened earlier by the murmur of voices but pretended to be asleep. What is Harolde's secret? Poldus wondered. More important, what is Jonathan hiding? All during their march, Poldus had watched Jonathan carefully; plainly, he was not like any of them. Now, almost positive that he had discovered the mystery, Poldus plotted ways to trick Jonathan into exposing himself.

The melancholy sound of the ten-foot-long alpenhorn wound through the forest, rolled up the mountainside, and carried across the expanse of Lake Lucerne. Again and again the note sounded from the quay on Brunnen, summoning everybody in the forest cantons.

The advance guard waited impatiently at the tiny stone church. When they had arrived in Brunnen early that afternoon, they saw what the deacon of Lucerne had warned them of. Beyond Brunnen, the wild and ominous shores of the Bay of Uri were impassable; the sheer, twisted cliff plunged straight down into the lake.

Roger told his tale to the village elder, a grizzled man in stiff leather clothing. The elder thought the boy mad and told him to be gone. Then, as Roger had done in countless villages when they refused to believe, he reminded the elder that "the Holy Father in Rome has himself called for a Crusade to free Palestine and has guaranteed all such Crusaders protection."

The elder raised his hand, unsure whether or not to smack the impertinent lad, until Harolde, holding up his rosary, added "All this on pain of excommunication if charity is not given."

Then was the alpenhorn blown. The representatives of the forest cantons of Schwyz, Uri, and Unterwalden soon began arriving and, by day's end, were congregated in the town meeting house. An incredulous buzz swept the gathering when Roger repeated his tale. Farmers laughed in short, exasperated bursts; women giggled.

Herr Blutkopf, the most influential man in Schwyz, got up to speak. A burst blood vessel in his left eye gave him a squint-eyed, evil appearance. "Is this why we have been called here?" he demanded. "My boats lie at anchor, the fish go uncaught and I am made to listen to the nonsense of children? I have no time for this!"

"Ah!" Roger called out. "But you had time to ferry the armies of the Holy Roman emperors, did you not? Soldiers weighted with sword and spear? Well, I tell you that we, too, are soldiers, of the Lord. No doubt, you would transport us if we paid you—say thirty pieces of silver?"

Blutkopf, a man of fiery temperament, rushed at Roger, but Gunther and Harolde held him off.

"Nobody, *nobody* questions my love for the Lord!" Blutkopf shouted. There were many in the meeting house who might have argued this, but since Herr Blutkopf was by far the richest man in the canton and employed scores. . . .

"How many children did you say?" Blutkopf fumed.

"I do not know the exact number, since we may have lost some since Basle," Roger said. "Perhaps ten thousand."

"When do you say they will be here?" Blutkopf demanded.

"They are a day's march behind us," Roger said.

"And I say you are either mad or a liar, the Lord curse you!" Blutkopf exclaimed. He had only one purpose now, to show Roger up as a fraud. "I will set you a bargain, and the Lord be my witness to this. If by nightfall tomorrow, five thousand— nay, one thousand! If one thousand children arrive in Brunnen, then we will ferry all who appear down the Bay of Uri to Flüelen without charge! But, if fewer than one thousand appear, then you and your five cohorts in evil shall be our indentured servants for one year. Agreed?"

Jonathan nudged Roger. "It may be that the army will not be able to get here that quickly."

Roger nodded. He tried to bargain for more time, but Blutkopf, sensing victory, remained adamant. "Nightfall tomorrow, or nothing!"

The children held a hurried conference. "Can it be that somehow God has arranged this pact so that our army might have free transportation?" Roger asked. "How else would we ever be able to cross the lake?" The others came to the same conclusion.

"We accept then," Roger said to Blutkopf.

Blutkopf's jaw dropped. He had not expected Roger to comply, truly believing him to be bluffing. Now Blutkopf wanted to back down, but hard-and-fast positions had been taken and he was too important a man in the community to lose face— and to a child!

By a show of hands the members of the cantons voted to accept Blutkopf's wager. Free transportation against indentured labor for a year. The deadline: nightfall on the morrow.

Roger started to saddle Mirage. Blutkopf grabbed him and yelled, "Where do you think . . . ?"

Roger yanked his arm free. "I go to make sure that the army arrives on time. I am leaving you five members of my guard as surety." Mirage reared under Roger's spur, scattering the crowd as he galloped off.

"That is the last we shall see of him," Blutkopf said. He pointed to Gunther. "I will take that one there."

"A moment," Harolde interrupted. "You have made a bargain, is that not right?" He looked to the parish priest for confirmation.

The priest nodded. "Nightfall, tomorrow."

"So be it then," Blutkopf laughed, and headed for the tavern, with it's steep-pitched roof and carved gingerbread decorations.

The advance guard did not sleep much that night. Their prayers were with Roger as he galloped through the darkness.

THE BAY OF URI

TENSION GREW THROUGHOUT THE DAY AS ALL Brunnen awaited the outcome of the children's gamble. Laurelle used the time to scrub herself and her clothes clean in the tingly lake, keeping a sharp eye out for Poldus.

But Poldus was otherwise occupied, for with Roger gone, he seized command and became very officious, ordering the guard about with insignificant tasks. Poldus strode to the stable where Jonathan was just finishing currying Tortoise.

"No matter how much I comb and brush you, Tortoise," Jonathan said, "you still look like the moths have been at you."

"Hurry up and finish with that stupid beast," Poldus ordered. "You must do my donkey next." When Jonathan did not respond quickly enough, Poldus punched him in the mouth.

After Poldus left, Jonathan gingerly tested his loosened tooth. "I did not fight back for the others' sake," Jonathan told Tortoise. Tortoise turned to look at him, lowered her lashes and peed on his foot. "You are right, Tortoise," Jonathan sighed, "I did not fight back because I fear him."

The sun seemed to speed across the sky this day, and before the children were prepared, it sank beneath the range of mountains. At the meeting house, the members of the Waldstatten drank their brews and ate thick hunks of cheese. Herr Blutkopf called to Gunther, "Gather your belongings, boy; we leave shortly."

Gunther looked helplessly at Jonathan, who kept searching the lake road. Already in the east, the deepening blue had filtered down the mountainside and into the valleys.

Herr Blutkopf shouted to the priest, "It is time?"

"Not yet," the priest called back. "But soon," the priest said to Harolde. "I cannot delay it much longer."

Blutkopf got up, stretched, then pressed his hand to his head and stood swaying on his feet.

Jonathan saw this. Desperate for time, he hurried to Blutkopf. "These dizzy spells you are having," Jonathan said under his breath.

Blutkopf started, almost losing his balance. "What—? There is nothing wrong with me!" he grunted.

But Jonathan would not be put off. "The dizziness when you get out of bed, or throw your nets too quickly; I know of things that can cure it. Listen to me. Otherwise, who knows what may happen when you are out alone on your boat?"

Blutkopf backed away from the boy. Jonathan followed, whispering urgently. "And your eye? You know the left one is the eye of the soul? See how red and angry it is."

Blutkopf crossed himself, frightened that Jonathan might be a witch. He had told no one of these spells, not even his wife.

"You must be bled," Jonathan confided. "Yours is a body too rich with the dark blood. Not with the knife, leeches only. They must be applied here and here," Jonathan said, touching Blutkopf's throbbing temples. "Further, do not eat of the red meat, nor innards, and avoid all arguments that anger the blood; especially do not beat your wife and. . . ." As the twilight deepened, Jonathan kept on talking, concocting a remedy half fact, half fantasy. Soon the first star appeared, joined by another and another.

The other villagers, hearing Jonathan prescribe for Blutkopf, thought the child gifted with healing powers and pressed their own ailments. The attention snatched from him, Blutkopf snapped back to the moment. "Enough!" he said. "It is an hour beyond the appointed time!"

"Listen!" Jonathan said.

Blutkopf cocked his head. "I hear nothing."

"Listen to the silence," Jonathan told him.

In truth, an unnatural quiet had fallen over the land. Then, faintly at first, no more distinct than the wind rustling through the larch, came a distant murmur growing with each heartbeat. The villagers rushed down to the lakefront. They saw it then, a long line of torches weaving in and out of the trees while thousands of children lifted their voices to herald their arrival. Their song echoed between the narrow cliffs of Uri and rose toward the night sky:

> Fair is the sunshine
> Fairer still the moonlight
> And the sparkling starry host . . .

Now the first legions came upon the townpeople, banners and crosses raised on high, torchlight haloing their heads. Higher rose their song and as they marched into the village, the members of the advance guard joined in spiritedly:

> Jesus shines brighter
> Jesus shines purer
> Than all the angels heaven can boast!

The men of the forest cantons shook their heads in wonder. Where reason would have dictated otherwise, faith had prevailed. When the priest knelt by the roadside, every villager knelt also, and a contrite Blutkopf was among the very first.

Flamonde and her brood of young were the last to file into Brunnen. Flamonde carried a new addition: an infant cradled in a sling around her shoulders. The babe's mother, no more than a child herself, had died in childbirth and Flamonde labored to save the infant. "She reminds me of you when you were first born," Flamonde said to Laurelle.

Laurelle spent the night with her sister, tending to the children's needs, crooning them to sleep. She gave Flamonde her rabbit skin slippers and Flamonde promptly cut them down to make a pair each for Rudolph and Little Luke.

The villagers of Brunnen worked through the night making hurried preparations for the crossing. Every boat was commandeered; hulls were caulked, sails patched. The fleet would not fish the next day, though it be Friday. Instead, the priest proclaimed a fast in honor of the children and their mission.

Range upon range of mountains lit up with dawn, until it seemed the whole world must be made of mountains. Cautious sailors sniffed the air and searched the sky. "Misty, that is good," Blutkopf said, "the weather is more likely to hold. If the day be clear, then may the Foehn winds strike suddenly."

Though every skiff, rowboat, and sailboat had been pressed into service, the army numbered so many that repeated trips would have to be made to ferry all across. Nicholas and his lieutenants stood in the lead boat, Nicholas at the prow, holding high his Greek cross. As the church bells rang out the good tidings, the boats set sail through the swirling mists of the wild and ominous lake.

All day long the men of Brunnen rowed and sailed down the eight miles of the Bay of Uri, unloading the children at the hamlet of Flüelen. By noon, the mists evaporated and the lake turned such a serene blue it seemed joined to the sky. More than a third of the army had been transported by then. Later that afternoon, only one thousand remained waiting on Brunnen's wharf, but now billowing thunderheads massed on the southern horizon.

Roger and his band were in the last boats to leave, for Roger, who had not slept in thirty-six hours, collapsed after leading the army into Brunnen. The guard would not sail without him. Poldus fretted, preferring to go with Nicholas, but Nicholas had ordered him to stay with the guard.

To prove that he harbored no ill feelings, Blutkopf arranged to transport Roger and his band in his own large boat. The horses had to be coaxed on board, but Tortoise refused. After precious minutes of light had elapsed, Harolde let go of the reins. "Then I must leave you, my girl," he said, and climbed the gangplank, whereupon Tortoise promptly scrambled after him.

The last scores of boats set sail. They had gotten about a quarter of the way down the lake when the wind dropped. Blutkopf looked to the slack sail. "We must row," he said urgently. "Hard!" And they bent their backs to the oars. At the halfway point Blutkopf cried, "No use! We must turn back!" but a sudden gust of the Foehn wind snatched the words from his lips.

"Is it not the same distance?" Roger yelled.

Black clouds raced across the heavens, turning day into dark. A weird gray glow cloaked the mountainside and the lake took the color of the lowering sky. No turning back now, for whirlpools of wind tossed the boat about at will.

Gunther stared up at the striated rock of the cliff face, towering on the left. "The Lord crushed that mountain in His hand before flinging it into the lake," he gasped, the muscles in his back cording as he pulled on the oars.

Flüelen came in sight when the storm hit with full force, a hot wind straight from the mouth of hell that uprooted trees and sent them flying across the whitecapped waters. The wind scattered the boats, dashing some against the cliffs, smashing others together to sink with their cargoes of screaming children.

The mast of Blutkopf's boat cracked under the assault. The boat shuddered, then the lake came up to meet them as they capsized.

Laurelle hit the water and immediately got fouled in the rigging. Roger swam about, searching frantically, until he caught sight of her bobbing head. He managed to free her of the ropes, got an arm around her neck and started swimming for shore.

Air became trapped in Harolde's long robe, buoying him; when he stopped struggling he discovered he was being carried toward land. The cross strapped to Gunther's back served to keep him afloat; once a wave threw him against the cliff, but the wood of the cross broke the blow.

Mirage whinnied his anger at the wind as he fought the waters. Jonathan managed to catch the stallion's stirrup and hang on as Mirage swam vigorously toward land. Poldus thrashed off to Jonathan's right, but Jonathan did not see him; his eyes were fixed on Herr Blutkopf, who floundered just ahead. As Mirage swam past, Jonathan caught hold of Blutkopf's jerkin with his free hand, Mirage hauling them both along. Jonathan's arms felt as if they were being torn from his sockets, but he knew that if he let go, both he and Blutkopf would drown.

The townspeople of Flüelen plunged into the churning waves to rescue all they could. A wave washed Poldus into the arms of a cobbler, more dead than alive.

Campfires dotted the beaches of Flüelen. The leaders of each battalion reported back to Nicholas; when the roll calls were tallied, they found that the storm had taken more than two hundred sixty children to the depth of the wild, enchanted Bay of Uri, "There to rest until that day when the earth and sea shall give up its dead," Harolde intoned at the funeral services.

Fewer than nine thousand children remained.

Flamonde, her face haggard with grief, could not be consoled. She had lost three of her charges to the storm.

"At least God allowed you to save the baby," Laurelle said gently. "Now come, we must not lose any more to hunger and cold." Laurelle set about drying and feeding the shivering bunch. Flamonde wiped her eyes and with a righteous rage at God and the devil and whoever else she could think of, set to work also, and the two sisters labored to give what little comfort they could to the living.

With his matted hair, protruding eyes, and incoherent babblings, Poldus appeared as one possessed. In turn, he collared the members of the guard. "I must tell you what Jonathan did! I was drowning and he came riding by on his horse . . ." Poldus's harangue became so unintelligible that the others, beset with their own problems, soon drifted away.

"He has cast an evil spell on them all," Poldus muttered, glaring at Jonathan. "I must bide my time, wait until the moment is right . . ." Poldus broke off and furiously honed his dagger.

Blutkopf, much chastened by his brush with death, huddled before Roger's campfire. "And the worst is yet before you," he said. "If only I were younger! I would guide you through the pass myself." Instead, he spent the next hour explaining in detail the dangers ahead. The torturous defiles of the Schonellen gorge; the Devil's Bridge, the suspension catwalk that hung from an otherwise impassable cliff; and finally, the hell of the St. Gotthard itself, swept by blinding storms at its seven thousand-foot height.

"Be warned of wolves and bears," Blutkopf said. "Food is so scarce that they have taken to raiding livestock, even attacking farmers."

Roger tried to remember all that Blutkopf said, but his crammed head would take no more. "We thank you for all you have done," he said, embracing the stocky man. "As for the dangers, we will have to trust each day to take care of itself."

The rest of the night Blutkopf organized the villagers of Flüelen and collected every available article of heavy clothing: woolen capuchons and shawls, cloaks made of sheepskin and other furs, and distributed the garments among the army. "Would that we had enough for all the children," he said, shaking his head sadly. "For when you climb to the St. Gotthard pass, it will be as if you are marching through the dead of winter."

THE DEVIL'S BRIDGE

THE ROAD OUT OF FLÜELEN LED THROUGH A NAR-rowing gap to Altdorf, and then began its steady serpentine climb into the barrier mountains. Confronted by the foreboding series of brutal, snowcapped peaks, the advance guard was over-whelmed by the enormity of their undertaking.

Poldus, voice quavering, said, "How can we ever hope to climb this?"

"By putting one foot in front of the other," Roger answered, with a confidence he was far from feeling.

They penetrated deeper into the bare, hostile gorges carved by the Reuss River. By day, the sun shone warm enough for them to slip off their overblouses, but in the shade of the overhanging cliffs, their skin prickled with the chill. At night, when their frosty breaths joined with the ground mists, they huddled together, using the animals as windbreakers.

By the time they had eaten their meager morning fare, the land, suspended between darkness and dawn, slowly gave up its secret shape.

The sun lanced through the needled foliage; prisms of color sparkled off beaded spider webs and the dew-diamond grass.

The shifting, evaporating colors reminded Laurelle of light streaming through stained glass. "But this is a living cathe-dral," she said to Gunther, who immediately understood.

Edelweiss grew along the narrow path, its delicate yellow and white petals somehow defiant against the outcropping of granitic rock. Gunther picked an alpenrose and held it to the sun so that the velvety membrane glowed, alive with light.

"It is beautiful, is it not?" Gunther said to Laurelle.

She nodded. "And witness to the Lord's handiwork."

Gunther gazed at the flower, put it on his tongue and said, "This is my body, this is my blood," then ate it.

Their slow climb led deeper into the gorges of the Schonellen. Poldus pointed out the tracks of wildcat and boar and the spoor of bear. They dismounted to lead the animals over the treacherous path, fording glacial streams lined with delicate ferns. The high noon sun beat straight down into the defile and their clothes were soon stained with sweat. On they trudged, marking the trail for the army to follow.

The air grew as sharp as the blade of a sword. Harolde felt his heart thud mightily in his chest. He could not get enough air into his lungs, yet his head remained clear and his feet moved automatically, one after the other, just as Roger had said. On and on, his feet finding purchase on the rocky path, up and up toward the top of the world.

Gone the twitter of forest birds, gone what little game there had been. Beyond exhaustion now, still they managed to drag their way onward.

Poldus slipped on the path wet with the run-off of ice, and would not get up. "I must rest or my heart will burst."

Roger took his switch and beat him across the shoulders until he stumbled on to rejoin the others: Roger went up and down cursing, wheedling, helping those who had fallen until they finally dragged their way to a clearing.

"Never before have I beheld anything like this," Harolde whispered. Great monoliths of stone rose all about them. Looming high above the divide, an enormous mountain whose ice-capped peak pierced the sky. Below, the foaming cataracts of the river Reuss.

Harolde fell to his knees and clasped his hands. "And on the third day He made the seas, and caused the mountains to rise up."

"And it was good," Gunther said, touching his forehead to the stone.

Jonathan raised Gunther's head gently. His shirt was bloodstained, the ropes of the cross having cut deep into his back.

Jonathan searched his wallet for herbs that might help, but Gunther smiled and said, "It does not matter."

Roger allowed them to rest for a bit. They watched enviously as a hawk wheeled against the sky, rising and falling on a column of warm air. Clouds with fantastic faces and shapes swept across the opening of the defile, darkening the sky.

"It might be the approach of a storm," Roger said, the gale that had drowned so many in the Bay of Uri still fresh in his mind. Charged with his feelings of leadership, he urged the guard forward.

The trail they followed led to a dead end. They marked the correct path so the main army would not waste time and strength making the same mistake. The road continued to twist and turn until they came to a treacherous two hundred-foot chasm over which arched a fragile stone bridge. Below, the rushing river tore at the supports.

"This must be the Devil's Bridge Herr Blutkopf warned us about," Roger said.

Legend had it that for many centuries men had tried to span this divide, but always met with failure. Finally, the devil said he would build the bridge, but in payment demanded the soul of the first traveler to cross it. The people agreed. The following day, after the bridge had magically appeared, they sent across—a billy goat. Outraged, the devil hurled a great boulder down to destroy his handiwork. But the boulder missed and now stood just to the right of the structure.

Gunther took the cross off his back and held it high as they approached, hoping to exorcise the demons of the bridge. Still, no one would venture across first.

"We do not have a goat," Harolde said, "but we do have a donkey!" The others heartily agreed, and with encouraging slaps urged the confused Tortoise across. The donkey reached the center of the span and promptly sat down.

They shouted and waved, Poldus hurled rocks at her, but Tortoise brayed back and would not budge.

"One of us must get her across," Roger said.

"Send Jonathan," Poldus said. "Is he not responsible for the animals?"

"That is not fair," Laurelle said. "Let us pick straws."

Blades of grass were searched for. Jonathan picked the shortest. "You see?" Poldus said. "It was destined."

Trembling, Jonathan took a deep breath and inched out on the narrow causeway. Very carefully, he avoided the crumbling edges. At last he reached Tortoise. Below, the river roiled against the arched supports, spuming high into the air to soak Jonathan and the donkey. He pleaded, cajoled, pulled and pinched her flanks, trying to force her across. Tortoise lumbered to her feet only to kick at him.

The others yelled encouragement. Desperate, Jonathan grabbed Tortoise's ear and bit hard. She screeched, then docilely allowed herself to be led to the other side. Safely over, and still owner of his soul, Jonathan did a triumphant jig.

When they had first begun the climb over these mountains, Jonathan had seriously questioned his ability to keep pace with the others. But the rigors of these past months had toughened him, and now as he stood on the far side of the bridge, his doubt seemed a vague thing of the past.

Poldus was beside himself with envy over Jonathan's success. He snatched Mirage's reins from Laurelle and began to lead the stallion forward. But Mirage forced his way back, almost toppling Poldus off the cliff. With a curse, Poldus unsheathed his dagger and slashed at Mirage. The stallion reared. Poldus panicked and threw the knife at him, but it sailed harmlessly past the horse to fall into the chasm.

"Look!" Laurelle cried, pointing into the ravine. They peered down and saw the broken bodies of men and horses. "It must be the merchant caravan that disappeared," Laurelle shuddered. Apparently they had fallen into the gorge, been covered by a snowfall and were just now revealed with the thaw.

The rest of the guard hurried across the bridge, this time with Roger leading Mirage. They crowded around Jonathan, clapping him on the back.

Poldus's face flushed with resentment. He growled to Gunther, "Don't you see? Jonathan *must* be in league with the devil to have accomplished such a thing!"

"Could it be that he just understands donkeys?" Gunther asked.

The path twisted around the face of the escarpment. Some miles later they reached a precipitous, wood-slatted suspension bridge hanging from the face of the cliff by iron pikes driven into the stone. The guard managed to cross without incident.

Shortly before dusk, fog began to roll down the mountainside, settling to obscure the valley. Their eyes strained against the mists which cloaked the landscape in a mourning shroud. "How beautiful," Laurelle whispered as the fog swirled and eddied around them.

After a few more miles Roger realized they had blundered off the beaten track. "We should have reached Andermatt by now," he said, worried.

"Are we lost?" Poldus cried, bringing down a fall of fine snow.

"Quiet! Or you will start an avalanche!" Roger warned him.

Then they heard the distant tolling of a bell and followed the sound until they reached the Hospental Tower, some two miles beyond Andermatt. The sixty-foot bell tower had been constructed eight years before to lead lost travelers to safety.

Harolde read an inscription carved in a plaque of wood over the outside door. "Here is the way, oh friend, where are you going? Will you go on to look down at holy Rome, or upwards toward holy Cologne on the German Rhine, or toward the west, are you going to France?"

At the mention of Cologne a somber weight of sadness settled over Roger. Father, he thought. Will I ever see him again? There was so much he wanted to tell him, so much to thank him for. Strange, Roger reflected, for when I had the chance . . . At the memory of all the lost opportunities his eyes welled and he rubbed them angrily. "You are too old for such nonsense," he reprimanded himself, sounding oddly like the baron.

"Or are you going to France," he repeated slowly, as the letters of the sign swam before his eyes. He wondered what had befallen the crusade of French children and his blood brother, Guillaume. "Only the Lord knows," he sighed.

Laurelle moved quietly to Roger and slipped her hand into his. "You seem lonely," she said softly.

He gripped her hand. "Have you ever wondered at the strange sequence of events which has brought us to this remote edge of the world?"

"I think of it without pause," Laurelle said. "But now I no longer question it, for it has brought us this far." What she did not tell him was that this mountain air made her feel somehow cleansed, and nightly she had debated whether or not to sleep with him.

The children spent the night huddled in the lee of the tower. Poldus and Jonathan had the watch; to stay warm, they kept patroling around the tower base. On the far side, away from where the others lay sleeping, Poldus grabbed Jonathan's arm.

"The others did not notice," Poldus said, "but I saw you cross the Devil's Bridge first, not the stupid donkey, for you dragged her over. So now your soul is forever in danger from the devil. But I have this . . ."

"Leave me alone with your stinking holy water!" Jonathan cried and tried to move away.

Poldus grabbed Jonathan by the throat. "I am not talking about that! What I have is a suspicion. You and your kind are in league with the dark one, aren't you? You knew I suspected the truth and that's why you left me to drown in the Bay of Uri."

Jonathan looked at Poldus, not comprehending.

Poldus said, "You do not need to pretend anymore. You see, I have found out your secret."

Jonathan's stomach contracted into a tight fist. What he had feared most on this pilgrimage. . . He jerked his arm free and tried to escape, but Poldus wrestled him to the ground and pinned him.

Poldus breathed heavily, "I shall expose you to everybody!

To the others, to Nicholas, and to the authorities in every town we come to! Unless you do as I say."

Jonathan struggled under Poldus's unsparing weight. "What do you want?" he choked.

"I have not seen my Germaine in over two weeks, and I am fit to burst. All you have to do is . . ." He whispered in Jonathan's ear. "Do this and I will keep your secret."

Their heartbeats thudded against each other, one in anticipation, the other in fear. "Well?" Poldus said.

Head averted, Jonathan nodded.

When Poldus stripped off his clothes and stood shivering in the dark, Jonathan broke and ran. He raced around the tower to where the others lay sleeping and with a headlong dive, burrowed his way between Harolde and Gunther.

Poldus came tearing around the corner, one hand holding up his hose, and tripped over Harolde's feet. Harolde woke with a jolt, started to say the prayer for complin, then saw Poldus. "You will catch your death of cold." He shook his head in a daze and went back to sleep.

In the morning, Poldus waited until the others were occupied with their tasks, then cornered Jonathan and punched him in the stomach as hard as he could.

"That is for last night," Poldus panted. "But tonight, tonight you will obey, or I shall reveal who and what you are."

THE ALPS

HE FINAL CLIMB TO THE ST. GOTTHARD PASS began just beyond Hospental. The advance guard made their way through misted meadows dotted with cowslip, wild carrot, and bluebell, much to the delight of the munching animals. On either side of the narrowing col pressed jagged mountains, gashed by glacial rivers.

As they walked, Poldus kept up a continuous stream of invective, possessed by the conviction that everybody had turned against him.

"What is the matter with you?" Roger asked.

"He knows," Poldus snarled, indicating Jonathan.

Jonathan shrugged helplessly. Roger moved Poldus to the front of the column, hoping the separation might calm things. All would go peacefully; then Poldus would burst forth again yelling such curses as, "God will punish those who try to commit murder against good Christians!" One time his shouting brought down a shower of stone and snow and Roger warned him once more about making too much noise.

As the band continued their climb, their ears popped. Then the mists began slowly to thin; in another hour they had broken free and found themselves above the cloud cover. All around them, mountains carved by wind and ice bruted above the cloud line, their icecaps blinding against the radiant sky. The billowing sea of clouds looked so thick that Laurelle said, "One might step off the ledge and walk across it. We must be at the top of the world."

"And see how it stretches to forever," Gunther added in wonder. "Do you think it is Jerusalem at the other end? Or heaven?"

Poldus suddenly whirled and screamed, "He saw me call for

help! He *saw* me! But he would have let me die, God curse him! Because I knew his secret!"

Poldus's shouts reverberated against the mountain, and then a deep rumbling noise born of his endless echo sounded high above them. The children looked up, hypnotized, as a great mass of ice cracked loose from the mountainside and started slowly to fall toward them.

"Everybody get back!" Roger shouted. He grabbed Laurelle and flattened himself against the cliff wall. The others followed. Jonathan held on tight to the reins of Mirage and Tortoise. But Poldus's mule bolted forward. With a deafening roar, the avalanche swept down, shearing away everything in its path. The curtain of ice and snow cascaded before their eyes to fall into the valley as, for what seemed like an eternity, they clung desperately to the cliff face.

With a final rumble, all was quiet. A fine mist of snow powdered everything.

"Is everybody all right?" Roger asked, counting heads.

Everybody was, except for Poldus's mule, who had been swept away.

"It is the spirit of the mountain warning us to go back!" Poldus cried, his hair and eyelashes ghostly white.

"Oh, no!" Gunther interrupted, "surely we are being guided. If we had been fifty feet further along the path . . ." His hand made a graceful swooping motion downward.

"We must move with great care," Roger said softly. "And no more noise, Poldus, or you will bring the rest of the mountain down on us!"

They could no longer walk two abreast, but proceeded single file where the avalanche had torn away the outer ledge.

"Do not look down," Roger warned them, but not even he could resist the dizzying look into the chasm below. Roger led Mirage, but the stallion came to a portion of the path so narrow that his ribs scraped the cliff wall. Mirage reared back, eyes rolling, his hooves sending a shower of stones into the valley.

They listened, waiting for the stones to hit bottom, but no sound came.

"Straight to hell," Poldus whimpered.

"Then take some of your holy water," Jonathan said, unable to resist.

Poldus fixed Jonathan with a murderous glare.

Roger pleaded with Mirage, even whipped him, but the stallion fought back. "What can we do?" Roger asked, beside himself with frustration.

"Animals *know*," Poldus said. "He is warning us to get away from this evil place. Nothing will make him cross that ledge. Let us go back."

"Never," Roger muttered. "Even if I have to leave him here."

"We must try to fool him," Jonathan said, and backed Mirage to a place where he could turn him to face into the sun. Mirage blinked and quieted somewhat. Jonathan took off his blouse and slipped it over Mirage's head, blindfolding him. Mirage stamped the ground, nostrils quivering.

"Come with me, my beauty," Jonathan said soothingly, as he led the stallion forward. "You know I would never do anything to hurt you. If we remain here, we shall all freeze or starve to death. Come, I have a carrot for you," he lied.

Once more Mirage balked as his ribs touched the cliffside, but Jonathan urged him on, step by step, until they cleared the section sheared away by the avalanche and stood on less treacherous ground.

"Now do the same with Tortoise," Jonathan called.

Harolde blindfolded her and gingerly led her across, with Laurelle holding on to Tortoise's tail. Roger followed behind, ready to grab Laurelle should she stumble. Tortoise plodded her laconic way, sure-footed as a goat.

Only Gunther and Poldus remained on the other side. Poldus pressed himself against the rock and would not move. "Hold on to me," Gunther said, "and I will lead you across." Gunther took Poldus's hand and started to make his way along the shelf. Midway, Poldus froze.

"I cannot, I cannot!" Poldus sobbed, and pulled back.

Gunther turned to reassure him, and as he did, the transverse arm of his cross banged against the cliff wall, throwing him off balance. For an instant, Gunther balanced precariously in space, his hand reaching out in a slow motion for the cliff, and then in a move as graceful as a falcon's, he fell, the cross on his back dwindling to a speck.

Poldus screamed and dashed blindly for the other side. He made it across and threw himself on the ground. The others searched frantically over the edge of the cliff. They could see nothing, or hear nothing, save their own sobbing and the moaning of the mournful wind.

The tears turned icy on Harolde's cheek as he searched for something to say. At last he managed, "He died for the Lord. There is no nobler death."

"He could have lived for Him!" Jonathan exclaimed. "That would have been nobler!" A blinding fury convulsed him, for he had loved the blacksmith boy. He could not imagine their journey without Gunther, without his simple goodness. While this other one. . . . Jonathan whirled on Poldus. "You—!"

"It was not my fault," Poldus blubbered. "He brought it on himself, carrying that cross. We all warned him. . . ."

"Hold your tongue!" Jonathan shouted, and a shower of stone and ice tumbled down again. Feeling helpless because he could not vent his rage, Jonathan started to tremble and gasp for breath.

Laurelle put her arm around his shoulder. "We all knew such a thing could happen to any of us," she murmured.

Jonathan nodded, gulping back his tears. "It is just that it is so unfair. Of all of us, surely Gunther deserved to live."

Yet, much as Jonathan hated to admit it, deep within himself he knew that Poldus spoke the truth. Gunther had made his own fate come to pass.

They might have stayed there for hours, staring down into the chasm, grieving for Gunther. But finally the howling wind picked up in intensity, forcing them to continue.

On they plodded, heads bent to the wind, Poldus muttering with every step. Icy ground water trickled through the stone, making the path even more treacherous. Somewhere over the crest of this mountain, or the next, lay the sea which would lead to Jerusalem.

"Sooner or later, there must be an end to mountains," Harolde panted, "if only we have enough faith."

"We will reach it," Roger muttered through his teeth. His head throbbed with guilt that as leader he stood accountable for Gunther's fate. He beat his fist against the cliffside. "We *will* reach it! My eyes will look upon the Holy Sepulcher! I will worship at the tomb and pray there for Gunther! By my eyes, I swear it!"

Night found them nowhere near any shelter. The wind turned bitter. They reached a flat rocky area where stunted bushes clung to a protected lee of the mountainside. Poldus, with his uncanny woodsman instinct, searched and shouted, "This way, there is a cave here."

Under ordinary circumstances, the band would never have entered the cave. "It might be the lair of a mountain lion, or worse, some monster," Laurelle breathed. But night and unrelenting wind forced them to take the chance. Roger lit a torch and he and Poldus crept inside.

In the gloom of the inner recesses, Poldus picked up some bleached bones. "A mountain goat." He sniffed the air. "From the smell of the place, I think this the den of a bear. But see here?" Poldus said, leading Roger to a small passage at the rear. "We can escape by squeezing through this opening should the beast return."

Roger debated and said, "We do not have much choice. If we stay out in the cold all night, we shall surely freeze. What we must do is build a fire in here to frighten any beasts off."

Jonathan staked Mirage and Tortoise near the mouth of the cave. The animals were skittish and gave him a great deal of trouble until he finally managed to calm them.

The children searched the mountainside to gather the little wood available; a meager amount, only bramble bushes and some dried pine cones. In the cave, they emptied their saddle bags and burned everything they could to keep the fire going. Roger looked covetously at Harolde's Bible, but the monk clutched it to his bosom, aghast.

For dinner, Jonathan rummaged through his wallet and gave them each some dried mushrooms. When he handed a portion to Poldus, he knocked the mushrooms from Jonathan's hand.

"I will not eat that poison!" Poldus shouted, his hollow voice filling the cave. "Gunther is dead because of you! We are being punished because you march with us! I suspected you right from the start, for you acted like you were better than any of us. And you would never go into a church, never! Then in Strasbourg, I knew for sure. For I watched you very carefully when the heretics were burned—and you cried! You knew I suspected your secret, so you left me to drown in the Bay of Uri. But God saved me so I could expose you." Poldus pointed accusingly at Harolde. "He knew it, too, for I heard him talking to you one night."

Poldus grabbed Roger's arm. "Ask him to deny it if he dares. Anyway, there is a sure way to prove it. Remember at Strasbourg? Let us see if he will kiss the crucifix!" Poldus thrust his cross in Jonathan's face and Jonathan started back. "See? He won't! For he is a heretic, he is a cursed Albigense!"

Jonathan stared at Poldus, then threw back his head and laughed.

"Do you hear how he mocks our Lord?" Poldus cried.

"Poldus, leave be," Roger said. "We have more important things to do than argue amongst ourselves."

"How can I leave be?" Poldus demanded, "when we march with an enemy in our midst? When our comrade is dead because of this disciple of the devil!" He whirled on Jonathan. "Do you deny you are an Albigense?"

Jonathan's laughter enraged Poldus all the more. "Deny it," he yelled, shoving the boy.

"I deny all those things," Jonathan said. "I deny that I am a heretic. I deny that I am an Albigense. But I will no longer deny that I am a Jew."

Laurelle had sensed this was coming from the moment Poldus began baiting Jonathan. But with the terrible truth uttered at last, her face twisted with pain, for what she knew would happen.

Jonathan's words sent Poldus into a crouch. "A Jew?" he repeated incredulously, and crossed himself.

Harolde checked the instinctive movement of his own hand.

Roger started to move between the two boys, but then some deeper instinct held him back.

"A Jew? God curse you!" Poldus cried. "No wonder misfortune has stalked us! I avenge Gunther!" he spat, and lunged at Jonathan.

Poldus was heavier and taller than Jonathan, and wiser in the ways of survival. Jonathan, who had spent his youth poring over books, knew next to nothing about defending himself. Poldus's fist caught Jonathan on the side of the head, knocking him to the ground. Poldus circled the fallen boy. "Stand up and fight, Jew!" he snarled. "I will show you the agony you visited on our Lord." He aimed a kick, but Jonathan rolled away.

"Stop them!" Laurelle cried, knuckles pressed to her mouth. She started toward the boys but Roger caught her arms and held her fast. Laurelle fought to be free, crying, "Is this what our march has come to?"

Roger shook her. "Listen to me! You too, Harolde! If we stop them now, Jonathan will never be rid of his fear. He must learn to fight back, or he is lost. Whichever way this ends, it is in God's hands."

Poldus yelled to Roger, "Throw me your knife and I will finish him off once and for all!" But Roger did not heed.

Jonathan stood up and Poldus knocked him down again. The next time, Jonathan sprang for Poldus's knees. They rolled on the floor of the cave, the firelight casting their disjointed shadows on the walls. With a twist of his torso, Poldus caught Jonathan in a body lock. He pinned his forearm against Jonathan's throat. Jonathan squirmed, trying to breathe. He managed to work his chin under Poldus's arm and bit down hard.

Poldus yowled and let go. Jonathan scrambled up. They crouched low, one on the attack, the other defending. Poldus's rage gleamed in his eyes. Again and again he had Jonathan down.

Laurelle struggled in Roger's grip. "Harolde?" she cried. "Do something!" When the monk started forward Roger exclaimed, "Harolde! You must leave this to God! You know I am right in this."

Laurelle sobbed, "Are you both so hard-hearted that you would see him dead?"

But Poldus was wearying, his arms grown heavy from hitting Jonathan so often. Jonathan's face was a bloody mass, and he lurched about on his feet. Still he came on, no longer waiting for Poldus to strike, but carrying the fight to him. He charged again, butting Poldus in the stomach, then fell to his knees. Poldus leaned back against the cave wall, gasping for air. He tried to kick the kneeling boy, missed, and sprawled to the ground. The two of them lay there, unable to get up.

Finally, Jonathan dragged himself to his feet and looked down on Poldus. Jonathan's mouth worked and he spat out a tooth. Then he collapsed.

Twice during the night the animals set up a fearful row, whinnying and straining to break free of their ropes. Roger and Laurelle woke and soothed them while they searched the darkness, but the children could see nothing.

Laurelle hugged herself against the cold. "What troubles them, do you think?"

Roger hunched his shoulders. "Perhaps the beast who owns this cave wants it back."

For a long time Laurelle looked up at the stars through the mouth of the cave. "What will happen now?" she asked finally, and Roger knew that she spoke of Jonathan.

Roger hunched his shoulders. "We are all right as long as we stay ahead of the army. But once Poldus gets back to Nicholas. . . ."

"What will he do?"

"Nicholas may refuse to let Jonathan go on with us. Worse, if our leader—or his angel—takes it into his head that the evil which has befallen us is because of Jonathan—that he is to be blamed for Gunther's death—then God knows!"

"Is there no way we can save him?" Laurelle asked. A long moment passed and then she said brightly, "I know! What if Jonathan became a Christian?"

"Hah! That is too easy!" Roger snorted. "You do not know

this boy, he is more stubborn than Tortoise. Harolde tried for a whole month but could not talk God's sense into him."

Roger moved closer to Laurelle. She leaned back against him and then with a sudden jerk started away.

Roger set his mouth. "Laurelle, it is very cold. Is it so wrong if we lie close together to keep warm? Is that not better than freezing? I have sworn not to touch you, yet you cringe from me. Do my vows mean that little to you? Have we learned nothing from Gunther's mistakes?"

Laurelle hung her head. How could she tell him it was not him she feared? Tentatively, she reached for Roger's hand and pressed it between hers. Her wounded eyes searched Roger's face. "Do not be angry, I beg you," she whispered. "Help me, please. I love you . . . but I am so frightened. . . ."

"Oh, my heart," Roger exclaimed, embracing her. "Rather would I die than cause you one moment of pain."

Laurelle curled up then and Roger lay down beside her, molding his body against hers. Heart overflowing with the closeness of her, he lay very still, restraining himself from any sudden movements that might frighten her. Fighting off his drowsiness, he tried to remain alert to the warnings of the night.

DAWN HAD NOT YET LIT THE MOUNTAINS WHEN the animals acted up again, Tortoise screeching in a frenzy. Roger roused the others. "We must get moving, or Tortoise and Mirage will go mad."

"What are we going to do with him?" Poldus asked, pointing to Jonathan, whose battered, swollen face was barely recognizable.

With the discovery that the others were not going to leave Jonathan behind, Poldus grabbed his belongings and announced, "I will not go another step! Unless you cast him out, I will return to the main army and tell Nicholas that you harbor the Christ killer!"

"You must do what you believe right," Harolde said, coughing uneasily. "But come with us at least to the next village. It is too dangerous to be in these mountains alone."

"Not another step," Poldus insisted, determined to shame them into accepting his demands. He never doubted they would. After all, the boy was a Jew, and he a Christian.

"We must not waste time arguing," Roger said. "Poldus, you know yourself that wild animals prowled this area all last night."

"We heard them, truly," Laurelle said. "See how nervous Tortoise is? Poldus, you can take the lead; Jonathan will stay in the rear."

"Are you trying to trick me?" Poldus cried. "Hoping I will change my mind? Well, I will not!" He sat down at the mouth of the cave.

"Suit yourself, then," Roger said, losing patience. He started out, the others following. "Poldus is bluffing," Roger said when they were out of earshot. "Just let a mouse cross his path and he will come running."

Roger looked at Jonathan's bruised and discolored face. "But you did well last night," he said softly, "and gladly would I choose you to be on my side in any battle."

Jonathan tried to smile, but winced in pain.

They turned a hairpin bend in the trail and had not gone another quarter mile when they were stopped in their tracks by a series of fearful screams. They rushed back to where they had left Poldus. There they discovered that a half-grown brown bear had returned and taken possession of its lair again, trapping the screaming Poldus inside. Poldus retreated as far as he could while the growling animal rose menacingly on its hind legs and then charged the boy, knocking him down.

"Fire!" Roger cried, looking around wildly. But they had burned every stick of wood last night.

"Distract the beast!" Harolde shouted. "I will try to get Poldus out the back way." He spurred Tortoise to the rear of the cave.

Armed with stones and their palmer's staffs, Roger, Jonathan, and Laurelle advanced warily on the cave. The small brown bear held Poldus down with one paw and snarled as the children hurled rocks at him.

Jonathan climbed to the ledge above the cave entrance and when the baited bear charged out, hit him on the back with a small boulder. The bear reared and made for Jonathan just as Roger struck it on the snout with another rock. The children kept up their barrage of stones and shouts.

With the bear's attention diverted, Harolde crept into the tiny opening at the cave's rear. He grabbed Poldus under the arms and dragged him out. Harolde got Poldus over to Tortoise and managed to heave him over the donkey's back. "I have him!" Harolde yelled. "Get away!"

The band slowly retreated. The young confused bear followed them to where Roger had tied Mirage. The instant the stallion saw the beast, he went wild, rearing and striking at him with his hooves. Stallion and bear circled each other, then the bear turned and slunk back to its cave, thinking to protect its catch. By the time the bear discovered his prize gone, the band had gotten a safe distance away.

Poldus's bloody right arm hung awry from its socket. His face looked ashen and his eyes rolled back into his head.

"Can you save him?" Harolde asked Jonathan.

Jonathan threw up his hands. "He is losing so much blood." He jammed a piece of cloth over the spurting wound. "We must keep him warm," Jonathan said.

"We cannot stop here," Roger said urgently.

Propping Poldus on Tortoise, Harolde walked on one side of the wounded boy, Roger on the other to keep him from falling off. They continued their journey this way, while the blood seeped through Poldus's makeshift bandage, soon to leave a red trail on the barren ground. Mercifully, Poldus lapsed into unconsciousness.

Only the bare rock now as they continued their climb toward the St. Gotthard pass, moving through the watershed area of the mighty Rhine and Rhone rivers. The clouds above them looked as if they had been snagged by the peaks and were straining to break free. August, the height of summer. They could not imagine what it would be like in winter. If the fires of hell had an equivalent in ice . . .

Their senses became numb. Mirage was first to know that they had reached the snow line; the stallion lowered his head and began to munch at the patches of white. The children scooped up handfuls of snow and slaked their thirst.

As they struggled on, a thought tormented Jonathan. If I try to save Poldus, I put my own life in jeopardy. All I need do is loosen the tourniquet . . . no one will ever know and I will be safe.

And then the Code of Maimonides that his father had so often quoted came to mind. "May the love for my art actuate me at all times . . . May I never forget that the patient is a fellow creature in pain . . . for the mind of man is puny, and the art of healing vast. I have been sanctioned to care for the life and health of man . . . I am ready for my vocation."

Through the pounding pain in his own body Jonathan whispered, "I am ready for my vocation . . . I cannot decide this.

God must judge," and then he carefully checked Poldus's bandages to make sure that they were all right.

All day long they marched, without food, without rest, knowing that if they stopped they would not have the strength to continue. When Poldus slipped off Tortoise's back, they tied him back on. The children no longer felt their hands or feet, numbed as they were by the cold, and the footprints they left in the snow were tinged with blood.

"If Herr Blutkopf had not given us these sheepskins we would surely have perished," Roger panted, as he helped Harolde to his feet after he had fallen.

By dusk, as they stumbled onto a wind-swept plateau, it seemed that they had not the will to drag another step.

"Is this then the top of the St. Gotthard pass?" Roger whispered.

Glacial blue lakes, with paler blocks of floating ice, spread before them in the cup of the pass. The lid of the sky pressed down, massed with lowering blue-gray clouds. For a moment, the setting sun broke through the cloud cover to ignite the glacial ice. Then the valleys filled with twilight until the darkness crept up the mountainside to envelop the pass.

A sudden gust of icy wind swept over them. When the first pellets of hail struck, the falling children would have laid down and consigned themselves to their maker. But the animals, sparked with some last instinct for survival, struggled on. The children grabbed the tails of Mirage and Tortoise and stumbled after the beasts, who veered to the left around a dark blue lake. The hail storm increased, stinging their faces until they winced with pain.

Then, in the slanting fall of ice, the dark shape of a hospice took form.

Two startled monks swung open the wooden doors in answer to the children's pounding. They carried Poldus immediately to the infirmarium; the other children were hurried into the main room and set before the crackling hearth. The monks took turns rubbing them with coarse cloths to get their blood circulating. The wind howled around the small stone building atop the seven-thousand-foot-high pass, and as the children sipped their mulled wine, they gave thanks to the Lord for having led them here. The hospitalier brought food but after a few mouthfuls, the children discovered they were too exhausted to eat and fell asleep where they sat.

Brother Xeno and Brother Kar fussed over the sleeping children, straightening blankets, starting with every moan. Forty years ago when the brothers had first taken their vows, they had been fast friends, but the decades had seen the friendship diminish. Each accused the other of infuriating habits. Brother Xeno cracked his knuckles constantly. But he had been driven to this because Brother Kar clacked his wooden spoon against his wooden bowl—at every meal! A small enough habit, but Brother Xeno knew it to be directed against him personally. In one week, three sittings a day, he counted twenty-one clacks. In one year, 1,092 clacks. And in the span of forty years, Brother Xeno had tallied 43,680 clacks. He did not know how much more he could stand. A hundred more clacks, perhaps ten, or even one, might shatter his patience and cause him to commit violence. Contemplating this possibility, Brother Xeno nervously cracked his knuckles.

Early the next morning, the children wolfed down the meal set before them. Then Jonathan and Harolde, with great uneasiness, went to the infirmarium to inquire about Poldus.

The infirmarian shook his head. "The boy grows worse. Once during the night he regained consciousness, screaming. I tried to comfort him but all he could do was babble that the Anti-Christ pursued him. Then he passed out again. I fear he may need to be exorcised."

"But will he live?" Harolde asked.

"That is in God's hands," the monk said. "To my mind it is a miracle that he has survived this long."

"Let me stay with him a bit," Jonathan said. "I know a little about such things and I may be able to help him."

Harolde left; while the infirmarian went about his other duties, Jonathan took up the bedside vigil, beset with conflicting emotions. What if Poldus regains his senses by the time Nicholas and the army arrive? Jonathan thought. If I help save him, do I not then place my own life in jeopardy? But the most compelling question that tormented him was, Did somebody like Poldus, so brutish and vindictive, did somebody like that really deserve to live?

Jonathan tore himself away from these thoughts. "I will worry about all that later," he said. Right now there were cold compresses to apply to bring down the fever, and bandages to change.

The arm savaged by the bear had turned gray and felt stiff to the touch. Gangrene had set in; if the infection spread, Poldus would soon be dead. Jonathan questioned the infirmarian about the possibility of amputating the arm, but the monk shook his head. "Such skills are beyond me." Jonathan did not know how to perform such a drastic thing either, not having progressed that far in his studies, and felt relieved that this decision had been taken out of his hands.

All that day, while the advance guard waited for the army to arrive, the monks questioned them about their mission. Roger told the tale and the good brothers could not hear enough of it.

"Inspired!" Brother Xeno exclaimed with a knuckle crack. "Why has nobody thought of this before?"

"Our good Lord did," said Brother Kar. "But the world must be made ready for such tidings. Perhaps we are ready for it now."

Brother Xeno told Roger, "From now on the march to the sea will be comparatively easy, for it is all downhill. To Lugano first, then Como, and thence to the plains of Lombardy."

"Avoid Milan at all costs," Brother Kar said, "for no matter how holy your mission they are hostile to all things German."

"From Milan," Brother Xeno finished, "it is only a few days march to Genoa. Where you say the sea will part for you? A wonder!"

Roger listened attentively as the two monks argued the relative merits of the best route to Genoa: via Pavia, or Piacenza. Roger thought this hugely funny, since neither monk, in all his years here, had ever left the monastery.

By late afternoon, the army still had not appeared. Roger paced the cloister endlessly. He trudged around the half-dozen lakes to the northern sector of the pass and scanned the approaches until a howling gale and darkness forced him back.

At dawn the next day Roger and Laurelle rode out on Mirage to search for the army. Just past noon they saw them, a black line stretched out below along the winding mountain trail. The strong carried the weak; others collapsed in the snow and lay still where they fell. Many had perished trying to cross the ledge where Gunther had fallen. Since leaving Flüelen, more than one thousand had died.

But there were eight thousand remaining. The brothers of the hospice regarded them with amazement as they dragged their way into the compound. Despite their ragged clothes, despite their gaunt bodies, a light seemed to shine from them. They had withstood every test, and these children—who now stood at the crest of the St. Gotthard—these children were indeed the champions of the faith.

Roger reported the death of Gunther to Nicholas, and told him what had befallen Poldus.

Nicholas barely reacted. "I am too tired to see Poldus now," he complained.

Roger did not press the matter. "The less explaining we have to do about Poldus, the better," Roger said in an aside to Harolde.

All that day the army rested. With darkness the monks crammed them into every available space—cells, chapel, crypt, stables—until all lay safe within the walls of the monastery.

Poldus wakened to see the hospital room filled with children and realized that the army had arrived. A surge of energy made him cry out, "Nicholas!" One of the monks hurried to fetch him, but could not get past Nicholas's lieutenants.

The children slept while the monks passed the night in prayer. Brother Xeno and Brother Kar huddled against the cloister wall, having given up their cells to the rows of children sleeping on the floor. The wind quickened, the sky shone brilliant with stars.

"These little ones," Brother Xeno said, "make me recall my youthful passion for the Lord. Ah, me," he sighed, and in the act of cracking his knuckles, stopped. "Brother Kar," he said, "I know I have long grieved you with my habit." He stared at his big-knuckled hands. "So I have prayed to St. Paul to help me control this."

Brother Kar's eyes sparkled. "Truly, there is something wondrous about these little ones, for at evening services I took a vow to St. Peter. Never again will I clack. . . ."

The brothers touched hands briefly, then said complin under the stars, feeling lighter in heart than they had for many years.

The morning of the children's departure, the monks gathered at the main gate. A day of fasting had been proclaimed; a necessity in any case, for not a crumb of food remained in the hospice. As the army left the mournful setting of St. Gotthard's gigantic boulders and scattered lakes, the rejuvenated children took up their song. Some monks tried to hum along; others waved. Many, including Brother Xeno and Brother Kar, felt the siren call of the adventure. But old vows and older bones kept them at the monastery. Not so the stable boy and a youthful novice, both of whom sneaked off to join the army.

The song grew fainter, the children smaller, until the bobbing heads, some red, some brown, some blond, were like so many wildflowers strewn down the mountain.

The monks undertook the sad business of burying those children who had died during the night. Eleven in all, including the wounded boy in the infirmarium. His death had been the most somber, for in his final moments he had not responded to the last sacraments, but instead had ranted and raved, first against bears and then against Jews.

THE LOMBARD PLAIN

OWN THE PRECIPITOUS WINDING PATHS, THROUGH aromatic forests of evergreen and spruce, and into the Trembling Valley the children marched, covering their popping ears. Though they mourned the many who had fallen, they soon discovered it impossible to remain somber on this mellow, sunny side of the Alps.

Some of Flamonde's children found the strength to run down the grassier slopes, tumbling end over end, honeying the air with their laughter. And Flamonde joined in.

From his canopied char, Nicholas pointed to the fruit trees and berry bushes and sang, "At last we have come out of the wilderness and into this land of plenty. An angel hovered over my bed last night and said it would be thus all the way to Jerusalem."

"If we had a bed, perhaps an angel would hover there too," Flamonde said to Rudolph, Ursula, and Little Luke, and they all fell to giggling.

But for the most part, the army still adored their leader; somehow his growing remoteness made him that much more mysterious and worthy of worship.

"Is this Jerusalem?" Rudolph whispered to Flamonde when they reached the hamlet of Airola. The child's face looked translucent in his wasting body.

"Not yet, my love," Flamonde said, stroking his hair. "Are you tired then? Come, I will carry you a little ways."

Harolde, witnessing this, brought up Tortoise and handed the reins to Flamonde. She thanked him and loaded four of her little ones on the donkey's back. "So you have a heart after all?" Flamonde said, and Harolde blushed furiously.

Flamonde had grown very thin, the bones in her face showed sharp, making her look severe and saintly all at once.

During the day, her irrepressible spirits buoyed everybody. Only at night, when she lay alone, did Flamonde allow her feelings to surface, and then did the tears fall, hot and silent. She had buried more children than she dared remember, and daily fought the devil to save those remaining.

Through the towns of Faido, Giornio, and Biasca the children descended. The peasants who gaped at them were olive-complected, with dark hair and bright dark eyes. Nowhere near as dour as their northern compatriots, they joked as they ran alongside the children, offering them cheeses and goat-skins of heady red wine. They spoke a language more melli-fluous than the guttural German; Italian, they called it, for the children had moved into the Ticino, an area long contested by the Holy Roman emperors and the League of Lombard Cities. The forest cantons, caught in the middle of the interminable battles, had set about defending themselves. Now with the civil war raging in the empire between the Welf (Guelph) Otto IV and the Waiblingen (Ghibelline) Frederick II, all Ticino appeared to be in a building frenzy. Nowhere was this more evident than in strategic Bellinzona. The formidable Castle Uri was being erected on a two-hundred-foot promontory while corps of masons and carpenters constructed walls to connect the towers studding the ridge line.

"Desist!" Nicholas called to the laborers. "And prepare to beat your swords into plowshares. For when I reach Jerusalem . . ."

The workers stared at him as though one deranged and then resumed their building.

For five days the advance guard had marched with the main army. With the territory once more turned treacherous, Roger and his guard rode out again to find safe passage.

Under the mid-August sun, Roger's hair and eyebrows bleached white; Laurelle's nose, bridged with freckles, caused her endless concern. Roger teased her, "If you get but one more freckle, then I may not marry you," then he set about counting them.

Since leaving the St. Gotthard pass they had descended almost six thousand feet. It had gotten hot again and Mirage took to prancing, as though the heat had lubricated his joints. He deviled Tortoise constantly, biting her on the neck and rump, until the long-suffering donkey lashed out with her hind legs, tumbling Harolde through the air.

Long before the advance guard reached Como they saw the one-hundred-thirty-foot Torre de Porte Vittoria, the principal lookout tower in Como's encircling fifty-foot walls. In the thriving noisy square of San Fidele, the guard sought out the podesta at the municipal palace, Broletta. The *maestri comacini* were building it in their distinctive Lombard style and the children gazed in wonder at the white-and-black banded marble.

"The shortest route to Genoa," the podesta told them, pointing south through the graceful arch of the triple-mullioned windows, "lies directly via Milan, Pavia, and Allesandria. But these cities of the Lombard League are hostile to all from the Holy Roman Empire. Milan, especially, has never forgiven Barbarossa for burning their city to the ground, for strewing their fields with salt so that nothing would grow, or for his greatest outrage, stealing their most sacred relics, the skulls of the three magi."

"But we have just two months ago worshipped them in Cologne!" Roger said.

"It is as the Bible foretells," Harolde sighed, "that the sins of the fathers are now visited on the sons."

"My advice," the podesta said, "is to circle wide around Milan, keeping a wary eye out for their patrols, and make for Piacenza. It is two or three days longer, to be sure, but perchance you will find the Piacenzans more hospitable and sympathetic to your cause."

After informing Nicholas and the main army of their new route, Roger and his band set out on the four-day journey to Piacenza. Streams which ordinarily irrigated the fertile Lombard plain were no more than sluggish trickles ending in dry river beds. Skeletal cows foraged in the baked fields; and poplar and willow wilted in the hazy heat.

On Monday, August 20 ("the birthday of St. Bernard of Clairvaux," Harolde informed them), the army of children, led by the advance guard, crossed the Po River. Instead of hospitality in Piacenza, the children met with confusion. The townspeople did not know what to do with them. Eight thousand additional mouths to feed in this time of drought? They gave what little food they could, but it was a hungry army that camped in the Piazza del Duomo at dusk.

Swallows zigzagged through the twilight sky, scooping up the swarms of mosquitoes that bred along the banks of the Po. The low monotone of a Gregorian chant threaded from the Duomo. With the tolling of the Angelus bell, the gates were shut; at nightfall, the toper's bell signaled the taverns to close. A short time later a final bell clanged curfew and Piacenza locked itself up tight.

In the light of the moon, Harolde gazed up at the Duomo, marveling at its many wonders: the smooth pink and white facing stone, the lions couchant that supported the columns of the central portal, and the greatest wonder, the massive red-brick Romanesque campanile which had, near its very top, an outside iron cage, the *gabbia,* in which criminals were exposed, naked, to the taunts of the crowd. An adulterer, pacing the cage this very moment, had gone stark raving mad from sunstroke.

When the main army had arrived in Piacenza, Laurelle and the guard, as was their custom, had sought out Flamonde.

"You must get some sleep," Laurelle said to her sister, distressed by her wild-eyed look.

Flamonde sat leaning against one of the gargoyles, rocking Little Luke in her arms to make him forget his hunger. Rudolph's head rested against her thigh.

"How can I sleep when these little ones are dying?" Flamonde asked, her voice heavy with fatigue. "Is there no food anywhere?"

Laurelle shook her head sadly. "I brought you all we had."

"If one more dies, I shall go as mad as that one there," Flamonde said, pointing to the adulterer rattling the bars of his cage.

Little Luke soon fell asleep and Flamonde set him down gently. "There must be food in the monasteries," she mused, "for I smelled bread baking earlier." She slipped the sling cradle from her shoulder and handed the infant to Laurelle. Then she stepped gingerly over the small sleeping bodies.

"Where are you going?" Laurelle cried after her, but Flamonde had already disappeared into the shadows.

Flamonde moved stealthily, ears alert to the rounds of the night watch. She waited in a darkened alley until the sentries had passed, then crept to the door of the monastery. She looked up at the stars. "Forgive me, Father, for what I am about to do," she whispered, then scratched at the locked door. Harder, until a muffled voice at the other side asked, "Who is there?"

Flamonde faked a whimper. "For the love of God, sanctuary! I am being pursued."

The door opened a crack, just enough for Flamonde to push aside the startled monk. "My children starve," Flamonde said, her hands reaching out in a gesture of supplication.

The monk retreated, shaking his head vigorously. "We have no food, the bishop has forbidden—"

"One loaf only," Flamonde pleaded as she advanced. Sensing that he was about to give the alarm, Flamonde hit him. The brother fell back, striking his head against the wall. Flamonde dashed past the stunned man into the kitchen. She flung open the cupboards, searching, and at last found a loaf of stale bread meant to feed the birds.

Flamonde heard a voice call from within, "Ezzelino? Who is at the gate? Ezzelino?"

Flamonde ran back out into the courtyard, clutching the loaf. She raced by the monk just stumbling to his feet; he promptly flattened himself as she ran by.

Flamonde fled through the twisting alleys, hearing the alarm sounding behind her. When she reached the Piazza del Duomo, she zigzagged around the bodies of the sleeping children and finally reached her own charges. Rousing them, she tore off pieces from the loaf and stuffed it into their mouths.

"Quickly, eat, they are coming! Finish before they get here. Rudolph, here; Ursula, Little Luke, eat!"

The children shook off their sleep and gobbled the bread.

The monk Ezzelino hurried into the piazza with the night watch. They searched out Flamonde and immediately arrested her. The children with her were also arrested, the law being very clear on this matter: those receiving stolen goods were just as guilty as the thief.

Tormented with guilt that he had not acted to find food for the starving children, Harolde spent that night in prayer at the Duomo. Harolde stared up at the crucified body of Christ, the painted blood that ran from his pierced palms and feet.

"Only let her and the children go free," Harolde whispered, "and I shall do what ever penance is require, give up anything asked of me." Harolde thought of the greatest sacrifice he could make, pondered it for a long moment and then swore, "I shall give up my dream of rising high in the church. Henceforth, I shall do only Your bidding."

Harolde felt a momentary flood of peace, but it was soon followed with the recognition that he, personally, would have to risk much more to save the children and Flamonde.

PIACENZA

THE CITIZENS OF PIACENZA GATHERED IN THE piazza to hear the sentence passed by the tribunal of the commune. Count Lomello, a member of the tribunal, said, "The punishment for theft is mandatory. The hand which perpetrated the crime is to be cut off at the wrist."

A gasp went up from the army and from the crowd.

Malaspina, another member of the tribunal, added hastily, "But because of the special circumstances of the accused being pilgrims, we mercifully decided to commute that sentence."

The crowd's sigh of relief was interrupted by Lomello. "However, to let the guilty go completely unpunished would make a mockery of justice. Therefore we sentence the woman and the children to be imprisoned naked in the *gabbia* for two days."

Flamonde grasped her throat. "But the children did not know the bread was stolen."

"Let the children go," came cries from the crowd.

Lomello said to Malaspina, "Put this sentence aside and who knows what ugliness will break out next. Why, the poor might storm the granaries any time they got hungry. Or even set their children to steal for them."

Flamonde shielded Little Luke and Rudolph with her body. "Look at them," she pleaded. "They have barely enough strength to stand, let alone be imprisoned naked in the blazing sun. They will surely die!"

"Woman," the podesta interrupted sternly, "you should have thought of that before you sinned."

Flamonde cursed and tore at her hair. Then, with a violent downward motion, she ripped open her blouse, exposing her breasts. The crowd gaped. A priest rushed forward with a robe, but Flamonde pushed him aside. "You would see me naked anyway, why not here and now? Is this the price you exact for a crust of bread? I beg you, imprison me if you must, but spare the innocent."

"Take them all away!" the podesta ordered the guards.

Laurelle bit her knuckles. "We cannot, we must not let this happen again!" she cried to the others, the terror of Strasbourg springing to mind. Laurelle flung herself on the Piacenzian guards, to save Flamonde and her children or die in the attempt.

The company Flamonde traveled with surged forward also, but the soldiers were many and fought them back.

Then Harolde pushed his way through the crowd, eyes glittering with fever. As he approached the tribunal, Harolde felt a moment of panic and prayed, "Dear God, allow me to speak to them without spitting blood."

"My lords," Harolde called, in a voice so suddenly full of resonance it shocked even him, "we have done wrong and we do confess to that wrong. But surely the church—who gives us all absolution—expects that this tribunal, too, can be forgiving?"

"The commandments say, 'Thou shalt not steal,' " Lomello interrupted impatiently, "and they have broken that commandment."

"All too true," Harolde agreed. "And our Lord Himself instructed His disciples to 'Honor the commandments.' But He also said, 'I give you a new commandment—one greater than all the rest, That ye shall love one another.' Oh, my fellow brothers in Christ, when you pronounced your sentence against these innocents, was it Jesus who whispered in your ear? Or Pontius Pilate?"

Ezzelino clapped his hand to his mouth and the word *Blasphemy!* slipped through his fingers. But the people of Piacenza listened intently to what Harolde was saying.

Harolde turned to Ezzelino and, playing to the crowd, called in a deep voice, "Remember, our Lord said, 'Do nothing to harm these little ones, for they are dear to me and to my Father who lives in heaven.' But good monk, if you must have your eye for an eye, then I offer myself, poor unworthy sinner that I am, in their place."

And as the words left his mouth Harolde realized that he was no longer bargaining for the children's lives, he really meant what he was saying, and in that instant, tearing pains in his feet and in the palms of his hands brought him to his knees. In an agony of pain, Harolde remained motionless, staring at the sun; a radiance of such blinding sweetness pierced his heart that he stopped breathing and thought he must be dying. Dear Lord, do not take me now there is still so much left to be done, Harolde prayed in a rush while the world whirled before his eyes. An eternity later, seconds in the court of man, the blinding light gradually diminished along with the receding pain in his palms, bringing Harolde back to the moment.

In the piazza, men brandished their fists and shouts of "Let them all go!" ripped through the crowd.

Though they had tried to hide it, the members of the tribunal had been sorely moved by Flamonde's impassioned plea. Now with this monk preaching in a voice to move a stone to tears, and the citizenry so unruly, the tribunal grew afraid of provoking an insurrection. They hurriedly conferred with the podesta.

"If I am to save them, the moment is now," Harolde whispered as he struggled to his feet. He glanced obliquely at Jonathan, and then Harolde bit his lips as he remembered.

Harolde cleared his throat and shouted to all in the square. "One question and one question only do I ask you, and I beg you, good and merciful citizens of Piacenza, be guided in this matter by your answer. If our Lord were to appear right here and now, and weigh the loaf of bread against the lives of these children, what would be *His* judgment?"

A hush fell over the crowd. Then, without waiting for the tribunal to respond, Harolde gathered the children and Flamonde, pushed past the guards and led them back to the ranks of the army, quickly melting into its mass.

Laurelle flung herself at Harolde, endlessly praising him for his eloquence. Roger and Jonathan could not contain themselves. Everybody was laughing and crying all at once. Only Flamonde remained silent, regarding Harolde in a new and different light.

In a daze, Harolde confessed, "All my life have I dreamed of addressing such a crowd, dreamed of impressing them with my knowledge of church doctrine. Instead, God gave me voice to preach the gospel in behalf of His children . . . my children."

Harolde pressed his fingers into his palms, staring at them. They were unblemished. He shook his head in wonder and then collected himself. "Let us be gone from here, and quickly, lest they change their minds."

The army, along with Roger's guard, departed Piacenza and commenced the final leg of the journey to Genoa. They skirted the foothills of the Apennines. Wheatfield and vineyard withered under the sun; a haze of pollen and dust choked the air, and the faces of the peasants were faces of hunger and fear.

"It will rain soon," Nicholas sang to the farmers from his char. "As soon as the sea parts and we reach Jerusalem, the Lord will cause it to rain, for we are his children of the rainbow."

The peasants did not understand him, but the crosses raised on high, and the cry "Jerusalem!" made them bow down.

The countryside gradually became hillier and soon they were marching through a gap in the Apennines.

"These paths are nothing compared to the terrain we have already conquered," Roger said, as the hills were eaten up by their legs.

Village and hamlet emptied to line the roadside and marvel at the barefoot, near-naked children carrying their tattered banners and crosses. The joy in their faces, their sense of impending victory, and their voices raised in song made them appear as if a heavenly choir.

"Two days to Genoa," said the hospitalier at a monastery along the way. The children's steps grew lighter with each mile as they followed the twisting road through the craggy hills. All sensed they were close to their destination and each wished to be among the first to behold the great sea.

The next day they came upon the final ring of hills guarding the approach to the seaport. The air, perfumed with jasmine and honeysuckle, which had been with them since Lugano, was diluted by strong breezes laden with the smell of salt. Above the crest of broken hills rose a swirling mist, as though the invisible sea were some vast boiling cauldron from which all the waters would evaporate.

On the children hurried, no longer keeping to the paths, but fanning out all over the hillside. They hauled themselves up, tree by tree, bush by bush, extending their hands to their weaker comrades.

"If I could just see the water," Rudolph said, clinging to Flamonde, "I could go to heaven happy."

"Hush," Flamonde scolded. "You shall see the sea and you shall go to Jerusalem with us." She lifted him up and carried him piggyback while Little Luke held onto her skirts. The babe gurgled in the sling cradle around Flamonde's chest.

Nothing could stop the children now, their hearts beating to the bursting as they ran for the final hill. At the crest of Mt. Righi, one thousand feet above the sea, they squinted through the mists at the flaming, hazy-edged ball of the setting sun.

As the children—seven thousand in all—watched, the veil of mist evaporated, revealing campaniles and castles and palaces jammed within the ring of Genoa's great wall. Then, as though by design, the mists retreated still farther to show the lighthouse on Cape Foro, and beyond, the wonder of the waters reaching and reaching farther than the eye could see.

The sun sank into the slot between sea and sky, turning the waters a molten copper. "How red the sea looks," Rudolph said to Flamonde. Another child overheard Rudolph, repeated it, and the words *Red Sea* sped from mouth to mouth.

A shudder swept the army. Some children fainted, others cried and danced about. They had accomplished the impossible. Nicholas kneeled on the soft cushions of his char and clasped his hands. As one, the entire army fell to its knees and gave thanks.

"Did I not tell you we would look upon this?" Flamonde said, pressing her cheek against Rudolph's. "And tomorrow, we shall see the waters part, as Nicholas has promised."

Rudolph's head hung listlessly on her shoulder. Flamonde eased him down. She tried to rouse him, then with the slow realization screamed "No!" and crushed his limp body in her arms.

Jonathan helped Harolde off Tortoise. The wheel of color that was the world gradually came to rest as the monk sank wearily to the rocky ground. "I thank thee for having allowed me to come this far," Harolde whispered.

"We could not have done it without you!" Jonathan said and kissed Mirage on the nose. The stallion curled back his upper lip and nibbled at the boy's ear. "And you too, Tortoise," Jonathan said hurriedly, in response to her indignant butt.

Roger stood behind Laurelle, hands resting lightly on her shoulders. She turned and looked at him. Roger reached down and gently touched her cheek with his lips. Then he gazed out at the waters with a faraway look.

"Jerusalem," he said resolutely, and Laurelle, looking deeply into his eyes, whispered, "Jerusalem."

PART

The Age
of
the Holy
Spirit

THREE

GENOA:
SATURDAY, AUGUST 25

GENOA THE PROUD, THE REPUBLIC WHOSE NAVY had humbled the Saracens and made the Mediterranean safe for Christians, whose cargo fleets brought the riches of the Mideast to her wharves—Genoa had seen much in her time, but never anything as strange as these wild and possessed children tramping through the Soprano Gate into the city.

As they passed through the arch, Harolde read the inscription carved above the portal: "I am provided by strong men and surrounded by admirable walls . . . If you bring peace you may enter these gates. But if you seek war you shall be repulsed and vanquished."

"Peace is what we bring," Nicholas called to the staring crowd from his litter. "Not only for Genoa, but for all men."

Emissaries from Genoa's ruling Senate had informed Nicholas that his army would be allowed to remain one week within the city. Heartened by this splendid welcome, the children now hurried to the Cathedral of San Lorenzo where the podesta was to inform them of further details concerning food and shelter.

If the Genoese were astounded by the army, the children were likewise overwhelmed by the city, more fantastic than any fairy tale.

Mouth agape, Laurelle stared up at the great palaces, counting, "Four, five, six stories tall!" Beyond the ground floor porticoes she caught glimpses of inner gardens with palm trees and splashes of bright orchid and anemone.

The houses, whether palace or hovel, were built primarily of the dark gray native premonton stone, lending an air of mystery and foreboding to the spired city jammed within the cincture of its fortifications. As the children trooped through the winding alleys they sensed that the hour of their miracle was growing ever nearer and gave voice to their joy:

> *Fair are the meadows*
> *Fairer still the woodlands*
> *Robed in blooming garb of spring*
> *Jesus is fairer*
> *Jesus is purer*
> *Who makes our saddened hearts to sing!*

An hour before the children were due to arrive at the Cathedral of San Lorenzo, Frizio entered the church. He blinked his eyes against the gloom; alternate black and white marble banded the interior of the distinctly Byzantine-looking church. Striding down the marble floor of the nave, he passed many pilgrims at prayer, having come to worship the treasures which Genoa had won for her part in the Crusades: the ashes of St. John the Baptist, and the cup hewn of emerald, said to be the Holy Grail from which Christ had drunk at the Last Supper.

Incense curled up from silver censers, hazing the sunshafts lancing from the clerestory windows. Inhaling the scent of frankincense and myrrh, Frizio said under his breath, "If all goes well, I shall soon be home in Outremer, and as rich as a sheikh."

He proceeded to the chamber in the north transept, where the Genoese consuls were hearing petitions. He joined the small group there and listened intently as Senators Grimaldi, Piccamiglio, Embriaci, and Spinola put aside all other matters and wrestled with the problem of what to do with the thousands of children streaming into Genoa.

When Frizio had reached Marseille a week before, he contacted the merchant shipowners Hugo Ferrus and William Porquierres and told them of the German army of children. To his amazement, the merchants informed him of the imminent arrival in their port of another such army, this one French. Though both merchants had reputations as God-fearing Christians—indeed, both had fought in the Crusades—they were first and foremost shrewd traders who knew the Saracen appetite for fair young Europeans. And so they had immediately seized upon Frizio's idea, which had not been too far from their own thoughts. Plans for the disposition of both the French and German armies were made, Ferrus and Porquierres agreeing that Frizio would personally oversee the German-Genoese operation. Ships were hired; then Frizio sailed for Genoa on a swift caravel. He had arrived two days before the children. Now all he needed to complete his grand scheme was the approval of the Genoese consuls.

Senator Grimaldi addressed the chamber. "True it is that these children have accomplished a miraculous feat marching from Cologne to Genoa, and surely the good Lord must have been watching over them. But the inventory of our granaries indicates there is not enough to feed seven thousand additional mouths for an entire week! Could it be we were too hasty in allowing them to stay that long?"

"Yet dare we deny fellow Christians?" the dour Piccamiglia said.

Silence fell over the assembly and Frizio used this moment to step forward. "Perhaps I can be of some service in this matter."

The consuls looked at him, almost grateful for the interruption.

After identifying himself and the merchants he represented, Frizio quickly outlined his plan. "And so I am authorized by my company to offer these children free transportation to the Holy Land," he finished.

Grimaldi smiled. "Have you not heard? Ships will not be necessary for these voyagers, for the sea will part for them!"

Embriaci and Spinola nodded appreciatively at this little joke and even the sad-eyed Piccamiglia seemed amused.

"To be sure," Frizio said, smiling back with his delightfully crooked grin. "But what if that day the Lord should be otherwise occupied?" He shrugged eloquently. "Genoa would find herself with seven thousand hungry children. Less than two weeks ago an army of twenty thousand children from all parts of France arrived in Marseille. The waters did not part there and much of that army disbanded. But my confreres Ferrus and Porquierres were so moved by the plight of these young warriors for Christ that they gave those remaining free passage to Palestine. Seven ships are already on the high seas, transporting five thousand children in all."

"And what, may we ask, prompts this selfless generosity?" Piccamiglia asked.

"The bishop of Marseille has assured Ferrus and Porquierres, and myself, of course, that our time in purgatory will be much lessened by such an act of charity," Frizio said, lowering his eyes and crossing himself. "Your own bishop will attest to the same, for I have already had speech with him."

Grimaldi made a steeple with his hands and rested his chin on it. "Does the leader of the German army know of your generous offer?"

Frizio shook his head. "I thought it best to discuss the matter first with you."

"Commendable," Piccamiglia said, "particularly since no boat may sail from Genoa without our approval. Where in the Holy Land would you take the children?"

"Tyre," Frizio said promptly, "that being the only port in Palestine still in Christian hands. As you doubtless are aware, my master Porquierres is a native of Genoa, so you may rest assured that these children will be delivered safely."

Grimaldi said with more than a trace of irritation, "John de Brienne pleads for men and ships and arms to save his beleagured Kingdom of Jerusalem, and you want to bring him— children? By what strange reasoning do you think that *children* can help?"

Having already anticipated this question, Frizio said earnestly, "Do you remember when the first Crusaders faced certain annihilation at Antioch? The Saracen forces were vastly superior, yet did not the discovery of the Holy Lance give our knights fresh hope, enabling them to win not only the battle for Antioch, but to go on and conquer Jerusalem as well? In such a way, these thousands of French and German children could bring new hope to the Kingdom of Jerusalem. Only God can tell what wondrous effects their demonstration of faith may bring."

Grimaldi stirred uncomfortably, reservation written all over his swarthy face. "So. But the Lord may indeed part the seas, in which case your offer will not be needed. We can discuss this further when we see what tomorrow brings."

The other senators nodded their approval and Frizio recognized the dismissal. For a moment, he considered leaving a discreet bag of gold on the table, then decided against that. These hard-nosed, calculating traders would immediately recognize the bribe. Above all, his donation of the ships must appear an act of selfless Christian devotion.

Outside the cathedral, where Baalbek stood waiting for Frizio, the first platoons of children were beginning to fill the piazza. From an alcove where the two of them could not be seen, Frizio and Baalbek appraised the gathering army. "Considerably fewer than were in Basle," Frizio said, "but prime flesh." Then his hand tightened on Baalbek's arm. "There they are," he said hoarsely, "and Mirage also."

Laurelle and Roger passed close enough for Frizio to see them. The boy held a bunch of grapes in his hand and every so often popped one into Laurelle's mouth. She looked thinner and taller and begrimed with the dust of the march, but her gray eyes sparkled with happiness. Their intimate, easy attitude with each other tormented Frizio and his body grew turgid with fantasies of how they spent their nights.

"The little thieves have ruined Mirage," Baalbek muttered, "see how wasted he looks and how drab his coat."

"At least he is alive," Frizio said, "and in another day or two I shall have him back."

After Frizio had left the consul chamber the senators reluctantly returned to the problem of the children.

"Have you seen them?" Piccamiglia asked. "Wild-looking they are, half naked and unruly. There is no telling what such an element might do to the morals of our citizens, let alone to the safety of the republic."

Grimaldi interrupted, "Still, if properly handled, these

young could prove a valuable addition to our populace; such an infusion of healthy northern blood could not help but revitalize Genoa's stock."

After further intense discussion, Piccamiglia presented the decisive argument. "Do we know if these children support the Guelph, Otto IV? Or are they loyal to Pope Innocent? Suppose the Holy Father discovered that we gave refuge to seven thousand of his enemies? Children, to be sure, but children grow up. Are we prepared to risk Rome's wrath?"

The senators then reached a compromise which pleased them all, and went out to the piazza to inform the waiting army of their decision. They found the bishop of Genoa leading the children in prayer; they had jammed the Piazza di San Lorenzo and were spilling into the side streets.

When the bishop had finished, Grimaldi came forward and said, "We welcome you to Genoa. Unfortunately, our earlier offer to allow your army to remain for one week must be rescinded. One night within our walls is all we can allow. Tomorrow, your army must be on its way. But if you children will swear to become good and loyal citizens of the republic, then you are welcome to stay and rebuild your lives. You will find Genoa most protective and generous, and you shall be safe."

Nicholas drew himself up haughtily and through an interpreter said to the consuls, "Do not concern yourselves with our safety, for we are protected by a higher ruler. As for the length of our stay, we did not need a week in the first instance and we do not need it now. One night is more than enough. For we have not marched this far merely to live in this city. Tomorrow we will go down to the beach, you shall see the waters part, as my angel has promised, and we will be on our way to fulfill our holy mission. And my doubting consuls, I tell you this; those Genoans who wish to march to glory with us, young and old alike, will not be refused."

The consuls looked at each other and frowned. "Never have I encountered a more willful child," Grimaldi said, and Piccamiglia added, "I would not be surprised to learn that the devil had his ear."

"Talk to this contentious child," Embriaci said to the bishop "and make him see reason. Even if the sea does part, can they walk the thousands of miles to the Holy Land?"

"Dare we interfere if the child has truly been chosen by the Lord?" the bishop asked, his need to believe winning over his good sense. Then he made the sign of the cross over the army. "It is all in God's hands now," he intoned. "Tomorrow the Lord will reveal His plans for His young warriors."

The rest of the day the children spent exploring the city, poking their noses into the dank, moisture-beaded churches, and crowding into the pungent waterfront marketplace of Sottoripa. Roger and Laurelle stared at the stalls loaded with wares from the world over. Jonathan haggled with an apothecary for a quantity of Irish moss—consumption moss, as it was commonly called—for Harolde, bartering some of his mandrake root for the medicinal herb.

Genoa, at the height of her power, had every conceivable vessel anchored in her harbor: galleys and galleons, caravels, carrocks and cutters. Some made their way through the sea by means of sail, others had slaves chained to the oars who would live and die at their posts.

The city boasted a babel of people. Broad-nosed Negroes strode the quays, with skin so dark it shone purple in the sun. And slant-eyed men from a land so distant it took years to journey there. They told awesome tales of a vast horde of Mongols led by a khan named Ghengis, gathering itself to sweep across Asia and Europe. Arabs in flowing jalabas rubbed elbows with turbaned Jews and the short, dark-haired Ligurians, natives to these parts. Unique as all these people were, everybody turned to stare at the golden-haired, blue-eyed striplings swarming through the narrow streets.

As they walked, Laurelle kept looking apprehensively over her shoulder. "I cannot get over the feeling that someone is watching us," she said.

"But you are being watched," Roger said, laughing. "They have never seen anybody with so many freckles."

"You!" Laurelle exclaimed, and laughed good-naturedly

along with the band. Still, she could not shake her apprehension.

"Never have I seen so many cats," Harolde said. They sat lounging on palace steps, in doorways, in the gutters, preening themselves in preparation for the night hunt. Many Genoese who relaxed in the intermittent sunshine also seemed to be marking time, for there was in the air a brusque masculine quality that bespoke exploration and commerce and conquest. And something more, an undercurrent of danger, and the barest hint of illicit traffic in goods and flesh.

A calico kitten tumbled head over heels out of a fish market, booted into the gutter by an irate fishmonger. The kitten shook her head in a daze and attached herself to the first passer-by; it happened to be Harolde. She followed the monk on wobbly legs, complaining loudly until he picked her up.

Her body was banded with beige and brown shot with orange. She sported a brown patch over one eye and an orange one over the other, giving her piquant face a look half in shadow, half in light. She wore a white bib around her neck and four white stockings, one of which she had forgotten to pull up.

Harolde said a prayer to exorcise any evil spirits. "For cats are known to be notorious familiars," he told the others. The kitten's enormous green eyes blinked slowly and with Harolde's amen, her scrawny body began to purr in his palm.

"You are the prettiest kitty in all Christendom," Harolde said, "but your fur . . ." He sneezed and put her down, but she yowled and clawed her way halfway up his habit.

"Oh, well," Harolde sighed, "yesterday was St. Bartholomew's Day, and he had his pig, so what am I to do?" He made a great show of annoyance but secretly he was delighted, for this was the first time in his life that an animal had not run from him.

"What will you call her?" Laurelle asked as she petted the kitten. "Her fur looks like it is all patchwork."

"Then I shall call her Tanis," Harolde said promptly, "for that is the Latin for patches." He put Tanis on his shoulder;

the kitten soon found her way into the nest of his hood where she rode along contentedly.

Before the children realized it the sun had set. But even with the ringing of the Angelus and curfew bells, the streets remained crowded with people, the wharves humming with activity beneath torch and moonlight. The lighthouse began to gleam on the promontory of Ponte St. Giorgio, named for Genoa's warrior saint. To survive, Genoa needed a constant lifeline to the wheatfields of Provence and the granaries of the Nile, so the city rarely slept.

Many of the Genoese, good and kind people, took the children into their homes and put them to bed with their own little ones. But elsewhere, the fears of the consuls were coming to pass. A flaxen-haired twelve-year-old girl was spirited into the palazzo of a nobleman, never to be seen again. Some adventurous boys explored the quarter around the Vacca Gate, where prostitutes serviced the navies of the world. Gaudy women of all colors called down to them from their balconies, offering their favors for the love of the Lord. A number of older lads and even some clerics slipped into the brothels, there to spend their energies seeding Genoa with the cream of northern Europe. In the dark area of the Molo Vecchio, a band of children, inspecting the waters which would soon part for them, were set upon by mercenaries bound for the Albigensian wars and cruelly used.

Flamonde had been deeply affected by little Rudolph's death. Now she feared for the tiny infant she had kept with her. This child too would not survive. That evening, she left the Piazza di San Lorenzo and walked along the narrow Via Orefici to the Benedictine convent. At the foot of the door stood a stone cradle where unwanted infants were left. Flamonde had half a mind to ring the bell and run. "No, that is the coward's way," she chastised herself, and yanked the bell cord.

A small wooden window in the door opened and a face framed in white wimple peered out. The door swung open and Flamonde stepped into a cloister of calm, with a neat vegetable garden and a whitewashed chapel glowing with altar candles. The sisters were at prayer and their gentle chant blended with the night breezes.

Fortunately, the mother superior spoke many languages, and Flamonde explained her predicament to her. "Traveling with the army, I cannot give the child proper care," Flamonde said.

The nun took the infant. "It is a sweet babe. Are you sure you want to give it up? After all, it is flesh of your flesh."

"Oh, but it is not mine," Flamonde said hastily, and told her of the circumstances. "I have cared for it since Lucerne."

"Then surely you are doubly blessed," the reverend mother said. "Rest assured, the child will grow well and strong here." The mother superior looked at the gaunt beautiful woman and sensed her weariness. "My child, you too can remain here if you wish. Our life is not easy, our pleasures few, but we truly love one another, and our Lord."

Tears started to Flamonde's eyes. She knelt and kissed the reverend mother's hand. "Thank you," she whispered, "but there are still so many I must care for."

"Bring them too," the mother superior said. "There is always room for one more in God's house."

Flamonde murmured, "If they would come, then gladly would I bring them and gladly would I stay. Alas, the children have their hearts set on Jerusalem. They will have it no other way, no matter how many fall. They have taken the vow, and so I must march with them."

The nun nodded. "Only you know wherein lies your own salvation. Here we believe that Jerusalem is in the heart. We thank you for bringing us this precious gift. Go with God."

Flamonde had gotten to the door when the mother superior cried out, "Wait! How is the little one called?"

Flamonde hunched her shoulders. "The mother died before she could be named."

"What is your name then?" the nun asked, and when Flamonde told her, she said, "Then we shall baptize her with the name of her godmother, Flamonde. Though you are not mother of her flesh, surely you are of the spirit."

Outside the convent, Flamonde leaned against the rough hewn stone wall and wept. Then she dried her eyes, and with her arms feeling light, started back to the cathedral.

Somehow, Flamonde managed to get lost in the blundering streets. She passed a tavern wild with music and laughter, and paused in the doorway, her blood beating to the call of her old life. Two boisterous sailors reeled out of the inn, caught sight of Flamonde and danced around her. Arms akimbo, Flamonde stood frowning at them.

The taller of the two sailors walked a silver coin through his fingers. "Yours," he said, "provided you are nice to us."

"There is more where that came from," the shorter sailor said, flipping another coin.

Both of these men are merry with wine and harmless enough, Flamonde thought, gauging them. She watched the silver coin spin up and down, seeing all the milk and bread it would buy, and in one fluid motion snatched it from the air and dropped it into her bodice. When the sailor made a grab for it she clouted him on the head. "That is what you get for teasing decent folk," she scolded him. "Now off with you before I call the night watch!"

When Flamonde got back to the Square of San Lorenzo most of the children were still awake, talking excitedly about the miracle that the morrow would bring.

GENOA:
SUNDAY, AUGUST 26

AT DAWN, THE YOUNG WARRIORS RUBBED THE SLEEP from their eyes and hastened to a large beach just outside the walls, there to witness, as it had come to be called, "The Miracle of the Parting of the Waters."

News of the event had spread throughout Genoa and its environs, and hosts of people, young and old, noble and peasant, flocked to the shore. The sick and the lame hobbled there also, for as with any miracle, there was always the chance of residual cures. The churches of Genoa stood empty; lacking worshippers, bishop and priest sped through an abbreviated Sunday Mass, then hurried to the gusting seaside where a curious atmosphere of carnival and vigil prevailed.

Some enterprising peddlers hawked rice water and pork and cheese pastries, others sold religious trinkets, while pickpockets and cutpurses weasled their way through the throng. The podesta and his guard came to keep order and many members of the Senate also made an appearance. "Merely out of curiosity," Grimaldi told Piccamiglia.

At last Nicholas arrived. A hush fell over the assemblage when he stepped down from his char. Two attendants caught the trailing ends of his magenta cape as he walked toward the waters. The sea shimmered, deep blue on the horizon, paling to aquamarine near the shore. Against the brilliant panorama of sea and cloud-swept sky, Nicholas looked even younger than his ten years. He stopped at the tide line of the wind-whipped waves and stared out at the Mediterranean.

Roger's advance guard stood a little distance away from Nicholas, nerves stretched raw in anticipation. "One could not ask for a better day for a miracle," Harolde said hopefully to Jonathan.

Jonathan nodded, his face a contradiction of his desire to believe and a deep doubt.

Little Luke tugged at Flamonde's skirts. "Will the sea really part?" he asked.

"It had better," Flamonde said grimly.

Laurelle's hands felt icy and Roger took them between his and rubbed them. "It will happen," Roger said resolutely, "I *know* it will!"

Nicholas lifted his arms to the sky, and in his sweet melodious voice recounted his first vision of Christ. He brought to mind the exodus from Cologne and all the trials the army had endured. He begged Jesus to clasp those children who had fallen to His bosom. For the living, Nicholas asked only for the chance to serve. So compelling were the evangelist's passionate words that the army wept, as they had wept when Nicholas first called them to crusade.

Many tearful citizens of Genoa also yearned for the miracle to happen and bent their prayers along with Nicholas's.

"And so my Lord," Nicholas said, "we have come this far in your behalf. But we cannot walk on water the way you did, and so we humbly beseech you to part the seas as you did for the children of Israel. That we may walk across to the Holy Land and bring about your Kingdom of Heaven on earth."

The innocence of Nicholas's request had moved the entire crowd, Genoese and children alike. But the sea was made of sterner stuff and rolled forward relentlessly, touching Nicholas's toes.

Nicholas would not budge, carried away as he was by the powers that his father, disciples, and lieutenants had sworn were his. "I will not move until the sea has parted," he insisted, stamping his foot. "Thus has my angel sworn to me and I will have nothing less."

In a fit of temper, Nicolas ripped the Greek cross from his neck and holding it high, advanced against the waves. A breaker swirled around his ankles, reached higher to his calves and then swept him off his feet. Nicholas's lieutenants plunged into the water to rescue him, all wet and sputtering.

Then did the Genoese, their sympathy turned to derision, roar with laughter. "Is that your miracle? Why, any one of us can do *that*."

The priest of San Giovanni de Prè cried, "The child set himself above the forces of heaven!" while another cleric called, "God punishes him for his sin of pride!"

Slowly then, a great lament rose up from the children, and as the waves continued to roll, the heart of the army withered with the realization that their glorious vision had led them not to Jerusalem, but to this sea of fools.

The children began to shout, demanding an explanation from Nicholas, but now he looked as one struck dumb. With the army jeering and hooting, Nicholas rode off with his entourage, speeded on their way by a hail of stones. Some said that in his shame Nicholas had gone to throw himself off a cliff. Others claimed he was riding back to Germany, terrified that the army would turn on him and kill him. Still others whispered that the earth had opened up and the devil had spirited his child-servant back into the underworld.

"Nicholas!" a wild-eyed Roger spat, making the name sound like a curse. He picked up a fistful of rocks and threw them one by one into the sea, which swallowed them with a gulp.

When Roger had calmed a bit, Jonathan asked softly, "Did you really believe that the sea would part?"

"Is our cause not just? Did the Lord not do it for the Israelites?" Roger demanded.

Jonathan rubbed his temples. "It is all in my head, but I do not know how to explain it. Roger, would you ask somebody to teach you how to swim?"

"Of course not! For I learned that as a child!"

"That is it," Jonathan said eagerly. "Once the Lord teaches a man to do something for himself, He no longer intervenes. The days of descending angels are over. In these times, seas are parted by ships!"

Roger smacked his head. "Jonathan is right! Why should the Lord waste His time with something man already knows how to do? What fools we were to believe the false little prophet!"

"Let us go home," Flamonde said, nudging Laurelle.

"To what?" Laurelle asked impatiently. She could not bear the thought of returning to her old life, for Jerusalem had become her dream, her salvation; and only through this could she and Roger ever hope to be together.

"We must *not* disband!" Harolde said, nervously fingering the red cross sewn on his habit. "Do you not realize the tortures that await us in purgatory if we deny our sacred crusading oath?" He attempted to go on but violent coughing seized him.

The children looked uneasily at each other.

When the spasm passed, Harolde said. "Only Pope Innocent can release us from our vow. And unless he does, we are doomed."

"Then here is what we must do," Roger cried. "Ship and sail and arm and oar, that is what parts the sea, and we must beg the Genoese, for the love of God, to give us passage!" And so saying, Roger began to shout, "Give us ships that we may do the Lord's work!"

Groups of children took up Roger's cry until the entire remaining army was shouting its demand.

The podesta came forward then and addressed the leaderless body of children. He told them of the merchants Ferrus and Porquirres and their offer of free passage to Palestine. The children's hopes soared, only to be dashed again when he said that the Senate had refused its permission. The republic could not spare any vessels, involved as she was in her perpetual forays against Pisa and her navy. Without an armed escort, their ships would be easy prey to the pirates who roamed the Mediterranean. Capture meant certain slavery and Genoa could not permit that to happen to kindred Christians.

Once more the podesta repeated the offer of sanctuary to the army. "Swear to settle down and become good citizens," he said, "and the gates and hearts of Genoa will be opened to you."

Whole troops of children gladly accepted this offer, for they were bone weary and could travel no more. Others, fearing the derision of the Rhinelanders, who were sure to mock them for their folly, also remained in Genoa. Many, though, felt too homesick to stay and slowly drifted from the beach to begin the trek north before autumn storms closed the Alpine passes.

But several thousand children remained who did not know which course to take.

"Terrible things will befall us unless we go home," Flamonde kept grumbling.

Jonathan said, "If they will not let us take ship from Genoa, is there no city in this whole land that will allow us? Do not pilgrims journey to Palestine all the time? I do not know what the rest of you plan, but I have not walked this far to be turned back. One way or another, I am going to Jerusalem!"

Harolde sat down on the pebbly beach and unrolled his map. He traced the coastline route from Genoa to Rome. "See? It is not very far, ten days, two weeks at the most. Now I propose that we march directly to Rome and lay our case before the pope." Harolde looked up at the circle of faces crowded around him. "Has it not been Innocent's unceasing call for crusade which stirred our hearts from the very beginning? Who better than Christ's vicar on earth can aid us in our quest? You will see," Harolde said, growing more excited, "once the pope learns first-hand of our sacred mission he will rally all Christendom around our cause!"

Harolde's enthusiasm fired Roger and he said, "Oh, would that you were right in this. For with the pope's blessing it is possible that people of *all* ages will answer our call for peace." Roger looked around for confirmation and saw Jonathan heading south along the boulder-strewn beach. "Jonathan, where are you going?" Roger called.

Jonathan yelled over his shoulder, "We shall none of us ever get to Jerusalem just standing here and talking!"

"Wait! We are all going." Roger turned and shouted to the scattered bands of milling children. "Will you deny your crusading vows? We have been led astray by the devil in the guise of a child. But do we love the Lord so little that we will allow the evil one to triumph? Are we the children of darkness or the children of light? I say we go on! If God wills it, then somewhere along this coast we shall find passage to the Holy

Land. Failing that, we shall march directly to Rome and petition the Holy Father. Now, who will come with us?"

First one band then another straggled after Roger and his guard, until a goodly number were following, shaken out of their lassitude and despair by the prospect of a goal, any goal. Even Flamonde tagged after with her children, grumbling with every step. A bewildered group they were with no clear leader save Roger.

As the remnants of the army headed south down the craggy coastline, Roger began to experience a new resolve. He stood up in his stirrups and looked behind him at the column of children stretched out along the narrow trail.

Of the twenty thousand who had started out from Cologne, there were only about one thousand left. But these one thousand—they could be the nucleus of a new crusade. And as he rode at their head the seed of a new thought began to grow within him. Had destiny at last chosen him to lead them all to glory?

Roger was not the only one with renewed hope. As Frizio had watched the children disband on the beaches of Genoa he could barely control his rage, for he literally felt the gold slipping through his fingers. But with Roger and his followers marching south, Frizio felt revitalized.

"Make haste," he said to Baalbek and headed for his vessels in the harbor. "We will follow the children down the coastline, and then as soon as they are away from Genoa's protection we shall have them!"

ALONG THE COAST:
LAST WEEK IN AUGUST

THE CHILDREN REACHED THE PENINSULA OF POR-
tofino long after nightfall and found refuge at the
Monastery of St. Jerome of Cervea, in the hamlet
of Pariaggi. The air being balmy, they camped
out in the cloister and swapped tales with the intrigued and excited monks.

"Pariaggi has sheltered many an illustrious visitor," an old
monk, eyes milky with cataracts, told them. "When I still had
sight, I myself saw Richard Coeur de Lion in our monastery.
While he was on his way to free Jerusalem a storm forced his
ship aground here."

"Is that not an omen?" Roger asked Harolde. "That our king
should have stayed here? Perhaps my father also?"

Harolde readily agreed.

"It is as if we are following in their footsteps," Roger said to
Harolde and Laurelle, "only this time we shall free Jerusalem."

In the morning, the army clambered down the rugged hills
to the harbor; but the Genoese Bank of St. George controlled
this port also, and once again passage was denied.

Undaunted, the children pressed south along the craggy
coast. "Sooner or later," Roger told them, "we must come to a
place where Genoa does not hold sway."

Only the healthiest, hardiest, and most determined of the
young crusaders were left. They became as sure-footed as
mountain goats as they traversed the rocky coastline of the
riviera, covering almost fifteen miles a day. The mornings
were usually foggy and damp, but by noon the mists burned
off to reveal yellow lupine and wild geranium splashing down
the hillsides. In the rare times when they stopped to rest, they
sought shade beneath strange flat-topped sea pines and
pungent cypress and cedar. With dusk the off-shore breezes

changed and quick winds flowed down from the Ligurian Apennines.

Soon they were passing through a rugged part of the coast, the Cinqueterre. Food remained scarce, the sea a haphazard source yielding fish, crab, and occasionally squid. One afternoon, Laurelle clambered among the wave-washed rocks and came back with a sack of mussels. Flamonde outdid herself concocting a mussel stew, while Tanis prowled around the steaming pot in a frenzy.

Flamonde tossed the empty shells to the kitten, who licked them clean.

"Thank you," Harolde said stiffly to Flamonde, his eyes avoiding her pale bosom near exposed by the tatters in her blouse.

Flamonde scooped up Tanis and rubbed noses with her. "Ah, if I had eyes like yours I would be covered all over with precious gems," Flamonde said, while Harolde reflected that indeed their eyes were very much alike. Then Flamonde dropped the kitten into Harolde's lap. "She is an enchantress, monk, and devoted to you," Flamonde said, then added with a teasing afterthought, "so you cannot be all bad."

Harolde felt the blood rush to his face and quickly buried his nose in his Saint's Day Calendar, searching for an appropriate grace for the meal. "Today being the Feast Day of St. Augustine," he said, "we will dedicate this meal to him."

Try as he might, Harolde's eyes kept drifting to Flamonde. "Lord, make me chaste—but not yet?" he murmured, quoting St. Augustine in his *Confessions.*

"I could renounce my vows," he said to Tanis, who had settled into his lap. Then he chided himself. "She does not even know that I exist." Another disconcerting thought entered his head. "Would the Lord love me less if I were an ordinary mortal instead of a monk? Tanis, which way would you love me more?"

The kitten yawned and then began to purr under his stroking fingers.

"It does not matter to you, does it," Harolde said. "You love me as long as I love you, and even when I don't. Perhaps that is the way it is with the Lord?"

Days later a range of mountains came into view with peaks so white they looked snow-capped. "That must be Carrara," Harolde said, pointing to the area on his map.

Laurelle wandered into the fields to pick wildflowers, then came back to Flamonde, arms laden with vibrant color. "Did you think I would forget your birthday?" she asked, kissing her sister.

"Oh, so it is," Flamonde said, feigning surprise, though she had sulked all morning, thinking the world had forgotten. She walked back along the line of children handing out the flowers, and all wore them in their hair in honor of Flamonde's day.

That night the children pooled all their food and prepared a meager feast. They sang songs of their own provinces and played prisoner's base and blind man's bluff. The children under Flamonde's special care had collected tiny scalloped shells, and Tintoro, a clever craftsman who had joined the army in Genoa, threaded them into a necklace. When Little Luke presented the gift to Flamonde, she let out a great cry and hugged and kissed each child in turn.

A reed flute appeared, then another, and then a lad beat upon a kettle and music was made. Around the campfire Flamonde danced a dance of joy, necklace whirling as she did. The children began to clap and she picked up her pace and spun until her skirts flared to show her long shapely legs and she spun ever faster, a woman possessed, possessed with the spirit of joy. She turned so fast she fell laughing to the ground, her fall cushioned by daisies yellow and white.

"Is there no one who will tell my fortune for the coming year?" Flamonde cried as she tried to stop the spinning world.

"You will marry and have many children!" a voice called. "Say the word and we start tonight!"

Jonathan said, "If today is your birthday, then you were born under the sign of Virgo, the Virgin, and you are as pure in spirit as you are in body!"

Flamonde threw back her head and laughed until the tears streamed down her face. She wiped them away and saw two Haroldes moving before her dizzy eyes. "And you?" Flamonde asked in a gently mocking tone, "have you nothing to say to me on my day?"

A thousand compliments burned on Harolde's tongue but the years of church doctrine locked his cloistered heart. What's more, when Flamonde had danced, he had been beside himself with jealousy that others had seen her naked legs. He cleared his throat and tried to make his voice stern. "Only to warn you that it is unseemly in the sight of God for a woman not to be discreet. As we all know, the church forbids dancing, and it is written . . ."

"It is written, it is written," Flamonde mimicked him. "What do monks know of the world save what they read in musty old books?"

Harolde barely resisted an overwhelming urge to seize Flamonde and shake some sense into her.

Flamonde stretched her arms skyward to stop the pinwheeling stars. "I know more of God in a blade of grass, I know more of God in a lamb nursing, I know more of God in the curve of a man's thigh than you shall ever know for all your precious words."

Harolde made a forked sign to ward off the evil streaming from her mouth. He knew his somber attitude was casting a pall over the festivities yet he could not help himself. "Would you be the devil's handmaiden? For it is the devil who speaks through your mouth, Flamonde. Take care lest one day you find yourself in purgatory."

Flamonde thumbed her nose at Harolde. "No doubt I will," she said, laughing, "though it will not be because of your threats. Besides, on this day especially I do not have time to listen to your nonsense of purgatory and perdition. I have danced for my children, I will dance for them again!" Snapping her fingers, Flamonde called for more music and with a toss of her skirts, began once more.

Watching her, Harolde trembled with anger and misery. He said to himself, "The Lord placed her in your path so that you might conquer your baser nature. And conquer it you must, or it is you who shall find yourself in purgatory."

In the middle of the night Harolde walked in his sleep, exactly to the spot where Flamonde lay sleeping. Flamonde woke, passed her hand before Harolde's glazed eyes, then drew him away from camp lest he be shamed before the others when wakened.

She shook him gently; Harolde blinked and then he focused on her with a look that burned. Flamonde had seen such a look before in too many men's eyes to mistake its meaning. Still, she was startled when Harolde lifted her in his arms and carried her down to the beach.

There, the blind eye of the moon watched them make love. Flamonde had expected only the most casual of concourse, she knew instinctively that Harolde was a virgin. But what she did not know was that her touch would release a decade of dreams in him, dreams so potent that the two of them were swept along to a place neither had ever imagined.

Later, when every lovemaking fantasy had been exhausted, they lay side by side on the cool sand. Harolde said, "We have committed a sin which will add eleven thousand years to our stay in purgatory. So it is written . . ." he broke off, blushing furiously.

Flamonde smothered her giggle, but it proved infectious, and Harolde joined her. Then he grew serious again; he took her hand and said, "I forced you to do this and I beg your forgiveness."

Flamonde absently brushed the sand from her legs. "You did not force me. Furthermore, I do not believe it a sin to love, no matter what you monks say." Then she ran her finger along the line of his sharp chin. "I have slept with many men in my life, more than I care to remember, and for reasons I would sooner forget. But never have I slept with a man such as you."

Harolde squirmed uncomfortably and cleared his throat to say something, but Flamonde put her finger on his lips. "Do not fret, I know your vows. I know what the church would do to you, and to me. But I cannot, I will not believe that what we have done is wrong. How can something of such beauty be a sin? Would the Lord permit such a thing?"

She took his fevered hand and pressed it to her lips. "I make you this vow. I will never sleep with anybody else, or dance again, or do anything to displease you. If I had to spend eleven thousand more years in purgatory, gladly would I do it to lie with you once more. For I know we reached a moment when our souls touched."

Torn with conflicting emotions, Harolde said nothing. He leaned back exhausted against the cool sands and closed his eyes while the battle of church and manhood raged within him.

Flamonde watched the autumn moon rise from the sea and send its silver shimmering beams across the waters toward them. She felt the breeze ruffle her hair and she sat very still, close to tears.

Show me who invented the human heart, she thought ruefully, then show me where he is hanged. She had fallen in love . . . deeply and impossibly in love. And with a monk! she thought, exasperated. How capricious the fates that have made God my rival. Not that I would ever ask him to renounce the cloth, she thought, but even if he did, it could never be. For she sensed that he did not have very long on this earth. Could that be why I did not resist him? she wondered.

She gazed at the nascent moon pearling the waters, touched the necklace of shells around her throat and heard the quiet breathing of her lover sleeping beside her. His face, washed with silvered light, looked unblemished with guilt. "Oh, Mary," Flamonde whispered, "I do love him. Let me have him a little while longer. At least until he sees his child born."

With the secret knowledge of her sisterhood, Flamonde felt that her prayers had been answered and that this night she had conceived. "Lord," Flamonde murmured, her heart overflowing, "If you were to call me tomorrow, I would die fulfilled."

Harolde hummed as he walked along, all smiles and kind greetings for everybody. He studded Tortoise's forelock with purple and pink verbena, and suffered Tanis to climb all over him, including to the top of his tonsured scalp. At his devotions, even his once-somber Te Deums had a new lilt to them.

Roger and Jonathan did not know what to make of this new Harolde, what with his sudden vigor, flushed cheeks, and eyes dancing with gaiety.

"Could it be that his sickness is cured?" Roger asked, but Jonathan could not say.

Harolde's mood continued to lift everybody, and the days passed with much laughter and jibbing.

One week after their debacle in Genoa, the children reached the alluvial plain of the Arno River. In the distance, where the river flowed into the sea, they saw the spires and palaces of Genoa's greatest rival, the Republic of Pisa. The closer they came to the city, the more distinct became the scores of ships anchored in the harbor.

"And none of them appear to fly the flag of Genoa," Roger said excitedly, squinting against the sun. He increased their pace until the children broke into a run. Their hope sounded in the jar of their feet against the baked earth, it sang in the rushing wind and throbbed with the surety of each heartbeat. At last, they sensed, they had come to a place where they would find passage to the Holy Land.

PISA:
SATURDAY, SEPTEMBER 1

*I*F GENOA WILL NOT ALLOW YOU CHILDREN OF THE Lord to serve Him, then rest assured, Pisa will!" the Consul Obertenghi proclaimed to the little army gathered outside Pisa's walls.

Obertenghi, who represented the ruling Senate of Pisa, told the children the exciting news. "Shipowners who had their vessels anchored in Genoa heard of your plight and ordered their ships to Pisa. Three are anchored in the harbor at this very moment, waiting for you. Furthermore, because they believe so fervently in your mission, the only payment they ask is that you pray for their souls after they have delivered you to the Holy Land."

Hosannas and hallelujahs were mingled with tears and embraces as the children went wild.

"I knew the Lord would not turn His face from us," Roger said. "Here is the miracle we have all prayed for."

When the children had quieted, Roger addressed the consul. "Where are these worthy captains that we may thank them?"

"They are in the shipyards of the Citadella, making last minute repairs," Obertenghi said. "You will meet them when you board."

"When?" Laurelle cried. Roger took up the question as did the others, until all the children were chanting, "When?"

The consul raised his hand to still them. "If all goes as planned, you sail Monday at dawn. The ships will begin to load Sunday night. Meanwhile," the consul informed them, "you are to consider yourselves Pisa's guests. Food is being made ready in the market district of Piazza della Berlina."

The band proceeded through the Gates of Santa Maria into the city. Coming immediately upon the panorama of the Piazza del Duomo, the children were struck dumb. Three gigantic white marble buildings of varying shapes and sizes were in the process of construction and a cloud of marble dust, lime, and sawdust hung over the square.

"To the far left of the piazza is the Campo Sancto," Obertenghi said, "our sacred cemetery, formed of soil taken from the Hill of Calvary by Archbishop Daimbert during the First Crusade."

"Barring Jerusalem," Flamonde joked, "that is not such a bad place to be buried."

The three hazy structures took shape as the children came closer. The nearest was a huge, round, roofless building with the outside scaffolding reaching to the galleried third story.

"This is the largest baptistry in the world," Obertenghi said proudly.

Just beyond it stood a monumental cathedral in the cruciform shape, of a marble so white it dazzled. "And as you know it far surpasses Genoa's Church of San Lorenzo," Obertenghi said.

"It is beautiful, yes," Jonathan said in an aside to Harolde. "But all this talk! Our business is Jerusalem."

Harolde shook his head and sighed. "You are right, yet how can we be rude to our benefactors? Let us pray for patience."

Beyond the cathedral, the children saw the greatest wonder of all, a campanile that defied nature, for it leaned at such a sharp angle that the children expected it to topple even as they watched.

Laurelle held her breath, waiting. Still it did not fall. "What holds it up?" she asked Harolde, but for once he did not have an explanation.

"People from all corners of the world come to marvel at our leaning tower," Obertenghi said, and recounted its origins. Enemies of the republic circulated the tale that the architect, Bonnano Pisano, had designed the campanile to mirror his own hunchbacked affliction, and as such it symbolized Pisa's fated decline. But all loyal Pisans knew that the sandy soil was unstable, and by the time the fourth story had been completed in 1200, the campanile leaned so dangerously that work had to be suspended. "Even now new architects are devising methods to complete the last three stories without toppling the structure," Obertenghi finished.

"We must climb it," Roger said excitedly. "Surely from the top we will be able to see the whole world."

"Have you taken leave of your senses?" Flamonde cried. "Look how it leans! You will fall off and break your heads!"

"You go on," Roger shouted to the others. "Laurelle and I will meet you at the Piazza della Berlina."

Then Harolde began to cough so violently that his face turned bright red. Flamonde hovered over him anxiously, beside herself that she could not help.

"It is the dust," Jonathan said, sneezing. "We must get away from all this construction before we suffocate." Then Jonathan went to Roger and took him aside. "If you are a leader, then you must lead. Is it not unseemly for you to indulge yourself in such childish pursuits when our whole army waits on your decisions?"

Roger squared his shoulders and scowled. Then he took Mirage's reins and led the column on. "I know Jonathan is right," he said to Laurelle, "but God's wounds! I am getting tired of his *always* being right!"

If Genoa projected a masculine vibrancy, then Pisa appeared mellow and almost pretty. On both sides of the Arno River, which cut the city's 280 acres in half, the streets were laid out in orderly fashion. To the northeast, beyond the red-tiled roofs of the mustard-colored brick and plaster dwellings, rose the craggy outline of the Apennine Hills. In the distant southwest delta, the children saw the Arno flow into the Mediterranean.

Roger pointed to the east. "There, from where the sun rises is our goal."

Laurelle gazed at the horizon for a long moment. "How long will the voyage take?"

"Harolde says that with good winds, less than four weeks, sometimes no more than three."

"Then I shall pray for good winds," Laurelle said, "for I cannot wait . . ." she stopped herself, blushing furiously.

Roger understood her meaning and gave her a crushing embrace. He stared at the waters, seeing not the limitless sea, but that long-ago black night atop Notre Dame Cathedral. "When I was a child," he said quietly, "I stood poised on a great height, thinking I could not go on. I demanded that God decide the course of my life. Now He has brought me this far, and He has brought me you."

Roger and Laurelle led the band of children down the Via Santa Maria to the Arno River and then turned left along the quays to the heart of the city, the Piazza della Berlina. The two- and three-storied inns surrounding the square housed merchants and travelers from all over the world. One side of the piazza fronted the river; stocks lined another side of the square. One imprisoned a sailor caught smuggling contraband; another held a shopkeeper guilty of selling his wares before sundown on Sunday. The piazza buzzed with activity; monks from the Benedictine and Carthusian monasteries arrived with carts loaded with food, and Cistercians set up a soup kitchen.

In the square, Harolde saw for the first time the mendicant friars he had heard tell of, the barefoot Franciscans in their coarse brown habits who walked the streets begging their food. As these monks helped the weary children, bathing their feet and feeding the little ones, Harolde talked to them and learned of their calling.

"If we were not going to Jerusalem, surely I would join these Franciscan monks," Harolde murmured to Flamonde later that night as they lay in a barn. "Never have I seen monks so loved by the common people. But then after all, whom would the Lord chose—these simple men who preach His Gospel? Or the church prelates who grow fat battening on the poor?"

Flamonde nodded as she nestled against his shoulder, but her mind was on other things.

Harolde continued, "Though the Franciscans are not yet a recognized order, they believe that Pope Innocent III will soon grant them that privilege. You see," he explained excitedly, "the pope had a dream in which he saw the church of Rome crumbling. But before it could fall, a monk he had never seen before rushed forward and held it up on his frail shoulders. The next day, who should seek audience with the pontiff but this very same man! The pope immediately recognized this Brother Francis as the monk of his dream. Is that not a wondrous tale?"

Flamonde agreed, but felt her usual pang of jealousy whenever Harolde talked about his calling. These past days had seen her drawn deeper into the well of love. She could not bear the thought of sharing him with anybody—not even God. God will have him soon enough, she thought. Yet for the first time since this crusade had begun, Flamonde wanted to believe that they would reach Jerusalem. That is what *he* wants, she thought, that is what will bring him peace. And the Lord might grant them a year, perhaps two in the Holy City.

She flung her arm across his chest. She could not get enough of him; every touch must be savored, every blissful moment stored up for her lifetime without him. Flamonde moved closer to Harolde and soon they had forgotten all else save the wonder of each other.

"Did you see them?" Frizio demanded.

"Yes, master," Baalbek said.

"Mirage too?"

"Stabled in the barn just behind this inn."

"You are sure?"

Baalbek nodded emphatically. "I saw him myself."

Frizio paced the room in the inn just off the Piazza della Berlina. Tension corded the muscles in his neck.

"Do not upset yourself," Baalbek said. "At this time tomorrow Mirage will be safely on board and in your hands again."

"Nothing must go wrong this time," Frizio said. "Stupid Genoese, they have cost me a fortune."

Fair winds had brought Frizio to Pisa fully three days before Roger's tiny army arrived. In presenting his plan to the Pisan Senate, Frizio had not missed the opportunity of underlining Genoa's refusal to help the little ones. Having some knowledge of the firm Frizio represented, and believing all concerned to be reputable Christians, the Pisans had no reason to be suspicious. And so the Senate had decided that if the children accepted Frizio's offer, they would have no objection to his transporting them to Palestine.

The only possible danger, Frizio thought, was that Roger or Laurelle or one of the others might recognize him. Frizio had debated long and hard whether or not to kill the boy. For a number of reasons he had decided not to. Not the slightest suspicion must shadow the delicate matter of the offer of ships. Frizio was also counting on Roger to lead his children aboard; the boy himself would fetch a handsome sum in the slave markets. Most important, Frizio believed that fate had drawn him together with these wanderers. The intertwining of their lives seemed destined, as it were. And it would give him unspeakable pleasure to have Roger in his power at last.

As for Laurelle, Frizio's feeling for her had grown during these weeks into such a confusion of contempt and desire that he could scarce bear to think on it. Drink and drugs had not helped, nor the girls in the brothels along the way, for their faces all turned into her face, leaving him trembling with frustration.

"I have arrangements yet to make," Frizio said to Baalbek. "Keep the children under close watch but make certain that you are not discovered or I will flay the fat from your bones."

Frizio went out the back entrance and hastened to the Citadella shipyards, there to supervise the nightworkers repairing his drydocked vessels.

Baalbek threw a long black cloak over his jalaba and went down into the piazza. Frizio had put the fear of Allah into him and Baalbek anxiously began to search for Roger and his cohorts. He saw them all, save for the red-haired woman and the monk. And Mirage? Baalbek thought, suddenly uneasy. Was he still in the stable?

Baalbek had to make sure. Stealthily, he moved around the building to the rear. He opened the barn door and slipped inside, to be met by quiet and the pungent smell of hay, manure, and horseflesh.

As Baalbek crept toward the stall, Mirage suddenly reared, kicking at the wooden slats and setting up a fearful racket.

Harolde roused himself in time to meet Baalbek's fist crashing down on the back of his head. He never saw the eunuch. Flamonde did. She scrambled to her feet, drawing her wits and shift about her in the same motion. Shock delayed the scream in her throat—surely this same nightmare had happened long ago—then Baalbek's hand tightened around her throat and all went black.

Baalbek trembled with fright. He did not know if the monk were alive or not. Not that it mattered, for he knew that Harolde had not seen him. He dumped the monk behind some bales of hay. But what to do with the woman? Strangle her? Frizio had said no killing.

"Oh, merciful Allah, what will he do to me?" Baalbek blubbered and in his panic threw Flamonde over his shoulder. Sneaking through the deserted alley behind the inn, Baalbek carried her up to Frizio's room.

L AURELLE THOUGHT NOTHING OF IT WHEN FLA-
monde did not appear the next morning. "Perhaps she has gone to light a candle for the souls
of the children who died," she said in answer to
Roger's impatient questions. "Yesterday she told
me she might."

"But where then is Harolde?" Roger asked, annoyed.

Laurelle smiled. "Ah, you men. You have eyes but do not
see."

Roger's mouth fell open as it dawned on him. He slapped
his thigh, chuckling. "Why, Harolde, you sly old friar!" he
exclaimed, startled by this new turn of events, yet delighted
for the monk. For Harolde had suffered much with his illness
and this brief respite of joy seemed fitting. Then Roger felt the
dull ache in his own loins, from his months of frustrated desire. "Never did I think I'd see the day when I would wish you
were more like your sister!" he said, grinning.

Laurelle's eyes clouded with such pain that Roger immediately put his arm around her shoulder. "Forgive me," he said,
"I was only teasing. Come, then, let us search out the ships at
the Citadella."

"Jonathan, will you come with us?" Laurelle called.

Jonathan shook his head. "Tortoise is getting a case of the
heaves and I must steam some water for her," he said, and
waved good-by. He felt uneasy; it was not like Harolde to go
off without telling anybody. He feared that the monk might
have had an attack during the night. He searched the square
but could not find him. Then he went to the stables to feed
Mirage and take care of Tortoise. The animals were skittish
and he could barely calm them.

"Ah, Tanis, I did not know you were here," Jonathan said
when the kitten leaned against his leg, her tail bushed.

"Where is Harolde? What? You say he has left you for another woman? Well, never mind, I shall love you."

The kitten hopped onto a bale of hay, meowing in counterpoint to Tortoise's continuous plaintive bray. Mirage was so nervous that Jonathan could not curry him. Twice the stallion tried to pin him against the stall and Jonathan had to punch him in the ribs to break free.

"What is the matter with all you animals today?" Jonathan shouted. A moan startled him and led him behind the stacks of hay where he discovered Harolde.

"Flamonde," Harolde groaned, when Jonathan splashed a dipper of water in his face. "Flamonde? Where is she?" Harolde cried on a desperate rising note.

Jonathan helped him to his feet and Harolde promptly threw up.

"I do not know what happened," Harolde insisted, as Jonathan questioned him anxiously. "Flamonde and I were here— talking," he said hastily as he put on his habit. "The next thing I knew, oh, my head. She would not have left of her own accord. Somebody must have spirited her away."

The monk and the boy looked at each other, unable to hide their foreboding fear. They looked through every corner of the barn and then made their way into the square to continue the search. Jonathan sent a child running to the Citadella to bring Roger and Laurelle back. Then all the children began to look for Flamonde, calling her name through the arcaded shops and the narrow streets. When they found no trace of her, they went directly to the "Officer in Charge of Stray Animals, Children, and Other Lost Property," and the deputy mounted a city-wide search for Flamonde.

"If you have ruined my plans because of this," Frizio said to Baalbek, "I will chop off your fingers. Are you certain nobody saw you?"

"I swear," Baalbek said, pressing a cloth to the oozing cut across his face made by Frizio's whip. "The monk could not have seen me, for I hit him while he slept, and nobody was about when I brought her here." As Baalbek passed the chair in which Flamonde sat tied, hands bound behind her back, he pinched her viciously.

Flamonde moaned through the gag in her mouth.

Baalbek fingered the knife tucked in his wide sash. "With one stroke we would have no problem."

"Fool," Frizio said, "it must be made to look like an accident. Surely the children will report her missing. Here is what you must do. As soon as it is dark, splash some wine on her clothes and pour some in her mouth. Then brain her and throw her in the river. If the tide does not carry her out, then let them think that she met her end after a night of revelry. And do not mark up her body the way you did with that last wench!"

Baalbek fidgeted and looked abashed.

Frizio lifted Flamonde's chin with his thumb. "A pity to waste you," he said, "for there are still some years of pleasure left in you, as even I can testify. You would have brought a fair price on the block. Ah, such hate gleams in your eyes, it cries out for an hour's dalliance. But you are a risk I cannot take."

Frizio turned to Baalbek. "I must go to the harbormaster. The ships are ready, but the podesta left innumerable papers for me to sign: oaths, guarantees, and the like. Let them have their paper guarantees, we shall be in Outremer before they realize what has happened. After the podesta, I must see to the loading of provisions. If I have not returned by nightfall, do as I instructed. Remember, no knife marks on her body."

Frizio stopped before Flamonde and said quietly, "As you sit here awaiting your fate, I leave you to wonder how different all our lives might have been had you not refused me your sister that night."

Then Frizio went off, leaving Baalbek alone with Flamonde. Having been up most of the previous night and all of this day, Baalbek soon wearied of tormenting his prisoner and lay down to rest.

While Baalbek dozed, Flamonde worked furiously to free herself. The brick building had irregular shards sticking from its rough, unfinished walls. The back of Flamonde's chair stood against the wall, and feeling along the stone, Flamonde found a rough edge and began to rub her bonds against it. Whenever Baalbek roused himself to squint in her direction, Flamonde stopped, resuming only when he nodded off again.

Hours passed, leaving her hands scraped and bleeding, but Flamonde worked on. Toward the afternoon, Flamonde heard the children in the square below, calling her name. Sweat trickled down her brow as she increased her efforts. Shortly before dusk, she heard the tramp of feet and singing as the children marched to the river quays. There the rowboats would take them to Frizio's ships waiting in the harbor. Tears mingled with sweat as Flamonde worked desperately at the fraying ropes.

Twilight had turned the mustard-colored buildings a deep umber when Baalbek heaved his bulk up from the pallet. He opened the shutters a crack and peered out. The houses cast their long shadows and Baalbek said, "It is time. The tavern will be open now and I will be able to buy your wine. What is your preference?" he asked, grinning mischievously. "You may as well have your choice for your last bottle." With both hands, Baalbek pinched Flamonde so hard that corkscrews of pain radiated through her chest.

As soon as Flamonde heard Baalbek's descending footsteps, she renewed her efforts with a fury, paying no mind to the stone tearing at her flesh. Her arms, straining in their sockets, became numbed, but she continued to grind away at the ropes. When she thought she could not make another move, Flamonde felt the first strand break, then another, until finally she worked her hands free.

At first she could not move her arms, then gradually the feeling came back. Faster, she told her trembling fingers, as she tore the gag from her mouth and untied the ropes around her ankles.

She flung open the window and leaned out, searching desperately for Harolde and the others. She saw them then, at the farthest end of the square, and opened her mouth to scream. But so tight had been the gag and so dry was her throat that she could only manage a hoarse croak.

Baalbek's heavy tread on the staircase panicked her. Too high to jump from the window, she thought. She had just enough time to grab the water pitcher and get behind the door as the bolt snapped open.

As Baalbek lumbered into the room, Flamonde brought the jug down on his head with every ounce of her strength. The pitcher cracked and the water fountained over both of them. It stunned Baalbek only momentarily, but long enough for Flamonde to scoot under his flailing arms and run down the stairs. She tried again to scream the alarm, but her throat remained paralyzed. At the foot of the steps Flamonde turned and saw Baalbek come crashing down after her. She fled into the alley and raced toward the piazza.

Though her body was stiff and her legs cramped with pins and needles, each running step brought Flamonde renewed strength. Ahead lay the Piazza della Berlina and safety. I am faster than he! The exultant cry sang through her body as she reached the end of the alley. I will save them!

But she was not faster than Baalbek's knife; the blade sank deep within her shoulder blades, pitching her forward.

Flamonde struggled to her knees; she heard the eunuch running up behind her. "Oh, my Mary," she breathed, "if ever you had mercy, not for me, only let me warn the children."

Flamonde stumbled into the piazza, lurching past the sailor and the shopkeeper still locked in their stocks.

The children who had known Flamonde and been loved by her had waited until the last minute, hoping she would return before the final rowboats left for the ships. Close to three hundred children were at the far end of the square, drifting toward the quays.

Then Flamonde found her voice. "Harolde!"

The band of children turned, saw Flamonde, and streamed back across the square toward her. Baalbek had no choice but to slink away into the shadows.

Flamonde clutched Harolde's shoulders and sank slowly to the ground. Harolde's questions and Laurelle's scoldings were cut short when they saw the dagger sticking from Flamonde's back.

"Jonathan!" Harolde shouted. The boy fought his way through the press and came to Flamonde. She lay face down, head cradled in Harolde's lap.

"Frizio," Flamonde gulped, blood bubbling to her lips.

"Frizio?" Roger gasped. "Merciful God, it cannot be!"

"Do not talk," Jonathan said urgently to Flamonde. "I fear the knife has pierced the lung. Hold her," he said to Harolde, "I must pull it out."

"Listen to me," Flamonde begged, grabbing at Jonathan's hand. "Those are Frizio's ships in the harbor."

Laurelle began to tremble. "The Lord have mercy on us all! Why would he follow us halfway around the world? Could you not be mistaken?" she asked desperately.

Flamonde shook her head. "It was the eunuch's knife that did this. . . . Frizio plans to sell the children into slavery. You must do for the living. Warn them!"

"Slavery?" Harolde repeated dully. "The man is the fiend incarnate!"

Flamonde twisted her head. "Laurelle, where are you?"

"Right here," Laurelle said, kneeling at Flamonde's side.

Flamonde licked her parched lips and Jonathan moistened them with some water. Flamonde searched Laurelle's face. "I beg you, forgive me for any of the sins I have committed against you. I thought only to protect you."

"Do not even *think* such things!" Laurelle sobbed. "It is I who should beg your forgiveness," she said, and covered Flamonde's face with kisses. "Oh my wild and sweet heart, I will do anything you say, marry whomever you want, take you home this day, anything! Only do not die!"

Flamonde shook her head with a mournful smile. "The Lord calls, and I must answer." Then Flamonde searched the faces of those crowded around her and sought out Roger's. "Now it is you who must protect her. And also the little ones in my care. Will you do this for me?"

"On my life I swear this," Roger said hoarsely.

Then Flamonde looked at Harolde's shimmering face. Her hand found his. "You will reach Jerusalem one day, this I know. And then I will not have died in vain." She coughed and whispered. "Remember me in your prayers, monk, for I loved you."

A spasm arched Flamonde's back. Her eyes widened and then turned blank. After a moment, Jonathan put his head to her heart. He shook his head and brushed his hand over her eyes, closing them.

In life, Flamonde had been beautiful, but death added a serenity that transfigured her with grace.

Laurelle rocked her sister back and forth, wailing over her. Harolde knew a sadness so bitter he would have taken his own life had he not been such a coward. He stared down at the one who had taught him more about the meaning of love than all his years of prayer. His tears came then, hot and silent, falling on Flamonde's face.

Though Harolde was not ordained and had not the right, he defied church law and administered the last rites.

When the brief ritual was over Harolde turned to Roger and said in a voice blurred with tears, "I will see to her burial. You must do as she asked and take care of the living. Go warn the others."

They made hurried arrangements to meet at the Piazza del Duomo. Roger, still weeping, sprang on Mirage and galloped off to the quays, shouting for the children not to board the rowboats. Riding up and down the river, Roger managed to save another fifty or so of the children. But the hundreds already on board the three vessels in the harbor were already lost.

Meanwhile, Harolde, Laurelle, and Jonathan put Flamonde's body across Tortoise's back and hurried through the night streets toward the cathedral square, for Harolde had in his mind where Flamonde must be buried. "The Campo Sancto, the sacred cemetery," he told the others.

Laurelle found some small comfort in this. "If anybody tries to stop us," she said resolutely, "I shall hit them, I shall punch them with my fists."

The area around the Campo was deserted and they crept into the graveyard. In the light of the waning moon they dug a shallow grave, wrapped Flamonde in a winding sheet and laid her to rest.

Harolde took the rosary from his belt and placed it in Flamonde's cold hand. "Until we meet," he whispered, and covered her over with the soil which had come from the Hill of Calvary.

At a council of war held an hour later, Roger counted heads: 357 children. "All saved because of Flamonde," he said, and they all began to cry again. "We must not delay another moment," Roger told them. "It is too late to stop the ships; they did not wait for dawn but have already sailed. Furthermore, it may be that the people of this city are in league with Frizio."

Harolde nodded. "Even if not, they might not believe our tale, and by the time they gave pursuit Frizio's ships would have long disappeared into the darkness. We must leave those children to God's mercy." Then he spread out his map, and focusing on it through his tears, traced the route to Rome as he spoke. "It would not be wise to journey via the coast. Frizio might follow us by sea, come ashore at night, and plunder our camp." He paused and wiped his eyes. "Best to head inland. We can follow the Arno River until we reach Florence. Then head south to Siena, Viterbo, and then Rome. We have little choice now save to present our case to the pope. Only Innocent III has the power to release us from our vows—or to revive our mission."

"Let us go to him, then," Roger said. "He will see that we are righteous. He will sound the clarion call throughout Christendom so that *all* will march for peace!"

"And so now we have yet another reason to reach the Holy Land," Laurelle said with quiet resolve. "For Flamonde."

"To Florence then," Roger said, heading for the gate of St. Zeno. The constable of the watchtower let the children out, for already rumors abounded that the city had been duped regarding the transportation of the children and Pisa was eager to avoid further embarrassment.

On a slight hill outside the walls, the children saw the three ships, tiny in the distance, their white sails catching the light of the moon as they headed toward the open sea.

THE TUSCAN HILLS:
EARLY SEPTEMBER

ALL THROUGH THE NIGHT ROGER LED THE REMNANTS of his army on a forced march. But the band walked without its heart, for along with their fear of capture they were pursued by thoughts of Flamonde. Where was the jest, the laughter, the embrace which had breathed life into them?

Twice during the night they halted to allow the stragglers to catch up, then continued their flight.

Little Luke tugged at Laurelle's hand. "Where is my Flamonde?" he asked. "We must wait for her."

Laurelle swallowed hard. "Why, the Lord had need of her, my Luke. You see, some of his littlest angels were ailing and Flamonde has gone to help."

"When will she come back?" the boy asked. When Laurelle did not answer, Little Luke burst into tears.

"Do not cry," Laurelle said, her face wet with her own weeping. "She is with us, she will always be with us." Laurelle picked up Little Luke and comforted him as they marched, until he had exhausted himself and fell asleep on her shoulder.

After some miles Jonathan took the sleeping child from her and carried him on his shoulders.

Laurelle stretched her arms. "Without the child's weight, I feel I could float away. How did Flamonde ever do it? Day after day, mile after mile?" She shook her head in a daze. "Without her, we are like orphans."

Though still very warm, a subtle quality in the air suggested that summer had crested and that the days were descending irrevocably toward the melancholy season. In their penultimate moment, the flowers went mad with color along the marshy banks of the Arno, outlining the sluggish brown river with slashes of periwinkle, meadow saffron, and rose.

At the unlikeliest moments tears would spring to Harolde's eyes. He questioned Laurelle without end, drawing from her details of Flamonde's life, hoping thereby to imprint her on his mind. At times, he would slip into hallucinations in which Flamonde rode with him upon Tortoise, her back pressed against his chest. Night held the saddest hours, for then came the demons of his training to stoke the fires of conscience. But there were also those blissful moments when her shade would lie beside him and mold herself to his body, drawing his love from him. Because she had been taken from him at the height of their passion, Harolde remembered and loved her with an uncontrollable desire which he could not have sustained in life.

On the fifth day of September, midweek, Roger's ragged group reached Florence. The populace reacted with indifference. After Nicholas's army had fragmented in Genoa, legions of other children had taken the inland route and had passed this way before Roger's band.

"They too said they were going south," a Carthusian monk told Harolde, "to get as close to Jerusalem as possible. Rome first, then if necessary, Brindisi, for that is the closest land point to the Holy Land."

This news cheered Roger enormously. "For you see," he explained to Jonathan, "if all the scattered forces of our original army were to meet in Rome, then we will have a large enough core to form a new crusade."

Jonathan did not respond as they tramped over the Ponte Vecchio with its jumble of goldsmith shops overhanging the Arno.

"You have not listened to one word I said," Roger grumbled.

"Indeed I have," Jonathan answered, and repeated Roger's statement word for word. "What I do not understand is, can salvation come to us only if we are an army? I believe . . . that each of us must journey to Jerusalem alone."

"Day? Night! Black? White! Never have I understood your prattle. Must you always be out of step?" Roger stalked off to

Laurelle and Harolde to concentrate his enthusiasms in more fertile soil as they left Florence and journeyed south.

The Tuscan countryside lay clothed in subtle shades, siena hills, forest green groves of cedar, and a sky sometimes cerulean, sometimes palest yellow. The exhilarating air gradually proved a tonic, and under the assault of such beauty their spirits eased somewhat. They found the strength to ponder their debacle in Genoa, their betrayal in Pisa, and how the Lord, working through Flamonde, had saved them.

"Never have I seen a city more comely," Laurelle said, gazing at the three converging hills on which Siena stood. A three-day journey south had brought them to the rich and powerful banking center in the Tuscan hills. The inscription on the Porte Camollia read, "Wider than her gates does Siena open her heart to you," and the children prayed that the city would be true to its word.

With Roger in the lead, the army proceeded in disciplined ranks through the streets, for they had learned that the more orderly they appeared, the better their reception. Siena's dark-eyed, vivacious youngsters ran alongside the troops, first challenging them, then growing more intrigued with their evangelical message.

The small army encamped in the enormous semicircular Piazza del Campo, which took the shape of the hillside.

"I could live in such a place," Roger said, impressed with the red-toned brick palaces and fine merchant homes fringing the concave square.

"It is very beautiful," Jonathan agreed, "but I could never rest here. Jerusalem is—"

"You," Roger interrupted, "are getting to be a bore! We are only passing the time of day with talk."

Jonathan flushed. "If I am single-minded, it is because I know that is the only way I am going to get there," he retorted, and clenched his fists.

The boys squared off, and circled each other; Harolde quickly stepped between them. "No good can come of this," he said, admonishing Roger. Then he turned to Jonathan. "Since our goal is the same, it would be so simple if you would but see the light."

"What light is that?" Jonathan challenged him.

"Embrace the Messiah, renounce your false ways."

"So I shall," Jonathan said, "but only when He reveals Himself to me. Now, if your God had parted the seas at Genoa . . ." Jonathan shrugged eloquently.

A look of such anguish crossed Harolde's face that Jonathan felt sorry immediately. Taking a more conciliatory tack, Jonathan said, "Is it so important to you that I be converted?"

"Why, of course," Harolde said.

"Why?"

"Because I have come to . . ." Harolde could not bring himself to say *love* to the unbeliever and so said, "I have come to like you. I want you to be saved."

"From what?"

"Why, from damnation, naturally."

Exerting all the control he could muster, Jonathan said, "Heed me for a moment, Harolde. Sometimes I think you need to convince me in order to convince yourself."

"Why, that is the most absurd idea I have ever heard," Harolde exclaimed.

"Is it?" Jonathan asked quietly. "If I question the divinity of Jesus, who is one of my own people, then does that not make you question also? Anybody who refuses to conform to your ways, especially a Jew—does he not become a thorn in the flesh of your beliefs?"

Harolde shook his head sadly. "Oh, you are damned, and your whole race is damned. You may win all the arguments you want with your clever words, your tribe is famous for that. But unless you let the light of the Redeemer enter your life, you shall be struck down with the sword of the archangel."

Jonathan hunched his shoulders. "Who can say? Only it is not the archangel's sword I see raised, only man's. Where then is the commandment that you all say your Lord Jesus gave?"

He stood up abruptly. "Now I must go. There is little water in Siena and I must beg some for Mirage and Tortoise. I fear for Tortoise, her cold is getting worse."

Harolde watched Jonathan disappear into the stepped streets. "Always the Jew confounds us with his obstinate arguments. What a waste, for in all other things he is a good and kind lad. Why, one might never even guess he was a Jew. Well," Harolde sighed, "there is little one can do except pray for him. Redemption must come from within."

Leaving Tanis in the care of Laurelle, Harolde left the giant scalloped-shaped Piazza del Campo and trudged through the cobbled streets to the Duomo, Siena's pride and joy. The enormous ornate cathedral, further evidence of Siena's importance as the greatest banking center in all Italy, slowly neared completion. The foundations had been laid almost 150 years before, and as Harolde gauged the work yet to be done he thought, Soon, perhaps another century or so.

Though midday, the church was crowded. Water had always been a concern in Siena and the months of unending drought had made the situation perilous. Siena prayed. After Mass, Harolde used the meager coins left from the silver piece Flamonde had snatched in Genoa and bought a half-dozen candles. As he lit one for the repose of Flamonde's soul, he caught sight of a black-garbed woman kneeling in a nearby pew. The woman was so old she seemed about to turn into a heap of dust. Harolde tried to imagine Flamonde that age but could not. In her way, he thought, she had conquered time, for she would remain forever young in all their minds.

Then, in a rush of pity, Harolde took another taper from his precious stock and lit it. "For the ultimate salvation of Jonathan's soul," Harolde breathed into the flames. "Lord, his is too good a soul to waste."

Outside, Harold blinked his eyes against the harsh glare of the sun. The monotone of a somber Gregorian chant drew him toward a procession of penitents; they moved in slow rhythm, lashing their bare flesh with knouts of rope and barbs of wire. Stopping before the tympanum depicting the Last Judgment, they made their confessions, whipping each sin from their bodies as they pleaded for rain.

The slim green-and-white marble campanile turned its slow shadow with the sun. Harolde stripped to the waist and joined the penitents scourging themselves. Soon his bare back and chest ran red with blood. When they were done, three of the penitents lay unconscious, but the sky remained cloudless. Carrying their wounded, they dragged themselves from the Duomo to return another day.

Harolde struggled back to the others in the Piazza del Campo where the palaces glowed red in the setting sun. No, Harolde thought, feeling his robe sticking to his bloody shoulders, it does no good to scourge the body if the sin remains embedded in the soul. Had she not lain with me that night she would still be alive.

When the tattered army left Siena the following morning, their ranks were swelled by scores of new pilgrims, including a sparkling lad named Marcello. These children laughed and chattered, bright with their new adventure.

"Do you remember when we acted so?" Laurelle sighed to Roger.

Within the hour at least a dozen of the runaway children were hauled back to Siena by their parents. The unwanted, the escaped servant, the orphan, these remained to find their fortunes along with their new adopted family.

Ever south the children marched through the gradually leveling terrain. They learned to eat things they once considered abominations: roots, grasshoppers, all manner of beetles. If a horse or mule died, it was butchered on the spot and devoured. Jonathan took to sleeping near Mirage, for rumor had it that some animals had been dispatched even before they were dead.

Once more, heat, exhaustion, and famine took their toll. Instead of being trailed by birds and butterflies, the children left behind a shallow string of graves.

"We must not despair," Harolde said desperately, trying to keep everybody's spirits up. "If only we can reach Rome, petition the Holy Father . . ." Try as he might, Harolde knew he did not have Flamonde's gift for instilling life and laughter. Yet with all his heart he believed that the spark of their crusade must be kept alive so that Pope Innocent might kindle it into a beacon for the Lord. Only that conviction kept Harolde moving.

Dysentery struck; perhaps it was the tained horse flesh or the eels they caught at mosquito-ridden Lake Bolsena, or its brackish waters that many had neglected to boil before drinking. A whole camp, twenty-two in all, were wracked with the disease. Jonathan, Laurelle, and Roger struggled to save them, forcing boiled water between their swollen lips. By early light, ten lay dead. The other afflicted were left behind, too weak to continue.

One day after the Feast of the Seven Sorrows of the Blessed Virgin, the children neared Viterbo.

"Viterbo is a city devoted to the papacy," Harolde excitedly told Roger and Laurelle. "Surely we will find food and rest there."

The children were stunned when they were refused entry into the city, and then sent scurrying away from the battlements by a shower of garbage and offal. They did find sanctuary at the Convent of St. Mary, just outside the walls. Though it was Sunday, a day given strictly to fasting and prayer, the mother superior took one look at the gaunt children and organized her sisters to feed them. It depleted the convent's stores severely, and there would be no food for the sisters on the morrow. "But what is the sense in saving for tomorrow, if it means that others will be dead today?" the mother superior told Harolde.

To Harolde's bitter denunciation of the city, the reverend mother explained, "Viterbo has always been threatened by the enemies of the papacy. Five years ago, in this very place, Pope Innocent consecrated Stephen Langton as archbishop of Canterbury—"

"With the disastrous results we know only too well," Harolde interrupted.

"And just this last year Innocent had to barricade himself within our walls when Otto IV began his incursions against Rome," the mother superior added. "And so our soldiers did not know what to think when they saw so many strangers approaching."

"Children!" Harolde exclaimed.

The reverend mother nodded sadly. "Such is the misery of the times that we fear our own children."

During the night, Harolde dreamed that he had an audience with the pope. He saw himself robed in fine white vestments, pleading the cause of the children's crusade. Pope Innocent appeared agitated, glancing nervously at a growing crack in the wall of the Lateran chapel. All at once the walls began to crumble. Everybody rushed forward to shore them up, but not even Brother Francis of Assisi could hold up the church. Then Harolde strode forward, and putting his back to the walls, first supported and then straightened them.

The following morning, after Jonathan finished saddling Mirage, he went to get Tortoise and found her sleeping on her side. "Come, my girl," he said, "we have new worlds to conquer today." Tortoise did not stir. Jonathan went to stroke her nose and jerked his hand away from the cold hard flesh. He burst into tears and ran for Harolde. Harolde would not leave until he had seen Tortoise safely buried. He could not bear the thought that anybody might butcher the creature who had served him so faithfully these many months.

Laurelle had a few whispered words with Roger, who then insisted that Harolde ride Mirage.

"Rome," said the mother superior at the convent gate, "is just three days south. You will be safe there, I am certain of it, for surely you are messengers of the Lord and the pope will clasp you to his bosom."

"Of a certainty he will!" Harolde said. "Is his not the court of first and last resort in all Christendom? Has a day passed during his reign that he has not called for a crusade to free the Holy Land? And are we not here in answer to that call? Of course we will recognize the truth in our cause! Of course he will help!"

"Only three days now," Laurelle said, and started a chant soon picked up by the others. They strode to its rhythm as they marched along the Via Cassia, their legs eating up the miles.

ROME:
MID-SEPTEMBER

HREE MONTHS AND MORE THAN A THOUSAND MILES after setting out from Cologne, the ragged band of children stood gazing at the seven hills of Rome. Of the original twenty thousand in the army, only two hundred remained.

Since the crumbling Ponte Milvio was closed for repairs, the children followed the meander of the Tiber to the next access bridge. The torpid river was coated with green slime; a duck and one fuzzy duckling waddled in the malodorous flats, searching for grubs and frogs. The heat pulsated on the intermittent hot wind, and sweat streaked the children's bodies and faces.

"We must go to St. John Lateran," Harolde said, "for that is the church of the popes, and where Innocent resides."

"How far is it?" Roger asked.

"I make it less than a half-day's march," Harolde said, checking his *Mirabilia Roma*. "But what a mean and squalid city this is!" he said, trying to reconcile the fantasy of a lifetime with the reality before his eyes.

At the height of the empire, Rome had boasted a population in excess of one million. Now a scant thirty-five thousand lived within its walls. Where once the Circus Maximus had thundered to the beat of horse and chariot, now shepherds grazed their flocks. The marble and other fine stone of the ancient monuments had been stripped to build the Christian churches, leaving the city looking scabrous.

Rome was a dangerous city. The *ribaldi*, brigands, and every other criminal were drawn here to prey on the unending stream of pilgrims. Internecine squabbles among the nobility added to the civil turmoil; the Conti, Frangipani, Orsini, and Pierolini families struggled continually for power.

"What building is that?" Roger asked, pointing to the massive circular structure coming into view at the Tiber's bend.

"Castel Sant' Angelo," Harolde said, recognizing it immediately from the pages of *Mirabilia Roma*. "The emperor Hadrian built it as his mausoleum, but now it is the fortress for the popes."

"Fortress?" Laurelle asked quizzically.

Harolde nodded. "Oh, yes, there are many who would deny the pope's primacy here in earth."

"But should not Rome be the place for the most devout Christians?" Laurelle said.

"To be sure," Harolde said thoughtfully. "But it is in the nature of things, that the closer one gets to the source of light, the more the devil must try to destroy it."

"Then shall we not find that also true when we reach Jerusalem?" Laurelle asked.

"Without question," Harolde said. "There at the center of the world, prayers fly straight away to heaven, just as sins descend right down to hell. Since creation, it has been the axis where the battle between God and Satan forever rages. Thus has it been and thus shall it ever be."

They came to a wide street and saw in the distance the Hospital of the Holy Ghost (which Innocent III had founded and which was becoming the model for every hospital in Europe), and beyond that, the Church of St. Peter.

"The body of Peter lies buried somewhere in its catacombs," Harolde said. "It would be most blessed to light a candle for Flamonde in that church." He rummaged in Mirage's saddlebags for his last candle and groaned aloud when he discovered it bent and misshapen from the heat. "How could I have been so stupid as not to protect it?"

As St. Peter's disappeared from view, Harolde thought, God created giants in those days, men so illuminated by the spirit that they changed the course of empires. Whereas my goal? To secure a comfortable position in the curia! "My faith is as firm as . . . as this candle!" he cried and flung the taper away.

They crossed the Ponte Sant' Angelo then headed east, wending their way through the filthy streets. Every so often the contents of a chamber pot would sail through the air from an upstairs window, spattering whomever might be passing below. Mothers shouted, children cried, men argued, dogs barked, and a myriad of monks hawked indulgences, adding to the city's din.

The people were handsome, Roger thought, many with hair so black it glinted blue, and with dark roving eyes. The men always seemed to be scratching their private parts and Roger said to Jonathan, "Do you think it is some special kind of flea?" Jonathan did not know.

Through the centuries, Romans had grown inured to the hordes who came to worship at the seven major churches, all of whom wore a tiny replica of Veronica's handkerchief, symbol of their pilgrimage. But even the cynical turned to stare at these fair young pilgrims.

Litters stopped, windows were flung open. The crucible of the last months had effected the final purification, and in the children's expectant faces shone the beauty of absolute belief.

The yellow and orange brickwork of the houses concentrated the heat from the white-hot sky and people fled the baking streets. Even the omnipresent priests at every corner preaching crusades against the Albigenses and Saracens, sought shade.

When Laurelle fainted, Roger called a halt. "We must not be touched with sunstroke. We must have our wits about us when we petition the pope." They sought sanctuary nearby in an enormous round temple with a portico supported by sixteen soaring columns.

"The Pantheon," Harolde told them, "erected for the worship of Rome's pagan gods."

Huge bronze doors admitted them to an enclosed space so tremendous that the children gasped.

The temple was as round as it was high, and thank the Lord, cool. They looked to the source of the structure's only light, a great hole in the dome, and mouths agape, watched clouds drift over the opening. A sunbeam lanced through the opening and inched its way across the geometrically patterned floor.

Without knowing why, Jonathan threw back his head, and

with arms extended began to turn in a circle. Set in niches around the perimeter of the Pantheon, seven statues representing the seven planets and seven Roman gods revolved before his eyes. The shaft of sunlight inched closer and in a rare expansive moment Jonathan dashed through the light, then again; the other children began doing it also, running from light to shadow to light.

Something about this whole game disturbed Harolde; he tried to stop the children, but their laughter proved so infectious that he soon joined in. "As long as it is dedicated to the Virgin," he said, shrugging, "can there really be any harm?"

Then the children joined hands and formed a giant circle around the sunbeam, dancing one way then the other, whirling ever faster until Laurelle started to sing and the temple gave back her voice a hundredfold, soaring to the dome and up into the clouds:

> *Fair is the sunshine*
> *Fairer still the moonlight . . .*

When the heat abated, the band continued their journey. They reached Trajan's column, marveled at the ruins of Hadrian's market and the once all-powerful Roman Forum. Down the street they saw the stupendous arcaded mass of the Colosseum. At last they found the Via Major, the road which would take them to the Basilica of St. John Lateran—and to the pope.

" 'The Most Holy Church of the Lateran,' " Harold read the words engraved in stone at the basilica's main entrance, " 'mother and head of all the churches of Rome and of the world.' We must all give thanks," he breathed, his voice thready with fatigue.

They entered the dark church and slowly walked down the patterned marble floor of the nave to the papal altar. Above the altar, in a golden reliquary, were fragments of the wooden table on which Christ had eaten his final meal.

"His Last Supper," Harolde said, clasping his hands.

"The Passover feast," Jonathan murmured.

Harolde whirled at Jonathan's voice, realizing for the first time that he had accompanied them in. Then Harolde shrugged, for suddenly Jonathan's presence did not seem blasphemous, or even important.

Jonathan did not understand what had possessed him to enter this place. Curiosity? Or an effort to get over his fear and see for himself what had been forbidden to him all his life? Whatever the reason, now he stood deep within the church. Its rich gold appointments gleamed in startling contrast to the squalid streets outside. Everywhere, disciples, saints, and prophets in statue, mosaic, and stained glass vied for his attention. "It is a palace," he said in wonder. And so different from the stark simplicity of the synagogues he knew.

At last Harolde located the appointment secretary to the pope's appointment secretary, a handsome young monk named Fra Angelo.

"How clean he smells," Laurelle whispered to Roger, staring enviously at his crisp white skirts. She fumbled with her blouse to smooth it, only to have a piece of it rip off in her hands.

Fra Angelo regarded the children with an expression akin to distaste. "In answer to your questions, the Holy Father cannot see you this afternoon, being otherwise occupied with the architect Vasseletto, planning our new cloister."

"Tomorrow?" Harolde asked.

Fra Angelo rattled off a discouraging list of the pope's state appointments. Realizing that there was little to be gained from this ragtag bunch, he began to edge away from them.

Harolde's insistent voice stopped him. "Tell his holiness that we shall come back tomorrow. And the next day. And every day thereafter until he can see us. We have walked more than a thousand miles. Our matter is grave and of the greatest importance."

Fra Angelo suppressed a smile. "Surely you know that all who seek audience with the pope consider their matter of greatest—"

Harolde advanced on Fra Angelo, thundering, "This concerns the soul of Christendom!" For the first time in his life he felt moved to physical violence, and reached out to lay hands on the immaculate young man.

Fra Angelo started back. "I will see the pope's secretary immediately," he said, promising anything just to get away. When the children moved off he muttered, "What mad, dirty little creatures! What's more, they are penniless."

And to think that this is what I once aspired to, Harolde thought, still trembling with anger. Trying to compose himself he said, "Let us see if they will give us shelter for the night here in the basilica," and started off.

But Roger took this moment to follow after Fra Angelo and converse briefly with him. Then he rejoined the others.

The deacon told the troop that they could not remain overnight in St. John's. "The pope prays here! What would he think if he saw so many ragamuffins?" In truth, neither the deacon nor anybody else at St. John's knew what to do with the children; until the pope himself rendered his judgment about them, the wisest course lay in not committing oneself.

The band left the church by the rear exit; cripples and beggars, who usually fastened themselves to anybody leaving the basilica in the hope of alms, shunned the children, so destitute did they look. Fringing the brick square stood dozens of booths set up by ship captains selling passage to the Holy Land, and the children were irresistibly drawn to them; Jonathan above all, for somehow he felt that with the pope's imminent involvement, his future was being decided without his leave.

One agent in particular, a short, swarthy man named Rainero, engaged the children. They listened to him extol the virtues of his swift, clean vessels and cheap rates.

"Early spring and late summer are the best times for the long sea voyage," Rainero told them, "the weather being generally fair."

But since the children had no money at all, even Rainero's reasonable prices sounded astronomical to them and at last they wandered from the booths and went searching for places to spend the night.

Everywhere they went they were turned away; Rome earned its living from pilgrims and only those with money need apply.

"Then this night we shall sleep in the Colosseum," Harolde said resolutely. "Where is there more hallowed ground than in the amphitheater where the first Christians were martyred?"

But even the Colosseum was denied them; the great stadium had been turned into a fortress by the Frangipani family in their feud with the Contis and Pierolinis. At last the bone-weary children sprawled out in the ruins of the Roman Forum. The moon rose early, casting its half light on the broken columns and gutted buildings.

"I wonder if the pope will really see us," Roger said to nobody in particular.

"O, ye of little faith!" Harolde exclaimed.

"That may be," Roger said, "but I went back anyway and talked to Fra Angelo and—well, even should my father ever find out that I parted with his blue enamel cross, he would understand that I gave it away for a good cause."

"There was no need for that," Harolde insisted. "As soon as the pope learns . . ." he broke off and began to choke.

Jonathan held Harolde's head until the seizure passed. Fever glazed his eyes and his skin appeared so translucent that Jonathan could see the pulsing network of veins.

The moon turned from pale white to pale gold and everybody bedded down. After a bit, Jonathan approached Harolde, who sat propped up against a column, the better to breathe.

"This morning in your anger, you threw this away," Jonathan said, and handed Harolde the last taper.

Harolde balanced the candle in his palm, shaking his head in disbelief. "But how? It is as straight as an arrow!"

"It is, is it not?" Jonathan said eagerly, evidently delighted with his work. "I let it soften in the sun, straightening it a little at a time. Then I set it in the shade to reharden. I knew you would want to light at least one candle to Flamonde while we were in Rome. Dear Harolde, I have a favor to beg of you. Will you remember me to her in your prayers?"

Harolde nodded and touched Jonathan's arm. "Thank you,"

he whispered. Harolde stared at the candle for a long time and then said, "Sometimes I think we are all like this . . . a little twisted and bent. But if one is patient and works hard enough, a little at a time, as you say, then it is possible not only to retrieve, but to make anew. You have taught me something, Jonathan, and I thank you."

Jonathan toed the ground. "You have taught me much also," he said and glanced up to meet Harolde's gaze.

Then in a faltering yet impulsive move, the monk and the boy clasped hands.

"However, this does not mean that I will not keep trying to convert you," Harolde said with a gentle smile.

"Nor I you!" Jonathan answered, and they both laughed.

The children were already on their way to St. John Lateran when church bells throughout Rome tolled prime. All morning long they waited without being summoned, though Fra Angelo, now wearing the blue enameled cross, assured Roger that he had mentioned their presence to the appointment secretary.

Throughout the afternoon the children waited and fretted, then finally at vespers, a very surprised Fra Angelo informed them that the pope could not see all two hundred of them, but had consented to hear a small delegation from their army. The pontiff would hold the audience in the Patriarcum, the papal palace next to St. John's.

After a hurried conference, the children decided to send Roger, Harolde, Laurelle, and two other boys.

Harolde yanked Tanis out of his hood and handed her to Jonathan. "We must be of good cheer," he said, his voice quavering. "We have nothing to fear, for we need only to speak the Gospel as our Lord did and the Holy Father will listen."

ROME:
THE FOLLOWING DAY

FRA ANGELO LED THE CHILDREN INTO THE LATERAN Palace. As they approached a flight of steps leading to an oratory, Harolde started when he saw a group of pilgrims climbing the stairs on their knees. He looked quizzically at Fra Angelo.

"It is the scala sancta," Fra Angelo said, "the holy staircase from the praetorium of Pontius Pilate. Up these very steps Jesus ascended to þe judged, and then was dragged down again after being condemned."

Harolde crossed himself and then sank to his knees. "We must make this our final act of devotion before we see the pope, and pray that the Lord will see fit to intercede in behalf of our cause." Kneeling, he dragged his way up the stairs, repeating at each step the prayer:

> *Holy Mother pierce me through*
> *In my heart each wound renew*
> *Of my Savior crucified.*

Laurelle glanced at Roger, and then the children of the delegation followed Harolde's example. Fra Angelo remained standing, looking slightly bored as he pared his nails.

Halfway up, Harolde faltered and would have fallen backward if Roger had not grabbed him. Roger held him until his dizziness had passed and then they proceeded on their knees until they reached the final, twenty-eighth step of the scala sancta.

Exhausted and gasping, Harolde found himself before the Chapel of San Lorenzo, the Sancta Sanctorum of the popes.

"You are to wait here," Fra Angelo said, pointing to a wooden bench outside the chapel. "The pope always comes to pray here at twilight; perhaps then he can spare a moment for you."

The children watched Fra Angelo disappear down the long marble corridor. Then they were alone, dwarfed, and frightened by all the surrounding magnificence.

After a time, Roger could not restrain himself and peeped into the chapel. "Come see," he whispered to Harolde and Laurelle.

Gold and silver and satin and silk adorned the sumptuous chapel. Above the pink marble altar hung Christendom's most famous painting, the portrait of the Savior "not done by human hand." Innocent III had encased the entire portrait in gilded silver, leaving only the face showing through the precious armoring. The eyes looked soft and decidedly Oriental as they stared out into the room, slightly bewildered.

"Those eyes, do they not look familiar?" Roger asked Laurelle. He stared at them for a long time, finally getting lost in their sadness.

It had been a hectic, difficult day for Innocent III, though not very different from any other in his fourteen-year reign. A willful, determined man, he made up for his lack of health with unrelenting drive. Physicians had warned him that such physical expenditures were shortening his life, yet Innocent could do nothing else; too much remained to be done. Who else except the church could save this world in crisis?

In his youth, Count Lothario Segni Conti had been considered handsome, but now his pallid face was given to puffiness, the once-patrician nose now looked pinched, and fatigue veiled his large brown eyes. A formidable authority in both canon and lay law, Innocent ruled Christendom's court of last resort with a firm hand which could be tempered with mercy or moved to vengeance.

A zealous guardian of the church's rights, Innocent quickly reviewed the status of the Holy See throughout Europe. With King John's final refusal to accept Stephen Langton as archbishop of Canterbury, Innocent made ready to signal Philip of France to invade England. The Holy Roman Empire? A sword aimed at the heart of the papacy, and Innocent could only pray that his annointed boy-king, Frederick II, would be able to save the Papal States from the mad Otto IV. From Spain, splendid news indeed! A great battle had been won by the Christians against the Saracen Almohads on the plains of Tolosa. Fought on the sixteenth day of July, the news had taken many weeks to reach Rome. From the extent of the victory, Innocent believed that the Moslem power in Spain would soon be crushed forever.

With the tolling of the bells at twilight, Fra Angelo tiptoed into the papal study. "Your holiness," Fra Angelo began, but the pontiff waved him away and then also dismissed his bleary-eyed amanuensis. In the growing gloom he concentrated on his most grandiose project, the convening of a Fourth Lateran Council.

An ordered man, Innocent needed beauty and mystery in his worship and planned many astonishing innovations in the Mass. He intended to declare as church doctrine the miracle of transubstantiation: that at the moment of communion, the bread and wine did literally change into the body and blood of Christ. He had also decided that every Catholic must go to confession at least once a year to receive Holy Communion, and he had chosen the season of the Resurrection to be the fitting time for this Easter duty. In this way, every living soul in Europe would be tied to the church.

For centuries, the church had tried to reason with those who strayed from her fold, going so far as to hold open dialogues. But heresy continued to raise its horned head everywhere. The Waldensians in central France, the Beguines and Beghards in Flanders, and of course the Albigenses. Within the body of the church itself dangerous schisms proliferated; witness the pantheism of Amaury of Bene, or the confabulations of Joachim of Fiore's Three Ages of Man. All of these Innocent planned to declare heretical at the council.

But nothing threatened the serenity of the spirit more than the question of the Jews. Nor would it be amiss to say that most heresy flowed from their rigorous refusal to embrace the true faith. It lay in the nature of their special relationship with the Lord of the Old Testament. Since Jesus Himself was of the royal house of David, if His own people refused to accept Him as the messiah, then that kernel of doubt would forever flower into the evil of heresy. Therefore, Innocent decided that all Jews must be isolated, the way one isolated any sickness. "They shall be made to wear distinctive dress," Innocent planned to decree, "a star of David on their sleeve, and a horned hat to remind all that their obstinacies are inspired by the devil." In Rome, a wall would be built around the Jewish quarter on the via Gaetae, and they would be locked up at sunset and let out at dawn. Such Gaetaes, or ghettos (as they came to be called) would be built in every city in Europe.

Finally, Innocent hoped to use the Lateran Council to call for a holy crusade to wrest Jerusalem from the Saracens. For he cannily recognized that the papacy's claim to universal dominion rested in many respects on its ability to recapture the Holy City. How could one claim that God was a Christian god if His holiest places remained in the hands of the unbeliever?

But if the papacy could reconquer Jerusalem? Then Europe would become the fief of Rome and the church the conscience of the world!

The bells signaling darkness began to sound. Innocent laid down his stylus and rubbed his eyes.

Once more Fra Angelo tiptoed to the desk. "Your holiness, it is past time for your prayers. And some children await your pleasure."

Innocent stood up and straightened the folds of his robe. "Ah, yes, the children, I had forgotten about them. Well then, let us hear what these little ones have to tell us."

When they saw the pope approaching down the long marble corridor, Harolde, Roger, and Laurelle were struck dumb. Everything Harolde had prepared himself to say vanished from his mind; strength fled from his limbs, leaving him weak-kneed and trembling.

Never before had Laurelle seen anybody so richly dressed. The pope wore a white linen chausable shot through with threads of silver; a heavy gold crucifix hung around his neck and precious gems sparkled on his fingers. Quickly, she put her own begrimed hands behind her back. And though Laurelle thought she had long ago laid her guilt over Frizio to rest, this confrontation with her supreme judge made her drop her gaze, lest the pontiff discover in her eyes the extent of her secret shame.

Despite his agitated state and the conviction that he would stutter as soon as he opened his mouth, only Roger managed to keep some semblance of his wits about him. Why, the Holy Father is so much shorter than I imagined! he thought. And his color! How pale he looks!

After the appropriate devotions were made to the pontiff, Roger haltingly began an account of the children's crusade. Courage returned with each word until soon his natural passions fired his tale. Innocent listened with growing, profound shock.

"So we have come to you," Roger finished with the phrase Harolde had taught him to memorize, "knowing that your holiness will recognize the righteousness of our cause and call for a new crusade, a crusade of love that will free Jerusalem."

Innocent shook his head sadly. Deeply wounded by their tale, he led them into the Sancta Santorum. "We must pray for guidance," he said, his hands lingering on the chest which held Christendom's most sacred relics, including the heads of St. Peter and St. Paul.

The pope clasped his hands and knelt at the altar, and the children and Harolde dropped to their knees also, Harolde so overcome by the thought of praying with Christ's earthly vicar that he grew faint.

During the pope's low monotone, Roger felt something staring at him. He peered out from under his bowed head and locked eyes with the portrait "not painted by human hand." Then Innocent's concluding prayer penetrated Roger's thoughts.

"God, thou who disposeth everything by thy admirable providence, we pray beseechingly that thou shouldest restore to the Christian cult the land which thy eternal son consecrated with His own blood, and which is now being held by the enemies of the cross, mercifully directing the vows of the faithful to its immediate deliberation for the sake of eternal salvation. Amen."

Innocent crossed himself and stood up. His starched white skirts whispered as he paced the chapel. Then he said, "These children shame us. While we sleep, they march!"

A look of hope transfigured Harolde's face. "Then you will—" he blurted and immediately clapped his hand over his mouth for his temerity in speaking without permission.

Innocent kneaded his hands. "I am overwhelmed by the faith and purity of your quest. But this is not the pure world that you have imagined. For example, innumerable times have I written to the Sultan Saphadin demanding that he surrender Jerusalem to us, its rightful heirs. But has he heeded?" Innocent shook his head vigorously. "You see, my children, you cannot argue with the infidel, the only thing he understands is the sword."

"But our Lord said," Harolde began, only to have Innocent stay him with an upraised palm.

The pope lectured the children further on the deceit and duplicity of the Saracens. "Each day they slaughter more of our fellow Christians in Palestine, they exact enormous sums from those wishing to worship at the Holy Sepulcher." On and on he went, until he had exhausted the crimes the Saracens had committed. When he was finished he said kindly, "Oh, my little ones, sad though it may be, you must give up your idea of a crusade of children. You must return home where your mothers and fathers mourn you."

Roger felt as though he had been struck in the stomach and Harolde's face turned very white. Roger yanked Harolde's sleeve, "But what of our vows?"

Harolde nodded and explained this predicament to the pope, feeling sure that he would now have to see the light and support their quest.

"Yes," Innocent said, stroking his chin, "there is the matter of your vows. But be of good cheer, the years have a way of passing more quickly than you think, and soon you shall all be grown men. Then will I call upon you again to fulfill your crusading oaths. Fra Angelo, make a note, only those children too young to have understood what they were doing are to be absolved; the others remain bound by their original oaths and are to await my call to arms."

Satisfied with this solution, Innocent finished, "With the Lord guiding our swords, together we shall march to Jerusalem and win back the land which our Savior bought for us with His precious blood."

While the pope spoke, Harolde stared wildly at the walls; had they begun to crumble yet? Surely, Harolde thought, God will intervene at this very moment and allow me to demonstrate the strength of our faith. But the rich hangings remained motionless and the walls did not fall.

In a moment of tenderness, the pope gave each child the papal ring to kiss. Then, with a prayer for their safe return, dismissed them.

"Wait!" Harolde cried. "Your holiness, it must not end this way! Thousands of children have suffered much. . ."

"Be at peace, my son," Innocent said. "God would never allow anyone to be tried beyond his strength."

"So many lives have already been lost for this holy cause," Harolde exclaimed. "Is it all to be in vain?"

Innocent said, "The trials of this life are as nothing compared to the rewards which the little ones have won in the next."

But Harolde would not be put off and his voice rang with rebellion: "The Lord Himself said, 'Suffer the little children to come unto me'!"

Innocent tapped the ends of his fingers together. "Yes, but by way of faith, not through a venture doomed to failure from its very outset."

With a mighty effort of will Harolde fought back a cough. "It is within the church's power—*your* power—to make this crusade a success! Because we marched for all our Savior preached, to unite the world in brotherhood!"

"I command you to return to your homes," Innocent said firmly, "there to wait for my call to arms when you are grown men."

Harolde's voice rose to a near scream. "There is not one place in His Gospel—not one—where our Lord calls for blood!"

A signal from the pope brought the papal guard; they and Fra Angelo herded the children out of the chapel even as Harolde continued to shout, "Our Lord Himself said, 'That unless ye shall become as children you will never enter the Kingdom of Heaven'!"

The doors of the Sancta Sanctorum clicked shut.

In the Lateran Square, Jonathan and the rest of the army waited for the delegation to emerge from the papal palace. Tension had built all through the day. At last Jonathan saw the band come out of the palace; the minute he saw their faces he knew. The children crowded around the delegation. An apoplectic cough seized Harolde; he eased himself down, speckling the ground with his blood.

"I cannot comprehend this," Harolde choked, the chords in his neck standing out as he strained to give voice to his fury. "Ordering us to disband? After we have come all this way? I *know* our cause is just! I cannot believe that this is the advice our Savior would have given us."

The moon retreated behind the clouds, limning their edges and fanning rays of pale light across the sky. Harolde looked at the faces of all who had marched with him these many, many miles. "You have been good and true friends to me," he whispered. "More than friends, brothers of my spirit."

Jonathan knelt beside Harolde. "Do not talk, you only weary yourself. We must get you to a hospital. Roger, bring Mirage."

Harolde shook his head. "There is nothing left to weary. I cannot go on, not another step. Do not shut me up alone in a small dark room." He coughed again, strangling on his blood. Laurelle started to cry. Harolde tried to move his head toward her but it sank to his shoulder. "There is no reason to weep, not for me. All my life I have waited for this mystery . . . besides, now I shall behold my beloved."

"A priest," Roger said, starting toward the church.

Harolde motioned him back. "No, no priest," he whispered.

Roger protested, "But you must make your confession! And what about the last rites?"

Harolde murmured, "Flamonde died without making her confession. If I do likewise, perhaps I will find myself in the same level in purgatory as she. After we have done our penance, however many thousands of years that will take in hell's fires, God may then permit us into His presence. Though in the eyes of man and the church we were sinners, the good Lord knows we were betrothed in spirit."

Harolde's eyelids flickered and Roger cried, "Harolde, oh my Harolde! What shall we do?"

"I cannot speak for you," he whispered. "You must listen to your own hearts. Only this. All my days I have lived in awe of the Holy Father. Today, when at last I saw him, I saw a man. Beneath the robes and the jewels, a man like you or me. Doubtless he is wiser than we. Doubtless he has our safety at heart. But for myself," Harolde said, his voice raspy with the effort, "if I had the strength . . . we dreamed a glorious dream. All else seems unimportant."

Harolde's fingers scrabbled at his leather wallet and Jonathan helped him. His hand closed around his Bible. "Bury this with me," he said, "but not the *Mirabilia Roma.*" Then Harolde gave a little cry, "Will somebody watch over Tanis?"

A spasm of pain gripped him and he clutched Jonathan's hand until it passed. "And you, Jonathan," he said, smiling wanly. "You have been a worthy adversary." He patted the boy's arm. "One thing I ask of you."

"Anything," Jonathan said, tears streaming down his face.

"One day, when it crosses your mind, read those things that Jesus preached. Not the way other men have interpreted Him, but only what He said. There is much there for all of us. Will you do that for me?"

Jonathan nodded and a peaceful smile came over Harolde's face. "Then I will not have failed totally." Harolde tapped the map Brother Gottfried had given him in Cologne. "Roger, whatever you decide, to go back or to press on, this will help."

Harolde fought to keep his eyes from closing and said in an aspirate rush, "And one last thing. Remember, if there be one righteous man . . . he can change the world."

Then Harolde turned his eyes to the drifting radiant clouds. "My Lord," he whispered, his words barely audible, "I have tried to work in your service. You alone know my sins of pride and my many sins of the flesh. Within me at every moment, the forces of darkness battled the forces of light. I say only that I desired to serve you better than I did. As for my refusing confession, priests are men, and it is to you alone that I must answer."

So saying, Harolde closed his eyes and gave up the ghost.

OSTIA:
MID-SEPTEMBER

T HE CHILDREN BURIED HAROLDE IN A NEARBY CEM- etery; then for lack of a better place to go, they returned to the torchlit square in front of St. John Lateran.

With no possibility of the pope's intervening on their behalf, most of the small army had already drifted away. Only eighty-five remained, not knowing what to do. Without their realizing it, the children had been sustained by Harolde's wisdom and faith; now they did not even have that, and bereft in the oppressive lonely night, they gave vent to their fear and grief. A group of curious Romans gathered around the children.

"No, I will not!" Roger said suddenly, kicking at a pile of rubbish. "I have not come this far to be put off by a man! And as Harolde said, that is all he is. What does he know of the thousands who have perished so that we few might march on? Only somebody who has walked with us . . ." Roger did not think he had any tears left for Harolde, yet still they came, causing everybody to cry all over again.

Then Roger looked to the palace of the popes and set his jaw. "Harolde will not have died in vain, nor Flamonde. By my eyes, I swear it." He unrolled Harolde's map and spread it on the ground. "Read it for us, Jonathan," he asked.

Jonathan's finger moved from Rome down to the heel of the Italian peninsula. "If we can get to Brindisi, we shall be that much closer to the Holy Land," he said. "I make it a journey of another month, perhaps longer, depending on the terrain."

"I say we walk," said Marcello, who had joined them in Siena and was still full of energy and optimism.

Laurelle studied the map. "I do not know much about these things, but even if we reach Brindisi, shall we still not have to find passage from there to the Holy Land?"

"Oh, surely the Lord will part the seas by the time we get to Brindisi," Marcello said, and with that the children of the advance guard regarded him with a jaundiced eye.

Roger paced back and forth. "Money," he said, "if only we had money. Is all the good in the world always to hinge on money?"

"I will give you the money," a resonant voice called out from the crowd of onlookers. "Enough to secure passage for at least four of you." Rainero, the ship's agent, came forward as Roger took an excited step toward him.

"I would buy your horse," Rainero said.

Jonathan started. "Impossible!"

"The stallion is skin and bones," Rainero said, poking Mirage's ribs, "and not worth half of what I will pay. But I fancy him. I would bring him back to health. And you would get to Jerusalem."

Marcello piped up, "Why not sell the animal? It is only a horse."

Roger and Laurelle exchanged glances. Seeing this, Jonathan blurted, "You cannot! Has he not saved our lives many times over? Laurelle, you would have been captured by the robber barons at Reichenstein Castle if not for him. And Roger, what of Poldus and the bear? He is our talisman. Sell him and we are lost."

"We are lost anyway," Laurelle said wearily. "You are right, though," she said, running her hand over Mirage's flank. "It would be like selling one of us."

Roger nodded soberly. Rainero argued a while longer then shrugged his shoulders and said, "Well, if you ever change your minds. . . ."

Jonathan heaved a sigh of relief.

As he started back to his booth, Rainero called over his shoulder, "Of course, there are other ways one can get to Jerusalem." Once at his station Rainero got very busy, telling the crowd about the superiority of his vessels.

"What did he mean, 'other ways'?" Laurelle asked.

"There is only one way to find out," Roger said, and proceeded determinedly to Rainero's booth, the others following.

To Roger's questions, Rainero answered, "A boat lies in the harbor of Ostia, taking children such as you aboard. I myself saw it yesterday when I took a band of pilgrims there."

"Who does this thing?" Roger asked guardedly.

"A good samaritan," Rainero said. "The captain of this vessel had a son who died on crusade and he is so moved by your mission and your plight that to honor the memory of his son, he has offered to transport you all to the Holy Land, even those without money. However, you must work for your passage, helping to load cargo, scraping the decks, and perchance even rowing should there be no wind."

"That does not frighten us," Roger said, "we are no strangers to work." He looked to the others. "What do you think?"

"Is this ship from Pisa?" Laurelle asked. "Have you heard mention of a man named Frizio?"

Rainero shook his head. "None of these things do I know. So many questions when all one offers is a good deed? Do not listen then, whether or not you go is all the same to me. I make no commission on this," and he turned away.

Roger took the man's arm. "When does this captain sail?"

Rainero said, "His ship has been in Ostia for the past four days, waiting for the stragglers coming down the coast. They will sail in another two days, three at the most. Remember, you must be prepared to work, and hard. I journey to Ostia tomorrow. Follow me, if you wish."

Arguments flew back and forth. Finally Roger said impatiently, "Since Ostia is only ten miles distant, why not see for ourselves? If it seems at all suspicious we will not board, but continue on to Brindisi. But if the captain be a good and true Christian—oh, would that not be a miracle?"

Laurelle moved to Roger's side and stood shoulder to shoulder with him. "After what happened in Pisa, I confess I am terrified," she said. "Yet what Roger said makes sense. We must not allow our old fears and old disappointments to hold us back from salvation. But let us be forewarned, for in this matter, we are dealing with the devil."

The following day, the last remnants of Roger's army left

Rome. One group, led by Marcello, headed south toward Brindisi, still convinced that the Lord would part the seas. The other band, led by Roger, followed Rainero through the leveling countryside to the coast.

When Roger's footsore, soul-weary band arrived in Ostia, they discovered to their joy that Rainero had spoken the truth. A small, broad-beamed vessel of some two hundred tons, the *Paradise*, lay at anchor in the harbor and hundreds of children crowded its decks. They learned that for some weeks, Captain Lamberte had sailed down the coast from Marseille to Ostia, picking up remnants from the disbanded crusades of the French and German children.

When Roger questioned the children already on board, they assured him that Captain Lamberte treated them with kindness, and had begged them all to pray for his son. Roger's suspicions were further calmed when these children said that they had never heard of Frizio, or seen anybody answering his description, nor had they ever docked in Pisa.

Roger began tentative negotiations with Lamberte, and when the captain grudgingly agreed to transport Mirage, Roger's joy knew no bounds and he questioned no more.

True to his word, Captain Lamberte made the children work loading cargo; poultry to keep them in eggs and meat for the three-week journey; goats for milk and cheese; and casks of wine and water. For two full days before sailing, the children were lowered over the sides to scrape barnacles from the hull. They worked with a will, grateful that the Lord had provided them with this opportunity to earn their passage.

Only Laurelle remained uneasy, inspecting each new sailor or supplier boarding the vessel. But soon even she relaxed and joined in the games with the others. They played tag on deck, climbed through the rigging, and poked their noses everywhere, including the dark, slimy cargo holds.

One section of the boat was restricted to the children—the captain's bridge—for the captain swore he could not bring them to safe harbor if they were forever interfering with his work. Also, a holy man who desired to be buried in Palestine lay dying in the captain's quarters. Roger had seen him carried on board in a stretcher, and he cautioned the other children to tread softly whenever they came near that section of the ship.

The seamen hoisted the anchor in rhythm to their singing of the hymn "Veni Creator Spiritus." Other sailors climbed the twin-masted galley and unfurled the canvas of the lanteen sails. They billowed with a sharp crack as they caught the wind. With an invocation to God to guide them safely to Palestine, the captain carefully steered the *Paradise* through the sandbars in Ostia's silted harbor.

Roger, Laurelle, and Jonathan stood at the stern castle, watching the shoreline grow smaller. "I cannot believe that we are on our way at last," Laurelle cried, and she grabbed Roger's and Jonathan's hands and whirled them around in a little dance.

The boat followed the shoreline some four bowshots distant; far enough at sea to avoid the rocks and reefs, close enough to head for land should they be attacked by pirates, whether Christian or Saracen. As long as they sailed within sight of land the children were not frightened. For the most part, the seas remained calm. By day, the gentle rocking motion soothed them and the quick breezes proved a delight after the inferno of their march. One night a sharp wind came up, tossing the boat about; scores of children hung over the side, green-faced with seasickness.

Roger could not help chortling with glee, "What would they think of my English Channel, where the waves can reach as high as these masts?"

For amusement, the children watched fish dart by alongside the hull, then set about catching them. They brought up strange monsters, one with bright red armor and giant claws, another creature with eight squirming arms. Seagulls piped their haunting, melancholy cry and followed in the ship's wake.

"That is Ischia," a sailor told them, pointing to an island on their left. Hours later, they passed Capri. The sea shone like beaten silver in the early autumn sun; lazy clouds drifted over head. The days ripened and Roger knew such contentment that he could not restrain his singing as he worked high in the rigging, replaiting rope.

Jonathan spent as much time as he could in the hold with Mirage. One morning Captain Lamberte told Jonathan he could walk the stallion around the top deck.

"I would not want it on my head if such a fine horse died from lack of exercise," the captain said.

Mirage had never liked the sea, and let Jonathan know this with some well-aimed butts and bites. Jonathan traded everything he owned with the sailors in order to get extra food for Mirage; despite the stallion's cantankerousness, the enforced rest was doing him good, for each day he was looking better.

"What shall we do when we reach the Holy Land?" Laurelle asked dreamily. She and Roger sat on the rear castle, watching the first stars appear.

"Why, marry, of course," Roger said.

"Besides that," she said, poking him. "I mean, how shall we live?

"Why, consider the lilies of the field," Roger said, chuckling.

"Oh, do be serious," Laurelle said. "Do you think we should go directly to the Saracens with our message? Or preach first to the Christians in Outremer?"

"I do not know," Roger said. "But surely the Lord who has guided us this far will make His will known."

"Of course He will, if we but keep our faith," Laurelle agreed. Her glance took in the scores of very young children sleeping on the decks. "Do you think we might keep the very young ones with us? At least for a little while. How else will they find their way in a strange land?" She blushed then and said, "Listen to me, I am becoming my sister."

Roger squeezed her hand. "We shall do anything you want."

Laurelle laced her fingers through Roger's. She felt the breeze lift the edge of her hair; it had grown so much longer since she had chopped it off back in Liege. I am becoming a girl again, she thought, with a kind of wonder.

A shooting star blazed across the sky and Laurelle reached for it impulsively, only to see it fall through her fingers.

Roger rested his head against Laurelle's shoulder. "My father once told me that falling stars were God's tears, for the evil that man commits. But tonight I do not believe it. Every time I think of how we met, of what we have been through—can there be any doubt that we are destined?" He felt her nod and said, "We shall be in Jerusalem soon."

"Soon," she murmured, though some uneasy premonition wakened by the shooting star cried out, Now! Love him now! Who knows what the turn of the wheel will bring? A storm, pirates, or a monster up from the deep to devour us in one gulp. Then you will never have known him. But in Laurelle's mind there also lived the fear that if she broke her vow to remain untouched until they reached Jerusalem, she would bring some terrible evil down on all of them.

The *Paradise* tied up briefly at Messina to take on fresh food and water and was gone the same day, making its way carefully between the rocks and whirlpools of Scylla and Charybdis. Another day saw them reach the southern tip of Sicily and by nightfall they had sailed out of sight of land.

"The whole world is made of water," Laurelle said to Roger and Jonathan. "We could go around in circles and grow old before we ever reach Palestine."

Roger laughed. "Oh, girls know nothing. Captain Lamberte has a magic instrument that came from the far-off land of the slant-eyed men. In a bowl of water he had a special needle which floats on the surface and always points toward the north star. From this, he can tell in which direction to head."

Laurelle looked at him dubiously.

"On my honor," Roger insisted, "he showed it to me yesterday when I was caulking the deck. Do you know what else? The holy man has recovered somewhat, though he still cannot walk. Anyway, he has taken a vow of silence and our chatter is painful to him. So the captain said."

"This holy man," Jonathan said, "has he been to Jerusalem before?"

"I do not know," Roger said, shrugging his shoulders. "Why?"

"A pity he is sworn to silence," Jonathan said thoughtfully. "For if he has been to Palestine he might give us valuable information. There is so much about that land that we do not know."

Roger mulled that over. "Do you think he might break his vow, just this once, if we explained?"

"A vow is a vow," Laurelle said, "never to be broken, or it is worthless."

"It could be that this holy man knows letters," Jonathan said, "and would be willing to write down what he knows?"

Roger nodded eagerly. "I will ask the captain about it as soon as I can."

They sailed for five days without seeing land. The children became fretful with boredom. Soon the sailors could not control them, for they were everywhere at once, getting into everything. Captain Lamberte had to reprimand them sharply, threatening to throw some of the worst offenders into irons.

One night, Jonathan could not sleep for the snoring and the groaning and the evil winds from the sailors. He climbed up to the castle on the stern; Tanis soon joined him there, settling into his lap.

Jonathan stroked the calico kitten. "I miss Harolde also," he murmured to her. "For without him, there is no one to argue with, no one to keep my mind sharp. Nobody I ever met knew as much as he did. He believed in one god and I in another, and yet I truly came to love him. How is such a thing possible?"

Jonathan stared up at the stars in all their multitude. Is the Lord watching us this night? he wondered. Does he have more in store for us? Is there a Lord? Jonathan thought, struck with sudden doubt. Or are the Albigenses right, is this material world the province of the devil? His head reeled with the unorthodoxy of his ideas and he wished fervently that Harolde were here; he could have explained this dilemma. God and the devil, were they in constant battle over the dominion of the world? Over the dominion of every man?

Then the murmur of voices interrupted Jonathan's troubled thoughts. He saw Roger and Laurelle leaning over the rail on the deck below. When the two children realized that Jonathan was on the aft castle, they climbed up and joined him. The three of them stood quietly, watching the *Paradise* racing the galleon moon in the waters.

"Let us make a promise," Laurelle said. "That we shall never part, the three of us, for as long as heaven shall allow."

"Agreed," Roger said immediately. When Jonathan did not respond, Roger nudged him. "What is the matter with you?"

Jonathan toed the planks. "Soon you will be wed. That is not the right time for a third person to be forever underfoot."

"Oh, but there are all manners of love," Laurelle said. "True, Roger and I will have one kind. But you are as a brother to me."

"And to me also," Roger said quietly, "even more."

I should be happy, Jonathan thought. Yet he felt so miserable he could not bear to answer. For he had never ceased to love Laurelle in the way that she had reserved for Roger.

"Please?" Laurelle asked.

Since he could deny her nothing, Jonathan said, "I swear then. That we shall never part, for as long as heaven shall allow."

The following afternoon, while Roger worked in the crow's nest, he saw the foreshortened figure of the holy man emerge from his quarters and begin to walk on the bridge. Roger scrambled down from the rigging and searched out Jonathan.

"The monk must be feeling better," Roger said. "Let us go and ask him about Jerusalem."

The two boys made their way to the forecastle. The captain appeared and shooed them away.

From the shadow of his cowl the monk whispered to Captain Lamberte. The captain nodded, then beckoned for the children to come up.

Roger and Jonathan climbed the ladder and knelt before the holy man. "Forgive us for troubling you," Roger said, "but we have heard that you journey to Jerusalem and wonder if you have been there before."

The monk nodded his head slowly.

"There is much we would ask you," Roger said.

"Ask, then," the monk said in a muffled voice.

With a start, Jonathan realized that the holy man was speaking. Just then, Tanis appeared on the forecastle, having clambered up after the boys. Attracted by the monk's habit, she scampered forward and rubbed her body against his skirts. The monk pushed the kitten aside with his foot. Tanis persisted, perhaps remembering the game she and Harolde had once played.

Jonathan went to get her but before he could, the monk lifted the kitten by the scruff of the neck. She hung limp in his grasp and started to purr. The holy man held her high in the air and then with a sudden motion flung her over the side.

Jonathan screamed and leapt to the rail, preparing to jump overboard, but the captain seized him and dragged him back. Roger attacked the monk, shouting and punching at him. Then the holy man's cowl fell and Roger found himself staring at Frizio.

ALEXANDRIA

HROUGHOUT THE FIRST NIGHT OF THE CHILDREN'S capture, Frizio pondered the fate of Laurelle. His first impulse, to drag her into his cabin and have her then and there, soon gave way to a more considered plan. For it would be unseemly if the others on board discovered his weakness—he could describe it no other way—for this child.

Better to wait until we reach port, he told himself, and then in the privacy of my quarters . . . The thoughts of the torments he had endured, the debasement he'd planned for her, all disappeared as he gazed transfixed across the weathered gray decks to where she sat bound. Though her clothes were those of a beggar's, still her beauty rivaled that of any houri in Frizio's fantasy. "There is no other way," he whispered to himself, "I must win her, I *will* win her!"

Laurelle gently massaged the knot on Roger's forehead; he had tried to lead a revolt against Frizio and his sailors and had been cracked on the head with a belaying pin for his efforts.

"When I think of you at that madman's mercy," Roger groaned.

"Do not torment yourself with such thoughts," Laurelle said. "Doubtless he has known many others since our encounter in Troyes. And that night he was surely out of his senses on wine or some other magic potion. Even if he has not forgotten, would he chose to be with anybody as ugly as I have become?" She rambled on, trying to convince Roger and herself that Frizio had long since lost interest in her.

Comforted somewhat, Laurelle rested her chin on her knees and stared out at the sparkling sunlit sea while Roger and Jonathan dozed off. After a time she thought she saw something and shook the boys awake. "Look, quickly, are those not sails off in the distance?"

They scrambled to their feet and leaned as far over the rails as their bonds would allow, shading their eyes against the blue-green glare of the sea. On the forecastle, Frizio had also seen the sails and sent a sailor climbing up to the crow's nest. The unknown ships quickly closed the distance.

"Alert everybody," Roger ordered, passing the word to the bound children on the deck. "When I signal we must yell as one. If they are Christian ships we may yet be saved."

But long before Roger sounded the alarm the children began to beat their fists against the planking, setting up a din. Then the wind brought the ships closer still and the children's screams died. Dhows, the strange vessels were, flying the flag of Islam, and the Arabian vessels took up escort positions on either side of the *Paradise*.

By day's end they sighted land and approached the shore-line of a city such as the children had never before seen, with domed mosques and slender minarets catching the sun's last light.

"Alexandria!" Frizio exclaimed, pounding the rail. "Beyond the reach of Christian hands! The children are mine!"

Two spits of land curved out from the harbor like the man-dibles of a giant spider. Above the breakwater flickered the signal fire of the Pharos, once the wonder of the world. Earth-quake and neglect had taken their toll of the lighthouse of Alexandria. Gone its four-storied magnificence, gone the giant reflecting mirror which had once guided the mighty navies of Rome and Greece into the safety of Alexandria's unique dou-ble harbor. Now a Mamaluke lighthousekeeper tended a small bonfire atop the remaining lower level and this lit their way into the western harbor of Eunostos.

By the time the *Paradise* dropped anchor, night had stolen over the city. Captain Lamberte was anxious to have his money and be gone, but Frizio refused to unload his cargo in the darkness.

"I have not followed these children halfway around the world to lose any more of them now," he said. "Mad little creatures they are, who would fling themselves into the sea rather than submit. We will disembark in the morning."

A short time later Baalbek boarded the *Paradise*. After attending to his master's needs, the eunuch took up his guard position outside Frizio's cabin. He squinted at Roger and Jonathan on the deck below, then stared at the empty places on his left hand where two fingers had once grown—Frizio had harshly punished him for having allowed the children to escape his snare in Pisa.

As he had tracked Roger's band from Pisa to Rome, Baalbek had come to despise these children and their dementia, for what else could their quest be but a kind of madness? Still, he reflected, it was all Allah's will, as it had been his will that enabled him to hire the shipping agent, Rainero, to lead the children to Ostia, where his master had a ship waiting to pick up the last of the stragglers.

Contemplating what lay in store for them, Baalbek licked his lips. He did not envy the blond youth. Too many times had he seen the fate of those who angered Frizio. Then Baalbek had an idea which sent shivers over his immense bulk. As a reward, perhaps Frizio would let him have his way with the dark boy.

On deck, the children huddled together. Jonathan gnawed away at the ropes which bound his hands. The thick plaits had been soaked in toughening brine and he knew it was near impossible to chew his way through. "But it is better than just sitting here and doing nothing," he told Roger.

The children started as a haunting cry threaded across the waters. "What is that?" Roger asked.

Jonathan cupped his hand around his ear, trying to decipher the prayer. It had been a long time since he'd read the Arabic texts of Avicenna, or hear the tongue from his father. "They are saying that there is no God but Allah, and Mohammed is his prophet."

With a moan, Laurelle clapped her hands over her ears. Despite her efforts to be brave in front of Roger, she felt sick with apprehension. Then strange new forebodings stole over her. For a moment, present and future blended; the dark sea turned to a brighter sea of sand. Under a relentless sun she dragged her feet through a sea of burning glass while Frizio pursued her. Roger ran after, calling her name on the wind, but his eyes were blind and unseeing.

She screamed and Roger shook her.

"Wake up," he said, "you were sleeping with your eyes open."

Laurelle moved her hand slowly in front of Roger's face and he followed her movement.

"Why do you do that?" he asked. "What troubles you?"

"Nothing, now," she said, sighing with relief and settling back against him. Still, it took a long time for her heart to stop racing.

Lying awake, Roger stared at the signal fire atop the lighthouse. It beckoned to his memory, conjuring the castle at Dover where they had made their escape from England six months before, though it seemed like a hundred years ago. A wave of homesickness washed over him, followed by a deeper wave of despair. To what strange ends has the Lord led us? he wondered. His father? Only God knew. Flamonde? Unshriven in her sins. And Harolde, a man of God denying absolution. And the thousands upon thousands of children. . . .

"For what?" Roger asked himself. "As long as we had the slightest hope of reaching Jerusalem and rekindling the dream of the Gospel, we would have marched to the last child. But to have it end like this?"

Guilt beat its raven wings around his head. "I am to blame for what happened," he muttered. "You trusted me, followed me, and I led you to this infidel hell!" A low animal sound escaped him and he began to rock back and forth, pounding his head against the bulwark. "And where is God in all this? Where. . . . ?"

At daybreak, the *Paradise's* pitch-sealed ports were opened and the human cargo unloaded onto the quays. The children were roped by the neck and arranged in double files. Then

Mirage clattered onto the dock, his nostrils quivering to the new yet familiar smells. He trotted to where Jonathan and Roger stood, butting the boys with his head. Frizio grabbed the stallion's reins to pull him away and Mirage reared, trying to kick him. Frizio swore and raised his whip.

"Mirage! Go with him!" Jonathan said sharply.

Mirage's ears swiveled; he snorted as Jonathan repeated the command, and then allowed himself to be led away.

With Frizio leading the column, Baalbek drove the children through the Gate of the Moon into Alexandria. Frizio had not been in the city for some five years. The air smelled sharp and fetid from the sulfurous mud flats; blight speckled the palm trees.

"No question about it," Frizio said to Baalbek, "this port is suffering the same fate as Ostia."

The silting of the Nile was fast destroying Alexandria's value as a seaport. Damietta in the east and Cairo to the south had become the prosperous cities of the delta. Yet Alexandria still boasted the busiest slave market in North Africa; from here the great slave caravans set out to the far reaches of the Saracen empire, stretching from Spain in the west to Baghdad in the east.

Because of the oppressive heat, Alexandria conducted its business during the morning hours and in the late afternoon. Now the streets were thronged with peddlers and shoppers, men in flowing jalabas and women veiled in black, their haggling voices strident in the thick air. The teeming population, some wearing round blue patches on their sleeves to identify them as Christians, many with the yellow star of David to mark them as Jews (the Arabs had devised this scheme the better to levy the *jizyah* tax on the unbelievers), paid scant attention to the ragged bunch of children. In the past months, so many young Frankish slaves had been brought into Alexandria that they had ceased to be a novelty.

The hollow shuffle of the children's footsteps sounded along the colonnaded street of Rosette. Little Luke did not understand what was happening; he knew only that they were marching again and began cheerfully to sing in his thin alto:

Jesus shines brighter
Jesus shines purer . . .

Jonathan saw Baalbek riding down on them, his cat-o'-nine-tails raised. Jonathan shielded Little Luke with his body, wincing in anticipation of the lash. But the blow did not fall; instead, Baalbek lifted Jonathan away from Little Luke, and the way his hands lingered on Jonathan's body proved more terrifying than the whip.

Roger sprang to reach them only to be jerked back by the halter around his neck. Just then Roger spied three black-robed monks hurrying along, their rosaries swinging from their belts.

"For the love of God, we are Christians!" Roger shouted.

Startled, the monks stared at the children, crossed themselves and then quickened their stride toward the Cathedral of St. Mark. "We will pray for you," one called just before he darted down a side street.

"How can this be that they live side by side with the heathen?" Roger asked, outraged.

"So much for your brave Christians!" Frizio called out mockingly. "To be saved, you must pray to Allah, for it is his will that is being done!"

Baalbek grinned and added his taunt, "Can you not see that my god is greater than yours? Else why would you be here?" Farther along the Rosette, the eunuch herded them past the white marble ruins of temples and palaces which had once been Alexandria's glory. Laurelle tripped and fell and Baalbek's scourge sang through the air, urging her on. Laurelle looked up at him. The Lord had instructed them to love their enemies, but with Baalbek she was unable to disguise her loathing.

Baalbek raised his whip again but suddenly Frizio was upon them and angrily snatched the scourge from the eunuch's hand.

"Do not mark her, idiot!" Frizio commanded. Then his eyes met Laurelle's and held. His lips parted in a slight smile. "Come," he said, "you can ride with me." He reached down to unfetter her but she cringed away, revulsion contorting her face.

Frizio's smile vanished; he wheeled Mirage and galloped back to the head of the line. Baalbek dragged Laurelle to her feet and she stumbled on, numbed with fright.

When they had covered half the distance to the slave pens, Frizio felt Mirage falter; he dismounted lest he tire the stallion, and ran his hands along Mirage's bony flanks.

"What have they done to you?" Frizio said, shaking his head. When he had first seen Mirage board the *Paradise* in Ostia, it was all he could do to keep from beating the two boys within an inch of their lives for the ruin they had brought on his stallion. "But you are of royal stock," Frizio said, stroking his nose, "and in three months, even less—"

Mirage lunged and bit Frizio's arm so hard it drew blood.

Frizio cried out in a flood of Arabic. Every time he had tried to comfort Mirage, the stallion had acted thus. In a cold rage, Frizio raised his whip and then at the last moment directed the blow at the file of children tramping sluggishly by.

In the slave market, additional pens had been constructed to contain the glut of children. As his share of the venture with Ferrus and Porquierres, Frizio had agreed to take seventy children of his own choice; whatever price they brought would be his. "A far cry from the hundreds I had anticipated, curse the Genoese," Frizio said to Baalbek, "but if market conditions prove favorable I will still make my fortune." He had already sold the two boatloads of children he had captured in Pisa.

An outbreak of tertian fever in the main camp made Frizio overly cautious. Though it appeared under control, he did not want to risk any of his children being stricken, and so had them quarantined in smaller pens adjacent to the main camp. The children were unfettered and separated according to sex. A makeshift fence divided the fifty-seven boys from the thirteen girls; Frizio did not want any of the girls to be with child, which often limited the price. After a final check of the children, Frizio set about finding accommodations private enough to carry out his plans for Laurelle.

. . .

It took Roger some hours to bend and separate the fence slats until he had made an opening large enough to reach through. His fingers tightened around Laurelle's hand and he said through the fence, "We will escape from this place, I swear it."

Laurelle clung to his hand. "I must warn you of something," she said, and told him of her vision of the sea of burning glass. "I do not know where it will happen, but it is not here."

Roger listened soberly. He did not like it when she talked this way, and yet she had been right in so many little things that he could not dismiss what she said. "Since we do not know what the omen means, all we can do is remain alert."

They stayed quiet for a bit, listening to the guards patroling the perimeter of the compound. Then Roger stood up and began to pace as far as his shackles would allow. He whirled suddenly and punched the fence.

"It is against nature for Christians to be imprisoned like this!" he shouted.

Jonathan tried to drag him away from the fence before the guards came but Roger pushed him off. "Coward!" Roger cried. "You sit there and accept everything that happens and do nothing? Do you not care that you are in a prison? That you are about to be sold like an animal?"

Jonathan clenched his fists. "I care," he said grimly. "I cared in London; I care in this slave pen. And I do not plan to spend my life in bondage to *any* man! But all your raving does is threaten to get us killed, and you are ruining our chances for escape!" He advanced on Roger, his knuckles white. "Now will you be still?"

"Oh, dear God, if only I had a sword!" Roger exclaimed.

"You are right," Jonathan said, "they have all the weapons and they are stronger. That is why we must remember what David said when he faced Goliath: 'The Lord saveth not with sword and spear.' " Jonathan tapped his forehead. "This is how we will escape. For there will surely come a moment when their guard will be down; we must be ready for that moment."

Roger slumped to the ground. His hands scrabbled in the hard-packed earth. "It is just that it is so unfair!"

"So it is," Jonathan agreed, "as so many things are unfair. But come now, do not dwell on the bad. Is this not the time for the faith you speak of so often?"

He held out his hand and pulled Roger to his feet. "Let us go and explain to Little Luke why he must not sing anymore. And then we must find out who those others are," he said, pointing to the milling children in the main compound, who numbered some two thousand.

ALEXANDRIA:
THE SLAVE MARKET

FIVE TIMES A DAY THE ULULATING PRAYER OF THE muezzin sounded from mosque and minaret. Throughout Alexandria all activities ceased as the faithful prostrated themselves toward Mecca, invoked the blessing of Allah, called for the continued good health of Sultan Malek Kamel, and ended with a fervent prayer for rain. When the melancholy incantation faded away, Alexandria got up from its knees and continued its business as usual.

The auction block for slaves stood adjacent to the camp, and Jonathan, Roger, and Laurelle could not help but witness the proceedings. A dozen children at a time were herded to the platform, stripped of their clothes and made to stand naked before the appraising eyes of the dealers and their searching fingers.

"Who has brought that group?" Jonathan asked Ibrahim, one of the young Bedouins whom Frizio had hired to guard his children, a boy little more than a year older than Jonathan. A number of Ibrahim's older brothers and cousins were also in Frizio's employ.

Ibrahim had been shocked when Jonathan first addressed him in Arabic. The Bedouin boy did his best to appear fierce to the captives, but such an air of curiosity piqued his burnished aquiline face that Jonathan suspected Ibrahim's heart was not really in his work. After a day of not responding to any of Jonathan's questions, except to jeer at him and laugh at his accent, Ibrahim chose to answer this one.

"That one with the strong back and split nose." Ibrahim said, "has been sold to the overseer of the Syrian copper mines. The scrawny girl next to him, she is too ugly to be anything but a kitchen maid."

"Your god is a cruel god if he allows such things to happen

to those who came in peace," Jonathan said. "Is this your much-praised hospitality of the desert?"

Ibrahim bloodied Jonathan's nose and would not speak to him the rest of the afternoon.

Nevertheless, as the days passed, the two boys formed an uneasy friendship. Ibrahim's discovery that Jonathan was not a Christian helped immensely, for the Bedouin lad had been brought up on tales of the cruelty of the Crusaders.

"Your barbarous Franks slaughtered the garrison of Acre, and *after* a truce had been declared! And also murdered the entire population of Jerusalem during the First Crusade, yet claim to worship the Prince of Peace?" Ibrahim said indignantly. "When I was a little boy, and sometimes bad, my mother used to say, 'Watch out, or I will send King Richard the Lion-Hearted to get you!' "

The two boys laughed. That Jonathan had been apprenticed to a physician and could read books in many languages made him akin to a magician in Ibrahim's eyes. The Bedouin became further indebted when Jonathan told him how to get rid of his body lice with an herbal tincture. But what cemented their friendship most was Mirage. No creature was of higher value to a Bedouin than his horse, for in the desert a horse could mean the difference between victory and defeat, life and death. Jonathan's love for Mirage was something that Ibrahim could understand completely.

"No, Frizio does not beat the stallion, in fact, he treats him well," the boy told Jonathan. "But the horse will not heed and each day Frizio grows more vexed. A strange one that Frizio is. Do you know what he does now? See that large stone house just beyond this compound?" Ibrahim asked, pointing it out. "Well, he has rented the upper floor and every day some new tradesman arrives with more furnishings, wonderful gauze curtains, and a Persian carpet, and thick mats and pillows, enough to sleep a dozen people. It is as grand as a sheikh's bridal chamber. Now why would he go to such trouble when we will not be here more than two weeks at the most?"

Jonathan shrugged. "That one is more than strange. Where do we go after this?" he asked.

"It depends on who buys you," Ibrahim said. "It is all in Allah's hands, so it is useless to worry. Best to resign yourself."

"Tell me this," Jonathan said, "who are the children in the main compound?" He and Roger had tried repeatedly to discover who the other prisoners were, for they had seen the red crusader's cross sewn on the garments of many children and clerics. But every time they came near the main compound one of the guards drove them back.

Ibrahim shrugged noncommittally. "When Allah sees fit that you know, you shall find out. But I will tell you the flare-up of fever has died down; it was not plague after all, Allah be thanked."

To pass the time, Ibrahim boasted of the glories of the free nomadic life. "I can walk barefoot over flint without being cut; I know how to find water in the desert. Already I have taken part in many raids against the Frankish castles along the Palestinian coast. Oh, we will drive the infidel out of our land, never fear."

Jonathan countered with the saga of the children's crusade and their special mission.

Ibrahim listened attentively then said, "I do not believe that it is in the nature of man to stop warring and anybody who thinks otherwise is a fool. What say you?"

Jonathan scratched his chin. "I can wish it to be so and I can pray for it, but," he said with a sigh, "you are probably right. The world is not yet ready. Otherwise, I would not be here!"

Ibrahim nodded sagely. "It is good that you are learning the ways of the world, instead of just believing things you read."

"Have you ever been to Jerusalem?" Jonathan asked.

"To be sure," Ibrahim said proudly, "many times. The city is holy, almost as holy as Mecca. And of a beauty without compare. All other cities are only cities; but Jerusalem? Well, you must see it for yourself to know what I mean." Ibrahim reflected for a bit and then said, "What I do not understand is why you stay with these Christians? You know yourself they cannot be trusted."

Jonathan smiled, "Do I have much choice?"

"Perhaps something could be done if you would embrace Allah. After all, we do revere common ancestors: Abraham, father of my tribe and of yours. And Sarah and Rebecca and Rachel. All you need do is recognize that Mohammed is Allah's prophet. So many Jews before you have done it. It is such a little thing to do, and then you would be safe."

Jonathan threw up his hands. "Another one trying to convert me! Is this to be my lot in life?" he asked good-humoredly.

Ibrahim shrugged and then tapped his chest with his fist. "If I were a rich sheikh I would buy you, on my word I would. Then you could be my court physician, the way your Maimonides was to my Saladin."

Jonathan salaamed in the Arab manner and the two boys grinned at each other.

"Those young ones," Jonathan said, watching a half-dozen children between the ages of six and ten clamber onto the block. Among them stood Little Luke. "Of what use are they to anybody?" Jonathan asked. "They will have to be fed for years before they can do any worthwhile work."

Over the auctioneer's singsong chant Ibrahim said, "See? You read and write and yet you know nothing. So far, these young ones will have fetched the highest prices. Alla-ed-din, the Old Man of the Mountain, will purchase them all, for he must have children as young as possible in order to train them in his ways."

As Ibrahim explained who and what the Old Man was, Jonathan's face grew white. In his mountain fortress, Alamut, deep in Syria, the Old Man of the Mountain would teach these young acolytes the mysteries of his sect. They would grow up to be human daggers, acting upon blind obedience, ready to fling themselves on prince, priest, or potentate at the Old Man's command. By using these terrorists, the Old Man was able to demand tribute from every ruler throughout Outremer. Count Conrad, would-be king of Jerusalem, had scoffed at the Old Man's power, only to fall to the terrorist's knife. Dreaded by Arab and Frank alike, these killers were known as *hashisheens*, from the hashish they used as a sacrament to induce their fearless madness. The Christians called them Assassins.

That Little Luke would one day grow up to be a killer—the thought was too much for Jonathan, and tears spilled from his eyes.

Ibrahim said derisively, "Like an old woman you act. It is unseemly to weep over something that cannot be helped." When Jonathan continued to cry, Ibrahim smacked him in the face and felt sorry at once. "I know who the children in the main camp are," Ibrahim said, "Stop crying and I will tell you."

"Children from France?" Roger said excitedly when Jonathan repeated Ibrahim's information. "Where are they from? Do any come from Paris? St. Denis?" Roger began to march along the dividing fence as far as his tether would allow. The fever scare being over, the guards did not stop him.

"Guillaume!" Roger shouted. "Is there a Guillaume among you? Does anybody know Guillaume?" He continued shouting until he grew hoarse.

Then a stocky lad with long arms and dark brown shoulder-length hair approached the fence. "My name is Guillaume," he said.

Roger stared at the youth. His nose had been broken in two places, giving his face a twisted look. It must have happened recently, for his lips were still puffed and the skin around his eyes shone an iridescent purple and green. "No," Roger said sadly, "I search for Guillaume of St. Denis."

"The same," the lad said, a quizzical look on his face. "But who are you?"

Then Roger noticed the threaded remnants of the stag-and-hound embroidery on the boy's shirt. Roger grabbed the lad's wrist and saw the hairline scar where they had mingled their blood. Roger pressed his wrist atop Guillaume's.

Guillaume let out a shout. He jumped, he leaped, he reached through the pickets of the fence and crushed Roger in a bear hug, then danced around the compound telling anybody who would listen of the miracle, and then came back to embrace Roger again.

Roger quickly told the stonecutter what had befallen the army of German children.

Guillaume listened, full of wonder. "There were rumors in France of such a movement along the Rhine, but never did I dream it would bring us together, and under these conditions," he said morosely.

"Now tell us of you," Roger said. "The last we heard, the masters of the university of Paris had decreed the crusade to be inspired by the devil."

Guillaume nodded, "And so Philip Augustus of France commanded us to disband. But one might just as well try to stem the tide, for by the end of June, more than thirty thousand children from all over the provinces had gathered at the village of Vendôme, our marshalling point."

Guillaume's tale was much like the German experience; hardship, hunger, drought, and desertion. The French army of children, including thousands of clerics, followed the Loire River until they were high in the central plateau. At Lyon they crossed the Rhone River and headed south, deep into Provence.

"All along our route we saw knights and foot soldiers of the pope with their great war machines, mangonels, towers, and catapults going to beseige the cities of the Albigenses. We begged them to lay down their arms, as the Lord commanded us, but they only laughed. In Languedoc, the heart of the heretic country, not a farmhouse was left standing, and every crop fired so as not to provide food for the enemy. Ravens weighted the limbs of dead trees and scavenged through fields of fallen bodies. At one captured castle we saw all the defenders—men, women, and children—being burned at the stake. Our priests claimed that as the heretics were burned all manner of devils flew from their bodies."

"Did you see these devils yourself?" Laurelle called from her side of the fence.

Guillaume shook his head. "I never did, but then I am not as holy as the priests. More children joined us here, orphaned by the war; many were rumored to be the children of the Albigenses but we did not question them on this." Guillaume lowered his eyes. "I am not wise in things of the spirit," he said. "But harken to me, if we were willing to go to the Saracens with open heart, could we deny the same to fellow Christians?"

At this, silence greeted Guillaume and he murmured, "You all hate me."

"Oh, no!" Laurelle said with a tiny cry and then related their own experience of the burning at Strasbourg. "Would that we had acted as you, Guillaume, and saved at least one child."

"You did," Jonathan said softly.

Guillaume looked questioningly at Jonathan. Roger cleared his throat and then whispered, "He is a Jew."

Guillaume shrank back and crossed himself. Roger gripped the stonecutter's arm. "Trust me, Guillaume, he is a good Jew."

Guillaume went on with his tale. At the end of August, after journeying three hundred miles, a weary army of twenty thousand remaining children had reached Marseille and gazed upon the Mediterranean. But here too the waters did not part as had been promised, and as the days passed thousands drifted back home.

"When all seemed hopeless, two merchants, Hugo Ferrus and William Porquierres, came forward and offered us ships to transport our remaining five thousand children to Palestine. They made their offer, they said, 'For the cause of God and without price.'

"Seven ships they supplied, mostly galleons of two hundred tons, and we were filled with hope again because of this miracle. The good people of Marseille cheered and waved from the city's walls as the wind carried us past Notre Dame le Garde, the chapel of the sailors and out into the open sea. Stephen's vessel took the lead—"

"Were you not on the same ship?" Roger interrupted.

Guillaume shook his head. "Stephen had changed much, encouraging everybody to idolize him. Those who did, fought and kicked to get on his boat; almost a thousand crowded on board though the captain warned them that they were riding low in the water. I had lost my taste for him by then and so boarded another ship.

"Never have I seen stars so bright as that first night; I confess I was sore afraid and prayed constantly to St. Cuthbert and St. Christopher. The next morning we sighted land on our left and praised the Savior for leading us to Palestine so quickly. The sailors laughed, we were passing Corsica, they said, an island owned by the Republic of Pisa. By dusk we could see the hazy outline of yet another island, Sardinia. Throughout the following day we sailed down its length. Then God caused a sudden fearful storm to rise and before we could reach safe harbor it engulfed us."

Guillaume stared straight ahead as he relived that moment. "Lightning rent the sky, thunder deafened, and mountains of waves washed over our decks, sweeping children into the sea. The wind drove our fleet toward a tiny island just off Sardinia's coast, San Pietro. The sea boiled around its reefs. Stephen's ship, so heavily laden with his favorites, could not maneuver well and was sucked toward the rocks. A second ship was also trapped by the currents. As they struck the reef, both vessels lifted high in the air and then split asunder. Above the howl of the wind we heard the pitiful screams of our brothers, but we could do nothing to save them. Some two thousand of us died that day."

Guillaume held his head in his hands and did not speak for a long time. At last he said dully, "God in His infinite wisdom allowed our other five ships to ride out the storm. Two days later we sighted land. We thought our trials were over, but instead of Palestine, the captain sailed us into the harbor of Bougie, a Saracen port. Then we discovered the terrible truth, that the two merchants, Ferrus and Porquierres, along with other Christian shipowners, had conspired with the Arabs and sold us into slavery. When we resisted—well, what can one do against men with weapons? That is how my nose got broken. Two of our ships anchored in Bougie. Those children on board were to be sold there; the other three ships, myself included, sailed here to Alexandria, a voyage of nearly two weeks. Many died on board, many have died in this camp, and here we remain, being sold one by one."

The muezzin's final call to prayer interrupted Guillaume. He looked to the delicate minaret, ghostly blue against the darkening blue sky, then turned to Roger with his deep trusting eyes. "Why are we being punished this way?" Guillaume asked.

Roger shook his head, unable to think of an answer.

"What great sins have we committed that God visits such affliction on us?" Guillaume went on. "To be sold into slavery by our own countrymen? Fellow Christians?" His arm swept around the compound. "Was it for this that we took the cross? Has God's arm been so shortened that it cannot save?" He was overcome and hung his head.

"Oh dear Guillaume, believe me, we have wrestled with these problems ourselves," Laurelle said. She pressed her fists to her chest. "It is bad enough for us, but for the very little ones . . ." She shook her head. She searched for something that would comfort him and said slowly, "When evil King Herod slaughtered all the newborn of the Jews? He did so hoping to thwart the prophecy of the appearance of the Redeemer. But they were all part of God's plan to herald the coming of the Messiah. In much the same way I have come to believe . . . that we are like those children. Being sacrificed for some greater glory that we cannot yet see or understand."

Guillaume looked at Laurelle intently. "You truly believe this?" he asked.

Laurelle nodded, an incandescent glow on her face.

Guillaume turned to Roger. "You too?" he asked hopefully.

After a long pause Roger said quietly, "What else can I believe?"

In the darkness, Jonathan's eyes glinted with anger at what Laurelle and Roger had said. The more he thought about it as they continued embroidering the idea, the angrier Jonathan became until he could barely control himself. He was on the verge of venting his rage when Baalbek suddenly appeared.

The eunuch went to Laurelle's pen and, without a word, loosened her bonds. Then, as she kicked and screamed, Baalbek carried her off, while the boys shouted helplessly after him.

ALEXANDRIA:
FRIZIO'S QUARTERS

AALBEK SET LAURELLE DOWN BEFORE THE ARCHED doorway of Frizio's quarters, nudged her into the chamber then quickly closed the door behind her.

Laurelle trembled like some frightened woods creature, her eyes darting to all corners of the room.

"Do not trouble yourself with thoughts of escape," Frizio called, "there is none. I have seen to it myself."

Then Laurelle saw him, lounging on throws of leopard and lion skins set beneath tented netting. He smiled at her, his lips glistening blood-red from a pomegranate he sucked.

Mixed with her terror was Laurelle's recognition that this was one of the most beautiful places she had ever been in. Soft light came from two oil lamps set on tripods, incense curled up from brass braziers, and pillows of varying sizes and designs lay all about. Try as she might, Laurelle's eyes always came back to Frizio; how can God cause this to be, she thought, that a man so blessed in appearance could be so cruel?

Frizio had taken pains for this meeting. He was as clean-shaven as his fine-honed knife would permit; the sheer billowy pants he wore showed off his physique to advantage, and his oiled upper body gleamed naked save for two silver and turquoise slave bracelets on each tanned, muscular arm.

Smoothing the leopard skin he reclined upon, Frizio called softly, "Come and sit here with me."

Laurelle did not respond.

Moving with animal grace, Frizio rose and strode toward her. She shrank back against the door, yanking on the latch. In one fluid motion, Frizio lifted her in his arms. Even as she struggled, punching feebly at his chest, Laurelle knew that she could not escape him.

He carried her to another part of the chamber where a large wooden tub sat on the floor, aromatic odors steaming up from its waters.

"Have you forgotten how we first met?" Frizio asked, his voice throbbing. "Never had I been so weary as when I reached Troyes. But your sweet fingers revived me, giving me life again. Now you shall see how I can return the favor." So saying, he began to remove her threadbare clothes.

Laurelle whimpered and clasped her arms around her body.

"You are strong for one so young," Frizio said, "and that is good, for you shall bear many healthy sons." With as much patience as firmness, he grasped both her wrists in one hand and with the other started to undress her.

She fell to the floor, begging him to leave her alone, pleading that she was worthless, that she had sworn a sacred vow, but his relentless hands deftly freed her of her clothes until she lay naked.

Staring down at her he murmured huskily, "Neither Aphrodite nor Isis . . ." and then undid the drawstring of his pants. As they fell around his ankles he kicked them aside. Laurelle quickly looked away from his rock-hard body.

He placed her in the tub and kneeled beside her. The soft warm water closed about her, tingling with its bath salts and oils, and Laurelle prayed desperately to the Virgin to keep her pure in thought and spirit. But try as she might, as Frizio's hands roamed over her body, scrubbing her clean, she felt herself become weak with dizziness, saw her nipples grow rosy and erect.

Hair, hands, feet, Frizio washed them all while Laurelle cried inwardly in litany to Mary: Protect me from this man, he sold innocent children into slavery, he killed my sister, he would kill us all without thought if it so pleased him.

With these prayerful warnings, she managed somehow to control herself and then moved into a state of being far removed from this room, from his touch. It did not matter when he lifted her out of the bath, nor when he rubbed her dry and laid her gently on the pillows, and only dimly did she hear the words of the song he hummed:

Live then like immortals
Worthy is the aim
To seek at love's portals
Heart's ease without blame . . .

But when his mouth ranged over her body she could no longer deny his presence and drew herself into a tight ball, punching and kicking at him.

Pinning her arms to the pallet, Frizio leaned over her, near overcome by her beauty and his ownership of it.

When she had not the strength left to struggle, he released her, then slipped off one of his silver bracelets and put it around her arm. "This one belonged to a princess," he said, "now it is yours."

Feeling gradually returned to her arms and then she ripped off the bracelet and struck him on the cheekbone with it, drawing blood.

Frizio's laughter belied the fact that his mood had been broken. "Some modesty in a woman is appropriate," he said, "but beyond a certain point it is tiresome. Must I have Baalbek teach you some manners?"

"Do what you will," Laurelle whispered, "for you will do it anyway, no matter what I say."

Stretching out beside her, he pressed his fevered body against hers, holding her immobile while his lips moved along the line of her neck and chin to find her mouth. But Laurelle remained as rigid as if she had been dead for a week. He wanted her, oh how he wanted her, but knowing he could use force at any time, Frizio set his sights on another, headier goal. How much greater his conquest would be if she gave herself willingly, with passion.

"Have you no need of love then?" he asked, a tenderness sounding in his voice. "Your life would be very different: the finest clothes, a soft bed, servants to tend to your every need. You need not want for anything ever again in your life. And you would have my protection and . . . devotion."

Laurelle fixed him with her clear gray gaze. "I am promised to another. We are to be wed."

Frizio barked with laughter. "Oh, you poor benighted child! Your lover has flattered you with such talk the better to have his way with you."

"My lover he is, yes," Laurelle said quietly, "but only in spirit. He has never touched me, not that night in Troyes as you claimed, and never once these many months though we have journeyed far."

The patent honesty in her voice made Frizio thrill with the realization that he and he alone was the only person who had ever known her.

He rolled from her and saw the tears glistening in the corners of her eyes. He kissed them away then said gently, "Enough of this for tonight. Tomorrow, perchance, will find you in a more receptive mood, and if not tomorrow, the day after; but one day soon, you shall open yourself to me."

"If that is your plan then you should kill me now and be done with it," Laurelle said, "for I will never submit to you. Never."

"Never is a very long time," Frizio said. "Too long for so passionate a maiden. Do you not understand by now that I can see into your heart? That I know what you yearn for? You are frightened, yes, but of yourself. Though you say you have sworn a vow, we both know that we are fated. The lesson you must learn is that it is holier to embrace one's fate than to fight it. Think on this, until tomorrow."

Then Frizio clapped his hands and Baalbek entered the room. He ordered the eunuch to confine Laurelle to her own chamber and to make sure that the serving women watched over her at all times.

During the next nights Frizio tried every way he knew to please the child. But she would not eat the choice tidbits placed before her, nor wear the fine clothes he bought for her. She huddled naked in a corner, saying her rosary over and over as though all reason had fled from her. Then she took to refusing food and drink until she was too weak to come into Frizio's presence unaided.

Her denial only increased Frizio's passion all the more, until it seemed to him that he too had slipped into a state akin to madness.

And then to compound his distress came a disastrous fall in the price of slaves.

For three days Frizio watched the market plummet. Never had he gotten less than six hundred dinars for a Turkish or Nubian child. A white-skinned Christian could bring anywhere from one thousand to fifteen hundred dinars, while a virgin (of either sex) commanded considerably more.

The governor of Alexandria, Maschemuth, bought seven hundred of the French slaves to till his vast farms along the banks of the Nile. His procurers bargained down to the last silver dirham for every child. Very few dealers dared bid against the governor, forcing Frizio to accept a ruinous price for ten of his own lot.

"It is this cursed drought," Frizio complained to Baalbek. "Will it never rain again?"

This season, the Nile had not overflowed its banks; even Lake Mariout, just outside Alexandria's walls, had completely dried up; with famine more than a threat, slaves were considered a dispensable luxury.

"It is entirely possible that I may not recoup my original outlay," Frizio grumbled.

Then carrier pigeons brought unexpected good news. The caliph in Cairo, Malek Kamel, planned to send his agents to Alexandria at week's end to purchase the finest specimens of children available. No one knew the reason for this extraordinary turn of events, but it was rumored to have the farthest-reaching consequences for Islam.

The news swept Frizio from his laconic, irritable state into determined action. "Here at last is what we have waited for," he said to Baalbek. "We must get our children into the best condition possible."

"The girl too?" Baalbek asked tentatively. When Frizio did not answer at once, Baalbek ventured, "If she refuses food much longer, who knows what her end will be, and then you will have lost not only her, but all the money she might bring."

Frizio chewed his thumb. "Yes, you are right. The girl also, then. Let her regain her strength, then we shall see what will be done. There is a way to reach her," he swore. "Somehow, that way will soon reveal itself. And when it does—after all, Baalbek, of what true value is any prize if it be too easily won?"

When Roger and Jonathan saw Laurelle being brought back to the slave pens they could not contain their joy. They rushed to the dividing fence and questioned her endlessly; in her weakened condition she told them what had happened as best she could.

After a bit Jonathan eased himself away so that Roger and Laurelle could be alone.

Roger crouched against the fence, his tears drying on his face. "The first day, when you did not return, I gave you up for dead; Jonathan said that for a time all reason fled me. I remember only that I prayed without end for your soul. But then the eunuch, well, he taunted me, saying that you had turned your back on us for life of comfort and had become Frizio's minion."

Laurelle shook her head weakly, "Never once did I break my vow. He could have forced me, but did not. Why I do not know. But we have not seen the last of this, for the man is truly obsessed. Oh Roger, I am so confused, so tired. I know not what to do!" She rocked back and forth ever so slightly. "Rather than submit to him, would heaven be denied me if I took my own life?"

Roger's eyes opened wide. "I do not know," he whispered, overcome with the very thought. He shuddered and tried to put it from his mind, but Laurelle went on.

"I try to imagine doing it," she said, "but I am so frightened. If only Harolde were here to advise us!"

"I tell you this," Roger said somberly, "if you die, whatever the way, I shall not be long following, for this life is nothing without you."

"Oh, but you must not!" Laurelle exclaimed. "One of us must live, if only to keep our dream alive."

The children sat this way for a long time, worrying the problem and never arriving at a satisfactory answer.

ALEXANDRIA:
ONE WEEK LATER

THE RULES OF THE MARKETPLACE WERE SIMPLE: IF a man would sell a house, he must apply a fresh coat of whitewash; if he would sell a horse, he must groom and curry the animal. The same applied to slaves, and Frizio invested the last of his dinars to this end. The children were amazed to be given ample portions of pita bread, goat cheese, and oranges. Twice a day Frizio inspected his lot, grunting with satisfaction as he watched their recovery. Flesh was added to bone; sores disappeared as the slaves ate voraciously; even Laurelle recovered, aided by the natural resilience of youth.

"Can this be a sign from the Lord?" Roger asked, as he devoured a green melon.

"Or some kind of trick," Jonathan said, sniffing the goat's milk.

Frizio took Baalbek aside. "The children are looking better already. Tomorrow, arrange for some exercise; their bodies must not be slack. But get rid of the deadwood," he said, pointing to three listless children too ill to respond to food.

Jonathan watched as Baalbek carried the children off. "What will happen to them?" he asked Ibrahim.

"Do not concern yourself with the useless ones," Ibrahim answered. "There is mercy in the swiftness of Baalbek's knife."

Jonathan turned pale. "I do not believe you," he said, though believing it all the time.

Ibrahim scowled. "They would have died anyway. What is the use wasting good food and water in a time of drought?"

Jonathan shouted, "They are children! Is this the way you honor Allah? To kill the defenseless?"

Ibrahim jabbed his staff hard into Jonathan's stomach. "Jew! Who are you to tell us what we can or cannot do?" He turned on his heel and stormed off. Throughout the afternoon, Ibrahim congratulated himself on the way he had handled Jonathan. "The slave took our friendship too much for granted," he told himself, "and I will converse with him no more." But Ibrahim could not understand why he felt so badly about the whole incident.

With a stern warning that any attempt to escape would bring severe punishment, if not death, Frizio had Baalbek untie the children so they might exercise.

Jonathan massaged his freed ankles, feeling so lightfooted he imagined that he could float away. The instant Roger was unfettered he turned into a whirlwind of punching, kicking arms and legs and broke for Laurelle's pen.

Baalbek unsheathed his dagger and raised his arm for the throw. Jonathan had but an instant to act. He kicked Baalbek as hard as he could, and then to complete the diversion ran for the opposite wall.

Baalbek howled, hopping about as he clutched his shins. Jonathan had gotten one arm over the top of the fence when Baalbek threw his knife. The blade pinned Jonathan's blouse to the fence. He managed to rip the dagger free, but Frizio's whip lashed through the air and wound around his ankle. Frizio jerked hard and Jonathan fell to the ground.

Meanwhile, Roger had reached Laurelle, only to stand there staring at her. The other Bedouin guards had rushed over at the commotion and Roger was quickly subdued. Both boys were brought back and tied up again.

Baalbek hulked over Roger, heaving with exertion. "Master, I can fix it so they will never try that again. Let me cut the Achilles' tendon."

"Oh, no, please!" Laurelle cried.

Frizio considered Baalbek's request. "Hamstringing him would limit the options for his sale; we would not get our full price if he could be used only as a field slave. But if, on the other hand, we sell him into the harem of a sheikh . . . what we would cut off then would make him docile enough. Better to wait another day or so. But Baalbek," he said, with a sideways glance at Laurelle, "whichever way it turns out, I promise it will be you who wields the knife."

Baalbek grinned broadly and thrust his head next to Roger's. "Then I pray it be Allah's will that you be sold into a harem."

The blood drained from Roger's face and for the first time since they had been captured, he looked frightened and unsure of himself.

Exceedingly pleased at the effect his threat had had on the boy and also on Laurelle, Frizio strode away, humming:

> *Fair is the sunshine*
> *Fairer still the meadows . . .*

Jonathan gingerly massaged his swelling ankle. "I do not think any bones are broken, torn ligaments, though," he said to Ibrahim, grimacing as he cautiously tested his weight.

"You were a fool to try it," Ibrahim scolded, but he was so confused he did not know what to think; for when Jonathan had dashed for freedom, Ibrahim had not tried to stop him.

"I could not let my friend die," Jonathan said.

Ibrahim spat on the ground. "Would he do the same for you?"

"I do not know. Does it matter?"

"Then you are worse than a fool," Ibrahim said in disgust. "I thought to teach you the ways of life, but will you heed? No. But now you must hear me; however you manage it, you must not let Frizio know you are hurt."

Remembering the fate of the sick children, Jonathan nodded. Searching through his wallet, he found some arbor vitae and swallowed two pellets of the pain-killing herb. "Ibrahim? Can you get me an extra ration of water? So I can make a poultice?"

Ibrahim shook his head vehemently. "The wells are low, there is not enough water for the faithful. And what if I am caught?"

"You are right. I am sorry I asked."

Later that night, when everybody lay asleep, Ibrahim crept to Jonathan's side and slipped him a small goatskin of water.

The moon was high when Laurelle saw the white-robed figure drifting toward her. Only when she smelled the familiar
bath oils and recognized the crooked smile did she know she
had not imagined the specter.

Frizio loomed above her and then reached down to stroke
her cheek. Laurelle bit his hand as hard as she could, but he
did not seem to feel it. He turned in the direction of the boys'
pens where Roger and Jonathan had wakened and were shouting at him to leave Laurelle alone.

Frizio approached them. Drugged or drunk, Jonathan did
not know which; but that Frizio trembled on the brink of
being possessed there could be no doubt. Scrambling, Jonathan did what he could to hide his injury.

With voice slow and slurring Frizio said, "You tried to escape this afternoon, so I would be within my rights if I put
you to death. But that would be too quick. Doubtless you have
wondered what plans I have for all of you?"

Pointing to Laurelle, Frizio said, "I had thought to keep her
for myself, for there is nothing more satisfying than breaking
an unruly filly. But I cannot afford to, for today a mighty sheikh
saw her and offered a king's ransom. When he is done with
her, he will pass her down to his soldiers and servants."

"He is only baiting us," Jonathan whispered to Roger, but
Roger sprang at his tormentor, only to be tripped by his
shackles.

Frizio jammed his foot on Roger's rump, pinning him to the
ground. "Each hour Baalbek begs permission to turn you into
a capon. Or perhaps you would prefer to be sold into one of
the male brothels throughout Islam—there to service those
who prefer the love of beardless boys? Many a Turk will pay
handsomely to sheath his sword in such fair scabbard. It may
be that you will grow accustomed, even like the vices of the
Ghilman, for I have seen that happen. You may last three or
four years before your flesh turns flaccid from misuse.

"Then you will be discarded," Frizio said, "to spend the rest
of your days rowing in the slave galleys, or chained to the

giant wheels that bring water up from the underground wells."

Roger squirmed out from under the punishing foot and dove for Frizio's legs. Frizio stepped nimbly aside and the boy landed in the dust.

"Oh, leave him alone, please," Laurelle cried. "I will do anything you want, anything, only do not torment him so."

Frizio stared up at the sky, his eyes the color of the heavy harvest moon. Almost buried was the memory of his defeat at the tournament in Troyes, and the fleur-de-lis burned into his arm seemed less a brand than a decoration. And when it came to him that he had inadvertently discovered the way to break Laurelle's spirit, he threw back his head and laughed long and low.

Stretching as far as their ropes would allow, Roger and Laurelle barely managed to reach each other's fingertips through an opening in the fence. When he whispered, "I love you," tears sprang to Laurelle's eyes.

Now that it seemed certain they would never reach Jerusalem, Laurelle burned to lie with Roger. Her daily trial with Frizio had wakened feelings in her that she never dreamed existed; the pulse of her blood beat, I cannot die without knowing Roger, I will not die without knowing him.

Laurelle felt a pang for her sister, for now she understood Flamonde in a way she never had before.

"I have thought long and hard about what we discussed earlier," Laurelle said, "and I have made my decision. You must promise me that if I am sold, and if I cannot manage it myself, then you must find a way to kill me. This afternoon when you went to escape, I thought . . ."

"It was on my mind," Roger said, "but when I reached you I could not." He shook his head wearily.

"You must not be frightened," Laurelle said. "If death can give meaning to my life, then I embrace it."

"But how?" Roger asked. "I could never lay hands on you, so how?"

"I do not know," Laurelle said. She thought for a while and then clapped her hands. "We will get Jonathan to concoct a poison! He is very clever with his herbs!"

Excited, they called Jonathan to their side. But when they told him of their plan, Jonathan shook his head violently. "No, I will not!"

Roger gripped his shoulder. "Are you on their side? Is it not better to be dead than to wind up the plaything of some filthy infidel?"

Jonathan pushed Roger off. "As long as we are alive, anything can happen. You saw yourself, there are Christians in this city, and Jews also. Surely we will find somebody who will give us sanctuary. All we need do is escape—"

"Escape!" Roger interrupted, yanking on his ropes.

Jonathan said hotly, "Do you trust so little in your Lord that you cannot bear His test? It is written in Ecclesiastes: 'It is better to be a live dog than a dead lion.' I tell you, there is a design here. Are we not that much closer to Jerusalem?"

"Yes, we are closer," Roger said derisively, "a handful out of the many thousands."

"If there be one honest man," Jonathan said, "then the Lord will listen, as He has listened before."

"I think you are right, Jonathan," Laurelle said eagerly, her spirits revived by his passion. "It is what I told Guillaume. Just as the holy innocents were martyred . . ."

With an oath, Jonathan pulled himself to his feet. "I will not believe we are going to be martyred. Believe such a thing and you will surely bring it to pass. Rather would I believe that we are being saved. For one final test. It may be to prove our faith in all that is righteous. It may be just to prove ourselves. I do not know, for it is not given to us to know. But for myself," he said, his defiant words ringing out the challenge, "I will never lose hope, and never will I be a willing sacrifice again!"

PART

The Last Judgment

FOUR

ACROSS THE NILE DELTA

N THE LUXURIOUS QUARTERS OF THE ENVOY FROM CAIRO, Frizio and several other slave dealers listened intently as the procurer outlined the caliph's desires.

Veiled serving girls silently proffered dishes of dates, sweet cakes, and lime sherbet made of snow from faraway Lebanon. The thread of smoke from cannabis leaves curled up from a hookah toward a ceiling mosaicked in designs of the zodiac. Through the graceful horseshoe arch of the windows, Frizio looked out to the atrium, where palm and olive, orange and lemon trees stirred in the vague evening breezes. A sacred ibis pecked at the flowerbeds and a white peacock spread its tail feathers to mirror the rising moon. Frizio eyed it all covetously. Patience, he told himself; for in the envoy's proposal Frizio saw the way of attaining it all.

The caliph of Cairo, Malek Kamel, had already contracted for all the clerics captured in the French crusade of children. For those who could read and write he had bid a handsome price and dealers were well pleased. Some four hundred slaves in all, including eighty priests, would teach the royal court in Cairo the ways of the Franks. With the repeated invasions of the Europeans during the past hundred years, the Saracens were avid to learn everything they could about their enemies, the better to defeat them.

"But the purchase of these clerics is nothing compared to the caliph's plan for some of the other captive children," the emissary told the slave traders. "For this he must have the most splendid specimens and you dealers have been selected because you own the best."

In all the centuries since Mohammed had been chosen prophet by Allah, only once had Islam been united, under the great Saladin. During the Third Crusade, his armies had fought the forces of Richard Coeur de Lion and Philip

Augustus to a draw, and the Moslem world had rejoiced. After Saladin's untimely death, his brother, Saphadin, had assumed the throne, but being neither as good a statesman nor general, the empire soon degenerated. After some years Saphadin abdicated, dividing the vast Ayyubid empire between his many sons; it was to his eldest son that he gave the eastern caliphate, with its capital in Baghdad; the western caliphate (formerly the Fatamid empire), with its seat in Cairo, he gave to another son, Malek Kamel.

Malek Kamel's ambition was to end the internecine wars beleaguering the Moslem factions and reunite the empire, for there was a new threat. The Franks had a new and vigorous king on their throne, John de Brienne, count of Champagne. True, the Crusader holdings had been greatly reduced in Outremer, but John de Brienne agitated constantly for one last crusade to reconquer the Holy Land, and his clamorings had already incited the European monarchs and the pope in Rome.

A council of all the princes of Islam was to be held in Baghdad, there to devise a war plan to crush the Franks once and for all. The call for *jihad,* holy war, had united Islam once before. It must do so again.

"A great demonstration of Allah's might is needed to arouse our war-weary people," the emissary explained. "Caliph Malek Kamel believes that Allah has delivered these children into our hands for just that purpose. For what better way to prove Allah's power than to convince these little ones to renounce their false gods for the true and only one? Such dramatic testimony will confound the Christians and ignite Islam. Then the Saracen armies will sweep across Palestine and annihilate the last Crusader enclaves still clinging to the coast!"

An exclamation of approval swept the chamber and Frizio's voice rang out the loudest.

The plan called for one hundred of the slave children to be taken to Baghdad, where in full view of the populace they would be made to deny their false ways and embrace Allah. Those who did would be freed immediately and would gain all the privileges of Islam. And those who refused would not refuse for long, after the necessary persuasions.

Overland, Baghdad lay more than nine hundred miles from Alexandria, a six-week journey across vast desert and desolate plateau, through terrain roamed by hostile nomads. Three of the dealers begged to be excused, claiming that pressing business matters prevented them from embarking on such a long trip.

But Frizio and another trader, Qabat, jumped at the opportunity. For though they knew it to be a hazardous journey, doubly so with such fragile cargo, not only would the caliph bear the cost of outfitting the caravans, including a guard of forty Bedouin warriors, he also guaranteed that in Baghdad the children would fetch five to six times their usual value.

Contracts were signed, down payments made. All Frizio had to do was deliver these Christian slaves and he would collect his money. Frizio did not know if these children would prove Allah stronger than Jesus. Nor did he care. What he did know, as he had known from the first day he'd seen them in Cologne five months before, was that they held the key to his fortune.

Three days later, the caravan transporting the slave children departed Alexandria via the Gate of the Sun, leaving the obelisks of Pompey's Pillar and Cleopatra's Needle dwindling in the distance.

The first leg of their journey, to Kantara on the Suez Isthmus, a distance of some two hundred miles across the Nile delta, would take ten days, barring accident, attack, or sandstorm.

Frizio rode at the head of his contingent of children, perched atop a camel; Mirage ambled behind on a long lead. The stallion had almost fully recovered, as though drawing strength from each step he took on his native soil.

"There is no need to tire him unnecessarily," Frizio said to Baalbek, who swayed precariously between the humps of a Bactrian. But in truth, Frizio remained uneasy about Mirage; the stallion had given him nothing but trouble. Determined to reestablish his dominion as master, Frizio knew this could only be accomplished with the greatest care. As for Laurelle, not a moment passed when she did not invade his thoughts, when he did not imagine conquering her in new and varied ways. But for now, the pressing business of whipping this caravan into shape occupied all of Frizio's time and energies. But soon, he thought, everybody would have learned his task, all would go smoothly, and then . . .

The slave children, the finest specimens culled, numbered one hundred and fifty. Frizio owned sixty outright, Qabat the same amount. The extra thirty children were to be sold along the route to help replenish the caravan's supplies. By some sharp trading, Frizio had added Guillaume to his lot, bartering two scrofulous girls for the sturdy French lad.

Camels and donkeys were the primary beasts of burden; four children shared each donkey, two riding while two walked. The better to keep his eye on the troublemakers, Frizio had grouped Jonathan, Laurelle, Roger, and Guillaume together. The children had been outfitted with loose clothes and burnooses to protect them from the sun. The animals were roped together in a line and each child was tied by a long lead to his donkey, allowing him to either ride or walk.

Jonathan's ankle was still badly inflamed, so the three other children insisted that he ride the majority of the time.

"If we could cut the ropes," Roger whispered to Jonathan, "we might scatter the animals and escape."

"To where?" Jonathan asked, looking out at the scrub-dotted dunes stretching endlessly before them. "If we are to escape we must do it near a city, otherwise we are sure to perish in this desert."

Like an earthworm, the caravan made its torturous way across the delta. What had once been the breadbasket of Egypt, the fertile triangle for which countless armies had fought, was now barren, baked earth. Gaunt fellaheens called to them from squalid mud huts, begging for food; swollen-bellied babies hung listlessly in their mothers' arms.

"Surely it cannot get any hotter than this," Jonathan said to Ibrahim. The Bedouin boy had ridden up alongside him.

"This?" Ibrahim laughed deprecatingly. "Why this is nothing compared to the desert of the Sinai and the wilderness of Judah." Ibrahim picked some withered almonds off a tree and

pitched a few to Jonathan. "They are good for you," he said.
"My father claims that he sired eight strong sons because he
chewed dates and almonds."

"Is there other food in the desert one can eat?" Jonathan
asked with forced nonchalance.

"Of a certainty," Ibrahim said. "Melons; sabra pears, they
are the fruit of the cactus. And from the sycamore, the tree
with the umbrella leaves, there is a fig which is edible, but
first prick the fruit with a needle and let it ripen in the sun."
Ibrahim's eyes twinkled mischievously. "You are not thinking
of trying to escape?"

Jonathan pulled at his tether. "Bound this way, is such a
thing possible?"

"For you, no," Ibrahim said, "but for a Bedouin, anything is
possible. In the desert, the sun is the enemy, the moon our
friend. I would travel only at night, conserve my strength."

"Water?"

"There is none—none that you could find, anyway. One
must make do with the juice from the fruit."

"Can such a thing be done on foot?"

"It is very rare; a camel is best. Once my father was lost for
days and desperate for water. He stuck a twig down his camel's throat and the water it gave up kept him alive. I have
heard tell of men on foot conquering the desert, provided of
course that the distance is not too far."

"If only I had my Tortoise," Jonathan said. "She was our
donkey," he explained to Ibrahim, "and a paragon among
animals. And with a disposition so sweet! She could climb a
mountain, ford a river, carry six children on her back with
never a complaint."

"What happened to her?"

"She died," Jonathan said, and added quickly, "but we did
not eat her, though we were sore hungry."

They rode along in silence for a while and then Jonathan
asked in a bantering tone, "In which direction would you go?"

"To Jerusalem," Ibrahim said promptly, "for there all the
people of the world meet and mingle, Arab, Christian, Jew.
One could easily lose oneself in such a place. Of course, you

might be able to vanish in Baghdad also, for though I have never been there I hear tell it is a vast, wondrous city."

"Baghdad?" Jonathan said sharply, "but that is at the other end of the earth! Why are we going there?" And then seeing the impassive look come over Ibrahim's face, said at the same time as the Bedouin, "When Allah wants you to know . . ."

Out of the corner of his eye Ibrahim spied Baalbek riding toward them on his Bactrian. Ibrahim swung and gave Jonathan a fearful clout on the head, knocking him off his donkey. He shook his fist at the fallen boy. "Don't ever let me hear you say such a thing again!" Ibrahim turned to Baalbek, hard upon them now, "One must be firm with these infidels," he said and galloped off.

Baalbek reached down and ran his fly whisk along Jonathan's face, tickling his ear. "Such things would not happen to you if you put yourself under my protection. See that lad?" Baalbek said, pointing to a towheaded Westphalian boy. "He has become the favorite of the Bedouin chief, and receives extra rations of food and water. Why should you not have the same?"

Jonathan brushed the whisk aside. Then he stood, and gritting his teeth to hide his limp, remounted. As soon as he was able, Jonathan told Roger and Laurelle what Ibrahim had told him. "I do not know why we are going to Baghdad," Jonathan said in exasperation to Roger's badgerings, "but my guess is that it must be for something very important to journey so far."

The days burned into each other as they continued across the delta. They woke long before dawn and rode until the heat forced them to halt. If an oasis chanced to be near they made for it, otherwise they took shelter in the shade of rock outcroppings or of their own hunkered beasts. When the sun was no longer direct they continued their trek past dusk, stopping only when darkness might cause their animals to stumble. In this way they covered twenty to twenty-five miles each day.

They forded the many branches of the Nile that compromised the delta. In most places the river was low enough to wade across; in those few areas where the current still ran strong, they took the available ferries.

At one such crossing, Frizio haggled with the ferry master over the cost of passage. The flat-bottomed boat traveled along guy ropes angled downstream; on the far bank, a scrawny ass walked in circles, turning a wheel which wound ropes around a creaky wooden drum, pulling the boat across. Finally Frizio and the ferryman reached an agreement: in exchange for transporting the caravan without charge, Frizio would sell him a slave at a good discount.

The boat owner walked up and down the line of slaves, inspecting them, prying open their mouths and tapping their teeth.

"I will have that one, he looks the strongest," he said pointing to Roger.

Laurelle drew in her breath sharply, feeling her stomach tighten into a knot.

Frizio let a long moment pass, looking from Laurelle to Roger, relishing the panic on their faces. Then he shook his head. "You may have any other male child. I have plans for him."

The ferry captain argued shrilly but Frizio remained adamant. Grumbling, the captain squeezed Guillaume's arm and poked his thighs and flanks. "Then this one will have to do."

"No!" Roger shouted, but Frizio bloodied his mouth with a backhand slap.

Guillaume tried to fight off the Bedouin guards but they quickly subdued him, untied him from his donkey, and then chained him to the great wheel along with the draft animal.

"The beast is getting old," the ferryman said, "and it costs too much to feed him. "Let us see what an infidel can do."

"You cannot make me, ever," Guillaume shouted, refusing to turn the wheel.

The ferry captain drew his knife. "Shall I put out your eyes then?"

Seeing that the man was not bluffing, Guillaume put his back to the spokes.

As the caravan started on its way, Roger dug in his heels,

shouting and swearing, but the line of animals plodded forward, dragging him through the sand until he lay stunned. Baalbek lifted him by the scruff of the neck and threw him across the donkey's back.

"It is hopeless to fight now," Jonathan whispered to Roger, "save your strength."

"Oh, yes, do as Jonathan says," Laurelle said, "and we will pray that the Lord will watch over Guillaume."

Roger looked back at Guillaume straining at the wheel. "We will meet again," he shouted, spitting out a mouthful of sand. Tears sprang to Roger's eyes; he had cried out these same words to Guillaume in Paris. Only now he did not believe them.

"Yes, we will meet again," he whispered, "but next time in heaven or in hell."

THE DESERT OF THE SINAI

INE DAYS AFTER LEAVING ALEXANDRIA, THE CARA-
van filed into the mud-and-wattle village of Kantara, the last inhabited outpost before the wasteland of the Sinai Desert. The Bedouin drivers
unhitched the animals and had the tents pitched
in a twinkling.

Frizio planned to remain in Kantara a full day, replenishing
supplies and tending to ailments, and resting, for the next day
would begin their five-day march through the Sinai. He took
special plans to make sure all was in working order, overseeing the caulking of weeping leaks in the water casks, the repairing of harnesses, and where necessary, the reshodding of
animals.

To his Bedouin guards' request that they be permitted to
visit Kantara's two brothels, Frizio said no, refusing any advance on their wages. "With the hell of the Sinai about to be
on us, it is best that a man conserve his energies. But if all
goes well," he promised them, "then you shall sate yourselves
to the full when we reach El Arish."

And so shall I, he suddenly decided. These past days, the
slow rocking motion of the camel between his legs, the heat,
and sense of success soon within his grasp, had brought pul-
sating daydreams of young flesh. Never before had Frizio
forced himself to so bridle his passions, and daily he had
grown more vexed under the savage sun. "But it will have
been worth the wait," he said to Baalbek. "You are my
witness that I tried kindness. That did not work and so I must
use other means. And now I know the way to bring her obe-
diently to heel."

The sea stretched away in full view of camp and the children
watched the brilliant colors fade as the sun set.

"I am so weary I could not have gone another step," Laurelle said, rubbing her feet.

"And these blisters," Jonathan said. Using the spine of a thorn, he pricked one between his toes and then tended to the other children's.

"Do not worry, in another few days your feet will be so tough that you will not feel anything," Ibrahim told Jonathan, showing him his own thickly callused soles. "How is your ankle?"

Jonathan screwed up his face. "Not good."

To spare him, Roger and Laurelle had walked as much as possible, and Ibrahim had taken great risks to bring him water for his poultices. Each night Jonathan applied his medications; the ankle would respond somewhat, only to be further inflamed by the next day's march. He had a decided limp now and could no longer hide it from Baalbek or Frizio.

That night the children watched the village fishermen go out to sea in their swift slim barks. The wolf fish, native to these shores, were elusive and could be caught only one way, by their attraction to light. One man held a lantern close to the water; when the curious fish rose toward it, a second fisherman scooped the catch into his net.

"We were like those fish," Laurelle said, "blinded by what we thought was the light."

Roger nodded sadly, but Jonathan scratched his head and said, "I marched for a different reason, yet I am also here. Could it be that something more drew us together?"

"Like what?" Roger asked.

Jonathan shrugged. "I know not, yet I do know that oftentimes the Lord demands that we journey along strange paths to reach salvation. All one needs to do is look at Job."

"Small comfort in the lot of Job!" Roger groaned. "Jonathan, remember you once asked me if I believed that salvation was something that could be gained only by an army?"

Jonathan nodded.

"Well," Roger sighed, "I think now that you were right. Each one of us must find that path for himself. But if our quest be righteous, why are we made to endure so much?"

"Why was our Lord made to suffer so?" Laurelle asked softly. "What was His crime—preaching brotherhood? And are all who preach brotherhood to be so crucified? In such a small way, in our march to resurrect His Gospel, perhaps we too took upon our shoulders the sins of our fathers. But our shoulders were too frail. . . ."

This gave them all pause; they did not converse for a time.

Roger leaned back against the sloping trunk of a palm tree. He pointed out to the sea, iridescent in the light of the half-moon. "Laurelle, if by some miracle you had the chance to go back to your old life, to relive it as if this never happened, would you?"

"Never!" Laurelle said without hestitation. "Would you ask me to deny you? Would you ask me to deny God? I would have found neither of these had I not made this pilgrimage. Of regrets I have but one."

"What?" Roger asked.

Laurelle drew a flower in the sand, and then a second, its petals touching the first. "That to you I was as cold-hearted as the Lorelei, that my ears were deaf to your pleas, and that I never loved you with my body as I do with my soul."

Roger closed his eyes. The nearness of her, the distinctness of her own sweet smell, was too much to bear. Yet he knew this was why Frizio held them captive this way, within arm's reach, yet unable to embrace.

"You must not distress yourself with such things," Roger said. "We are as one, this I know above all else. In Troyes, that night on the Rhine, and this very moment. And if I had to choose one life only, gladly would I choose what we have now."

Laurelle reached out for him as he reached for her, and it did not seem that such a wide space remained between their fingertips.

Later that evening, Ibrahim had the watch and soon gravitated over to where Jonathan sat. Ibrahim nudged Jonathan and pointed to a rock hyrax nosing out of its burrow. "It had best be careful," he whispered, pointing about ten feet further away. Coiled just out of sight, an adder waited with the patience of its kind, forked tongue flicking as it tracked its prey.

Baalbek too watched, his flat cold eyes glinting in the folds of his face. As the hyrax took a step outside, Jonathan threw a pebble at it; the hyrax scurried back into its den as the adder struck and missed.

Baalbek heaved his bulk toward Jonathan, grabbed the boy's ankle and slowly squeezed. Jonathan cried out and fainted. When Baalbek took his hand away he found it covered with the mud of the poultice. He hurried to Frizio's tent and brought him back.

Frizio slapped Jonathan back to his senses. "Where are you getting the water for this?" he demanded.

Jonathan did not reply.

Baalbek reached for the ankle again. "You will tell, or I will break it," he said, applying pressure. Jonathan screamed again.

Ibrahim came forward then. "I gave it to him, it is from my ration."

Frizio struck Ibrahim on the side of the head, sending him sprawling. "These slaves are my property!" he shouted.

Ibrahim got to his feet. "And I am not a slave to be struck by you," he said, trembling. "I am a Bedouin."

Baalbek lunged for him but Ibrahim dodged. "Lay a hand on me again and you shall answer to my kinsmen," he said.

"Come away," Frizio said to Baalbek, for he did not wish to provoke a confrontation; the boy had a half-dozen relatives among the guard. "He has learned his lesson, and we must keep a sharper eye on the water casks."

"Thank you," Jonathan said to Ibrahim when the two men were out of earshot.

Ibrahim rubbed his stinging ear. "We are not all beasts like that one," he said. "Even a slave is a human being, so says the Prophet. A man like that gives Islam a bad name."

"But he does not worship Allah, does he?" Jonathan asked, surprised.

"For sure he does," Ibrahim said. "I myself have seen him in the mosques of Alexandria."

"And I have seen him enter the churches of Europe!" Jonathan exclaimed.

Ibrahim looked scandalized. "You cannot be right. It is death for an infidel to enter our sacred places."

Pressing his advantage, Jonathan told Ibrahim of the trial by combat in Troyes, how Frizio had sworn on the Bible and other sacred Christian relics to obey all the rules.

"Perchance he did it only to fool the Christians?" Ibrahim said.

"That may be," Jonathan answered with an unconvincing shrug. He said no more, but he could see that the seeds of doubt had been firmly planted in Ibrahim's mind.

Outside Kantara, the caravan picked up the roadway of the Via Maris, which paralleled the Mediterranean shore. This was the preferred route across the Sinai for many reasons, foremost because the Via Maris lay only a few hundred yards from the sea. Though not potable, the mere presence of water made the desert seem less ominous. Pockets of underground sweet water made possible a handful of oases along the shoreline, affording occasional shade and drinking water.

They reached the inland sea of Lake Sirbonis and found it little more than a swamp. Gnats and mosquitoes darkened the morning air, intent on blood.

Baalbek fell back to ride alongside Jonathan. "You will wait on me tonight," he said.

Jonathan did not answer.

A fly buzzed around Baalbek's head and he caught it with a deft motion. "A favorite Turkish chastisement for an unruly boy," Baalbek said, "is to tie him naked to a stake and let the bugs have their fill of him. He that does not die of the bites soon goes insane from the sun, so it is all the same. You will wait on me tonight."

The rest of the day Jonathan alternately sweated and shivered in anticipation of the night. Having heard what transpired, Laurelle and Roger tried to calm him.

"That God lets that fat one live is a wonder to me," Roger

said. "Though I have sworn myself to peace, I would not grieve to see him dead."

Laurelle ran her hands across her eyes. "I do not know what to think anymore. The Lord tells us, 'Resist not evil.' Yet that evil will martyr us all. Is that what He intends? If only we had a sign! Some signal to tell us we are on the right path!"

"We are on the right path," Jonathan said grimly, then added under his breath, " 'O, Jerusalem, if I forget thee . . .' I will endure what I must from the eunuch," he murmured. "My Lord God will know that in my heart I did not sin."

The sun burned a hole in the parchment sky. The road seemed to go nowhere, hanging suspended between the yellow glare of sand and sky. In many places, wind drifts had moved entire dunes, obliterating the road altogether.

Sweat trickled down Laurelle's cheek. The dunes, hill upon hill, moved in her vision and lost their shape to the shimmering heat. At any moment it seemed that the sand itself would catch fire. "A sea of burning glass," Laurelle whispered, her eyes fixed not on this moment in the dazzling sun, but on the premonition she had had in the slave pen.

"Do not stare so!" Roger said.

She looked at him with unseeing eyes and said, "Closer, we are getting closer."

"To what?" Roger asked, shaking her anxiously. "You must stop talking like that! It only serves to frighten us the more."

Laurelle blinked her eyes and her recognition flooded back to the present. "What did you say?" she asked sweetly.

Baalbek did not get his chance to carry out his threat that night. Two of the slaves collapsed from dehydration shortly before they pitched camp; one died after midnight and the other the following morning. Frizio and Baalbek tried to save them; the money loss would be considerable. But the exhaustion of many months of marching, coupled with the crucible of the desert had proved too much.

Frizio had not anticipated the inability of these fair children to endure the desert, and his mood turned foul; everybody, including Qabat and the Bedouin guard, learned to stay out of his way.

"We must not relax," Frizio said to Baalbek as he increased the caravan's pace, "else we shall lose them one by one."

Two days away from El Arish they dragged their way into a small oasis. This day's march had been particularly brutal and Frizio even allowed the children an extra ration of water. Then he ordered that the girls, thirteen in all, be taken into his tent and rubbed down with the sap of the aloe plant; he did not want their skin blistered or turned leathery by the sun. Nor did he want any liberties to be taken with his merchandise and so he stood by, overseeing the proceedings.

The stems of the long, spiny plant were cut and its liquid allowed to ooze into a bowl. Then a Bedouin smoothed the balm over the body of each child. Soon it was Laurelle's turn, and though she shuddered under the Bedouin's touch, it was Frizio's penetrating stare that made her cringe.

The aloe cooled her skin, raising gooseflesh all over. The Bedouin's hand lingered for a fraction of a second and Frizio's whip whirred through the air; the Arab howled and scrambled away, holding his bruised and bleeding forearm.

Then Frizio herded everybody out of his tent save Laurelle.

"Beautiful enough to find favor in a sultan's harem," he said, circling her. His hand moved to stroke the soft hair, not quite red, not quite brown. Then Frizio reached up and caught her face in both his hands; he twisted it to him, gazing into the pale gray eyes that in their refusal to show passion or fear challenged him to break her to his will.

"You who believe so in omens and vows, shall I tell you your fortune?" he asked softly.

She did not answer but continued to stare at him.

"Well then, in two days' time we shall reach the oasis of El Arish. And there you will come into my tent and give yourself to me, all willingly."

Laurelle shook her head. "You may do what you want. Even kill me, but never will I do what you say."

"Ah, how greatly you Christians suffer from the sin of

pride. But you will do it," he repeated matter-of-factly. "For if you do not, then your betrothed shall have his manhood cut from him."

Laurelle's face blanched and then she was seized with violent tremblings.

"If, however, you are dutiful, and do what you must to please me, then perhaps I shall be merciful and set him free. His fate lies in your hands. Oh, and one last thing—under no circumstances is he to know of this. If I discover that you have told him, I shall set Baalbek on him at once. Now you have two days to think on this, and I shall expect your answer in El Arish." Then Frizio dismissed her.

After Laurelle left, Frizio stared out at the palms swaying gently against the star-pricked sky. He knew that he had broken through her remote reserve, and feeling the need for an expansive moment, went outside. His flowing robes caressed his skin in the quick sea breezes.

He walked to where Mirage was tied. In this very countryside he had first seen the stallion. Moving gently, he stroked the stallion's nose; Mirage shuffled and backed off. Frizio spoke to him, telling him of the pasture he would have outside the walls of Jerusalem. "As soon as this caravan is over you shall have the most beautiful mares and sire stallions known throughout the world. We will grow old together, you and I," Frizio said, his voice and hands caressing.

With great care, Frizio slipped the bridle and bit over the stallion's head, then untied him. Mirage kicked at the sand. Frizio knew that Roger and Jonathan were watching his every move, and this greatly pleased him. When Mirage calmed sufficiently, with a lightning leap Frizio vaulted onto his back. Mirage bucked, but Frizio locked his knees against the stallion's rib cage and gave him his head.

Mirage broke for freedom, galloping along the crest of the dune. His muscles corded as he tried to flee from the man atop his back. The wind whistled in Frizio's ears, he felt the warm, powerful flesh of the horse between his thighs, felt his body merge with the beast's as they raced the moon.

Mirage ran as he had never run before, seeming not to touch

the slipping sands. When Frizio tried to turn him back toward camp, Mirage grabbed the bit in his teeth and would not respond, though the iron cut his mouth and blood streaked his muzzle.

Frizio's knees grew numb with the strain as he fought to hold on. Grasping the reins tightly in one hand, he grabbed a fistful of the horse's white crest and pulled back as hard as he could. Still Mirage would not heed and raced on. Frizio lunged forward and sank his teeth into the stallion's neck, biting through the flesh. Mirage whinnied in rage, reared, and in a last effort to escape plunged into a wadi and rolled on his side, trying to crush Frizio beneath his weight. Frizio barely managed to leap free. The stallion scrambled to his feet and charged.

Mirage would have escaped had not the other Bedouin riders, alerted by Frizio's shouts, followed him out into the desert. They threw ropes around the horse until they held him fast. Mirage stood trembling, chest heaving as though his heart would burst.

When the men came back to the campsite, Frizio saw Jonathan, Roger, and Laurelle standing at the edge of the darkness, watching anxiously. Jonathan flinched when he saw the blood-spattered horse and Roger cursed Frizio.

Frizio's eyes swept over the three shackled children and then came to rest on Laurelle. He laughed then, and continued to laugh long after he had retired to his tent.

THE OASIS OF EL ARISH

A SWAYING STAND OF ROYAL PALMS, FIFTY TO SIXTY feet tall, lined the sand-drifted road leading into El Arish, capital of the Bedouin tribes in the Sinai.

Turbaned tribesmen sang out El Arish's noted wares: "The rarest ivories! Hashish of the finest grade!" Arab youngsters ran alongside the marching slave children, staring at and sometimes even daring to touch the fair creatures. Veiled women peeped from the doorway of the town's brothel, their throats throbbing in high-pitched greeting, finger cymbals ringing in scintillating rhythm, beckoning to the caravan's grinning Bedouin guard.

Never did Frizio's men pitch camp nor have done with their chores more quickly. They had survived the Sinai and nothing could keep them from this earned night of pleasure.

An uneasy heaviness charged the air. From the brothel came the music of lute and tamborine and the sound of raucous laughter. And from the black tents of the Bedouin guard wafted the acrid odor of hashish; Mohammed's injunction against alcohol had led his followers to the poppy and cannabis.

"All men must have their dreams," Ibrahim said to Jonathan, "and will find the means to them one way or another." So saying, he dipped some pita bread into a pot of a honeylike syrup made from the residue of cooked grapes and shared the intoxicating delicacy with Jonathan, Roger, and Laurelle.

Jonathan grew heady from the winy taste; he rested his head on his knees and stared out at the sea. The moon banded a path of sparkling light which seemed to lead directly to his eyes. "It is very beautiful here, and so peaceful that one might almost forget these," he sighed, shaking his bonds. "But we shall find the means to our dream one way or another."

"Yes, we shall," Laurelle said, trying to be spirited. "Now

come, we have been sad so long, can it be that we have forgotten how to laugh? How to sing?" In a quavering voice she
started on a rondelet, motioning for Roger and Jonathan to
join in the refrain. More children started to sing, until the
slave pen rang with song.

And then a dark heavy presence blotted out the moonlight.
The children looked up to see Baalbek hovering over them.

Laurelle cried out and scrambled to her feet. Baalbek leaned
close to her and said with the air of a conspirator, "My master
would have your answer now."

Though she thought she had fully prepared herself for this
moment, Laurelle could barely get the words out. "Tell him I
will come. Tomorrow."

"To where?" Roger demanded, trying to get as close to
Laurelle as his fetters would allow. "Where are you going?"

Baalbek shifted his gaze to Roger, eyes lingering over his
torso, then turned back to Laurelle. "My master says it must
be this night or never."

For an instant, Laurelle wished that God would strike her
dead where she stood.

"Well?" Baalbek said, his hand playing with the hilt of his
dagger.

Laurelle clasped her hands and slowly nodded. As Baalbek
untied her, Roger shouted questions at her, his face growing
livid. When she would not answer, he began to hurl violent
insults at Baalbek until the eunuch took a threatening step
toward him.

"Roger!" Laurelle cried out, "you only make it worse for
yourself, and for me. It is useless to fight any longer, can you
not see that? We must accept our fate." She dropped her gaze.
"This night I go to Frizio."

Roger's mouth fell open, and then he recovered and cried, "I
do not believe you! They are forcing you to do this! Tell me
this is so!"

"No one forces me," Laurelle said, fighting to keep her voice
steady, fighting to keep from flinging herself into his arms.
"Whatever I do, I do it of my own free will."

"That God should permit me to hear such a thing!" Roger

whispered. "This is how you swear our love?" His voice rose until he was shouting. "To deny all to me but to give yourself to the slave master? What has he promised you, an extra ration of water? I would have given you my blood! Laurelle, by all that is holy, we are betrothed!"

Though his words tore at her heart, Laurelle kept her face impassive. She followed Baalbek to the tent where Frizio had been waiting and listening intently all this time. When Frizio slipped his arm around her waist, Roger went wild, tearing at his bonds, to no avail.

"Oh, the Lord curse their whole wicked sex," Roger cried, tears of rage spilling from his eyes as he watched Frizio and Laurelle disappear into the tent. "For they are as changeable as the moon! I would have given my life for her, yet she does this to our love? She is not better than her sister!"

"Do not believe ill of her," Jonathan said, trying to calm him. "Somehow, Frizio is forcing her to do this, can you not see that? And as for Flamonde, have you forgotten so soon that she gave her own life to save ours?"

But Jonathan's words could not penetrate through Roger's grief. He threw himself on the ground, muffling his sobs against the sands.

In the tent, Laurelle stood trembling as Frizio's strong fingers massaged the back of her neck. She stiffened under his touch and Frizio stopped at once. "Remember," he said, "we do not have a bargain unless all is done willingly. And with joy," he added.

Then he disrobed and threw himself on the animal skins strewn about under the netting. When he patted the place beside him Laurelle came forward slowly. "Send the eunuch away, I beg you," she whispered.

Frizio snapped his fingers for Baalbek to be gone.

Then with a prayer to the Virgin that she would be able to fool him, Laurelle lay down beside Frizio.

He closed his eyes and for the space of many heartbeats did not touch her, savoring the moment, breathing in the intoxication of her sweet smell. His hands lingered over her body, touching her tender mysterious places, as if to imprint her every curve and hollow on his own flesh. This is mine, he thought, mine to have whenever I desire. And he could scarcely bear the ecstasy of it when at last he entered her.

He made love to her then, first passionately, with all the stored memory of his months of denial; then violently, recalling his humiliation at the hands of the children; and then at last with an unbidden tenderness, trying somehow to please her.

These many months Laurelle had feared for the wantonness of her own flesh, but her terror vanished when Frizio took her. The hard rocking motion of his body, the kneading hands, the heavy demanding mouth pressed against hers brought her only pain, nothing more. That place within her that God had reserved for her own true beloved, that belonged only to Roger. Knowing in her heart that she had not sinned, and that she had also managed to save Roger's life, made her feel strong, almost joyous, and her spirit floated serene and free.

When it was done, Frizio gripped her as though she might drift away. He rolled onto his side and through half-closed lids stared at her in a kind of wonder. Truly, she has bewitched me, he thought. His sweaty body slowly became aroused again, and he knew then that through the body of this child-woman he would find his own youth.

Laurelle regarded him, feeling a great sense of sadness for this man. It is so simple, she thought. Without love, it is nothing more than the rutting of beasts. Then she swallowed hard and asked the fearful question; "You will free him as you promised?"

He got up on an elbow and leaned toward her. "That depends entirely on you; for you see, there were moments when you held yourself back and that did not please me."

Laurelle grasped his hand. "Oh, but that is not true," she cried, "did I not do everything you asked?"

Frizio rolled over on his stomach. "Well, you are young, so

perhaps you will do better later on. But I will tell you this, there is much you must learn before you have fulfilled your part of the bargain."

At intervals during the night Frizio continued his demands and Laurelle struggled to please him until both her body and spirit grew raw from exhaustion.

In the morning, Baalbek led her back to the other children and roped her into place between Roger and Jonathan. Jonathan did not know what to do, what to say; he felt so sad for the anguish on her face that he could have died for her. Silently, he handed her some withered almonds he had picked, but she shook her head.

Roger sat motionless, mouth set, his face bloodless.

Laurelle reached out to him tentatively, but Roger did not move, did not speak, as though he had been turned to stone. Shortly thereafter, the caravan commenced the journey on toward Gaza.

"What scars the land like that?" Jonathan asked Ibrahim, pointing to the deep gullies running perpendicular to the road.

"You would not believe it to see this desert now, but during these autumn months there is usually much rain here. It is why the Franks and Arabs fight so fiercely over this Gaza strip. But we have had no rain for over a year. Unless we have some soon all the world will be nothing more than a cinder," Ibrahim said, pointing to the drifting sands which had encroached upon the once-fertile fields and well into Gaza itself.

The caravan camped near the old section of town, where the mighty exploits of Samson seemed to linger among the ruins. After their previous night's revelry the Bedouins were weary and irritable and the slave children helped them to put up the lean-tos, rude little tents barely affording enough protection to break the winds sweeping in from the northeast. Every crevice soon filled with fine sand, coating the children's hair and eyelashes and tasting gritty on the tongue.

"Still, you do not realize how lucky we are not to have been in a real sandstorm," Ibrahim told Jonathan. "Myself, I have barely lived through two, one in the wilderness of Judah, where we lost an entire mule train."

Water being outrageously expensive in Gaza, Frizio made the slaves dig for their own. Ibrahim held a dowsing stick in his hands and walked slowly along the sands. In one spot the pointer of the dowser dipped and a group of slaves started digging. After about seven feet water began to seep up through the earth, and soon there was enough at the bottom of the hole to water the animals. Then the children were allowed to slake their thirst.

"Ask him where one can obtain such a magic stick," Roger said to Jonathan, "for we shall need it when we escape."

Ibrahim told Jonathan, "The magic is not in the stick but in the ability of the holder to sense where the sap in the branch wants to join the water in the ground. Any branch will do, but if you are thinking of using it, forget it, you will never master the art in time."

That night, when Baalbek lumbered toward Laurelle, she firmly believed he had come to tell her that Frizio would set Roger free. Then he will know why I had to act as I did, she thought, he will forgive me.

But it was Laurelle that the eunuch untied, cackling that his master was ready for her again. "For myself," Baalbek whispered in her ear, "I beg you do not go, for then we shall have an evening's entertainment that you and the boy will never forget."

With the crushing disappointment heavy on her heart, Laurelle stood up; she reached out for Roger as she passed him. For an instant he seemed about to take her hand, but then stared right through her as though she were not there. Only when she walked away in the darkness did his hand jerk out involuntarily after her.

Laurelle dragged her way to Frizio's tent, fighting back her tears, for above all she must present a cheerful face to Frizio lest he find fault with her and set the eunuch to do his work.

. . .

Each night Frizio fell more and more under Laurelle's spell. Never had he imagined that he would not remain master through all this, but he had not reckoned with the child's innocence, nor with his own needs. In his battle to penetrate her purity, he found instead that he could not get enough of her. And even as he exerted his formidable powers, wearing her resistance down, still the secret place of her spirit grew ever more elusive. In his desperation to conquer and to own, he cast about frantically for that one final debasement which would place her forever in his thrall.

THE WILDERNESS OF JUDAH

THE THREAT OF SANDSTORM KEPT THE CARAVAN IN Gaza an extra day, and with each hour Jonathan grew more frightened for Laurelle. Her eyes shone with a light that seemed to burn ever brighter as her physical strength diminished; she barely spoke or took any nourishment.

"Do you not see that she is being martyred before our eyes?" Jonathan said angrily to Roger. "If ever you loved her, go to her, only you can give her the comfort she needs."

"So she is thinner," Roger said, "but she needn't be, for the eunuch tells me that Frizio gives her the choicest morsels."

"You are a fool!" Jonathan exclaimed. "The fat one tells you that to torment you, and you listen? Go to her!"

"Oh, the Lord forgive me, I cannot," Roger whispered. "Not knowing that she has lain with him, and will again and . . ." With a groan like a stricken animal Roger crawled off to a corner of a mud wall and sat huddled there.

On Thursdays Gaza held its open market; here a grain merchant exhibited his lean barley crop, there a wheat speculator his precious sacks, literally worth their weight in silver. Penned camels waiting to be sold regarded everybody with their supercilious expressions.

"They look as if they know something we don't," Jonathan said to Laurelle, trying to draw her into conversation.

"But they do," Ibrahim exclaimed, "any fool knows that." He clicked his rosary of ninety-nine beads. "Allah is known by a hundred names, but it is given to man to know only ninety-nine of them. Only the camel knows the hundredth, and that is why he looks so superior."

The morning fare consisted of bitter green grapes and sabra pears. Ibrahim showed them how to eat the pears, peeling back their thick prickly skin. They were sweet and juicy, though laden with pips that had to be spat out. Jonathan peeled one of the fruits for Laurelle but she refused it, telling him he could have it for himself.

A little distance away Frizio sat cross-legged on a mat, devouring skewered portions of lamb, followed by slices of melon and dates.

"May the Lord make him choke on it," Roger muttered. "Oh, what would I not give to have the strength of Samson that I might smite that fiend!"

"Do not say such things!" Laurelle cried, suddenly roused. She approached him and made a sign over his blue eyes to ward off any evil. "To regain his strength, Samson had to give up his eyesight."

Roger checked his instinctive move to embrace her and then moved away as far as his ropes would allow.

Laurelle seemed to shrivel and Jonathan said softly, "He does not mean it, it is just that he loves you so and is mortally wounded. If only you would explain to him. . . ."

Laurelle gave a sad little shrug. "I cannot. But then it does not matter, nothing matters anymore."

Just beyond Gaza the road parted; one leg continued along the coastline toward Ashkalon, the other branch headed east to link up with the King's Road leading into the interior. Frizio would have preferred the sea route, but though Ashkalon had been destroyed as a condition of the treaty between Richard Coeur de Lion and Saladin twenty years ago, islands of Crusader strength still existed along the coast, and Frizio had not brought his precious cargo this far to be ambushed by Christian knights.

Whatever small comfort the caravan had derived from the presence of the sea soon disappeared as the Mediterranean retreated behind a line of dunes. Miles of sand gave way to ridges and cliffs of chalk-white limestone. They climbed steadily into the wilderness of Judah along a road that wound through the denuded hills of the Negev plateau, bare save for the hardiest vegetation. It would take two, perhaps three days to reach Hebron, thirty miles to the northeast and some three thousand feet above the level of the sea.

"The animals are to be spared as much as possible," Frizio shouted to Baalbek, who rousted the children off their mounts.

Forced to walk, the dull pain radiated from Jonathan's ankle up his leg. Mercifully, the whole side of his body soon went numb. Some miles farther on they passed the skeleton of a dead horse, and Jonathan stopped long enough to disentangle a bleached thigh bone, which he used as a crutch.

Frizio looked back at the limping boy. "We shall have to sell him when we get to Hebron," he said to Baalbek. "He is too lame to go much farther."

"I would buy him," Baalbek said, "he pleases me."

Frizio regarded the eunuch in mild surprise. In all the years Baalbek had served him, never had he heard him express a desire for anything. "From slave to slave owner?" Frizio chuckled. "So is the world turned upside down these days. Well, we shall see what Allah decrees in Hebron."

"This is the most desolate place we have been," Laurelle said.

"Do not talk," Jonathan cautioned her. "This wind!" He squinted against the hot buffeting gusts that swept over them.

On they climbed. Dead trees poked bleached fingers at the blazing sky. The glare off the sand and the limestone gave everything the appearance of . . . what? Laurelle wondered. Have I been before, or have I dreamed this nightmare of desert and slave and Frizio into being? She searched the plateau for a recognizable landmark but nothing stayed in its place. Were those buzzards wheeling against the sun, or just spots before her eyes? Once she glimpsed a huge lake in the distance, only to see it evaporate as the caravan approached. Waves of heat shimmered up from the ground until the earth itself seemed to smolder, about to burst into flame. Step by step they dragged their way through a land as barren as a biblical curse.

"I am frightened!" Laurelle cried out, drawing Jonathan to her side.

Ibrahim came riding up on his camel and Laurelle moaned at him, "This is an accursed place! No trees, no animals, no birds!"

When Jonathan translated, Ibrahim shook his head vehemently. "That is sacrilege! This is a most sacred place. Jonathan, tell her."

"What?" Jonathan asked. "I do not know."

Ibrahim slapped his thigh. "Dolt! You say you read, yet you do not know? These are the fields of Adama, of the red earth, in Hebrew. Here the Lord picked up a handful of dust and into this red clay He breathed life, creating Adam. For all know that Adam was of a red complexion. And there is Hebron," Ibrahim said, pointing to the tiny pink-tinged houses clustered on a distant hilltop.

Hebron, one of the biblical cities sacred to both Jews and Moslems, contained four holy tombs. Three were of their common ancestors: Abraham and Sarah, Isaac and Rebecca, Jacob and Leah; in the fourth tomb lay the bones of everybody's ancestors, Adam and Eve. According to their religious laws, the Jews had constructed a simple, small rectangular mausoleum over the tombs. When the Crusaders conquered Hebron they built an enormous church, the Church of St. Abraham, over the mausoleum. Then the Saracens recaptured the city and stripped the structure of all the idolatrous statuary, paintings, and icons and converted the church into the unadorned Mosque of Abraham. The caravan set up camp against one of its stepped outer walls.

Shortly before the evening meal Ibrahim crept to where Jonathan was tied. "I have come to say good-by," he said, fidgeting nervously.

"Are you leaving us then?" Jonathan asked, feeling a sudden pang of sadness. The Bedouin boy had become a friend.

Ibrahim shook his head.

Jonathan understood then and let out a groan.

"What is it?" Laurelle cried, coming quickly to his side.

"I am to be sold," Jonathan said. "Is that not so, Ibrahim?"

"You would have found out tomorrow anyway," Ibrahim said, "and this way at least you can prepare yourself."

Roger came over then also, his anger at Laurelle momentarily put aside in the face of this immediate crisis.

Ibrahim said, "Earlier I heard Frizio talking to the fat one. They plan to auction you in the morning. But Jonathan, take courage, there are many Jews in Hebron and they watch out for those of their own faith. When they discover that you are one of their own, it may easily be that they ransom you back from . . ."

Sensing the distress in Ibrahim's voice, Jonathan asked fearfully, "To whom am I being sold?"

The Bedouin boy toed the sand, debating whether or not to tell all he knew. He took a deep breath. "Frizio has an order for a girl and a boy, both to be sold to the brothels."

Jonathan sat back, stunned.

"It is not possible!" Laurelle cried. "I will not let them do such a thing." She yanked at Jonathan's ropes to get his attention. "Have no fear, my brother. They shall not take you. I know of a means to save you."

"How?" Jonathan asked desperately, but Laurelle would say no more. He turned to Ibrahim. "A brothel?" he whispered.

Ibrahim explained. Hebronites were religious to the point of fanaticism; they tolerated no sex outside of marriage. Any Moslem girl suspected of such an abomination would be immediately stoned to death. Wives were expensive and a man might grow to middle age before he could afford one. So the bachelors had little recourse save to embrace the practices of Onan or pleasure themselves with the Ghilman love of boys.

Ibrahim said, "Frizio has chosen Jonathan not only because he is lame, but also because he is the only slave in the caravan not a Christian. And the princes in Baghdad have ordered that they want only Christian children to be put to the test in their trial by faith."

This statement brought forth a flurry of other anxious questions which Ibrahim explained as best he could. The children were stunned by this news and discussed it fearfully.

"Renounce our Lord?" Laurelle whispered and crossed herself. "Is it not enough that they own our bodies, must they also have our souls?"

"I will never reject the Savior!" Roger said angrily, throwing a rock at the trunk of a palm. "Let them do what they will. Well, one could die a worse death. We shall all be martyrs— those of us who have remained pure!" he said with a sideways glance at Laurelle. "And they shall sing of us in ages to come."

Their brave talk was interrupted when Baalbek came to fetch Laurelle. With Jonathan's predicament uppermost in her mind, Laurelle's stride became resolute as she marched to Frizio's tent.

"See how eagerly she goes now," Roger said, his voice cracking as he stared after her. "Women!" he swore, tears starting to his eyes over this wound that would never heal.

Jonathan pressed his fingers to his temples. "If only we could escape now, lose ourselves in this city. Ibrahim?"

Ibrahim spread out his hands in a gesture of helplessness. "Even if you could escape, Hebron is too small. You would be recaptured in a matter of hours. Jerusalem, that is the only place."

"But if I am to be sold *tomorrow*!"

"I must go now," Ibrahim said, shaking his head sadly. He grasped Jonathan by the elbows. "May Allah watch over you."

Jonathan spent a sleepless night trying to figure out a way to avoid his fate. He took various herbs in his wallet, hoping to precipitate some reaction, but nothing seemed to work. Here it is light, he thought, my head aches from thinking and I am no closer to a solution. He fingered two budding boils on his face and neck, trying to worry them to a head.

Frizio had told Baalbek that to buy the boy he must match the highest offer; Baalbek had little hope of that and so had resigned himself to the loss. But for Frizio, Jonathan's sale had provided unexpected delights, for Laurelle had pleaded that the boy be set free also, and was prepared to do anything Frizio asked if he would spare him. And though Frizio had asked much, in the end he had, of course, refused her.

Within the hour Jonathan and the slave girl were put up naked on the block. The brothel owners inspected the merchandise. Prying fingers searched and found; Jonathan blushed from the pain but more from the indignity. The girl was quickly approved, but Jonathan's choice was another matter.

"He is too thin," one dealer shouted. "Too dark," another called. "We were promised a fair one." "He is lame." The negatives flew around Jonathan's head as Hebron's young blades crowded around the block, adding their vociferous complaints to the negotiations. "Give us one 'who is uncut that we may circumcise him for the glory of Allah!"

Then somebody called out, "What are those spots on him?"

Even as the crowd watched, more angry red blotches erupted all over Jonathan's body, swelling and disfiguring his face.

"He is diseased!"

"It is a plague of boils!"

"Worse! It is plague itself!"

The crowd shuddered, for like every other city in the world, Hebron was constantly on the alert for the dreaded scourge.

Then Jonathan lifted his arms and called out, "O Jehovah, deliver me from this affliction!"

When the crowd realized that Jonathan was a Jew, their hostility increased tenfold. Surely the boy's kinsmen would buy back his freedom and they would be left with nothing.

Frizio was hurriedly forced to substitute the nubile, towheaded youth from Westphalia, who at first appeared terrified of the crowd and then relaxed to preen under its attention.

Jonathan was roped back into place with Roger and Laurelle, who alternately hugged and clapped him on the back.

Ibrahim said excitedly, "You see? I told you Allah would watch over you! If you would just put yourself under his protection—"

"I prayed to the Virgin," Laurelle interrupted, "I knew she would never let such a thing happen to you."

"And I to the Redeemer," Roger added, smiling from ear to ear.

"Those boils," Laurelle said, "it is not . . ."

Jonathan shook his head. "It is not plague. I too prayed to

the Creator, and all night long I dosed myself with thuja." He patted the wallet where he kept his herbs and medicines. "It is a beneficial herb when taken in minute quantities, but I swallowed all I had."

"Will you be disfigured for good?" Laurelle asked.

"It will disappear in a day or two. I hope!"

They all laughed at that. Then Jonathan grew serious. "I must make a great atonement for the boy forced to remain in my stead."

"Do not concern yourself overmuch," Ibrahim said. "That lad? He is known to many of the Bedouin guards. He did not get his extra rations of food and water for nothing. To my eyes, he did not seem too desperate about his lot. Allah sees that each of us gets what he seeks."

Then Baalbek came riding up and down the line shouting, "Make ready, we leave within the hour!" He stopped and patted Jonathan on the head. "You are clever," Baalbek said, "and we shall see where your cleverness gets you. Perhaps tonight; if not, then tomorrow, or the day after." Baalbek rode off with a jaunty toss of his burnoose, calling, "Allah has saved you for me."

The children stood up and gathered their meager belongings.

"To where now?" Jonathan asked Ibrahim.

"Bethlehem," Ibrahim said. "About twenty miles due north, less than a two-day march. After that, it is but a half-day's journey to Jerusalem."

The caravan continued its slow climb. Jonathan and Roger exchanged glances, their minds racing with the same single thought.

THE APPROACH TO BETHLEHEM

HE TERRITORY SURROUNDING BETHLEHEM WAS IN A perpetual state of flux, sometimes in the hands of the raiding Frankish knights, most of the time under the domination of the Moslems. Fortunately, both sides recognized the importance of commerce and taxation, so caravans were allowed to travel unmolested—provided they paid the heavy tolls.

Laurelle looked about her as the caravan approached the highest point in the Judean wilderness. The terrain grew more desolate, deep cracks fissured the earth, and jagged cliffs thrust into the sky, making the land look like it was still in the throes of creation. Though her body and mind ached with her ordeal, for some reason Laurelle felt closer to the Lord than she ever had in her life.

The caravan had covered half the distance to Bethlehem when twilight overtook them and they camped in the cup of a rocky plateau. On either side, precipitous cliffs fell away to stony valleys. In the distance a lion roared at the rising full moon and another beast answered across the rocky wasteland.

Night had brought quick mountain breezes, but Frizio remained flushed with heat. Believing himself fully sated, he had made no plans for the night, save to relax and perhaps dream with a measure of hashish. But uncoiling from his reverie had come the means whereby he could crush Laurelle's spirit, and with that growing surety he felt an irrepressible surge of desire. One corner of his mind warned him not to venture further with this, but the prospect of conquest spurred him on.

"Prepare my tent," he said to Baalbek. "This night shall see her mine completely."

Baalbek understood at once; he lit candles, burned incense,

and then took some implements from a small chest and laid them by Frizio's pallet. Frizio nodded with satisfaction and then went outside to where the children were fettered.

The moment Laurelle saw Frizio approaching, lips parted in his crooked grin, she sensed that this night would bring no ordinary encounter, for by his naked swagger and glazed eyes she knew that he had fallen into the well of his own madness.

Frizio leaned against an outcropping of rock, his body monumental in the moonlight. Directing his taunts at Roger, he said, "Pray, where is your God tonight? By now you know that you are being taken to Baghdad. There in the great square, in full view of thousands, you will be made to abjure your God, ycu will spit on the crucifix."

"No!" Laurelle cried.

Frizio shifted his weighted gaze to her. "Did you really believe I would ever set him free? Confess, you needed that as an excuse in order to pleasure yourself."

Hearing this, Roger started. Then understanding flooded over him. Moving as close as he could to Frizio, Roger spat at him.

Frizio wiped his cheek as though nothing had happened and continued, "Believe me, you will repudiate Him, for the Seljuk Turks are privy to certain means of persuasion." Frizio reached for Laurelle. "Come, I will show you," he said, untying her.

The blood drained from Laurelle's face; she kicked and scratched at him but he only laughed at her efforts, for they aroused him all the more. When he had freed her of her bonds he held her pinned in his arms.

The sight of Laurelle being so used enraged Roger, and with her continued struggle all his doubts about her vanished. "Leave her be, coward," he yelled, straining at his bonds. "You are quick to take advantage of the defenseless, but in a fair fight as in Troyes . . . Release me, you bastard, and I will show you!"

Frizio's lips thinned; his eyes flicked from Baalbek to the shouting boy and the eunuch jammed a gag in Roger's mouth. The Bedouin guards stopped what they were doing, shrugged, and then went back to their tasks. Except for Ibrahim, who did not hide his disgust.

Dragging Laurelle behind him, Frizio came up to Roger and thrust his face at the boy. "Bastard, eh?" he said softly. "When next you scream it will be with a high-pitched cackle. Baalbek, as soon as we reach Bethlehem, he is yours!"

Laurelle fought all the harder at this until Frizio stunned her with a slap. He said to Roger, "So now you know that this baggage thought to save you by pleasing me. Well, it is all the same. For a time I indulged her in this foolishness, but I am weary of this sport. I promise you, when I am done with her this night, she will deny you, deny your Lord, the Virgin, and whatever other gods you swear by, for she will know once and for all who her true lord is."

The remainder of the night Frizio experimented. Once Laurelle cried out "Roger!" and the name stung like a whip-lash across Frizio's heart. It was then he decided that he must rid himself of these two boys, lest their very presence remind her of anybody but him. The game of the denial of her God proved a spur and in Laurelle's resistance he discovered ways to plumb depths he had not known existed in him. The soft quality of the darkness, the light on the harsh white rock, and her pliant body all conspired to rob him of the boundaries of reality. He grew young before his eyes, with all the passion and endurance of youth; and there even came a moment when he convinced himself that he loved her, and she him.

Laurelle had gone into the tent in the penultimate moment of her youth. When Baalbek led her out the following morning she shuffled like a bent and broken woman. Baalbek retied her and left her lying on the ground. Laurelle's fingers raked at the earth and closed around a long, sharp piece of flint.

Jonathan knelt beside her. So fragile did she look that he expected her to blow away on the wind. He put his arm around her shoulder, asking gentle questions. "Are you hurt? Water?"

Roger moaned to her from where he sat, still bound and gagged, but Laurelle was too weak to respond. Her eyes were turned inward, the shutters were shut, no light might pass. She began to mumble and Jonathan bent closer.

"I did not renounce my Lord," she whispered. "No matter what he did I did not renounce my Lord."

By day's end the caravan had managed to climb more than fifteen miles across the burning plateau and were within striking distance of Bethlehem. Here in the shepherd's field Ruth had left her own people and followed Boaz to found the house of David; here the young shepherd boy armed with sling and righteousness had slain Goliath; here the three magi, guided by the star, had come to worship the infant; here King Herod had massacred the Holy Innocents.

Had he pressed, Frizio could have gotten the caravan to Bethlehem before the gates closed, but he chose not to, for all that day he had thought only of the coming night, thought of the terror on her face, terror that somehow held the key to his own prowess. At one point during the afternoon his desire reached such an uncontrollable peak that he dismounted and moved to take her right then and there, and only Qabat's sharp admonition stayed him.

Intent on repeating his success, Frizio anxiously wanted all the elements of this alchemy to be the same as last night; the distant roar of beasts in the wilderness of Judah, the blind eye of the full moon, the dark sky studded with a myriad of stars, all this he deemed more important than being within the safe yet sterile confines of Bethlehem.

Once more Frizio approached Laurelle. Another exquisite turn had entered his mind and he called to Roger, "Tonight you too shall enter the tent so that you may see men's work and hear for yourself how she rejects your Lord."

Baalbek undid Roger's bonds but held the boy fast in his round, weighty arms.

Frizio began to unfetter Laurelle. The instant the ropes fell she flew at him with the shard of flint she had secreted earlier and in a desperate motion stabbed for his eyes, managing only to rip open his cheek. She stabbed again but Frizio blocked her hand.

Laurelle turned and fled, heading for a nearby ridge. Frizio grabbed his whip and gave chase, further incensed by her flight. Laurelle ran, hearing Roger shouting after her, seeing her dream come true before her eyes, for just beyond the line of a stand of gnarled pines lay the stone-silent town of Bethlehem.

Frizio caught up with her at the crest of the hill. She stood balanced for an instant on the cliff, limned against the moon. Before she could make another move his whip lashed out and pinned her against the trunk of a pine. She tore at the coils and managed to free herself just as Frizio reached her.

"If you persist in this," he said, grinning, "then you shall really anger me and who knows—"

Her fingernails raked across his face, drawing blood.

Caught by surprise, Frizio lashed out. His blow, meant only to stun her, struck her in the windpipe, shattering it.

She fell to the ground, hands clutching her throat, gasping for the air that would not come.

In the confusion, Baalbek had relaxed his grip on Roger and the boy broke free and dashed up the hill. He came upon them, Frizio standing stunned, Laurelle writhing on the ground. Roger pushed Frizio aside, knelt beside Laurelle and cradled her head in his lap.

She clutched his hand, her lips moving to form the words *Help me*, but no sound came out. She had only so much life in her as had been in her last breath, and Roger saw it fading from her face with each heartbeat.

"Oh my God, help us!" he cried, and covered her lips with kisses as though his own breath would give her life.

Her eyes widened, the gray eyes which had reflected every color and every mood, and with the last of her strength her lips moved and Roger read, "Pray for me."

In the instant before oblivion a great radiant light blinded Laurelle with an ecstasy that pierced her entire body. One final spasm stiffened her and then her eyes darkened as the moon retreated behind the cloud cover.

"Dead?" Roger whispered, shaking her. "No, not dead, cur Lord is too merciful to permit such a thing. Laurelle? Oh,

Laurelle, forgive me. Dead?'' he screamed, and his voice echoed through the shadowed valley.

Roger lifted his eyes toward Frizio, then sprang at him with one thought only. Gone reason, gone the vow he had sworn to march in peace.

The force of Roger's charge caused Frizio to lose his footing and both of them tumbled down the wadi. Knocking the boy aside, Frizio stood up. Roger staggered to his feet, grabbed a heavy rock, and hurled it at Frizio, hitting him in the shoulder. He bellowed with pain. Roger reached for another, but Frizio's whip cracked through the air and caught him across the bridge of the nose. With a crunch of bone, blood fountained across his face and he fell unconscious.

Frizio dragged the boy up the wadi and dumped him at Baalbek's feet. ''When he regains his senses bring him to me,'' he ordered.

Overcome with grief, Frizio cursed and threw things about his tent and then finally broke down, pressing his knuckles to his mouth to muffle his sobs. All his days he had searched for such a one as this girl, and now he could not bear to think that he had lost her. ''A stupid accident!'' he choked, ''and one that could have been avoided if . . .'' The ifs came to torment him as he relived the scene again and again in his mind.

''It is the boy's fault,'' he swore, wiping away his tears, ''from the very start, all his fault! Well, this night he shall know what it means to rob me this way!''

Frizio thrust his head out the tent flap. ''Well,'' he shouted to Baalbek, ''is he conscious yet?''

''Master, he is,'' Baalbek began.

''Then why am I kept waiting?'' Frizio demanded, storming over to where Baalbek and the children were grouped.

Jonathan was tending Roger, trying to stem the bleeding that ran into the hollows of his eyes. As Frizio approached Jonathan dropped to the ground and clasped him about the knees.

''I beg you,'' he pleaded, ''by whatever gods you worship, have mercy on him.''

Frizio thrust Jonathan aside. "He has caused the death of my slave and must be punished."

"Your whip . . ." Jonathan said. "His nose is broken and he is blind."

"What new trick is this?" Frizio said, the cords in his neck throbbing. "Baalbek, fetch some light. If you are lying, Jew, then you too will suffer his fate."

When the eunuch brought a candle Frizio passed the flame back and forth before Roger's wide, unseeing eyes. They did not blink.

The death of Laurelle, and now Roger's blindness, shocked Qabat and the Bedouin guard, and their anger at this mindless, wanton destruction of property forced Frizio back to a measure of sanity.

Jonathan buried Laurelle on the ridge overlooking Bethlehem. The rocky ground made digging near impossible, and so over the shallow grave he began to build a mound of stones to cover the body. A tree grew close by, a bent and twisted pine, carved by the sharp, constant winds. In his desperate effort to control his grief, Jonathan cast about for any small comfort and hearing the gusts moan through the needles, felt better somehow for her being buried in this place, where the wind would always mourn her.

Roger crawled to the grave, his swollen, black-and-blue face streaked with tears. In his perpetual night Roger saw the last thing he had witnessed, her face, and heard the omen Laurelle had told him back in Troyes. "Innocent you are and innocent shall you remain and in the sight of that place where the Holy Innocents were martyred. . . ."

When Jonathan had finished building the mound he picked up a handful of dust and sprinkled it over his head and shoulders, and then with a sharp movement rent the right sleeve of his tunic. "I must not cry," he told himself, "this is the moment when I must be strong," for he feared for Roger.

Quickly, he clasped his hands and prayed, "O Lord, of all the thousands of children who marched, surely this your daughter walked in the straight path. And so we humbly beseech you, Lord of mercy, clasp her to your bosom so that all the goodness of her days will not have been in vain. Keep her then, O Lord, for in a world not yet ready for her goodness she has taken refuge in thee."

Roger groped along the rocky mound until he found the rude cross Jonathan had constructed; he rolled his head back and forth against the crossbeam. "My heart," he whispered, "if you would but listen . . . I loved you always, I swear it, and if I could see to do the deed would join you this moment. My own heart was closed because I thought you had stopped loving me. Do you forgive me? Hear me then, my love," he pleaded, and began methodically to tear the stones away, digging down to reach her.

"It could easily be that she is not really dead—stunned only! Yes, that is it! And yet we are burying her in this cold stone ground? Jonathan! Help me, quickly! We must not—"

Jonathan grabbed him and held him close until his uncontrollable sobbing had quieted.

"Make ready to move on!" came the shouts from the Bedouin drivers.

Hastily then, Jonathan finished with the psalm, ". . . He leadeth me beside the still waters. He restoreth my soul. Yea, though I walk through the valley of the shadow—"

With a strangled cry Jonathan broke down, and the two boys clung to each other. They cried for her, they cried for their dream, they cried for all the things that heaven had not allowed, and when they thought there were no more tears left, they cried for the cruel cheat that was life itself.

BETHLEHEM

ROM A CUT IN THE HILLS THE CARAVAN CAME UPON Bethlehem, nestled on the highest point of the mountains of Judah. A heavy stillness hung over the hills; the mules flattened their ears and brayed uneasily; horses and camels took up the cacophony, and then all at once the animals ceased.

"Why has it become so quiet?" Roger asked, cocking his head. He sat astride a donkey, holding on tightly to the halter so he would not fall off; his unseeing eyes were red-rimmed from his periodic crying.

Jonathan limped alongside him, using the thigh bone as a crutch. "You are right," he said, listening to the unaccountable silence, "something is very wrong."

The Bedouin guard scanned the horizon anxiously and began shouting at each other. Then Ibrahim galloped up and down the line shouting, "Windstorm!" He gestured frantically to the east where a gathering yellow cloud obscured the hills.

Cursing and shouting, Frizio whipped the caravan toward Bethlehem. "If we can make it to the walls we shall be safe," he cried. They had gotten to within half a mile of the gates when the storm struck, swallowing them in its blinding, buffeting gusts.

Pelted unmercifully by the hail of pebbles and sand, Frizio saw that any attempt to continue meant certain disaster and shouted the order to halt. The Bedouins brought their mounts to their knees, faced them away from the wind, then took shelter behind the kneeling beasts.

Frizio stood up to make sure all was secure, but the wind knocked him down. He crawled to Mirage and shielded the stallion's head with a length of cloth. The storm increased in intensity, ripping supplies from the backs of the pack animals and sending them flying, stinging everybody's faces and bodies and sucking the breath from their lungs.

Ibrahim crawled along the line of animals on his belly, making sure that the children were safely secured. "Frizio ordered us to do this," he panted when he got to Jonathan, "being too cowardly to see to it himself. This is how Allah punishes him. We are not all such beasts as he," Ibrahim coughed. "The girl was a good creature, she did not deserve to die in such a way."

A gust half-lifted Ibrahim off the ground and Jonathan grabbed him. Ibrahim shouted over the wind, "If ever you hoped to do it, now is the time. Never again will Allah send you such an opportunity."

Jonathan understood his meaning at once. His eyes met Ibrahim's. Gone the questions of nation and religion, gone the blind loyalties. In the elemental battle of young and old, Ibrahim was responding to his kind.

Jonathan embraced him and then was struck with a thought. "If Frizio finds out that you helped us, he will kill you."

"That is why you must do exactly as I say," Ibrahim said, and shouting staccato instructions, outlined what Jonathan must do. "Wait until there is a lull in the wind," he went on. "That will be the eye of the storm. Do not be fooled, for then the second half will hit. It is then that you must make the break. The sand will cover your tracks. I could not get you any water; they are guarding the water bags. Bethlehem is less than half a mile away. Avoid it if you can. Skirt to the right, through the shepherd's field. From there you will find many byways that parallel the road to Jerusalem. Above all, do not set foot on the main road; that is the first place they will search. We cannot know why Allah acts as he does, but ease your heart with this: if Frizio had not stopped last night to dally with the girl, we would be within the walls of Bethlehem now and you would not have gotten this chance. May Allah go with you. And your god too. And now you must do as I told you."

Ibrahim turned his back. Jonathan lifted his thighbone and with a prayer for forgiveness brought it down on Ibrahim's head. But it was only a glancing blow. Swearing, Ibrahim turned around and struck Jonathan hard. Jonathan's second blow knocked Ibrahim unconscious.

As Ibrahim had instructed him, Jonathan positioned the Bedouin so that his mouth and nose would not be clogged with sand. Then he took Ibrahim's dagger from his sheath and began to cut his way through the ropes. When he had freed himself he started on Roger's bonds.

"What?" Roger asked, feeling the tug.

"Freedom," Jonathan whispered.

Roger started, then slumped against the donkey. "Save yourself. Without her, I do not have the heart."

Paying no attention to this, Jonathan continued working.

"Of what use am I if I cannot see?" Roger said.

"I will be your eyes," Jonathan said. "But you must help me walk. I cannot escape alone. Together we both might."

The last strand of rope parted and for the first time since Frizio had captured them on board the *Paradise*, the two boys were free.

"What about the others?" Roger asked.

"Would that I could free them all," Jonathan said, "but I cannot get near any of them without being spied by the guard."

As Ibrahim had predicted, there was a slight lull in the storm. Fortunately it gusted from behind them as they crawled away from the caravan in the sand-darkness.

Once out of sight, the boys tried to stand but could not. They continued on their hands and knees, and when the wind dropped somewhat, managed to walk, Jonathan leaning heavily on Roger. Many times they were blown over, but at last they responded to each other's rhythm and managed to walk as one. The force of the storm remained so strong they knew they must seek refuge in Bethlehem or perish.

The gates of the city were open, the streets deserted as they dragged their weary, aching bodies through the sand drifts, going from doorway to doorway.

"We are coming upon a church, the Church of the Nativity, I think," Jonathan said.

"Could we not find sanctuary there?" Roger asked eagerly.

"I wish we could," Jonathan said, "but this city is too small and we would be discovered very quickly."

Moving as fast as they could lest they be locked within Bethlehem's walls, they struggled through the hilly streets. Just before darkness they slipped through the north gate and lost themselves in the surrounding wilderness.

For hours they moved slowly through the bleak terrain, following an aqueduct line. Millennia ago, abundant rainfall and snow had prompted King Solomon to build three reservoirs and an aqueduct here to bring water to Jerusalem, ten miles distant. Now the reservoirs were dry, the groves did not bear olive nor the vines grape.

Once great forests had covered the mountainside, but to prevent the Franks from building their castles and war machines the Saracens had put the forests to the torch. Decades of erosion had completed the devastation, leaving terraces of dolomite where the weaker limestone had been washed away. The route to Jerusalem lay downhill through this jagged wasteland.

All that remained of the sandstorm were small sand devils whirling like ghosts through the moon-bleached terrain. Hunger, thirst, and the sure pursuit of Frizio drove Jonathan and Roger on. A dozen times they fell, cutting and bruising themselves on the sharp rocks.

"We must not stop until daybreak," Jonathan said, possessed by his new-found freedom. "We must not be captured again!"

First light found them in a narrow valley scored by deep fissures.

"Now we must find a place to hide," Jonathan said. "Frizio is sure to have his trackers out after us." He searched for a hiding spot, rejecting this wadi as too shallow, that cave as too small.

"I do not think I can go any farther," Roger said. "Of what use is it anyway, without Laurelle?"

"You must go on," Jonathan insisted. "Would you give the lie to her sacrifice? And just when we have Jerusalem within our grasp?"

"But I cannot see!"

"The more reason to get there. Of all the physicians in the world, those in Jerusalem are the most renowned. So said my father," Jonathan went on, embroidering the truth somewhat to give Roger hope. "How do we know that your sight cannot be restored?"

He led Roger into a deep, narrow wadi, just wide enough for them to squeeze into. At the far end, the cleft opened into a sort of cave. Leaving Roger hidden there, Jonathan crawled around and searched the area until he found a stunted acacia uprooted by the storm. Dragging it behind him in sweeping motions, he obliterated their tracks and then used it to block the entrance to their hiding place.

"Sleep now, I will take the first watch, then you," Jonathan said.

"How? I cannot see!" Roger exclaimed, and the fissure reverberated with his echo.

Jonathan clapped his hand over Roger's mouth. "If you say that once more I will hit you! I cannot see either in this place, but I have ears. So do you. Now sleep!"

Protesting that he could not, Roger fell asleep almost immediately, his exhausted breathing filling the cave. Once in a delirium of sadness he cried out, "Laurelle!" and Jonathan held him, wiping away the sleeping boy's tears while his own streaked his face.

The sun rose higher and waves of heat beat down on their hiding place. The stone stored the heat and then gave it back until the defile seemed like an oven. Sweat dripped down Jonathan's face and stung his eyes. His tongue stuck to the roof of his mouth, the corners of his lips cracked and split; he felt as if his blood were being brought to a boil, yet he knew they dared not move. He let Roger sleep as long as he could, and only when he caught himself nodding did he rouse him.

"You must watch for a while," he whispered. "If you hear anything, anything at all, waken me."

It seemed like only moments later that Roger shook him out of his uneasy sleep. "What?" Jonathan cried out.

Roger inclined his head, finger to his lips.

Jonathan listened but heard nothing. Then faintly, he heard the Bedouin trackers calling to each other as they criss-crossed the wilderness, trying to pick up the boys' trail.

Making themselves as small as possible in the shallow recess, the two of them huddled together, holding their breaths. At one point horses' hooves thundered right overhead, and Jonathan saw the talus of stone sift down to the bottom of the ravine.

"They are not here," a man called.

Jonathan thought he recognized Baalbek's voice, but could not be sure.

Twice more horses jumped the defile, then the boys heard the Bedouins gallop off to continue the search elsewhere. After the sun had slanted away from the wadi, Jonathan felt it safe enough to move a bit. His leg had fallen asleep; pins and needles shot up his right side.

"That is good," he said, "for if there is still feeling in the leg then it can heal eventually. Now we must have water and food," he told Roger, "else we shall be too weak to go on. We must find a date palm or a cactus before it gets too dark to see."

They remained hidden until late afternoon, then Jonathan ventured stealthily from the cave. Every sound froze him in his tracks. At length he moved aside the branches, squeezed through the narrow opening of the cleft, and began climbing out. He got one leg over the top when fleshy hands grabbed him and yanked him to the surface.

"It was worth the wait," Baalbek said, grinning. "I knew you were hiding in there from the first, but I kept it from the Bedouins. Shall I tell you why? So that you and I could have our moment before I take you back."

Jonathan's stomach knotted in violent contractions. He

fought to break free but he might just as well have struggled against a behemoth. "Run, Roger, run!" Jonathan shouted.

"It is useless to carry on so," Baalbek said, as Jonathan continued to shout for Roger to flee. "I have waited a long time to get my hands on you." Quickly, he bound Jonathan's hands and feet. "Now for the other one." Baalbek sprawled out on the ground and stuck his arm down into the cleft, trying to ensnare the hidden boy.

Roger felt the hand clawing the air above his head and shrank back into the recess.

Baalbek heaved his bulk closer to the edge and reached down farther. He teetered there, once even managing to grab Roger's hair, but the boy yanked free.

Then Jonathan kicked out with his bound legs, catching Baalbek unawares. Jonathan did not know if it was his kick or the crumbling ledge or both that sent Baalbek tumbling into the fissure.

Baalbek bellowed like an ox when he fell; his thrashings only served to wedge him deeper into the tight space. His legs could not touch bottom; he grasped for the ledge to pull himself out, but his missing fingers betrayed him. Those that remained were not strong enough to lift his weight, and he lay there in the broiling sun, struggling like an upended beetle.

Ducking beneath Baalbek's form, Roger groped his way out of the cave and scrambled to Jonathan. "Take the knife from my sash," Jonathan instructed. Roger did, then felt along Jonathan's body until he found his bonds and carefully cut them. Roger's hand tightened around the hilt of the dagger. "Lead me to where he lies," he muttered.

Jonathan stayed his arm, "Let us leave him; the others are long gone and he will not be found this day."

"He killed Flamonde!" Roger choked.

"I know," Jonathan said. "But do you dare carry the mark of Cain for the rest of your life? And for something we cannot change? I beg you, let us get away from here while we can." Gently, he took the knife from Roger's hand.

Baalbek shouted from the vise of the rocks, "They will find

me. When I catch you, I will flay you alive! I will tear out your heart before your eyes!''

Jonathan stared down at Baalbek, whose face looked as if it might burst. ''What you say may come to pass,'' he called, ''or may not. Whatever your fate, content yourself with its being the will of Allah!''

Supporting each other, the two boys dragged on, leaving Baalbek wedged and screaming in the wadi, his voice more hysterical with each shout. From a large radius in the rocky plateau, jackals, hyenas, and other eaters of carrion gathered and took up their vigil, while a bull's-eye of vultures circled, spiraling ever lower.

Some miles from where they left Baalbek the boys came upon a date palm. Jonathan got up on Roger's shoulders and searched through the fronds, only to find that the tree bore no fruit. They had better luck with a cactus and Jonathan plucked a handful of shriveled sabra pears from among the spiny branches. He peeled the prickly fruit as Ibrahim had taught him, and he and Roger ate greedily, the juices also serving to slake their thirst.

Jonathan looked at Roger. ''We must do something to disguise you.'' Roger's skin, though tanned, was unmistakeably that of a Frank. Jonathan searched through his wallet and found some tannin bark. He mixed the dye with the sap from an aloe plant and smeared the dark mixture over Roger's face and hands. Roger wrinkled his nose.

Jonathan smiled. ''The smell will not last long,'' he said, reaching to cover Roger's sun-bleached hair with his burnoose. Jonathan stepped back and surveyed his work. ''There, you could pass for an Ethiopian, except for the eyes.'' So blue, they would give him away immediately in this land of dark, sloe-eyed people. ''When we get to Jerusalem, you must keep them closed, or else I shall bandage them.''

They set out again, bones stiff from the cramped position they had been in all day. Soon the rhythm reasserted itself and they picked up their pace. Beyond this ridge or the next lay the goal for which they had journeyed halfway around the world.

With each step, a little more of Roger's despair fell away. Supporting Jonathan while at the same time being led by him, he stumbled on, burning with a determination intensified by their ordeal, convinced that if just one child of the crusade could set foot in the Holy City, then it would not all have been in vain.

One last hill and they broke free of the wilderness. And there in day's last light lay Jerusalem.

JERUSALEM:
OUTSIDE THE WALLS

THAT THE LORD SHOULD HAVE BROUGHT ME TO THIS place yet deny me sight of it! Tell me, please,'' Roger begged, clutching Jonathan's arm.

The words caught in Jonathan's parched throat. "It is like no other place we have seen. The whole city rises like some monument to God.''

"Yet every evil man has ever dreamed has been committed here,'' Roger murmured, remembering Harolde's words. "Tell me *everything*.''

"Imagine this, then,'' Jonathan began. "A circle of hills surrounds a taller hill in the center. Jerusalem is built on the crest of this tallest hill. The stone walls that enclose it form a sort of diamond shape. And though the sun has long since disappeared, the city still glows.''

Desperate as they were for safety, Jonathan could not help but stand there, watching the changing, flaming sky. The light reflected off the stone-white city to the surrounding hills, only to be thrown back to Jerusalem until the land seemed bathed in an infinity of light.

"All we have suffered . . . ,'' Jonathan whispered, his eyes welling. "Those we have loved and lost, if only they could have glimpsed this as we do.'' Then he caught his breath with the realization of what he had said, and looked sadly at Roger.

Roger squeezed his hand, "Do not fret, I see it all through you.''

For one last moment, city and hills and sky seemed to evaporate in a molten golden glow that cooled to pale blues and darker lavenders. Picking their way carefully down the hillside stubbled with grasses and bushes, the boys started their final descent.

Jonathan could not take his eyes off the spired city, which

even as they approached seemed to move further away in the gathering darkness. " 'And when God appointed beauty to the world He gave nine parts to Jerusalem and one part to the rest of the world. But to compensate, when He appointed suffering . . . ,' "

"O merciful Lord, if only you could have allowed Laurelle to gaze upon this," Roger cried.

Jonathan gripped him. "Wherever she is, she *is* seeing it with us. And Harolde, and Flamonde!"

Roger lifted his head. "You are right! Then blessed are the peacemakers!" his voice rang out in the hush of night, "for they shall be called the children of God!"

"Amen!" Jonathan shouted.

About half a mile from the southernmost point of the walls, they came upon the caravanserie of the Khan, a way station built to shelter those merchants, travelers, and pilgrims who had arrived too late to gain entry into the Holy City.

Campfires burned within the compound; Jonathan led Roger to a secluded spot near a stable where the firelight did not reach. A polyglot of languages drifted on the night air: talk of drought, of new hostilities, of plague in Jaffa and nearby Beit Nuba. Jonathan limped away from Roger to beg for food; he returned a little while later with some unleavened bread and half an overripe melon.

Roger shook his head in appreciation as he ate. "Even if I could see, I do not think I could cope so well as you do here."

Jonathan flushed under the compliment, yet he recognized its truth. Though the land was foreign to him, some dream turned reality made him feel more sure of himself in this homeland of his ancestors, tempering his strength and resolve.

The night grew cold. Roger hugged his knees and shivered. "Is there no fire nearby?" he whispered to Jonathan.

"Yes, but better to be cold than discovered. Your eyes, do they feel any better?"

Roger touched his fingertips to his lids. "I cannot tell. The chill tells me it is deep night now, is it?"

"Half gone," Jonathan replied.

"And your leg?" Roger asked.

Jonathan kneaded his ankle. "Better, but I could not walk very far without you."

Roger shook his head with a rueful smile. "I have been wondering," he said quietly. "It is so strange, now that I cannot see, I *can* see. I thought we needed only to set the world an example and all would rally to our cause. Our parents, kings, the pope. Fool that I was, I believed love to be stronger than all else."

Jonathan touched Roger's arm. "If we believe it to be so, then it is."

"And Laurelle, then?" Roger murmured.

"Surely above all else, her life bespoke that."

"You loved her, did you not?" Roger asked softly.

The chirp of cicadas marked time as Jonathan struggled to answer. Finally he managed, "Yes, I loved her."

Roger nodded. "I suspected from the very first."

The boys remained silent for a bit. Then Roger said, "What shall we do once we are within the city? How shall we live?"

Jonathan hunched his shoulders, weighing the possibilities. "I can be a cook," he said. "Ibrahim told me they are in great demand because of the many pilgrims." Then another idea struck him. "Yes! Why can I not apprentice myself to a physician? Do not worry, Roger. God willing, we shall survive. Somehow."

Roger reached out in the darkness toward Jonathan's hand. "You know, I did not like you much when first we met in London," he said. "You were so clumsy, such a dolt!"

"That was so long ago," Jonathan said, laughing.

Roger nodded. "I have found many brothers on this pilgrimage—Harolde, Gunther, Guillaume—but I thank the Lord that no less than any other, He allowed me to find you."

Jonathan swallowed hard and impulsively embraced Roger. "Enough of this," he said gruffly.

All at once Roger started, his skin crawling with apprehension; he turned his head in the direction of the gate. "Something is happening," he whispered.

Jonathan looked around the way station; then he saw Frizio

gallop into the compound on Mirage, followed by a half-dozen of the Bedouin guard.

"Do not make a sound," Jonathan whispered. "Frizio and his men come this way."

The boys crawled to the rear of the stable. Jonathan's heart thudded wildly as he peeped through a crack between the boards and watched the trackers dismount and unsaddle their horses.

"Three times we picked up the trail," the boys heard Frizio mutter, "only to follow it to a dead end. How can that be? Are they wizards that the earth can swallow them up? And where is that fool Baalbek?"

Then Mirage whinnied; rearing, he tried to pull Frizio around to the back of the stable.

"Oh my god, he smells us," Jonathan gasped. "He will lead Frizio directly to us."

But Frizio, irritable from fatigue and lack of sleep, had no patience; and when the stallion continued to fight him, he beat the horse until his flanks were striped with blood.

Then Frizio strode to the various campfires, questioning the sleepy merchants and pilgrims about the escaped slaves.

Jonathan stood up, helping Roger to his feet. "We cannot remain here. It is only a question of time before somebody realizes who we were—oh, look! The Bedouins are lighting torches! Come!"

Hugging the shadowed walls of the compound, he helped Roger to a breach in the fence. The boys crawled under and slipped out into the darkness even as Frizio and his Bedouins, torches raised high, searched the Khan.

The boys half-ran, half-walked the remaining distance to Jerusalem. "If only the moon were not so bright," Jonathan panted as they climbed the incline of Mount Zion.

On the hill's rise stood the Dormition Abbey, built to mark the place where Mary had fallen into eternal sleep; abutting it, the Tomb of David Coenaculum, the room where Jesus and His disciples had celebrated the Last Supper. A mass of dark clouds scudded across the lower quadrant of the sky, but the moon sailed serenely above them.

As they hobbled toward the city the battlements grew taller. The road led directly to the southernmost corner of the walls, where it divided; the right path going to the Zion Gate, the left to the Jaffa Gate. But on the right, the land plunged so steeply into a valley that Jonathan realized they could never manage it in their weakened condition. He headed left, toward the complex of the Citadel of David, whose slim white tower rose above the city's walls, keeping a wary eye on the sentries that patrolled the battlements high above them. They managed to get past the white tower and reached the ponderous wooden doors of the Jaffa Gate.

"Of course they are closed," Jonathan breathed, "we expected that."

"Is there no way to climb the walls?" Roger asked.

Jonathan stared up at the sheer cliff face. "It is more than seventy feet high."

Roger stooped suddenly, listened, then spread his hands on the ground. "Horses," he said.

Jonathan strained to hear. "You are right!" he said "We must keep moving, find a place to hide."

Once more they ran. Proceeding from the Jaffa Gate they reached another corner of the walls and turned right, continuing north and east. As they climbed toward the Damascus Gate, the ground leveled off somewhat and their legs buzzed with relief. Then the path grew steep again. They had reached the farthest, northernmost corner of Jerusalem's walls when they heard the faint shouting of the Bedouins.

Roger turned, clenching his fists. "We will die bravely!"

Jonathan yanked him down. "Bravely, yes, though not tonight, if we use our wits."

He steered Roger around the north corner of the wall and then turned south. Instead of following the line of the battlements, Jonathan headed into a thicketed wilderness which was the garden of Gethsemane. Within a hundred paces their way was barred by interwoven brambles of Jerusalem thorns. The bushes grew as tall as trees, with needle-spines a finger long that tore at their clothes and flesh. They got on their hands and knees and crawled deeper into the dense thicket;

soon they were bleeding from cuts and gashes all over their bodies. Finally they reached a place where they could go no further, so impenetrable were the thorns.

From atop the wall, the sentries challenged Frizio and his band.

"We search for two escaped slaves," Frizio shouted up to the Saracen guards. "A Christian and a Jew; one fair, the other dark."

A guard yelled back, "We have seen no one this night, but we will remain alert."

The Bedouin trackers fanned out into the garden of Gethsemane and began to beat the bushes.

The silvery olive trees turned dark as a mass of clouds obscured the moon. Jonathan's heart was beating so loudly he felt certain the Bedouins would hear it as they passed, less than thirty feet from where he and Roger lay hidden. One tracker cursed as his horse shied, his hide lacerated by the thorns.

"Nobody could be alive in there," he swore, and turned aside.

As the boys listened fearfully, the signal cries grew fainter. The moon appeared, disappeared, and then shone again before the boys dared venture out of the thorny labyrinth.

"The cuts will heal soon enough," Jonathan said, stemming the blood from the worst of Roger's wounds and then tending to his own.

"Where are we now?" Roger asked, as they started up again.

"Following the northeastern wall," Jonathan said. "We dare not remain in this area, for the guards at these gates have been alerted and they would surely know us if we tried to enter here."

Pressing on, they soon found themselves in an ancient cemetery and ran a broken course as fast as they could, trying not to step on any graves lest the guardian demons lurking beneath every stone reach up and drag them down into the underworld.

They passed the bricked-up portal of the Golden Gate, where Jesus and His disciples had entered the city on that long ago Sunday, waving their palm fronds. Hard by, above the walls, loomed the Dome of the Rock, the mosque built over the stone where Abraham's hand had been stayed by the Lord as he prepared to sacrifice his son Isaac. By the time the boys had turned the easternmost corner of the wall and headed south and west, the first band of dawn's light became visible.

The pathway swung sharply into the valley of Kidron, and they had to brace themselves to keep from slipping down the incline. Then Jonathan saw the lowly Dung Gate. As they approached, they heard a cock crow, and then another, and soon, throughout the city, the roosters were heralding the new day.

The Dung Gate creaked open; a load of garbage, detritus, and offal came tumbling through the open doors to fall into the steep valley. A dung collector and his helper went to a wagon piled high with more of the city's refuse and prepared to dump it.

Using this unguarded moment, Jonathan and Roger slipped through the open doors and into Jerusalem.

JERUSALEM

ONCE WITHIN THE DUNG GATE, JONATHAN LED Roger along a dusty road which climbed up to a large, irregularly shaped public square. A gigantic wall made of huge blocks of rosy beige stone reared up before him, and Jonathan stopped.

"Is something wrong?" Roger asked, sensing Jonathan's indecision. "What is it that you see?"

"Nothing, only a section of a wall," Jonathan said, continuing to stare at it. "It stands higher than the battlements of the city, yet is not part of them. It goes nowhere, encloses nothing."

Then Jonathan caught sight of perhaps a dozen people, faces turned to the wall, bodies swaying with prayer. With a sudden blow to the heart he realized that these were devout Jews, praying at the Wailing Wall, the last remnant of the western wall of Solomon's Temple.

Dragging Roger along, Jonathan rushed headlong to reach it. Each layer of block comprising the wall stood higher than his head. White doves and pale blue pigeons nested in the tufts of grasses, and wildflowers grew in the crevices.

He pressed his body against the ancient stone, giving himself up to it. His knees buckled and the last of his energy drained from him. And then the wall seemed to give back its strength. The memory of the Passover ceremony swept over Jonathan and the fervent prayer: "This year, O Lord, I wander in a strange land, but next year, Jerusalem."

Slowly, he straightened and recited the prayer for the dead for his parents. "In peace," he whispered, fighting back his choking sobs. And then he offered up prayers for Harolde, Flamonde, and for Laurelle, shedding new tears for each of them.

Even as he prayed Jonathan knew it was too dangerous to

linger here; he would come back another time when it would be safer. He hesitated one last second, resting his head against the stone. "One last thing," he breathed, "if it be possible, dear Lord, restore his sight."

As he wiped his eyes, the square came once more into focus. He looked around, trying to decide what to do next. With the city awakening and going about its business, the square was becoming more trafficked. "Come," he said, taking Roger's arm, "it is too open here."

Avoiding the main thoroughfares, he chose a narrow pathway that climbed on half-a-hundred steps to a street high above the square. When they finally reached the top Jonathan looked down about him. From this height the golden Dome of the Rock shone resplendent, its mosaicked facade visible above the top of the Wailing Wall. A river of shimmering morning mist filled the valley of Kidron.

Then Jonathan saw a band of black-garbed riders galloping through the Dung Gate. "The Bedouins!" he cried, "and there is Mirage, with Frizio!"

Hobbling as fast as he could, Jonathan guided Roger along the Street of the Chain and into a dark alleyway. They turned left onto a narrow street, hoping to lose themselves in its dingy recesses.

"We must disappear," Jonathan panted. His ankle was hurting so badly he thought he might faint. "If only we can find the quarter where the Jews live; Frizio cannot search every house."

"Or the Christians," Roger said; then he stopped suddenly, sending Jonathan sprawling.

Jonathan got up and made a move to go on but Roger would not budge.

Roger grasped his shoulders. "Frizio will find us, we both know this, as we have known from the first moment we escaped. Before he does, you must take me to the Church of the Holy Sepulcher."

"Are you mad?" Jonathan exclaimed. "Let us leave here. People are beginning to stare at us."

"You have been to your holy place," Roger insisted. "Would

you deny me mine? I have sworn to pray for my mother there
. . . and now for Laurelle."

"I do not know where it is!" Jonathan cried, tugging at him.

"Ask then."

"And what if Frizio questions those we ask? He would
know where we went for sure. When we are safe, and they are
gone, I will take you there."

"You swear?"

"Yes, only come," Jonathan pleaded. "If we remain here arguing, then we are as dead."

Roger relented and they started out again. They hopped and
hobbled through the narrow, stepped streets that smelled of
goats and chickens and humanity pressed together in a place
too small for their numbers. Shops began to open; the warm
smell of baking bread filled the air, tormenting the boys'
growling stomachs.

A mule train carrying jugs of sesame oil clattered toward
them, forcing them against the stall of a shop where fruits
stood pyramided. A cantankerous mule kicked at Roger; the
stand upended and the fruit cascaded all over the street. Jonathan and Roger fled from the commotion, but not before Jonathan managed to grab an orange and a pomegranate.

When Jonathan thought they were safe, he sliced the orange
and gave half to Roger. They gobbled that down and started
on the pomegranate, clacking their lips against its tartness.

"Where are we now?" Roger asked, suddenly alert.

Jonathan wiped Roger's chin and checked to make sure his
burnoose hid his blond hair. "I do not know," he answered,
looking around. "This street is not like the others, it is
quieter."

"Yes," Roger said eagerly. No possible way could Roger
have known where they were, yet he did. In trying to lose
themselves they had been drawn deeper into Jerusalem's
heart. "The Via Dolorosa," Roger whispered, "the way of the
cross."

Even as Roger said it Jonathan knew he was right.

Roger would have it no other way but that they follow this
winding street to its end. "Have we not been guided here?"

he insisted. "Have we not lost Frizio?" Since Jonathan could not walk without Roger's help, he had no recourse but to give in to him. He told himself it would be all right, that their route was still leading them into the darker, more mysterious sections of the city.

Dwellings atop dwellings—Jerusalem was built in many levels here, and they passed beneath a network of arched bridges connecting the upper stories of the houses. Stumbling, whimpering with fatigue, they dragged their way along in the footsteps of one who had gone this way before them.

They came to a small hill, which in the Hebrew was called Golgotha, the place of the skull. When they reached a flight of steps leading down into another square, shouts reached them, and then a crowd of people tore up the steps. Christian pilgrims and Saracen guards, their eyes rolling in terror, were fleeing before some common threat. Behind them came a group of monks carrying a dead pilgrim on their shoulders. As the people charged past, the boys flattened themselves against the walls.

"Now what is happening?" Roger asked, listening to the cries and the retreating footsteps.

"I could not make it out," Jonathan said. "Something about the old dead man, but I cannot be sure." Then he gasped and quickly replaced Roger's burnoose, which had been knocked off in the melee. He looked around to see if anybody had noticed, but the streets had emptied because of the sudden alarm.

With one hand braced against the wall and the other clutching Roger's shoulder, Jonathan eased himself down the flight of steps, twenty-four in all, worn to a groove in the middle. When they finally reached the bottom, he was bathed in sweat. They came suddenly on an open space about seventy-five feet by ninety feet, the courtyard of a church.

"You do not have to tell me," Roger said excitedly, "I can feel it! We have reached the Church of the Holy Sepulcher!"

"Find them for me and each of you shall have a gold dinar this day," Frizio said to the Bedouin trackers. Only three of them were left with him. Three others had gone searching for Baalbek; when they found his remains, they buried what the vultures and scavengers had left. Then, disgusted with Frizio and his aberrations, which had brought this all about, they had returned to the caravan.

"Spread out," Frizio ordered the remaining trackers. "Search the Christian quarter, and that of the Jews." He made arrangements to meet them in two hours. That was when Qabat, the other leader of the caravan, had insisted that they resume their journey to Baghdad.

"We are behind our schedule as is," he had complained to Frizio. "Why should we jeopardize this entire venture searching for two insignificant slaves?"

But Frizio could not let the escape of Roger and Jonathan go unpunished. He guided Mirage along the narrow steps on which Jerusalem rose and fell in this quarter. "I will find them," he muttered aloud, "for I know each street and alley, each lane that turns into a dead end. They shall not escape me." He tried to guess where the boys would go but his mind went blank. "Somebody must have seen them!" he swore.

He had suspected that Ibrahim had aided the slaves in their escape. But Frizio could not risk proving Ibrahim's guilt, for the boy had many kinsmen among the Bedouin guard and Frizio dared not alienate them all. So Ibrahim had gotten off with a few blows from his uncles.

The slaves' escape and then the discovery of Baalbek's body had lowered Frizio considerably in the eyes of his fellow countrymen. What kind of man could he be to be outwitted by two children, one blind, the other lame, the Bedouins had muttered to his face. Frizio understood that nothing less than recapturing these slaves could restore his leadership.

But it meant much more to him than that. It was a question of will, of his beliefs over theirs, and long before this day had dawned, Frizio had decided that he must kill them.

But I will use them first, he thought, rabid with rage, mutilate them while they still breathe. I know how to make boys beg for mercy. Were it not for them, the girl would still be alive.

As he rode along, he saw his future. He would sell the rest of the slaves in Baghdad and make his fortune. He would move then to Jerusalem, find another young girl like Laurelle, marry, sire legitimate sons. He would grow old and be venerated in this most important city in all the world.

"All this I will do," Frizio said aloud. But first, he thought, I must free myself from the malevolent spell these slaves have cast over me. I will make them suffer the same fate they brought on her; I will strangle them so that the strength of their spirits will be added to mine.

So engrossed had Frizio become that he did not see the mule train plodding along the street. The lead driver shouted for him to get out of the way and in answer Frizio freed his whip and slashed all about him, driving the animals from his path. The asses brayed and kicked and all at once Mirage was scraping against the narrow walls trying to unseat Frizio. When the fracas was done, an earthenware jar on a mule's back had cracked open and splashed Frizio's loose tunic and pants with oil.

Frizio rubbed his scraped shoulder and looked down at his ruined clothes. He cursed aloud, trying to blot the oil stains spreading over everything. He brought the butt of his whip down hard on Mirage's ears. "Betrayer," he hissed.

Then he reached out and stroked Mirage's neck. "And I loved you more than all else in life," he said. "It is plain to see that those children have worked their evil on you also." Unable to bear the thought of anybody else's ever owning the stallion, Frizio decided that as soon as this was over, he too must die.

Frizio rode on, stopping shoppers and merchants, asking about the slaves. "One limping, the other blind?" Nodded heads and pointed fingers took him first to the Via Dolorosa and thence to the hill of Golgotha. There he dismounted and led Mirage down the steps toward the courtyard of the Church of the Holy Sepulcher.

THE HOLY SEPULCHER

ONATHAN AND ROGER LIMPED SLOWLY ACROSS A courtyard. "It is dangerous to be here, I know," Jonathan said, "but without some rest, I could not have gone any farther." He looked down at his ankle, swollen again to a frightening size.

Ordinarily the church doors were barred and guarded by Saracen warriors, who exacted a six-ducat fee for every Christian pilgrim seeking to enter the shrine. The worshippers were allowed to remain overnight in the locked church; with cock crow the following morning the doors were open and the pilgrims were let out to make room for the next group.

But this day had seen great confusion. An elderly pilgrim who had entered the church the previous night had been found dead in the Chapel of St. Helena. Not so unusual an occurrence; many of the worshippers used their last bit of strength to reach the holy place, and once there, died. This death, however, had thrown the Moslem guard into a panic, for the dead man carried out by his companions bore all the signs of having died of the plague. Saracens and Christians alike fled, leaving the church empty and the door unguarded.

Jonathan and Roger approached the double-arched entryway; one door had been walled up, the better to control access. The other massive wooden door stood slightly ajar, and the boys edged through it and into the musty gloom of the church. Roger pulled back his burnoose lest his head be covered in God's house.

Directly to their right, Jonathan saw through a haze of incense the Chapel of Calvary, built over the place where Jesus had been crucified. In a hushed voice, he described everything to Roger.

The patterned marble of the floor felt cold beneath their bare feet as they moved slowly into the transept and apse of the church. The steep dome of the rotunda soared high above, dwarfing them.

"It is near, I sense it," Roger breathed, his voice tremulous with awe.

In the center of the rotunda stood an oddly shaped structure, some forty feet in length and perhaps twenty feet wide, the edicule of the tomb of Christ. One end widened into a curved wall decorated with blind arches.

Jonathan tried to look into the first room of the tomb, but a low archway blocked his view. He hesitated a moment, and Roger, trembling with anticipation said, "You must take me into it." Jonathan told Roger to stoop down and led him into the first chamber, the Chapel of the Angels.

Roger clasped his hands, his face shining. Then he felt his way around the chapel. "It is small," he said.

"No more than three or four people could fit in here," Jonathan told him.

In the center of the room Roger touched a pedestal; his fingers roamed over a large fragment of rock that had been placed upon it. "What is it?" he asked.

Jonathan read the inscription. "It is said to be from the original wheel of stone used to seal the crypt of Jesus."

Roger pressed his forehead against it so that its imprint was left upon his skin. He prayed for his mother and Laurelle then, that the journey of their souls might be eased.

Hanging from the rounded ceiling, silver and brass censers burned aromatic oils of many colors, lighting the chapel with delicate hues. Jonathan stared at the lanterns and the circle of candles surrounding the fragment of stone, hypnotized by the flickering light which constantly changed the shape of the small room.

Roger had slipped into a state that was part exhaustion, part reverie. "Laurelle," he whispered, and then said her name again.

At last, Jonathan blinked his eyes. He nudged Roger. "There is another room just ahead. Watch yourself." He helped Roger stoop under a second archway, this one less than four feet high.

They entered the Inner Sactum of the Holy Sepulcher, a room about seven feet square. The arched ceiling reached higher, but here too, dozens of lamps hung down, so low they almost touched the boys' heads. The heat from the burning lamps radiated throughout the small space, making the chamber uncomfortably hot. Taking up the whole length of the right side of the chamber was a marble sarcophagus.

"Of a size to hold a man's body," Jonathan murmured.

Roger turned slowly in the cramped space, listening raptly as Jonathan described everything; the walls, floor, the banked candles burning on the lid of the sarcophagus.

As Jonathan spoke, Roger gripped his hand and energy surged between the two boys. "I can see it," Roger whispered, "I can!"

Jonathan could not tell if Roger actually saw or if he was hallucinating, but it did not matter; whatever way, Jonathan knew that Roger was seeing it with his inner eye. Then he stared, thinking he too might have begun to hallucinate. Even now he imagined he saw a figure materializing in the doorway, all in white, staring at them. Then Jonathan screamed.

Frizio crouched in the archway between the Chapel of the Angels and the Inner Sanctum, the sleeves of his tunic spread wide like the wings of some fallen angel.

Quickly, Frizio took in the room; one entrance only, and he was blocking that. "Let it be done with now, once and forever," he muttered to the boys, with the oblique thought that it was somehow fitting that they should meet their fate here.

Keeping his head low and clear of the hanging lamps, Frizio came forward carefully, arms stretched lest they try to dodge past him.

For an uncertain moment Jonathan debated whether or not to beg for mercy, but the look in Frizio's eyes told him it would be useless. But more important was his vow that he would never beg for mercy again.

His hand closed around the hilt of Ibrahim's dagger. "Get behind me, quickly," he said to Roger.

Frizio feinted toward the boys and when Jonathan started, he threw back his head and roared with laughter. Frizio's hand shot out again, this time seizing Jonathan by the throat. Jonathan swung with his knife but Frizio saw the move, and with a sharp chop knocked it from his hand.

"Roger, the knife!" Jonathan gagged. "On the floor!"

Roger dropped to his knees and frantically searched the floor. A quick kick from Frizio sent him sprawling against the sarcophagus; the banks of candles shuddered but remained upright.

Frizio's voice reverberated in the tiny chamber of the Inner Sanctum. "If anybody uses a knife it shall be me. What say you, Jew? Shall I turn you into another Baalbek so you may grow fat and service me for the rest of your life? Let me hear you beg for the honor of serving me!" He released his hold on Jonathan's throat a bit lest he strangle him too quickly. Jonathan coughed and drew in great gasping breaths. Just as he began to breathe freely again, Frizio tightened his grip.

Roger got up from the floor and flailed wildly about. Frizio kicked at him again to keep him off, but this time Roger caught Frizio's leg, his fingers closing around the loose cloth of the trousers. He hung on desperately, climbing up Frizio's leg, then finding his arm and shoulder. As Frizio beat at him with his free hand, Roger sprang for his jugular vein with his teeth.

So surprised was he by the violence of the assault that Frizio dropped Jonathan to concentrate on this blind lunatic trying to tear out his throat. Had the space been bigger, Frizio could have dispatched them quickly. But because of the hanging lanterns he was forced to crouch and could not fully use his arms. With a deft move, he caught Roger's wrist, twisted his arm behind his back, and pinned him against the wall.

On the floor, Jonathan clutched his throat and tried to come to his senses, making sounds like a beached fish. He saw Frizio reach for his own dagger, saw the curved blade flash in the light of the lanterns as he slowly raised it, preparing to bring it down on Roger.

With a croaking cry of rage Jonathan charged up from the

floor, butting Frizio in the stomach. He punched and kicked at his groin.

Frizio doubled over with the excruciating pain, then bolted upright, slashing about with his dagger in a sudden mindless fury. As he did, his head cracked against one of the hanging lamps. It swayed precariously and then the hot flaming oil splashed down on his already oil-stained clothes. A finger of fire connected the lamps to Frizio and in the next instant his clothes burst into flame. His eyes opened wide in disbelief— that this could be happening to him—even as the shroud of green and gold and blue flame roared all about him.

Jonathan grabbed Roger's hand and dragged him through the arch of the Inner Sanctum while the fire pursued them. Frizio tried to escape by the same route, but lantern upon lantern blossomed into flame, cascading fire all about and engulfing him.

The two boys fell into the tiny Chapel of the Angels and then crawled out of the edicule and into the rotunda of the church.

Jonathan turned back once and saw Frizio at the entrance of the tomb, standing like a pillar of fire, the black hole of his mouth stretched in a circle of horror as his face melted into the flames.

END OF THE JOURNEY

TUMBLING INTO THE CHURCH COURTYARD, THE boys beat at the drops of oil burning holes in their clothes. At last they had smothered them all.

They clutched each other, choking and gagging for breath, trying to assimilate what had happened. "We must get away from here," Jonathan said urgently, "before Frizio is found."

"And what of the fire?" Roger asked.

"The tomb is unharmed," Jonathan said, "for there was nothing in it to burn, save Frizio."

Roger straightened then. "Thank the Lord for that. The light," he said, shaking his head, "I am so dizzy."

"Can you see then?" Jonathan cried. "It *is* daylight!"

"Wait," Roger said morosely, blinking his eyes, "it has all gone dim again."

"Yes it has!" Jonathan exclaimed. "A mass of dark clouds has just passed over the sun." He moved his hand in front of Roger's eyes and Roger's head turned ever so slightly to follow the movement.

"God is merciful," Jonathan breathed. "The main thing is that you can tell dark from light. Trust me, it is only a question of time before your sight is restored!"

"Do you really believe this? You are not just saying it?"

"I would not lie about such a thing," Jonathan said.

"God willing you are right," Roger said soberly. "We will wait then and see what happens."

They dragged their way out of the courtyard and were just about to climb the stairs when they heard a whinny at the far end of the square. Mirage stood tethered to a rail.

"I do not believe it!" Jonathan exclaimed, as they hurried toward the stallion. "Do not make a scene," he warned Roger, all the while hugging the stallion's neck. "I am going to untie him as though he belonged to us. Remember now, no fuss. Mirage! Stop biting!"

Roger's hands roamed over the stallion, stroking his forehead and nose. Jonathan grabbed the reins and mounted. Then he reached down, grasped Roger's arm, and hoisted him into the saddle behind him.

"Go, Mirage," Jonathan said softly. "We must not be discovered here," he said over his shoulder to Roger. "The other slave dealers may be about and they know that this is Frizio's horse."

At the top of the steps they met the troop of Saracen guards and Christian pilgrims returning to the Holy Sepulcher. Physicians had examined the dead pilgrim and determined that he had not died of the plague, merely of old age and boils.

One of the Saracen guards looked back curiously at the two ragged urchins mounted on the magnificent stallion. "Stop!" he called out, but Jonathan made believe that he had not heard, and digging his heels into Mirage, wheeled him into the first side street and then into another until they had lost the guard.

"What can we do to disguise him," Roger asked, "stain him as we did with me?"

"Impossible, the dye would soon fade," Jonathan said. "You heard how the guard called after us; we would be stopped. And now that we are in Jerusalem we must be as anonymous as a thorn among the brambles."

"Then what?" Roger asked. Suddenly it came to him and he gripped Jonathan's shoulder. "You mean to turn him loose."

"I mean to set him free," Jonathan said. "Does he deserve anything less?"

Roger's heart sank. He rubbed his head with the dizziness of light and then rested his forehead against Jonathan's back. "I cannot think," he said. "I cannot bear to give him up, and yet I know you are right." He heaved a sigh and said, "What will happen to us now?"

Jonathan hunched his shoulders. "I do not know. What matters is that we are here. And I cannot, I will not believe that God has led us through the wilderness to abandon us."

They made their way through the torturous, winding

streets. The oppressively humid heat of noon had forced most of the Jerusalemites indoors and the boys were not challenged.

When they got to the Wailing Wall, in sight of the Dung Gate, Jonathan dismounted and removed the saddle, bit, and reins from Mirage. A sudden gust of cool wind whipped the dust about; Mirage shook his head and then held it high, muscles bunched, skin quivering in anticipation.

Jonathan stroked the stallion's nose and murmured, "When I had no other, you were my friend." He hugged him one last time then stepped back and said sharply, "Go!"

Mirage did not move.

Jonathan slapped him smartly on the rump and Mirage bolted.

Two guards lounging near the open doors of the Dung Gate saw the stallion bearing down on them. They ran forward, arms waving, but Mirage dodged them and galloped through the gate. The guards gave chase.

"Wait here for me," Jonathan said to Roger, "I must make sure that he is safely away."

Leaving Roger standing near the foot of the battlements, he climbed the narrow stone steps to the top of the wall. He scanned the hillside and saw Mirage plunging down into the defile of the valley of Kidron.

"Like the wind," Jonathan said exultantly as he watched Mirage, neck low, legs moving in a blur, outdistancing his pursuers. Deeper into the valley Mirage ran, and then up the farther slope of the Mount of Olives. Through welling eyes, Jonathan saw the golden dappled hide blend into the desert landscape until he could see him no more. "Mirage is free!" he called down to Roger.

Far in the distance Jonathan thought he could make out the line of a caravan snaking north, in the direction of Baghdad. He shuddered for what he knew would befall the other slave children.

Turning, he looked at the city stretched before him, the domes, minarets, and bell towers dazzling in the dazzling light. And the scarred but immutable monument of the Wailing Wall.

"Home," Jonathan whispered, "I am home."

On the northern horizon, racing black clouds roiled, pierced with jagged shafts of lightning. The cloud bank swept toward Jerusalem, heavy with the promise of rain.

EPILOGUE

According to the chroniclers of the times, a caravan of slave children from the Crusade finally reached Baghdad. There the children were promised their freedom if they would renounce their faith. When they refused, eighteen were martyred.

When the news reached the citizens of Cologne that the sea had not parted for Nicholas and that most of their children had been lost, they hanged Nicholas's father for his instigations.

Some years later, the merchants Hugo Ferrus and William Porquierres were executed in Sicily for their slave tradings and for complicity in a plot to assassinate Emperor Frederick II.

At the Fourth Lateran Council in 1215, Pope Innocent III successfully had all his tenets adopted by the ecumenical council, including the Miracle of Transubstantiation and the Easter Duty. Anti-Semitism became codified church policy, Jews were required to wear distinctive dress and were segregated into ghettos. The preachings of Joachim of Fiore and his Three Ages of Man were declared heretical. Nevertheless, that concept remained the single most powerful philosophic idea in Europe until the nineteenth century.

To date, two parts of the prophecy in Revelations have come to pass: That there be a new nation of Israel, and that the Jews be once more established in Jerusalem. Only the third condition, that the Temple of Solomon be rebuilt on its original foundations (now occupied by the Moslem Dome of the Rock), remains to be fulfilled before the world, according to the biblical prophecy, shall witness the Kingdom of Heaven on earth.

ACKNOWLEDGMENTS

The source books consulted for this project are too numerous to list, but my special gratitude to the New York Public Library, the British Museum and their map department, the Bibliothèque Nationale, the Vatican Library, and the Hebrew University Library in Jerusalem.

In following the route of the children's crusade, my journey in England was made easier by Shelley Munjack Stephenson, Leslie Jenchel, and Father George Minnox; on the continent by Robert B. Beardsley and George S.B. Morgan; and in the Mideast by Ambassador and Joan Comay and Moshe Pearlman. I am grateful to L. Arnold Weissberger and Milton Goldman for making these Mideast contacts possible.

For their expertise in the preparation of the manuscript I am indebted to John J. Young and Sabina Iardella, and for their moral support to Isabel Leighton Bunker and Diane Sokolow, the godmother of this book. The novel could not have been completed in its final form without the sensitive insights and formidable talents of my gifted editor, Joyce Johnson.

And finally, my deepest thanks to Antoinette Marie Bunker, whose generosity helped to underwrite my research and explorations.

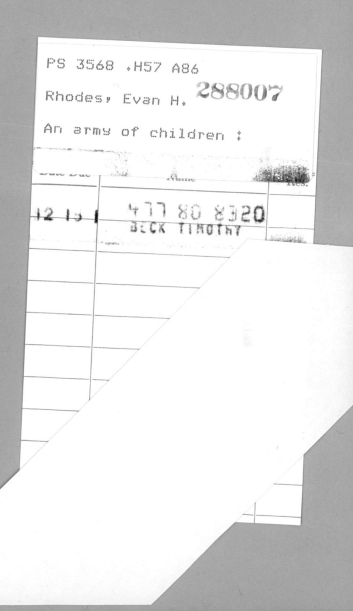